THE ~~EAGLE~~ OF THE HILLS

Lady Churchill was waiting with her committee of ladies to receive Mary Sinclair in Grosvenor Square, and she was welcomed as if she were a poor relation who owed more service.

'I do not know if you have family there,' Lady Churchill said. 'My young son Jack is out there with the South African Light Horse, and, as you know, Winston is a war correspondent for the *Morning Post*. He was captured on an armoured train, but he is alive, thank God. And knowing Winston, I very much doubt if the Boers can keep him for long. We could never keep him at home. Always breaking out. You know what young men are, to be sure.'

'I do that,' Mary Sinclair said, 'though I have none of my own. But I have two nephews, Hamilton with the ships — he looks for the engines — and Hamish Charles with the Seaforths like my poor brother was — he was killit at Magersfontein.' Mary could not stop her Scots tongue breaking out, faced with the high condescension of the aristocratic voice. 'And I hear another is coming from Canada — Robert, my brother Bain's boy — all the way from his farm on the prairies. It is no' his war, but he will come, for he is a cowboy, you could think he had hoofs, not two feet. And this Lord — Strathcona, do you ken? — he asked for the Mounties and the cowboys to ride for him over the water and teach the Boers there was other hard men on ponies as good as they were.'

About the Author

Andrew Sinclair, the well-known novelist, biographer and social historian, was born in 1935 and is a member of the clan Sinclair. This is the second novel, following THE FAR CORNERS OF THE EARTH, about the history of the family. His own forebears were cleared from the Highlands of Scotland in the nineteenth century and served the British Empire for five generations, until its end.

His other novels include 'The Albion Triptych': GOG, MAGOG and KING LUDD.

ANDREW SINCLAIR
THE STRENGTH OF THE HILLS

CORONET BOOKS
Hodder and Stoughton

Copyright © Andrew Sinclair
1992

First published in Great Britain
in 1992 by Hodder and
Stoughton Ltd

Coronet edition 1993

A John Curtis Book

The right of Andrew Sinclair to be
identified as the author of this work
has been asserted by him in
accordance with the Copyright,
Designs and Patents Act 1988.

British Library C.I.P.

A CIP catalogue record for
this title is available from the
British Library

ISBN 0 340 58032 1

Printed and bound in Great Britain
for Hodder and Stoughton Paper-
backs, a division of Hodder and
Stoughton Ltd, Mill Road, Dunton
Green, Sevenoaks, Kent TN13 2YA
(Editorial Office: 47 Bedford
Square, London WC1B 3DP) by
Clays Ltd, St Ives plc.

CONTENTS

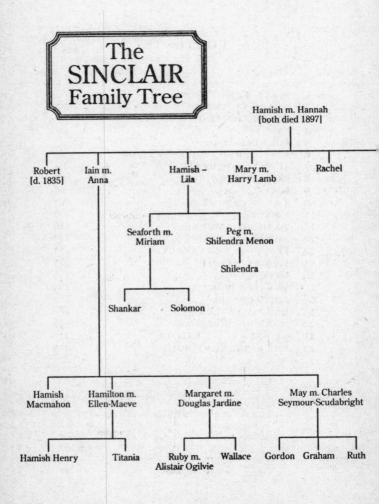

The SINCLAIR Family Tree

Hamish m. Hannah
[both died 1897]

Robert [d. 1835]

Iain m. Anna

Hamish – Lila

Mary m. Harry Lamb

Rachel

Seaforth m. Miriam

Peg m. Shilendra Menon

Shilendra

Shankar

Solomon

Hamish Macmahon

Hamilton m. Ellen-Maeve

Margaret m. Douglas Jardine

May m. Charles Seymour-Scudabright

Hamish Henry

Titania

Ruby m. Alistair Ogilvie

Wallace

Gordon

Graham

Ruth

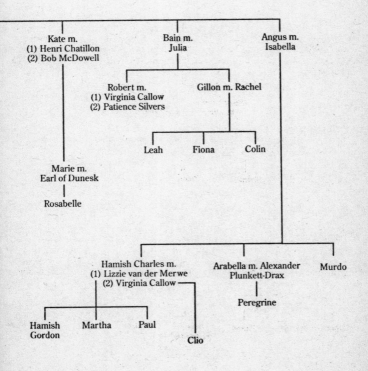

Kate m.
(1) Henri Chatillon
(2) Bob McDowell

Bain m.
Julia

Angus m.
Isabella

Robert m.
(1) Virginia Callow
(2) Patience Silvers

Gillon m. Rachel

Leah   Fiona   Colin

Marie m.
Earl of Dunesk

Rosabelle

Hamish Charles m.
(1) Lizzie van der Merwe
(2) Virginia Callow

Arabella m. Alexander
Plunkett-Drax

Murdo

Peregrine

Hamish
Gordon   Martha   Paul

Clio

I

BLACK WEEK

Even in Black Week the starch on the nurses' bonnets had to be whiter than white. Mary Sinclair saw to that, just as Miss Nightingale had seen to that. A snow peak on the nurses' hair as pure and stiff as one of those Alps. "If you dinna show clean," Mary used to say to the novices, "you canna be clean. If the patient, he looks at you and sees a dirty sister, will he no' think he will end in a dirty grave? I will no' say, cleanliness is next Godliness, but I will say, keep your aprons proper, wash your hands, and thank God for the carbolic."

The first of the wounded from the Boer War had begun to reach St Thomas's Hospital after the long voyage home on the hospital ships. Mary had seen it all before in India and the African campaigns, the men without a leg or an arm, still thinking they had one and saying, "Move the blanket, it's hurting my foot," when the foot was not there at all. The soldiers bandaged round their head with their jaw or cheek shot away, and they had to eat through a funnel or suck through a straw. And the lying bodies that were alive, but had the shrapnel or a bullet in the spinal column, and so they could not move, but the young nurses had to shift them on the hour to stop the bedsores and to use the bedpan. Ach, a man was a man for all that, and there was not a bit of a man that her nurses did not know.

But she could not bide here, in the office that had been Harry Lamb's before he died, her poor husband. She stroked the oak desk with her fingers, his desk where she had sat all afraid on the other side on their first meeting, the wood so smooth it put the wrinkles on her ageing hands to shame. Poor Harry! He would have had his work cut out, trying to repair the damage done by the field surgeons out in the veld after all the disasters of trying to fight the Boers. But now she might be sent out herself on a last mission, the only matron they could trust with the experience to run a floating ambulance. Lady Randolph Churchill and her rich American friends were equipping a hospital ship, the *Maine* was its name. And there was nobody to manage the nurses, nobody but her old self that the War Office would

I

trust. For had not Miss Nightingale put her trust in Mary Sinclair, who had never let her down?

Mary rose to take her cloak and call a hansom cab. She had never liked the rich ladies. She had never forgotten her first days as a parlour maid in London, after the clearing of her family from the Highlands and its scattering to the far corners of the earth. All those airs and graces the duchess had used to put her down, all the dirty linen below the frills and the flowers. But Lady Churchill was better, being an American, though sometimes those not born to it were the worse for it. For when they took on their new high position, they went too far, fearing they would be found out to be not what their lifted noses said they were. What had Harry told her? "Some are born noble, some achieve nobility, and some have it thrust upon them. Those are the true scum, the guttersnipes in coronets."

The crowds in Westminster and Mayfair were hushed and draggity, with only the watercress-girls and the muffin-men crying their wares. "Cress, cress, penny a bunch!" and "Who'll buy my lovely hot crumpets?" The illness of Queen Victoria, nearly ninety now, and the three defeats in a week in South Africa had cast a black veil over the end of the year. You would have thought in the weeks before Christmas and the turn of the year into a new century in 1900 there would be singing in the streets and bright colours on the pavements: the red tunics of the bandsmen still not turned to khaki, as the new uniforms were now; the players blowing the brass and the pipes in the gay tunes of war. But no music sounded in this late afternoon of Black Week, only the rattle of the carriage wheels and the crack of the coachman's whip on the hindquarters of his stumbling horse.

Lady Churchill was waiting with her committee of ladies to receive Mary Sinclair in Grosvenor Square, and she was welcomed as if she were a poor relation who owed more service.

"I do not know if you have family there," Lady Churchill said. "My young son Jack is out there with the South African Light Horse, and, as you know, Winston is a war correspondent for the *Morning Post*. He was captured on an armoured train, but he is alive, thank God. And knowing Winston, I very much doubt if the Boers can keep him for long. We could never keep him at home. Always breaking out. You know what young men are, to be sure."

"I do that," Mary Sinclair said, "though I have none of my own. But I have two nephews, Hamilton with the ships – he looks for the engines – and Hamish Charles with the Seaforths like my poor brother was – he was killit at Magersfontein." Mary could not stop her Scots tongue breaking out, faced with the high condescension of the aristocratic voice. "And I hear another is coming from Canada – Robert, my brother Bain's boy – all the way from his farm on the prairie. It is no' his war, but he will come, for he is a cowboy, you could think he had hoofs, not two feet. And this Lord – Strathcona, do you ken? – he asked for the Mounties and the cowboys to ride for him over the water and teach the Boers there was other hard men on ponies as good as they were."

"My son is in the Hussars." A lady in a green shroud spoke now. "And I have a nephew in the Lancers. I am sure we do not have any need of this colonial cavalry."

"My brother Iain did say, when he was with the Highlanders in the Crimea and the Mutiny, that devil a bit the regular cavalry did, on their fancy gee-gees riding into the guns. Horsemeat with ribbons on."

Lady Churchill coughed discreetly. "Strategy is not our province. Let us leave it to the men."

"And look what a fair mess they have made of it," Mary said. "Losing to the Dutchmen three times in a week."

"You have the best reputation in London, Matron Lamb, for managing a hospital. Lord Roberts himself has heard of your services in past campaigns. Through the generosity of these ladies present –" a slow sweep of Lady Churchill's mauve silk arm indicated the other members of the committee with their pinched waists and swelling corsages, "– the *Maine* has been fitted with the very latest in medical equipment. There is even something called an X-ray, I believe, that can actually see through the body and detect a broken bone. Splendid, is it not?"

"If it is only a bone broken," Mary said, "a soldier will thank his luck for it."

"And we have plate glass on our operating table. And we have room for more than two hundred patients in four large wards and an isolation ward for dangerous cases."

"Typhoid," Mary said. "Cholera and malaria. Enteric and blackwater fever. They'll carry off more than the bullets ever will."

"There are also splendid quarters for the nurses and the doctors and the medical orderlies. We see no reason that they should suffer as well as our soldiers."

"Most considerate," Mary said. "In my experience it is not many that think a nurse may suffer too."

"American women know it," Lady Churchill said. "We know it is our function to foster and nourish the suffering. And we are more adept at it, we believe, than any others."

"Will any of your ladies," Mary asked drily, "be coming with us

3

the now to do what you are adept at? Or are you sending us to do it for you?"

There was a silence in the drawing-room, then a woman in a long cerise skirt and red bodice said with severity, "We have our duties here. Our husbands, our commitments. We would all welcome the opportunity to do what you will do. Do not think that because a woman's place is in the home, that she does not nurse the sick and the dying there. I have lost three children, matron, in my time. Very slowly with many tears. Have you?"

"No' personally," Mary said, "but I have watched die the hundreds of children of other mothers. You are right, I ken that. Every home is a hospital. We have no' enough of them. And a big home like this –" her eyes moved up a marble pillar to the lofty ceiling with its frieze of fleur-de-lys and stucco roses below the chandeliers "– what a lot of dying there must have been in here. All those people, all those rooms, and it nearly the size of St Thomas's. Where there's high living, there's a high dying too. Now, Lady Churchill, if we can get to the detail. The how, when and where. And as for the why, as you say, it is the province of the men. I dinna ken why we are fighting some dirt farmers in slouch hats for a piece of dry veld, but I ken that there's never a good enough why to fight any war, but if there is a war, why we must go in and patch up the poor men that are fighting. Or if they do not ken the why, the order is good enough for them, as it is good enough for me."

"You do not sound very patriotic," Lady Churchill said.

"And you Americans are so?" Mary smiled at the circle of ladies around her. "For our Empire? Is that no' a strange thing?"

"I have sons there as I said." Lady Churchill rose. "I would not fall behind in my duty." She reached out her hand to Mary. "They said you were most direct, Matron Lamb. And as you are, I will direct you to the how, when and wherefore of this hospital ship. For arguing the whys will not cure a single soldier."

"That it will not," Mary said, taking Lady Churchill's hand. "But bless you all for doing all you can do for them."

The Dutchmen had put barbed wire under the Tugela River. It was a damnable trick. It hooked your puttees and dragged you down. If the Mausers and the Pom-poms didn't get you, the waters choked you. A fire storm above, a snare below. When a bullet or shrapnel didn't stop you, drowning did. Why, he could make the Irish Brigade charge over mountains and deserts and marshes, Colonel Thackeray knew that. But running into a loop of sandbanks opposite the Boers in their trenches the other side of the river, it was sticking your nose into a noose. So the survivors of the Dublins and Connaughts and Borderers and Inniskillings were trapped on a skillet, grilling in the glare of the sun. And if they poked their head up to fire back, *ker-phut* the bullets were a whiplash in the sand or a hole in the brain-pan. All to save those damn-fool navy guns that had gone too far forward, and now the Dutchmen were swimming the river and hauling them away. And the Irish had to stay put and lie low like badgers in the earth, only this was powder. Dust to dust and ashes to ashes, Thackeray thought, into the tomb the colonel dashes. His laugh at his jingle turned into a cough. And the moaning of his wounded men and the neighing and rattle of the shattered horses in their harnesses were the winds of dying.

Funny that the Red Cross should save them from surrender. The Irish never surrendered, but even so, behind the stretcher-bearers coming up with their white flag and the bloody crucifix set on it, there was a cordon of Dutchmen tightening the hangman's knot. But Thackeray wasn't having any of that. It was as sneaky as the wires under the water. The bearded burgher in the slouch hat might shout out, "Surrender, *kakies*, or we will kill you, by God." But Thackeray was ready for him. He jumped up and gave the Dutchman a dressing-down. "That's not sporting," he said. "Coming up behind the Red Cross. That's not a fair fight."

Now the Dutchman laughed. "Dom fools," he said. "We shoot you like *diuker* – stembuck – "

"Not behind a white flag," Thackeray said. "The devil you don't. You go back where you came from. And we'll begin the battle over again."

Again the Dutchman laughed. "Well," he said, "I won't look at you while you take your men away." And he turned his back on Thackeray to face his own cordon of men. "We don't want prisoners," he said. "Let the *kakies* go. Dom fools – but brave fools."

And so Colonel Thackeray called up his men from the sandpits they had made with their prone bodies, and each soldier who could stand and even the walking wounded, they were the crutches for those who had stopped one in the leg or the body, while the stretcher-bearers took up the maimed and the mutilated who still breathed and could not hobble. And as Colonel Thackeray walked among them, he saw that the carriers of his shattered brigades were Indians, *char-wallahs* and coolies. Had this war against bush farmers and small town burghers brought the Empire down to that? Brown hands strapping the bloody khaki with white bandages, brown arms and brown legs bearing the heavy bodies of the Irish to the field hospitals, brown heads wearing old helmets and bowlers and tam o' shanters. It couldn't happen in Connaught.

Now they reached the ambulance waggons, which would take the wounded back to the field hospitals and the operating tents. The stretchers were shipped aboard, the non-walking wounded hoisted on. And the mules pulled the vehicles over the rocky ground, pitching and tossing like drunken ships on a choppy sea. The walking soldiers and the bearers running behind heard groans and shrieks and curses, a barrage of pain. Blue flies hovered over the canvas flaps in clouds that buzzed. And when the soldiers reached the three operating tents to the rear, it was a factory. The victims were laid out in rows on straw, waiting their turn under the knives of the teams of surgeons. Every man who could drink was given a mug of hot Bovril from boiling cans outside. And Dr Seaforth Sinclair, taking a break after three hours of hacking and stitching at the operating tables, saw a drummer boy no more than fourteen years old, as he sat against a wall by the boiling Bovril with his left arm a mangled mess. With his right hand, he was eating a biscuit. And one of those staff officers, who never saw enough of a fight to ruffle a side-whisker, he took half-a-crown from his pocket and gave it to the drummer boy. The lad said, "Thank you, but would you mind putting it in my pocket. I mustn't let go of the biscuit."

Fury at the boy's taking of the condescending gift sent Seaforth into the field hospital. Dr Treves, Surgeon to Queen Victoria herself, was already there before him. He was kneeling beside a small young man, lying almost like a baby in the womb, strapped round the groin with a bright red loincloth. This infant had to be important for Treves to be there, giving him chloroform to dull his agony. Seaforth knelt too, not in mercy, but in curiosity.

"May I help, Mr Treves?"

"Hold the pad over his mouth." Treves offered Seaforth the soaked gauze, and Seaforth slipped it between the face and the knees of the shape, doubled in a ball on the straw. With his palm, he smothered the breathing of the dying youth, forcing him to inhale, choking and sneezing.

"That will ease him," Treves said.

The two doctors knelt and waited for the gasping to die to a low grunting. Then Treves stood up, followed by Seaforth.

"That's Freddy Roberts," he said. "Lord Bobs's son. If we could only get *him* out here. Instead of that butcher Buller."

"I agree," Seaforth said. "Another frontal attack at Colenso. It was as bad as Magersfontein." He paused and gave the thin smile that always warned the British of a surprise. "My *father* was killed there."

6

"Father?" Treves was surprised. "I thought you were an —" Treves stopped himself in time. "Of course, your name is Sinclair."

"You thought I was an Indian," Seaforth said. "My mother was. My father was in the Seaforths. That explains my name."

"You're a fine surgeon," Treves said diplomatically. "Where did you train?"

"St Thomas's in London. Do you know my Aunt Mary? She was married to Harry Lamb. He was a doctor there."

"Of course. The best, Harry was. Simply the best. And your aunt, too — all that work she did for Miss Nightingale in India. Now we must get back to work."

He looked down at the unconscious Freddy Roberts, then he led the way towards the door of the field hospital. Already rain was tapping on the roof, and it was nearly dark. "We must get tarpaulins over the men out there," Treves said, then heard a voice at his feet, "Doctor, I can't move them." And Treves dropped on his knees again, where a wounded gunner with a blistered red face was sitting against a bale of straw, looking at his legs laid out in two logs in front of him.

"Where were you hit, man?" Treves asked.

"In the back. In the spine. I must walk again. Man the guns."

"We will try. I pray that you do." Treves stood up again and walked away, and as Seaforth followed him out into the wet he heard the gunner say to himself, "So I was in time for the fun."

The stretcher-bearers were already covering the soldiers waiting for their operations with canvas and tarpaulins. They were themselves drenched, their tattered khaki tunics sticking to their thin backs. And as Seaforth came up to Treves, he heard him say to the Indian bearers, "Good work. Keep it up. We'll operate on them all and get them ready for you to put on the hospital train as soon as we can."

"Perhaps you think I should be among them." As Seaforth said the words, he wished he had not said them. "As an Indian I should know my place." He could have bitten his tongue out.

Treves looked down at the lying soldiers spitting out the rain that fell in their open mouths. "Perhaps you think I should be among them," he said.

Seaforth was shocked into a straight answer. "Of course not."

"Your place is curing them with me, Mr Sinclair."

And so they went back to the operating tent, where the sound of the fusillades of heaven on the canvas was louder than the Pom-poms and the Mausers, and the amputation of limbs was worse than the scything of human bodies by shrapnel, and the dropping of human arms and legs into the waste buckets thumped on the zinc like mortar shells. Seaforth took his own skills for granted, but now he marvelled at the steadiness of the surgeons and the silence of the soldiers under the saw and the scalpel. Chloroform helped, but courage had much to do with it.

The eight hundred men in need of immediate surgery were not all treated until dawn, when the rain at last had stopped. Some fifty of them died, the rest were to be shifted by train to convalesce down at the Cape. Going outside red-handed and red-eyed, Seaforth saw the Indian bearers waiting patiently on the grass, wrapped in drenched cloaks they had improvised from tent flaps. He went over to the nearest of them and squatted beside him.

"They are treating you like dogs," he said. "Why are you fighting their war?"

"Why are you?"

"I am a doctor. I must."

"Gandhi tell us – "

"Gandhi?"

"Mohandas Gandhi. We are from Natal. He is barrister. He says, if we show loyal to the Empire, then – then they give India back to us."

"When's *that*?" Seaforth was incredulous.

"When the war over."

"Your Gandhi's a fool." Seaforth stood up. "We will have to take India ourselves." He saw Treves walking towards him from the operating tent. "These men have been out all night. They are being treated like animals."

"War turns us all into animals," Treves said. "Dogs in the rain. There is no shelter for them. We do what we can."

"It is because they are Indians. *Volunteers* for the Empire."

"You do not pity them, Mr Sinclair." For the first time, Treves's voice was as sharp as a blade. "You pity yourself too much. You really shouldn't. I had a patient once – now he had every reason to pity himself – but he never did. He even met the Royal Family – "

"Oh, your freak!" Seaforth grimaced with his black lips. "The Elephant Man! All his patrons, his noble patrons. They went to see him for his deformity – "

"For his dignity, actually." Treves looked at two bearers putting a soldier with two legs gone onto a stretcher as delicately as a baby into a cot. The only sound was their feet slushing on the wet grass. "Does anyone complain here? Only you, I think. We help one another. Or we will become animals, like elephants and not men – even when the war is over."

Seaforth was ashamed, but he was also bitter that he was ashamed. That damned conscience his Aunt Mary had implanted in him. That

8

hook the British could always tweak to make their subjects feel small. And he felt even lower when Treves put an arm round his shoulder and said, "I'm whacked. Help me in, Sinclair. We need a hot drink. And thank you for all your help."

If you could give the Strand and Piccadilly the name of London, then London had never seen anyone like Marie Sinclair, and she had never seen a city like London. It was her Crow beauty, the bronze flush in her cheek under the slant of the bone, the green eyes that slit in laughter and blazed in song, the body that quivered as a knife flung into wood, the stride as lithe as a Greek runner, the whip of her step and the leap of her dance and the shake of her loose red hair. She was the first woman to wear Indian buckskin leggings on stage, and she off, in the street, without being a male impersonator. With her slipper, she could kick a champagne glass raised to toast her out of a swell's hand, and she could do hand-springs and back-flips all across the Domino Room of the Café Royal. Then her body was reflected a hundred times in the opposing mirrors, brighter than the infinite vista of exuberant gilding and crimson velvet, a caryatid of grace fallen down from the wall to somersault through the blue cigar smoke. And she never made even one domino fall on the marble tables of the artists and gamblers. Monsieur Gérard should have escorted her away, but how could he exclude such talent and beauty any more than he could throw out that outrageous fawn Augustus John with his gold earrings and red shirt, almond eyes and quicksilver lust?

When she had come to London from Vancouver, Marie had made her way straight to Charles Morton and his Theatre of Varieties. He looked like a fat cherub of a banker or a solicitor, yet Morton knew his Music Hall. In fact, he had invented it at the Canterbury over the river and had saved the Alhambra and the Tivoli on the Strand with his shows. Of course, Richard D'Oyly Carte had built the terracotta Palace on Cambridge Circus as The Royal English Opera House, but to tell the truth, only Queen Victoria had liked Sir Arthur Sullivan's opera *Ivanhoe* when it was put on there. After a time, the shares cost pennies, until Morton came along with his motto, "One Quality Only – the Best". Of course, it did depend what you meant by the best.

The trouble with Music Hall was the ladies could not go to it, and places like the Empire with its Lounge were really knocking-shops for the chorus girls and the young blades about town. But the Palace was a palace of the variety show, and anyone could take their grand-mother to tickle her fancy, if she could still remember she had one. Marie was a natural. She had faced down the frost-bitten miners coming back from the Klondike in Vancouver halls and she had none of that shy holding back that was the curse of the English artistes except for Marie Lloyd, she was all brass and sauce.

And the horses! She could gentle a gee-gee and giddy-up a stallion till they were hot wax to her act. The audiences went wild at her mastery of the beast, which they loved better than a wife or a husband or even a child. She would ride bare-back on her white pony onto the boards, then chant as she circled its body, first round its belly and back astride, then over its hindquarters and up under its tail, never touching the ground, while every man Jack thought a hoof would kick her head in. Then round the neck of the brute with its straining muscles swelling to the sex of her, and her song rising to its high note:

> *Pony of the prairie,*
> *Come for me –*
> *Indian Kathleen*
> *In my teepee.*
> *Pony of the prairie,*
> *Take me where*
> *The wind is wanton*
> *In my hair.*
> *Take me, take me –*

The white pony would be bucking and pawing now, sweating under the sinuous body encircling and embracing its hot hide, not daring to bolt; the energy as electric as the new house lights that blazed instead of the old spluttering candles; and Marie ending her enticement of the beast and the thousand spectators just a jot and tittle short of how far the Lord Chamberlain and his blue pencil would tolerate her show:

> *Take me true*
> *Over the prairie –*
> *I am you –*

Then Marie would catapult onto tiptoe on the pony's back, and cry, "Take me!" and the white horse would rear now, with Marie only steadying herself with one hand on its mane and her feet still on its spine. Then it would kick away off-stage into a stall full of bales of straw with Marie shouting, "Take me! Take me!" and the house thundering with clapping hands and hurrahs, the men's faces red with passion and the women's pink with jealousy and envy.

Going down Shaftesbury Avenue to the Trocadero, Marie could not stop the urchins yelling, "Take me! Take me!" and the mashers sidling up with their propositions, "Take you – I'd take you anywhere." But nobody dared molest her, the pride of the Palace, the toast of the Strand.

It took a while for Marie to persuade her Aunt Mary to meet her at the Café Royal for dinner after the show. It was not in the Domino Room – shades of Oscar Wilde and Bosie Douglas, scandal and ruin – but in the restaurant upstairs, where the best cellar in the world was lifted to accompany some of the better grub.

Mary found the way to that culinary heaven quite stimulating, but as she lifted the skirts of her long bombazine dress, she wondered if it was the right thing to wear. At least, black did not show the dirt if the hem dragged on the red carpet on the stairs. She did not know what the allegories meant on the walls with their swirls and symbols, but the gilt railings and little grove of shrubs and flowers in the waiting-room at the top of the stairs were bonny.

The big dining-rooms beyond were partitioned by screens of mirrors, but Mary did not dare sit down in one of the easy-chairs, scooped out by the weight of many a large man. She would never have got out of it again. Instead, she sat on a small cane chair and looked up at the domed glass roofing that gave the great room the look of a greenhouse at Kew. So tight was her dress that Mary felt like a potted plant, her feet crammed like roots into her button shoes. She needed some care from a gardener and she was glad that Marie came bounding up the stairs, her wide ochre skirt flailing round the skip and hop of her legs, her red hair burning in a comet's tail behind her.

"Aunt Mary," she cried, "I got you here – into the house of sin!"

Never was Mary better treated or fed. She was appreciated without flattery, heard without yawns. The two young men, whom Marie introduced familiarly as Bill and Algie, almost revered her as much as they fawned on Marie. There was no patronising or condescending, although Mary had rarely seen a pair of such precious young fops. Algie's hair was as red as Marie's and carefully curled: his pallor was unhealthy beside her tan. But he wanted to know every detail of the *Maine* and how our brave boys would be treated after they had been wounded by the beastly Boers. And Bill, who was a skeleton of drawling emaciation, wanted to listen to everything about her life: the looking after the Indian women in the closed *zenanas*, the marriage to Harry Lamb, and particularly how Marie had found her in London before setting up on her own as the belle of Cambridge Circus. "I must confess," Mary said, "I have never seen Marie ride her pony – "

"Take me," Algie giggled, "take me now."

"Theatre," Mary went on, "is not my line. I did see the ballad singers in the Seven Dials – "

"Darling," Marie said, "that does date you. But you never age – "

"And the Vic once. But a theatre of varieties, even though it's a Palace. But I ken Marie. She'll take the house by storm."

"More than we can do," Bill said, "against those boring Boers. Now, Mrs Lamb, try the terrine. I know the geese of Strasburg stuffed their livers and parted with them nobly for this, but we do give them a fond farewell. Those blocks of truffles look just like mourning hats."

Mary took the liver paste, but she did not like the talk. Dying was not funny, at least not in her trade. And Marie intervened with that quick sympathy that stopped her from being impossible about her beauty.

"La-di-dah, Bill. Food's food. Give my aunt some of that Cliquot *rosé*. It's better than Canada. What we got there was bear's blood and gunpowder with a dash of iron filings. But Robert's coming over, have you heard?"

"Yes," Mary said. "With Strathcona's horse –"

"Can he ride like you can?" Algie laughed shrill again. "Take him *anywhere*."

"His grandmother wasn't a Crow," Marie said. "And *père* Bain is no French trapper like my father. He's a dirt farmer in the prairies. But Robert, I must say, he always loved a horse. Born to the saddle, not plodding behind a plough."

"He should not be fighting," Mary said. "It is no' his war."

"It's not mine either," Algie said. "I do think fighting's for those who are fit for it."

"And dying?" Mary said.

"That's for others. I don't mind a *beating*, a good whacking –" here Algie's eyes glittered with amusement "– but death is going too far."

"Shut up, Algie," Marie said. "You can't shock Aunt Mary. She's nursed more dying people than you've had forty whacks."

"Yes, do shut up, Algie," Bill drawled. "We should support our soldiers. I didn't tell you, Marie, I did try and volunteer. Lovat's Horse, a family thing. But they said I was too skinny. The nag would bolt away with me."

"You Scots?" Mary said. "You dinna give the impression –"

"Been down South rather too long, really, Mrs Lamb. But the old heather has its pull. I mean, Marie says she's never seen Scotland, so I said I'll take her back to Sinclair country."

"Little of that is Sinclair now," Mary said. "Our own folk, there's no muckle in the crofts."

"All the same," Bill said, "we still have an acre or two. And one cannot change a moor or a mountain or a loch, whoever claims to have it. But one can choose a menu. *Caille cocotte*, I recommend, to melt in the mouth before we freeze our palates with a *pôle nord*."

"Ach, it's too rich for me," Mary said, only to give way to her niece's laugh.

"Mary, Mary, quite contrary – you deserve all the riches in the world." And she held up her glass of pink bursting bubbles. "To Mary – who has given more and taken less – the only generous spirit in all the world."

The two young men lifted their glasses and drank too, saying, "The only generous spirit in all the world."

Mary felt a prickle at the back of her lids. She groped in her little evening bag and found a handkerchief and dabbed at her eyes. She did not like Marie's young men – flimsy-whimsies and namby-pambies, not worth a curl of Marie's red hair – but they oozed charm enough to float the royal yacht *Britannia*. And they did want to hear about her life. And at her age, appreciation was pretty well all.

"Thank you," she said. "I try. And what do you do?"

And when it turned out that Bill was a painter and designer, for houses rather than the stage, she was more impressed. Particularly as he was also the Earl of Dunesk, and Mary never expected a nobleman to lift a finger to do anything. He did, though, lift his glass in one more toast, and rose with it.

"The Queen," he said. "May *She* live and prosper."

Algie remained seated with the two women, although he drank the toast with them.

"The Queen. But *She* is ninety."

"Yes," Bill said as he sat down, "but when *She* dies, it will be a new age – and not surely for the better."

With brass buttons gleaming like mint golden guineas, his braid shining and a rose in his buttonhole, his hunter chain across his belly button and his silver whistle in his waistcoat pocket, his flag furled for the last stop at Vancouver, Bob McDowell rode the Canadian Pacific Railway like a king, not a guard. But he was out of sorts, puffing and snorting through the heavy breathing that he said was asthma, but his wife Kate said was overweight. He had not liked the sly look in Charlie Mackinnon's eyes when the steward had handed him the *Illustrated London News* which some vacationer had left in his dining-car.

"Looks like your Marie, showing a leg," Charlie had said and smacked his lips. Yes, he had positively popped his lips in a wet kiss.

"Offensive noises," Bob had to reprimand him, "are not permitted in these premises."

"But girls' legs are," Charlie had said and scampered off. The young wouldn't know a manner from a water closet, not these days.

And the drawing in the magazine did show his step-daughter riding a rearing pony bare-back and half-bare herself. Naked limbs almost up to the thigh as her loose leggings were rucked high. That was the Indian in her. It had to come out. Blood always told. And his own blood was drumming high in his ears as Bob McDowell fought to control his temper. He wanted to bellow like a bull moose. But he clenched his hands on the tails of his frock coat and pulled it down. He would maintain his dignity, however much Marie tried to drag him down.

The huge locomotive came into the station in a storm of steam and a rolling grindstone of great wheels. The black face of the engine loomed like a meteorite, the funnel blew fumes high as a twister to the sky. The waiting Kate could only feel awe and a kind of worship for these iron behemoths which her man rode and commanded. She did not love him as she had Henri, the gentle frontier savage of her dream days, but Bob was steady, for sure, and he had fought for forty years to be where he was, nobody to help him, but only her now. And there he was, riding the end carriage on the steps, hanging on and blowing his whistle, then jumping heavily down – *plump* – *plump* – to unroll his flag and shake it over his head. He called, "End of the line – the Pacific!" He always did that, as if announcing a victory. And it was a victory of sorts, the crossing of a whole continent on a metal road, the spanning of the two great oceans of the world.

Kate ran to him and saw his red face and his fury. He pushed a rolled paper at her. "Marie – *your* daughter – shameful . . . shaming us . . ." He turned away to his duty, seeing the passengers off the train, and Kate ruffled the pages to find the drawing of Marie performing on her pony at the Palace. Her heart swelled. She could have sung with joy. Marie successful, Marie loose, Marie free. Henri would have loved that wild liberty in his daughter. But how to tell Bob? How to explain that women now – and maybe women always – needed to break out, if only for a time? There was no putting up with a man's world if a woman had never known how to ride fast and dance a fling and run her own wild way. But Kate knew the diplomacy between the two of them, Bob and herself, in the marriage bond. So she hid the delight in her heart, and she said gloomily to her husband, "She's doing terrible, terrible things –" and then she could not stop herself from adding – "thank God."

2

A BARE TABLE

Spion Kop had a flat top. Some giant seemed to have sliced its head off its shoulders like an executioner with his axe. For once the Lancashires and the Engineers and the Rangers were above the Boers after a night attack. But with the coming of the light snipers and sharpshooters, edging round the crust of the kop, peppered the British, lying uneasily between the flat rocks. The Krupp and Hotchkiss and Maxim-Nordenfeldt guns of the enemy artillery had made a target of the tableland on the height of the mountain. They deluged it with fire. From a distance well out of range, Captain Charles Seymour-Scudabright, on detachment from his battleship with his battery of naval guns, saw the bombardment from nearby Spearman's Hill. There was nothing to do but watch. And finish his letter home to his wife May in purple prose that would prove that he had himself been in the heat of the action. And it was hellish hot. So he wrote in pencil on the ruled pad on his knee:

Ping! ping! rang the rifles in chorus. Bong! bong! go the guns, with a *basso profundo* that reverberates in the hollows of these hills. What an awe-striking revelly! Shrapnel from Teutonic guns sprays hither and thither. Lyddite opens out umbrellas of earth far and wide. The roar and the roll of fiends in fury rends the clear air, scented with mimosa. Even the bosom of the placid silvery river shudders and quakes as it winds round Potgieter's Drift. Hour after hour, the tornado pursues its deadly course . . .

Stumped for his next lush patch of words, Charles looked up at the top of the kop. He could see reinforcements creeping as big as lice up the near steep slope, past the dressing station set up for the wounded below the ruin. They would hold the mountain, turn the flank of the Boers and use his naval guns to break through to besieged Ladysmith. He was there all night, in the thick of it, at risk. So he wrote on, the sweat from his fingers smudging the letters:

Death – mutilation – agony – thirst – these mean more here than

15

the word glory – and you know, my dear May, what glory means to me. Other than you, it is dearest to my heart. Officers and men alike can scarce lift a head lest they meet the doom that hangs over every creature in this murderous arena. We crouch and take cover and wait. And the Boers see the dance of death among us and sneak up and are upon us. But we do not flinch. We will not be able to hold much longer. The trenches that we are grandly defending are becoming our graves. The number of the slain is appalling to see. The dead lie literally in stacks at our Thermopylae, and they are the sole protection of we few who survive . . .

One couldn't beat a classical education at Eton, where Gordon and Graham already were, growing up like their father to serve in the army or navy. Greek gave one all the right adjectives. And the army gave him the right borrowed batman Higgins, who produced from nowhere biscuits and scrambled eggs in a mess-tin. It was smart, even though the egg was orange-yellow, perhaps from one of the ostriches Charles had bagged on his way up from his battleship *Terrible*. He had the tail-feathers in his bag for May's hats.

The British were certainly not going to show the white feather here. But there was precious little to view on Spion Kop until the evening came. Only then did his naval gunners receive the orders to drag their battery to the top of the mountain, just as the last of the heroes were retreating back down the last scarp. He still had time to end his letter home:

We reel from loss of blood – not mine, personally – but this is Victoria Cross time. Dozens of heroes have earned it all about me, and I do not boast about what I have done. A thousand are dead, hundreds live – yet I have come through to the other side. Fear not for me, for I will live to drub the Dutch. The next time is the time for the pounding of the guns until they beg for the mercy which they never grant to us. I will keep you all safe.
A kiss from Daddy to little Ruth
CHARLES

What was damnable about watching the battle was that he was actually wounded at it. While they were limbering up the guns, some dozy idiot dropped an iron spike and crippled Charles's foot. He felt he had five broken toes through his boot. It had to be Ingrams, and Charles was not so sure it was not deliberate, for he had had Ingrams tied to a gun-wheel every night for a month for falling asleep on picket. It was an act of mercy. He could have had Ingrams shot for dereliction of duty in the face of the enemy. And now the cretin breaks his captain's bones. And all he says with a smirk is, "Sorry, sir, must a' slipped outa me 'and," like a skivvy dropping a Dresden plate. Watch it, Ingrams. When I am back in harness, I'll have my eye on you.

The naval guns never reached Spion Kop, for its defenders had abandoned it already. But on his Calvary in the ambulance cart back to the field hospital, Charles wondered if he could get a medal for being wounded. It was in the course of duty. He might have to settle for a mere campaign ribbon – but that would be rotten luck. The pain in his foot was just as excruciating as it was for the other wounded soldiers lying bloody and cursing about him in language that gentlemen only used between each other. All who were harmed – however they were harmed – should be rewarded equally for their service to their country. If only he could find a friend in a high place who would write him a recommendation for his derring-do at Spion Kop. His letter to his wife May would be proof of his presence of mind.

So it was that Charles Seymour-Scudabright arrived at the field hospital, where he was not pleased to meet his wife's cousin, Seaforth Sinclair, that little mistake on the other side of the blanket by her uncle Hamish James in India. And Seaforth was in no hurry to treat Charles, who had to wait his turn in the lying line of sufferers, soldiers and commissioned ranks treated in the order of arrival. And what was worse, Charles saw Seaforth take his time off from sewing and strapping up the sick to jaw with a jumped-up Indian in a black suit, who seemed to be in command of the coolie body-snatchers who had assumed the title of the South African Indian Ambulance Corps. Charles could not hear what Seaforth was saying, but it was bad enough that he was saying it to one of his kind instead of saving British lives.

"You are doing a good job, Mr Gandhi," Seaforth was saying to the small Indian who was wiping mist off his spectacles, "you and your volunteers are doing a splendid job – but I fail to understand *why* you are doing it at all."

The voice that answered Seaforth was so compelling and reasonable that he was almost seduced into assent.

"We are showing our loyalty to the Empire," Gandhi said. "And then it will show its gratitude to us."

"We want liberty, not gifts."

"Like the Afrikaners," Gandhi asked, "you want to take liberty with guns? Like the Afrikaners, you want to discriminate between the races? The British, at least, claim we are *one* Empire and we are all British subjects. They give their domination over us all to some free Dominions – Canada, Australia . . ."

"Free *white* Dominions. Not to India."

"In the end, to India too."

"I cannot wait that long. Free India now."

"And have this?" Gandhi looked along the rows of shattered and bleeding men, as they groaned on the ground, with only the Indian bearers to give them water and comfort. "Which would you rather be, doctor? A live negotiator or a dying soldier?"

"I would rather be free."

"But we are. We are free of dying. We are excluded while white man fights white man. We merely bear the Empire as it kills itself. It kills itself by fighting itself. That is not the way. Sit down." The words were said as a quiet order, not as an invitation. So Seaforth sat awkwardly on his hams in the British fashion, while Gandhi sat cross-legged and easily, as he went on talking. "If I say, 'Sit down,' to all my ambulance corps, and they all sit down, what will happen to the British soldiers? They will die more quickly. If you stay on sitting here and do not go back to your operating tent with Dr Treves, more British soldiers will die. Fighting does not win wars. It only piles up bodies. Sitting makes for changes. Doing nothing can be a big action. Refusing is resistance. How would this Empire work, if the people who worked for it sat back and said, 'Work it yourself without us, until you set us free!'?"

Seaforth paused before replying to the persuasive force of the argument.

"We would be *made* to get up and work," he said. "Flogged into hard labour."

"I doubt it," Gandhi said. "The British have laws. I practise them as a barrister. They know what they do – and what they say they will do – and do not do. And when they behave badly, when they are guilty, I can play on that guilt. That is the way to make India free. We must make them depend on us. We must make them guilty. Then we must sit down, when they really need us. As they now need you, Dr Sinclair, and you are sitting down."

Treves had, indeed, appeared at the entrance to the nearest operating tent and was looking round, searching with his eyes. Seaforth found himself getting to his feet against his will, answering an unspoken call to duty.

"Have to stretch my legs," he heard himself mumbling as an excuse, but he was all too conscious of Gandhi, still sitting cross-legged on the ground and smiling at his going.

Just as Treves saw him coming and said, "Ah, good man, we need you –", Seaforth heard a shout from a familiar voice behind him, "Seaforth! When are you going to treat my bloody foot? I am a captain on the *Terrible*, you know, in the Royal Navy!" Seaforth was relieved from his embarrassment in front of Gandhi by turning and shouting at the intolerable Charles Seymour-Scudabright, "Wait your turn, captain! Being *family* won't do you any good." He found Treves laughing as he pushed his way past the Queen's Surgeon into the operating tent, then he heard Treves giggle as he spoke, "I must say, Sinclair, you do seem to have family *everywhere*!"

Charles had to put up with his foot aching worse than an attack of gout until past midnight, before he reached the head of the queue and was strapped up and given to the Indian body-snatchers to ship off on the train to a hospital ship, where proper due would be paid to his superior rank. From his train compartment, he saw a face he knew, pug-nosed and pugnacious under the Boer hat and cockolibird feather of the South African Horse. It was Winston, Lady Randolph Churchill's son. He must have escaped from his prison camp and wriggled his way into a cavalry post as well as war correspondent for the *Morning Post*. But he could write up Charles's role at Spion Kop.

"Hey, Churchill," Charles called. "Over here! Churchill, I say."

The young man sauntered over and looked through the open compartment window at Charles lying along the seat. He did not recognise the captain, who had to add his name, "Charles Seymour-Scudabright. With the naval guns at Spion Kop."

"You didn't see much action," Churchill said.

"Oh, I *saw* it, all right."

"They peppered you."

"Only my leg."

"I got up and down the kop *twice*," Churchill said. "One hell of a mess."

"Was it not."

"*You* were up there? We must have missed each other."

Charles swallowed. The lie had to be by omission, but he must be mentioned in Churchill's dispatch.

"I was wounded with the others. I have written all about it in a letter to my wife. Would you like to see?" Charles held forward his ruled pad. "I think I have captured the pluck and the glory . . ."

"Thank you." Churchill did not move to take the pad. "We lost, you know. We did not win. I have my own view and style. Get well, man, soon."

Then he turned and walked away. It was a puzzle how the captain had been wounded – the naval guns had never been in action. Churchill had seen no glory, nor would he match the style of Charles's letter home. In his own manner, Churchill wrote the next morning of his first pilgrimage to the summit of the bare table mountain. *Streams of wounded met us and obstructed our path. Men were staggering along alone, or supported by comrades, or crawling on hands and knees, or carried on stretchers. Corpses lay here and there. The splinters and fragments of shell had torn and mutilated in the most ghastly manner. I passed about two hundred while I was climbing up. There was, moreover, a small but steady leakage of unwounded men of all corps. Some of these cursed and swore. Others were utterly exhausted and fell on the hillside in stupor. Others again seemed drunk, though they had had no liquor. Scores were sleeping heavily. Fighting was still proceeding . . .*

Churchill put down his pen. It had not been much like glory, really. War was anything but.

A letter had come from home – or what the British in India called home, whatever that was. For Peg Sinclair at her hospital desk at Lucknow, home was wherever the few people she loved were. With a Scots soldier father and Hindu mother, she had no real country and no home, no more than her brother Seaforth did, in spite of his identification with India. Her Aunt Mary had been more of a mother to her than anyone else, putting her through her training at St Thomas's in London. But a "home" in England also meant a place where they put unwanted children to teach them to be good. Yes, Mary's letter to her was a letter from home.

Dearest Peg,

I must ask you to come home. They have asked me to go out to South Africa on a hospital ship called *Maine*. It has an X-ray machine that can see through bodies and tell us what went wrong. But there is no X-ray machine to see through this terrible war and tell us what went wrong, why there is more of this senseless killing, worse than Glencoe.

We need you here at St Thomas's. There will be many wounded from the war. I want my best lassies back here. You will have a ward to run. The poor soldiers – it is not *their* fault they are shot by Dutchmen holding onto their land.

My dearest Seaforth, as you know, is working with the wounded at the front line. He is with Dr Treves, one of our best surgeons. He serves the Queen, though she is poorly they say. I think Seaforth serves in the war because he loved his soldier father who died in South Africa. You love him, I know. Of course, Seaforth will never say it. No Sinclair can ever say he loves another Sinclair. Though some of the Sinclair women can. You and I, Peg, we can say it.

As I prepare to sail, it is all rich women and committees. You would hate it. This big city is empty without you. I miss you sorely. But your cousin Marie is the toast of London. She does something wicked on a horse, but she will not allow me to see it. Not for you, Auntie, she says. Cows and a milk pail are more your line. What does that mean? She has all kinds of friends, earls and such. But never a man like your father or your Uncle Iain. You must tell me of the news from Annandale.

But you must come *home*. The India Office and your cousin Margaret's husband Douglas will be looking to it. Do not say you will not come, even if we miss each other in London, for I may have sailed by the time you reach me. I do not ask you to come for the war or the Empire, but for me. I need you. Your hospital needs you. And don't forget to bring back that green chutney I muckle like. But not Bombay Duck. It is everything hygiene is not.

All my love
MARY

They were so unconscious about their orders, the people she loved, the British. They told you they needed you, they arranged for you to come "home", and then they said, "Of course, it is only if you want to." In fact, their command was your wish. To tell the truth, Peg knew that she wanted to go. Lucknow was all right, her position was good, almost an assistant matron to the whole hospital, but these were sad times with the Boer War, a rebellion in a colony. The Indian regiments were marching away under their British officers to fight in an alien conflict. And there were whispers of another mutiny in India in aid of the Boers. Her brother Seaforth would be working for that, for Indian independence. He was obsessed about it. But she – a soldier's daughter – she would move with the soldiers, as she always had, to take care of them.

Outside her window there was the sound of the neighing of horses, the jingle and clanking of guns. Peg rose from her desk to stand by the open window and peer round the edge of the canvas screen. A squadron of horse artillery was passing the hospital wall. She could see the heads of the horses, the plumes and banners of the mounted gunners and the covered barrels of the guns on their wheeled carriages. They moved in a cloud of dust as if they were already firing the earth. Their going was a quiet explosion. They were heading for the sea on a dictate from London, as she would be. And yet they were not unwilling. The horses' heads jerked and pranced, the gunners shouted and tossed their helmets. They were going somewhere, if not home. And she would also soon be at sea, going to do what she knew how to do. But the why of it, Peg knew no more than her Aunt Mary.

*

21

Robert Sinclair hated being a Mountie on a transport ship. Even sailors had an easier life. Revelly was half past four, a trumpet tooting at the dawn. He was sleeping on deck and he had to roll up his blanket and carry it down to the store-room. At five in the morning, he had a mess-tin of dish-water tea, and half an hour later there was roll-call in case a Canadian cowboy had gone for a swim off Africa. Then the worst, mucking out the stalls below decks, and feeding and watering the horses. It had to be done to drilltime. If one bronco was fed before the next bronco in line, there were ructions, and the whole herd of horses was fighting and kicking. The din of the hoofs on the buckboards was deafening. The order, "Stables!" meant swabbing out the alleyways between and behind the nags. Robert was enough of a farm boy to know anything you put into a horse came out worse at the back end and he laughed to see the gentlemen volunteers, the friends of Lord Strathcona himself, grubbing after manure to put in buckets, then banging their oily heads against stanchions and beams as they carted the dung away.

Slopping out was never done, but somewhere towards eternity, the bugle always called breakfast. The scrum in the wash-house wasn't for washing yourself. You needed a curry-comb and a frayed rope's end to get the muck off you. And as for a meal, you had ship's biscuits, a scrape of jam and tepid bilgewater with a trace of tea. And pickles – always pretty pickles! One day, there was a treat, a tin of sardines among thirteen men. If there was a bit of bully beef, the bully got it – and it was not Robert. All he got was a suck at the tin-opener . . . the man behind him had a look at the tin and the label for hereafters. Such was life on the ocean wave. Then there was the call of "Buckets!" and some bronco had kicked one over, and they all started up stamping and squealing, and woke up the sleeping Tommies, and Stripes leant over the hatchway and wanted to know what that son of a swivel-eyed sea-cook was playing at. And you were down to the horses again, which was why you were there, although you didn't know where you were, just in the middle of the godforsaken sea.

Washing-up was worse. You doubled over two pints of tepid water, trying to clean up forty greasy tin plates and mugs, and you were jamming rusty fork points into your fingers, while your tea towel was an old dirty jersey and your brush was the straw cover off a beer bottle. That was the time you blessed your wife, if you were old enough to have an old woman, or your mother, God bless her, how did she put up with it all! Men looking after men, it was the sorriest sight in all the world, except for men looking after horses, which was bloody murder.

The mess room was just under the main deck-houses and measured about forty feet square. There were thirteen long tables with a hundred and forty men seated at them. It was always noisy, but that was silence compared to the noise when the beer didn't arrive on time. The din then beat feeding time at the zoo into a cocked hat, every man Jack hitting the back of his tin plate and mug till the sparks flew and the plates and mugs looked like the order of the boot. And when the music started, it was "Swanee River" and "Beer, beer, glorious beer" and "We are not working now" and "Oh, listen to the band" until everybody choked and the tinware was bashed into smithereens.

The other sport was boxing. The Britishers reckoned it was kind of like war. Down in the stuffy hold, a ring of sorts, and a couple of idiots smashing their noses flat and thinking they were bashing Johnnie Boer, old Uncle Kruger and Botha and all. But that was all fossicks. Sport wasn't war. Play wasn't war. And this ship never got where it was going.

Fire and boat drill, that was a laugh. Three hundred men with four boats and two dozen life-belts five hundred miles from shore. If they had a fire or hit a reef, they'd see their Maker sooner than their saviour. They knew that. This bloody ocean, it went on too long. Where was Johnnie Boer? Here's luck and blue blazes to his good old *sjambok*, but when he saw the Canadian cowboys coming, he'd go hell for lather for home.

Funny, wasn't it, but however big the world was, and wherever you went, you could never get away from the good old kith and kin. When Robert was a kid, Cousin Marie couldn't say "kith". So she said, "kiss and kin". It was nice for him, he got kisses from Marie if he was kin. Which was something to say, now she was the belle of Piccadilly, the darling of the Strand. But who could reckon this chap would come up from the engine-room with the long Sinclair face and the mournful chops and say, "I saw you on the roster, Robert Sinclair. You must be Bain's son. I'm Hamilton, your cousin from India. We'll have a chat over the games."

The British navy didn't run on engines, whatever Hamilton said. It ran on three games which passed the time of day, if the horses didn't. Otherwise everybody would be overboard – sharkmeat – nothing else to do better. They played Under and Over, Crown and Anchor, and 'Ouse About, as 'Arry called it. Under and Over was a dead loss. A piece of canvas marked in three squares, Under Seven and Over. You put on sixpence, and if it was a seven on the dice, you got eighteen pence. If not, the game was over and you were under the odds, you couldn't beat them. Crown and Anchor had six squares: the crown, ace of spades, hearts, clubs, diamonds, and the ship's hook, the anchor. You had three dice, which meant you lost three times quicker. But at 'Ouse About or 'Ousey 'Ousey, you got an 'Arry for your money, because he was a riot, though you still lost. Talking to Hamilton while 'Arry was on the blarney, Robert didn't know which ear to use.

"How could you leave the farm, Robert? Didn't your father go wild? And your mother – I would have thought she would have chained you to your bed."

"'Ouse about," 'Arry was calling. "Come away, my lucky lads. 'Ouse correct. Oo'll 'ave a card? Sixty-nine, eighty-four, seventy-two. Oo's the lucky man? Twenty-nine, thirteen, unlucky for some – but top of the 'ouse."

"You got away," Robert said. "That farm of yours in the Himalayas. Iain couldn't keep you. You love them, your engines. You're a mad mechanic."

"'Ouse correct, gentlemen," 'Arry was calling. "'Oo says another card. Come on then! All of you ready?"

"It's not the same," Hamilton said. "My father wanted me to go. He wanted me to be an engineer. Ship's engines. Do something useful. He builds canals himself in the Punjab. He didn't want me to die like my brother Hamish – and my uncle – fighting for Africa, which we didn't want. It isn't any use, anyway."

"Three to one on the lucky seven! Now then, gents, you pays your money and you takes your chance. Now's your time to seize the brass bull hopportunity by its silver-plated 'orns – nifty fifty . . ."

"Pardon me," Robert said and put his coin on thirty-three. "You never ploughed a field behind an ox. You never cut corn or fixed barbed wire. I tell you, you can break your back on the land. I love horses. Christ, Ham, a horse – being on a horse – a gallop on the plains – it was the only way out. And when Lord Strathcona said, volunteers, anyone who could ride, shoot straight – and I've shot grizzlies – well, you would be here, wouldn't you? And not *there*."

"As you were, gentlemen," 'Arry was calling. "Number eleven, get to 'eaven. Ninety-nine, end of the line. Sixty-four, knock on the door, and no 'ouse yet."

"There's no need for cavalry in this war," Hamilton said. "It's all twelve-pounders and machine-guns. The poor bloody horses are all riddled with bullets before they get near the trenches. There are no lancers now."

"We don't have lances," Robert said. "We have six-shooters. We're cowboys. You've never seen anything like it."

"You've never seen anything like Johnnie Boer," Hamilton said. "He rides like the wind when you're after him. Then he'll suddenly sit in a donga or a spruit bed and knock you off with his Mauser like quails for breakfast. Don't count your chickens, Robert. You hang up your saddles to dry."

"Sixty-six, pick up sticks," 'Arry was calling. "An' no 'ouse yet. Oh, is it you, sergeant? 'Ave a tanner on a number. What? Game's over, and there ain't a winner? Strewth, what a bummer. Sorry, lads, and so long. Two pound five in the kitty, and I'll 'old it till next time. Cross me 'eart and 'ope to die. But if you care to join me, I'll get a jar out of Pills."

"What?" Hamilton asked. "A drink out of the doctor?"

"Stout," Robert said. "For rheumatism. We can get it for the broncos, when their withers don't work so good."

"And we can get it too? I mean, we are humans – or are we?"

"'Arry can," Robert said. "'Arry can get anything, including the fingers off your hand. I don't know, Ham, but 'Arry's taught me one thing about the mother country."

"What's that, Robert?"

"Sharp, they are. You must count your blessings. Because if you don't count them, the Queen – God bless Her – will lift them off you."

"I don't know," Hamilton said. "I thought what you learned was to play the game – whatever it was – whatever the rules were."

3

POUND THEM DOWN

Kitchener was a butcher. The problem was, he seemed to like killing his own men. Coming to South Africa late with Lord Bobs, he had to make the same mistakes all over again at Paardeberg, and make them worse. As though they hadn't before tried to charge across the chocolate-brown Modder River and make it redder. It was just like Magersfontein – Hamish Charles knew that – and there he had lost his uncle. Yesterday the Highland Brigade had marched more than thirty miles after the relief of Kimberley and then the Scotsmen were thrown straight at the huge snail of the Boer position in the morning. The Dutchmen had hidden sharpshooters in the willows and mimosa and brushwood and dongas along the river bank, but the laager of their waggons and trenches bulged out in a fortified shell on the north bank of the river. As usual, the Highlanders had to charge across open ground at Mauser rifles firing from dug-outs, and, as usual, they were pinned down and staked out among the ant-heaps, the backs of their necks and their bare knees below their kilts blistering in the sun, their throats drier than sand dunes with the dun river-waters mocking their thirst a hundred yards ahead. Hamish Charles did not even dare brush away the horse-fly that bit into his leg. If he had, likely as not a Dum-dum or a Pom-pom bullet would have taken away his relieving arm.

But this time, the Highlanders did not break and run. They knew they were not in a trap now, the Boers were. Old Cronje with his burghers and women and children, he had stopped trekking and was trying to fight it out behind the river. But he was being surrounded. And now the twelve-pounder naval guns and the howitzers were on the kopjes, and they were pounding the laager with lyddite and shrapnel. Waggons were blazing or else charred to black scrap. Explosions blew up eddies of earth and plumes of soil. Already the tempting beige waters had begun to smell, as the bodies of horses and men floated down and stuck on the banks to putrefy in the shallows. Vultures waited as gravely as undertakers to profit from death. But this time the Dutch were being peppered and they could not trek away.

Lord Bobs arrived that night after a tummy upset, and he would have none of death and glory. Dapper and tiny, not a pip on him to show his rank, he decided to win by shot and shell as the Boers had always done. There was one charge more for Hamish Charles across the river. The Seaforths and the Cornwalls went in with the bayonet into the brushwood and drove the snipers from their cover by the drift. One fat farmer was the first man that Hamish Charles had ever killed with the steel, driving it into his back as he tripped over a root, then putting a boot in the ribs of the lying and squirming Boer Johnnie so that the point could be pulled out. Then the corpse turned over like a porpoise and looked up at him, red froth coming from his mouth. "Why?" he said, and died in a spasm of crimson bubbles. And Hamish Charles found himself retching and swearing never to stick a human being again. He did not have the blood lust in him.

De Wet and his commandos took a kopje nearby but Cronje would not budge to join them. So they rode away, and the Old Man surrendered. It was chalk and cheese to see. The huge and portly Cronje slouching down suspiciously, his small eyes sly and darting between the brim of his grey slouch hat and his bush of a black beard, his pantaloons rolled up from his tan boots to the bottom of his bottle-green overcoat and his *sjambok* in his hand. Confronting him, the imperial whippet, Lord Bobs with his picquet cap straight along the parting of his white hair, a glossy strap slicing down his erect back to his swordbelt, and the sheath of his sabre arching forward to the gleaming toe-caps of his riding-boots. Lord Bobs held out his hand. "I am glad to see you," he said. "You have made a gallant defence, sir." Cronje engulfed the hand of peace in his large one as a dog might grab a bone. He did not speak, but stared in hate and shame. His little wife stood behind him, a thin and toothless woman in a rough straw hat and a dirty black dress, rather like a gypsy who had told her fortune wrong.

The beaten Boers themselves appeared to be refugees. In shapeless and muddy clothes, they carried pots and pans and parasols and Bibles as well as rifles. From the rolled blankets in their knapsacks, teapots and bottles and galoshes were hanging. Hamish Charles could not believe such a bunch of derelicts could have thrashed the British armies so often and so bloodily. There were about fifty women shrouded in reach-me-downs, some carrying babies on their hips. A tall Australian went among them, insisting on kissing every infant. And the Dutch women held up their children to be blessed by those foreign lips.

It was not the time of the concentration camps yet. The women and children were let go under safe-conduct, the men taken off to prison on the island of St Helena. And wandering into the remains of the stinking laager, Hamish Charles could not imagine how the enemy had endured the pounding for so many days. The whole camp was a dark chaos, slashed with zig-zags of green and yellow from the lyddite. Waggons were mere smashed struts and wheels or twists of black metal. The whole area was a rubbish heap of saddles and leather panniers, tin trunks and brass cartridges. And everything reeked, an open slaughter-house in the stench of the sun. Shrapnel had scattered the bodies of the oxen, and the horses were turned inside out as wet gloves are. Flies were heaving blue cloaks on the entrails of the poor beasts and unburied men. The very river stank like a sewer, and typhoid and enteric infused its waters with more deadliness than Maxim bullets. Hamish Charles was too sickened to pursue his hunt for souvenirs to send home, but he did poke under the flap of one upturned waggon, only to start back, his heart in his throat. For a dead man moved.

But he was no threat. The Afrikaner lay back, his leg caught under an axle-tree. His thin face was striped with ochre and soot from the lyddite shells, his breath was sharp as vinegar. But he smiled up at Hamish Charles and said, "Oy, *rooinek*, can you get me out?"

So Hamish Charles put down his rifle and tugged at the axle-tree and managed to heave it high enough for the Boer Johnnie to pull his limb free with his hands. He had grit all right. He pulled himself upright on the struts of the waggon and tested his weight on his injured leg. "Oy yoy, I can't . . . but it's better than your shells on our *schanses* . . . I must. Find me a stick, man." So Hamish Charles found a broken spar and gave it to the young Boer, who put it under his armpit and hopped out of the waggon. "Let's trek."

"You're my prisoner," Hamish Charles said.

"*Vrede*," the Afrikaner said. "Peace. Not *vlug*. How can I run, man?"

So Hamish Charles gave the Boer Johnnie his shoulder and supported him along the Modder bank towards the drift, where they could ford the river to the grouping area for the other prisoners. But in a clump of willow that the shells from the far *berg* had spared, the hobbling man asked for a rest and sat on a stump. His name was Piet Krug, he said. And he came from the Orange Free State, that would not be free much longer, after Cronje's surrender. With his crushed leg, he could not fight any more. For him *huis-toe*, the war was over. He would go back to his farm. Hamish Charles should try it, dry farming with cattle and mealies, it was a good life. The Kaffirs round there were not bad, if you could make them work. Nothing was like the *bushveld*. It was better than choking on lyddite fumes or the shrapnel they called hell-scrapers. Could Hamish Charles use Krug's slouch hat to get some river water and wash the muck off his face from the *klein kafferkies*, the lyddite shells. He looked a *swart* sight, he knew he did.

So Hamish Charles swabbed off the face of his enemy with dirty water, and then performed an act that amazed himself. Piet Krug said, "Hell, man, that drift, I don't know if I can make it across the Modder. Leave me here. Forget me. And if the other *rooineks* forget me, I go back to my farm, not to your prison camp. Look at the leg – I won't shoot you again." And Hamish Charles found himself consenting to the possible escape of Krug and even the thought of visiting him on his farm near Bechuanaland after the war was over. "I must be crazy," Hamish Charles said, "to trust you, Piet Krug." But he knew he could. For he had forgotten his Metford rifle when he had gone to the river for the water to wash Krug's face, and Krug had not turned the weapon on his helper. When it came to it, and if there was mutual respect, you could trust Johnnie Boer.

Hamish Charles did not have mutual respect for all of his own side. The Scots had never got on that well with the English, nor the Seaforths and the Highland Brigade with the cavalry. But now there were the volunteer colonials, come to help their mother country in a far corner of the Empire. They were good scrappers, the Australians and the Canadians – Hamish Charles had even heard from Aunt Mary in London that his cousin Robert might be coming out with Strathcona's Horse. But these colonial cavalrymen, the planters from Assam with their Hindustani words and their pony ambulance tongas with two wheels and their total contempt for the natives, they set Hamish Charles on edge. A joke was a joke, but not the joke that Hamish Charles heard round the campfire that night, when the pickets gathered for their scalding Bovril in tin mugs, before they relieved each other. Then a gangling planter told of the best laugh he had ever had, and that in the battle, too.

"I saw some Kaffirs right out to the side of us, watching the show. There was a man and his wife, two girls, and a collie dog. I let drive a couple of bullets right behind them. *Spout! Spout!* went the nickels in the dust close behind them – pretty fair for a sighting at eleven hundred yards. Even a Dutch parson would have laughed! Up went civilisation waist high, in the shape of three gaudy petticoats. And did those Kaffirs run!"

"So would I," Hamish Charles said, but he could not stop the planter's flow.

"Run! Why, you couldn't see their heels for dust. Away they went, hard as they could go, down the donga, up a spruit to the other side like so many black snipe. Then helter-skelter into their hut, banging the door against the white devils. Laugh! Laugh!" The planter laughed, but none of his hearers did. So he went on more hurriedly. "To see those black feminine limbs with nothing on but their big boots – while rolled up around their waists were those lovely Liberty Pattern skirts – I could have cried laughing. I could have died."

"Many did die," Hamish Charles said. "Or didn't you notice?"

The planter's face grew red with anger. And incredibly, tears ran from his eyes as if by order.

"What do you mean, Jock? My friend Eric, he was killed. Only a few hours ago, he was telling us what he was going to do when the show was over, when he went home to the Old Country." The ruddy cheeks of the speaker were as wet as puppies after rain. "Aye, he's gone home now, if ever a good sort of chap went home. And his sister and the mother he was so proud of, they'll only see him in our Eternal Home. Poor Eric, he's gone home."

"Get on with you," a sergeant said. "Change pickets." And as Hamish Charles walked away, he knew he would never understand it – the terrible mixture in them all of cruelty and sentimentality, crassness and feeling. He really did feel a sympathy for the Boers now – they did not know how to deal with what they were facing, these soft hearts and these harsh acts, these schoolboy japes and this careless violence. The Dutchmen knew what they were doing, as their president thundered his telegrams at them: *Officers and burghers, place all your faith in the Lord. He is our highest General, and the final victory is in His hand. You must not think that all who fight against us belong to the Beast. There are certainly hundreds of the children of God among them, who are forced to act as they do from fear of the Beast. But God knows all hearts. We did not seek that the blood that lies on the ground should be shed. But when they wished to murder us, we rose up against the Beast . . .*

The Boers knew they were fighting the Beast, and Hamish Charles did not believe that he was fighting the Beast, nor that he was the Beast. It had been simple at Harrow. He would join his uncle's regiment and come out for the show. But now he did not know the face of the enemy. For the enemy sometimes wore his face or even the faces of his own side. What he did begin to feel was the power of this strange land of trial and woe with its terrible beauty and bleak choice.

4

PAST IT

"I never thought I would see *you* here," Charles Seymour-Scudabright said. "I mean, aren't you a bit . . .?" His words died in his mouth. It was not only Mary Lamb's dour look, it was the fact that he was a gentleman, and no gentleman referred to the age of a lady, even if she was a hospital matron.

"A bit past it. That is what you were about to say." Mary was examining the plaster cast over Charles's injured foot. She tweaked at his protruding toes, which he had not expected.

"Ouch."

"Ach, you do feel something," Mary said. "I never thought you could feel anything. That means we can knock this cast off and get you back on deck."

"The answer to my prayers," Charles said.

"You do pray?"

"Of course I do."

"I am no' past prayer myself," Mary said, then she turned to the orderly, Maxwell. "You saw this cast off. Do not trouble Dr Sinclair. He has more important things to do."

As Maxwell left for the companionway of the *Maine*, Charles protested.

"You permit an orderly to take off my cast –"

"Seaforth has vital operations to perform. They may save lives – I think yours is safe."

"Your darling Seaforth – you sent for him to serve on this ship – *you* had him seconded here."

"He is the best surgeon there is. I know from St Thomas's –"

"He is your darling," Charles sneered. "And if you think I would look forward to him getting his hands on me –"

"Those coloured hands . . ." Mary smiled and shook her head. "You know, his sister Peg – she's a doctor now too – she's coming from India to London to help to take my place, while I am over here looking for you."

31

"You sound like a family recruiting sergeant," Charles said. "The wrong side of the Sinclair family, may I say." And he said it.

"That's what families are for," Mary said. "To help each other. And I am the head of what is left of our bit of the clan. Ach, Maxwell –" the orderly had returned with a huge pair of scissors and a small handsaw – "please cut off that cast. Not the foot, if you can help it. Captain Seymour-Scudabright does not want to hop between his broadsides from HMS *Terrible*." And as Charles spluttered from the bed, Mary left on the words, "My regards to my niece May Sinclair. She always said I had *bad taste* in men – poor Harry Lamb – but meeting you again, Charles, I wonder . . . your wife or me . . . who chose well?"

In the narrow companionway outside, Mary found her age beginning to tell. Her legs hurt too. There were blue veins in them, varicose they were called. She had to wind bandages round them to keep herself on her pins and in her duty. But her skirt was long enough to hide her body down to her boots, and nobody now would even care to see her ankle. Not like those ladies in Piccadilly, descending from their coaches outside the Café Royal in a foam of white lace petticoats, and the men writing sonnets about the swish of one foot. Ach, you're a daft old lady, Mary Sinclair, and you had better look to the leg of Jack Churchill. And his mother, she's a witch. How did she see he would be first on the *Maine*?

"There's no' wrong with your leg, Mr Churchill," Mary said, looking at a flesh wound in the calf. "I will be writing to your mother, who was giving us this ship, and saying there is no' wrong with you at all."

"Mother gave this?" Jack Churchill was surprised. "She never gave much except to the widows of the tenants. I never knew she cared about shows like this."

"I dinna ken she does," Mary said. "But she cares about you and Winston. Let me tell you, lad –" she stared down at the bulging Churchill eyes – "there's no' a woman cares for a country more than her own. And I dinna have sons – nephews only. But you can take all of Westminster and call it Pretoria, for all I care, as long as my own flesh and blood keep their own flesh and blood. And there's no woman in the world would not say the same as me."

She had finished changing his dressing, and she clipped shut the last safety pin. "You will live," she said, "and ride again."

"But we are meant to be fighting," Jack Churchill said, "for a woman, Queen Victoria, and our country, which She rules."

"Ach, that woman," Mary said, standing up. "More a mother than a Queen. Look at Her, trying to stop all those wars with Germany, because She canna have a grandson fighting another grandson like the

Kaiser. I tell you, Mr Churchill, if we are ever to have peace in our time, it will be while She lives. There's not a drop of Royal blood to be spilled – although perhaps some of ours."

"But her grandson Prince Victor of Schleswig-Holstein, he's on the staff of Lord Bobs –"

"Well back from the front line. The staff always are."

"And the Kaiser, he's sent out German officers to fight for the Boers."

"As long as he won't come – his royal selfishness – it will be no grandson against grandson."

"I mean, we'll soon be in Pretoria, and that will be that."

"I'm no' so sure, Mr Churchill. You may be riding again. It's a big country, I hear tell, and they have horses, and it will be no' so easy to track them all down." She rose and asked for her report. "Any complaints?"

"The ladies," Jack Churchill said.

"Ach, no' the nurses –"

"The ladies also come in to wash our faces and gossip. I had my face washed five times yesterday. And I know much more about Picca-dilly than the Transvaal. There's a girl rides a white pony called Marie Sinclair . . ."

"I have heard tell of her," Mary said severely. "But I canna stop the ladies – the visiting ladies from London. They paid for this hospital ship. I dinna approve, but they say, since all the men are here, they must come too – to mop your faces and chatter away. And what you need is rest and the carbolic."

So she left Jack Churchill thinking that Mary Sinclair was as direct a woman as his mother had written to him that she was. But she was thinking that the awful Charles was right. She was trying to make the *Maine* into a floating family hospital. Hamish Charles might be carried in from the front, and Robert was riding out there with the cowboys, Lord Strathcona's Horse. She had Seaforth ready to treat them, if they were brought in – and even Hamilton was waiting to ferry them home on his wonderful ship's engines. There was no harm in running the war like your own business, if you were called into it at all. Favouring your own, that was to be expected. And if the Queen lost her grandson, that would be the end of the war, to be sure it would.

Hamilton caught her between rounds before she had time even to visit Seaforth. He told her of shipping Robert across with his horses along with munitions and supplies and some of the visiting ladies from London. "Except for you, Mary, ladies are a pain in the neck in a war."

33

"I'm a mere wee working woman, laddie."

"They take ten times more looking after than a soldier and three times more than a horse. Some of them even brought their maids. And they told the stewards what to do, until one of them dumped a stewpot over a Lizzie and said, 'You want it all your way. Now you have it all your way.'"

"What do you think, Hamilton? The ladies – they never ken what war is. Nobody will ever ken, so nobody will ever stop it."

"The ladies are all off to Bloemfontein, now its ours and the field hospitals are there. Lady Roberts went up with her daughter and a whole special trainload of personal supplies – and we're not so sure that Lord Bobs wants it. The Queen doesn't like it, perhaps because She is too old to go herself –"

"I am not," Mary said.

"You deny time," Hamilton said gallantly. "And you make eternity blush."

"Where did you learn those fine words, Hamilton? Are you courting?"

Now Hamilton did blush.

"And where would I meet a lady in the engine-room of a transport ship?"

"You said they were all ladies on board with the horses and Robert."

"*Married* ladies. Now, Aunt Mary, I said the Queen did not approve of them. Mr Chamberlain sent out a dispatch, which I know of. The Queen regrets the large number of ladies visiting South Africa and the hysterical spirit which has influenced them to go where they are not wanted."

"Good for Her," Mary observed. "She only came out here on a chocolate tin."

"Ah, you heard of that. That Lancaster private saved by the Queen's Christmas chocolate tin. The Boer bullet hit slap in the middle of J. S. Fry's best indigestibles and was squashed flat. Fudge beat lead. I had to bring him out another tin, wrapped in red, white and blue ribbons. You know, the tins are selling for a fiver in Christie's – souvenirs of the war."

Seaforth now came in to Mary's cabin, the small centre of the hospital ship. His eyes were circled in soot, yet there was pallor under his brown cheeks. "Hell," he said, "it's hell here. Hello, Hamilton, you've brought in more of the Pom-pom fodder?"

"Only Cousin Robert and the Canadian cowboys. And some of the chit-chat ladies from Hades. Sometimes I wonder if we have a war on or a side-show. The Mauser Music Hall or Oom Paul Kruger's Palace of Varieties."

"Seaforth," Mary said, "you look dog tired. Have a rest in my bunk."

"I can't, Aunt Mary. The show goes on. We're still getting the Irish in from Hart's Hill. They were left lying out there between the lines for two nights and a day in the rain. Murder, sheer murder. But that's what you do to them in Ireland anyway, isn't it? Murder them in the rain. It solves the population problem. Fewer of the rebels to deal with."

Hamilton laughed.

"The same old Seaforth," he said. "Never a good word when a bad one will do. And never a cruel act when a kind one will do better."

"Ach, Seaforth's got the hands of a saint," Mary said. "With that needle and scalpel of his, he could raise the dead – God forgive me for saying it. And he does no' care whether it's Boer or Tommy or Kaffir or Jew, he'll put them back on their feet, he will."

Seaforth smiled his thin smile.

"But I might care more, Mary, if I was operating on an Indian, don't you think? But we're not allowed to fight for you. Only to patch you up."

"You are a doctor, Seaforth Sinclair, and you know it. Here, some Camp coffee. Put on the primus, Hamilton. That cousin of yours, he does more good with his bag of tricks –"

"Than I do with all my engines." Hamilton turned up the wick of the primus stove, struck a Lucifer match and started the little blue flame. Then he picked up the bottle of liquid coffee and looked at the label of the Highland soldier standing in his kilt with his tent and his *sirdar* and the Himalayas behind him. "When I see this," he said, "I think of Uncle Iain and the Mutiny, where we all began fighting for the British, in India, after we were cleared."

"You left your little legacy from there," Seaforth said. "My sister and I."

"And lucky we are for it," Mary said. "Look what you are doing for us."

Marie had been lassoed. The rope had caught her, and she was hog-tied. It was not so much the convention – she could buck that – it was the competition. Those lovely ladies sweeping from their coaches, the A La Girls. She had to admit, Sir George Davies's little number was even better than her own "Take Me":

> *Oh, the A La Girl is an English girl,*
> *With lots of A La talk,*
> *And when she goes down Regent Street,*

She has an A La walk.
She's an A La twinkle in her eye,
She wears an A La curl,
And she cuts a dash,
With an A La Mash,
Does the A La English girl.

And what a splash of a dash the A La Girl cut. As she frothed down
in the cascades of lace fringes on her countless petticoats, she swung
her padded curves below her tight long skirts like two foxes curled in
a bag. The men liked "a fine woman", and that meant adding to
bosom and behind rather than taking them in with corsets and stays.
The whole mystery of woman – or so the swells said – lay in the
undressing. You never did know what might be revealed: the Venus
de Milo or a skeleton from the closet. As each layer came off, the
excitement grew, the shape of Aphrodite was shown. Marie found out
that she showed too much. Of course, her body was perfection, but
the men knew too much about it. What was suggested was more
tempting than what was seen. So Marie bought herself a Directoire
dress, as soon as they were worn by the Lady Dandies. It was tobacco
brown with no belt and a bolero. Marie could not resist having a slash
in the long skirt, which did show rather too much of one leg – and
much too much for most of the London ladies.

The changing fashions demonstrated that Queen Victoria was
dying, and that her voluptuary of a sixty-year-old son, Edward, the
Prince of Wales, would not have to wait in the wings much longer
before reigning over an easier style of British life. The question was
whether the aged Queen would last out the Boer War. It now seemed
won, with Piccadilly a huge street party on Mafeking night, when the
besieged town was at last relieved. Bill Dunesk escorted Marie through
the mob and the Union Jacks and the squirts and the peacock-feather
ticklers – only a penny a plume. He looked rather like Banquo's ghost,
a thin and tall spectre at the feast. Then he invited her to Scotland
for the two weeks when the Palace was closed, changing its variety
acts. Marie accepted. "Back to my roots," she said. "And I've never
even seen them."

"There's a Sinclair castle and chapel down the glen," Bill said.
"The oldest Sinclair places."

So Marie came to Dunesk Castle without even a chaperon. She
would manage herself. The castle was near the paper-mills of Penicuik
and the coal mines, where the green glen of the Esk ran down through
red-orange gorges past two other castles, Rosslyn and Hawthornden,
down to the Firth of Forth by Edinburgh. The castle was elementary

and magical, a fortified tower with rounded turrets under pointed slate hats rearing from the pink rock walls. Inside, the stairs were bare stone, but carpets covered the guard-room and great hall now, while huge log-fires warmed the chilliness and there was even hot water from an old boiler in the sole bathroom with its enamelled iron tub on four clawed feet. "Designer I may be," Bill said, "but my old castle defeats me. Basic it was, and basic it remains."

But he had designed the new paper-mill at Penicuik, which Marie discovered was making him rich along with his mineral rights from the coal mines on his land. Green tiles embellished with pale lilies and water-nymphs decorated the square brick factory, but the stream running from it was livid with red and yellow chemicals, and frothing with caustic soda. Inside, swatches of esparto grass were treated with lye before they were mangled into rolls of thick paper, which were then sliced into pages. Village women shuffled the pages into reams, riffling the papers with fingers as fast as the flutter of the wings of larks. "They are never wrong," Bill explained to Marie. "They do not count, they feel five hundred sheets to the ream, and they are always right."

"What are their wages?" Marie asked.

"A living," Bill said. "Before this it was starvation except for the Midlothian mines. The work at the paper has saved them."

"But not the river," Marie said.

Marie was right. The lye and the caustic and the bleach ran down to the Esk and painted the brown waters. And as she walked with Bill down through the ash and oak and thorn that lined the gorge, Marie could see trout floating white belly-up in the dark rock pools. But past the rose-red walls and ruined tower and causeway bridge of Ross-lyn Castle, down in the zig-zag orange gorge across the rapids called "The Dreepers", she saw the blue flash of a kingfisher and even the ochre swirl of an otter in the stream. All of nature had not been killed by the spills of man.

"William Wallace lived here with his rebels," Bill said. "In caves the ancient Picts made. Then the English caught him and they hanged him – they drew and quartered him – all for Scots freedom. You know the Burns poem, do you?" And his English drawl suddenly became a Scottish rant, his passion changing his voice from a trickle to a torrent.

> *"Scots, wha ha'e wi' Wallace bled!*
> *Scots, wham Bruce has often led;*
> *Welcome to your gory bed,*
> *Or to victory.*

"Robert the Bruce did fight here, and the Sinclairs, and my people the Frasers. There's a place I will take you riding – the Shin-bones or Stinking Rig – where the Frasers and the Sinclairs beat three English armies in the same day – and we're still digging up their bones, for they litter the field there."

"My grandmother Hannah told me," Marie said, "when we were being cleared from the Highlands, the Sinclairs and the Frasers, we were at school together. My uncles were always fighting your uncles . . ."

"Sometimes we fought on the same side – at least against the English." Bill gave one of his rare smiles to Marie. It gave life to his pale skull of a face, where the bone almost seemed to push through the skin. "The Frasers and the Sinclairs – we can agree, you know. And look, there at the end of the gorge, there is Hawthornden." Another castle rose from the top of a cliff. "It is not a Fraser or a Sinclair Castle – the Drummonds have it. Of course, William Drummond, he was the first traitor – or a diplomat, as you might say. The first good Scots poet to write in English, Drummond of Hawthornden."

The third of the castles along the Esk was the most dramatic. Although only a fortified manor house now, it stood on the far bank a thousand feet sheer above the tumbling river. It brooded over the rushing water, evoking the fierce and free streak in Marie, the child of the wilderness that would not be tamed. Yet as she looked at these strongholds of the centuries above the glen, she felt the love and the security that their owners must feel in them, and that the people of their clans must feel about them. And as if answering her unspoken thought, Bill said to her, "This was raiding country. The English over the border, the steel bonnets of the other clans. You had to flee somewhere to be secure."

"We were a raiding nation," Marie said, "my other grandmother's people, the Crows. But when the raids came, we had nowhere to keep us safe. We had to pack camp, ride away with our teepees, begin again. I love it here."

"You know that they wrote of ancient Petra in Transjordan as a rose-red city half as old as time." Bill's hand swept towards Hawthornden as a bird in flight. "I think of our fortress in the glen as a rose-red castle twice as old as time."

On the walk back up the glen, Marie was taken up the hill to see Rosslyn Chapel, where Sir Walter Scott had confirmed that twenty Sinclair knights were buried in the vaults in full armour. Inside was the Third Day of Creation with every variety of fruit and leaf and plant carved over every pillar and arch and wall. A jungle of stone. The faces of green men shouted in dumb show or leered from the garlands and friezes. Marie was entranced.

"A Sinclair built this?" she asked. "It's as fierce as a forest."

And Bill nodded and said, "I do not think your ferocity comes only from the Crows. The Scots, you know, are a ferocious people . . ."

"Not you, Bill. You're so soft . . ."

"Try me," Bill said. "You might be quite surprised."

And Marie was surprised, when she went riding with him over the Pentland Hills in the afternoons. Although he looked like the Grim Reaper on a horse, he stuck on a saddle as if he were a spear in the back of his mount. When she galloped like the prairie wind on her pony, he went with her, neck and neck over the moor, and when she leapt the rough stone walls, he soared beside her. She threw back her head and cried her Indian cry, "Wah-heeee," and her red hair flew in a banner behind. And when they reined up in a bog and turned, panting and laughing to each other, Marie saw another man, the colour high in his cheeks and whipcord in his lanky frame. And when he said to her, drawling again, "You will be my Countess – actually – will you?", she was unsure whether it was a proposal, and anyway, she certainly did not know what to answer. So she turned her pony and walked him off the soft ground, then she drummed her heels into his flanks and shouted over her shoulder, "Catch me first." And he did not catch her before she reached Dunesk Castle again.

When Peg Sinclair reached London on the P & O steamer from India to help to replace Mary at St Thomas's Hospital, her first wish was to meet her cousin Marie. The fame of the Canadian actress had reached Bombay. The *Illustrated London News* stretched to the ends of the Empire. Not an officers' mess or club missed the long white magazine, in which the drawings had given way to photographs, and the tidings of the metropolis had become the chat of the globe, since the city was now an imperial hub, where the new god of love, Eros, stood erect with his aluminium bow and arrows above a fountain in the dead centre of the planet, Piccadilly Circus.

In fact, Peg met Marie under Eros. When they saw each other, they knew each other at once by their brown faces and prominent Sinclair bones. Marie bought Peg a posy of violets from one of the motherly flower girls who sat round the fountain in bonnet and boots, shawl and voluminous skirts. "I'd take you to the Cri," Marie said, "but it's men only, dirty rotters, and I have to be wearing my leggings to pass for male. So what do you want to try? The Troc or the Café Monico? But if you want to be really English –" giggling and looking at somebody who also said she was an Indian, Marie went on – "we should go to Snow's Chop House and have two poached eggs on finnan haddie and sit on oak pews. Or Scott's, of course, and have oysters and sole till we burst."

"Scott's," Peg said, "because we are not really."

So they left Eros and the painted façade of Swan and Edgar's towering over the horse-buses pulling round the Circus, and they walked to Scott's with only two swooning swells coming up and muttering, "I say – take me, take me anywhere." When they reached the restaurant the doorman swung the glass panels open as for royalty, "Miss Sinclair, how are you?" and Marie ushered Peg inside before her and said, "Nice to be known. If I wasn't, we'd be put out like two ladies of the street. It's just that now I am treated like a *man*." The *maître d'hôtel* did indeed defer to Marie as to a gentleman, taking her over to the best table, offering her the wine list, and bending over her every wish with fond attention.

Looking round the other dining tables in the expanses of white linen and polished wood, Peg saw that she and Marie were the only two women dining with each other. The few other ladies there all had male escorts. Marie was privileged, that she was.

"Sauterne," Marie said. "Whitstables and Sole Walewska. What do you think?"

"Choose for me," Peg said, and Marie gave the order.

"It will be normal soon," Marie said. "Women dining together or even alone. When we have the vote."

"The vote," Peg said. "You are not serious."

"Oh, I have friends," Marie said. "Through Bill Dunesk – he is a friend of mine. They are serious. After the war they are going to fight for female suffrage. Suffragists – that's what they say they are."

"But men don't have the vote in India," Peg said. "So how can women? Many of us still wear the veil."

"You're just a colony still," Marie said. "But I am going to vote before I die. You will see. Things change. Look at you – a qualified woman doctor. It was not possible, even for Aunt Mary."

"I know. She made me do it. And Seaforth, my brother. Marie –" Peg gave a mischievous smile which suddenly splintered her solemn face – "it is so comic to me; in your acting, you call yourself an *Indian*. And I really am an *Indian*. I know we're both Scots, too, but *Indians* – how can you believe that?"

The opened oysters were set before the young women on beds of cracked ice and vast silver platters with lemon slices in gauze to squeeze over them and Tabasco sauce to sprinkle on them and fingers of brown bread and butter to help them down.

"Some people say you can hear an oyster scream when you swallow it," Marie said nonchalantly. "Others say they are good for making love."

Peg smiled.

"We hear that in Bombay too. Although ginseng and powdered rhinoceros horn . . . not *medical* prescriptions, I assure you . . ."

Marie laughed.

"Buffalo horn for the Crows," she said. "We were called Indians only because that fool Columbus thought he had reached India, when he discovered America. Discovered? Actually, we discovered America rather before Columbus, and when we discovered Columbus had come, we let him overstay his welcome. Indians, I don't think we are. But the name has stuck." Marie swallowed an oyster in one gulp and then sipped the juice from the shell. Peg was closely watching her to follow her example exactly.

"But meeting you, Peg, I tell you, I don't mind being called an Indian, as long as I can be like you."

"Don't compliment me," Peg said. "You are the toast of London."

"I would rather be a doctor. Somebody useful."

"Not if you were one. The hours are terrible. And the human body . . . if you see too many, you even are disgusted by your own."

"Nonsense. A beauty like you . . ." Marie considered Peg's severe, but handsome face, lines of judgement already etched deep by her eyes and nose and only a full mouth to suggest any weakness. "It's only your hair, you know. You mustn't waste it and coil it up like that with that bonnet on. I reckon, when you undo it you can sit on it. That's what all the ladies want to do in London – sit on their hair."

"I am *not* a beauty –"

"You are."

"You're acting, telling me what is untrue."

"You are a beauty. And you can sit on your hair. Which is more than I can. I have a mane like a red pony."

"It is beautiful. All London says so."

"Well, I will not wear a hat. I know all London wears hats because the Queen does. But I will not. I think hats are only for people who don't care for their hair, so they hide it. Don't you?"

"I have to wear a hat," Peg said. "In my position . . ."

"Do you operate with your bonnet? Do you diagnose through your hat?"

"Oh, Marie, you know what I mean."

Marie swallowed another oyster, then she drained the salt juice.

"What other people do," she said, "you should never do. I never do. Except . . ."

"What?"

"Except – shall I tell you first?"

"Do, please."

"Only because we don't know each other. I believe in confiding in strangers."

"We are cousins."

"We lived a world apart. Until now. Peg, what do you think? Shall I . . . shall I . . .?" Marie prodded with her small silver oyster-fork at the flesh of the nearest shrinking mollusc. "Shall I go home to Sinclair country – Scotland – marry a Fraser and be a countess?"

"A countess. Marie, not really –"

"He is a good man. A fine man. I won't do better. And the influence I would have . . . the power. And I might be able to fight for the vote. But Peg, a *man* – to be bound to a man. I am free."

"The only free woman, Mary wrote to me, in all the world."

"Well," Marie said and drove the prongs of the silver fork into the raw oyster, "I reckon we're free to give our freedom away, if we want to. The Countess of Dunesk. That is something to crow about."

5

BURNING TIME

It was as Hannah had told him before she died. Only these were farms
on the veld, not crofts in the glen. But it was the clearances all over
again. The worst moment was riding up to the house. The Boer
women went to fetch a cup of milk. And the troopers had to say they
came to burn the place down. They gave them ten minutes to evacuate,
the women and the children. Some of the mounted men also gave the
Boers a hand with the beds and the chairs – they took out their Bibles
and the blankets themselves. Then the horsemen piled up the bales
of straw round the walls and set them on fire. The women did not
shout, they did not complain. They only opened their eyes until the
troopers saw the flames dancing in them. And the men said, "How
long will your men go on fighting? We only do this because you give
the commandos food and supplies." And the women answered, "How
long? Till you have gone away. We will still be here. We will be here
longer than you."

So the mounted men rode on after the Orange Free Staters and the
last of their armies. And they saw the mountains. They were blue and
purple and bigger than the mountains of Scotland. With the Seaforths
and the Highland Brigade were Lord Lovat's Scouts. They all felt
that giddiness in the head to see the mountains. It is almost like the
sea-sickness of a sailor, to see the strength of the hills ahead. Some of
the Wittenbergen and the Roodebergen, the White Mountains and
the Red Mountains, were smooth and round like our braes; but the
most of them were bleak and bony ridges of crimson and bleached
rock with stripes of snow in the gullies. Good lurking places for the
Boer snipers, unless they could corner these against the scarps and
the steeps. And whoever heard of cornering Brother Boer and certainly
not de Wet, unless he made another bad mistake and decided to fight
it out?

The Boers' weakness was their waggons. They would not leave their
oxen and their carts. They were farmers. They had these travelling homes. But they were boxed in now in the horse-shoe of the

43

Brandwater Basin with the imperial troopers commanding three of the four passes out and Basutoland behind them. And the troopers had told Chief Jonathan to stop them doubling back to the east. The Basutos hated the Boers, anyway. But trust de Wet: he did not stay in the trap, but rolled out over the open Slabbert's Nek with fifteen hundred men and four hundred waggons, rolling too fast even for the British cavalry. But the rest of the Dutchmen stayed put in their laagers. It was a hard fight carrying nearby Rietef's Nek, but nothing that the Seaforths and the Black Watch could not do. When Hamish Charles heard the first challenge, *"Wie gaat daar?"*, he knew it was to be the bullet storm and the murderous jets spouting disaster from the barrels of the Mausers. But the five-pounder cow-guns were in the rear, and they hammered the Boer trenches. Then it was the charge and the bayonet as usual, but Hamish Charles would not use his pig-sticker, and he swung his rifle as a club to knock the Dutch skittles down.

Now Brother Boer had his neck in the noose. While he dithered about his surrender, Hamish Charles rode over to see his cousin Robert in Strathcona's Horse. As he was not fighting now, he put off his khaki helmet and put on his full lieutenant's uniform: his white cockade over his bearskin bonnet, his red sash over his scarlet coat and pipeclay bandolier, the white and red criss-cross of tartan lines griddling his green kilt that fell as far as the top of his black riding-boots. He seemed quite a sight to the shaggy Canadian cowboys with their unclipped broncos, the only colour in their camp a guidon presented by the ladies of Ottawa – crimson silk with a broad white stripe through the centre, bearing embroidered letters, *Strathcona's Horse*, and the noble lord's motto *Perseverance* below a baron's coronet, a green maple leaf and a brown beaver.

"Very neat," Hamish Charles said to Robert when they encountered each other in immediate recognition, the long Norse features being as they were.

Robert was shy, although that was hardly his nature. His cousin was an officer, and he was a trooper. And the Tommies were meant to care about rank. But he did not salute, and Hamish Charles did not dress him down for it, but shook his hand and said, "Far cry from the prairie."

"It's good country," Robert said. "You could make a go of it here."

"I met a Dutchman at Paaderburg," Hamish Charles said. "He said farming was good round Ficksburg. We might see him again."

"He got away?"

"Not far. He had a broken leg. But, yes, I hope he got away. It's better than being in a prison camp, and caged like a fly in a beer-bottle.

St Helena's full up of Boer prisoners. I hear they're sending them to Happy Valley in Ceylon."

"It's better than fighting."

"Is it? Not if you're a farmer. You want to go back to your land."

"I don't," Robert said. "My father Bain, mum and brother Gillon, they're stuck on the soil. All they think of is crop yields and barbed wire. The sky's big here. And the mountains. You can kind of breathe."

Hamish Charles looked over to the livid knuckles of the bergs in Basutoland, the cruel blue heaven stretching away, infinite to the end of sight.

"You can stop breathing here, too," he said. "Brother Boer – will he throw his slouch hat in the ring again? Or throw in the towel?"

"He's had it." Robert spat. "I don't know why he gave you such a hard time of it. Till we came and did it right for you."

"We had to learn," Hamish said. "We're still learning. We don't know how to fight a war like this. And even if this lot give in, there is still de Wet and the commandos. Don't think the war will be over here."

And it was not, even when Prinsloo threw in the towel. The finale at Fouriesburg was almost worthy of the Palace of Varieties. All the generals and their staffs were mounted, while the Highland Brigade and Strathcona's Horse and the rest of the contingents stood in two lines on the hills overlooking the basin. Prinsloo rode in between the ranks and handed his rifle to General MacDonald. After him, the Dutch farmers slouched along on their little ponies, throwing down their Mausers and bandoliers with a swagger onto a weapons' pile. Then came the carts, dragged by the oxen and looking more like gypsy caravans, bulging with cook-pots and blankets. And on the back-board of one of them, swinging his good leg, Piet Krug sat sucking at a pipe and lean as starvation. Hamish Charles broke ranks to greet him.

"Krug, you devil," he said. "You did get away."

"Sinclair, man," Krug said, "my farm's here. You are burning the farms now. A man has to fight for his *huis*."

"They'll send you to Ceylon now."

"If they can keep me." Krug laughed as his cart rolled on. "I see you in Ficksburg."

Hamish Charles resumed his post. He admired Krug for going back to the battle with a gammy leg. That was the trouble with a brave enemy. Soon you valued them almost as much as your own. And Krug was right. It was a dirty business, the burning of farms. He hoped it would not become worse if the war went on against the commandos. Lord Bobs had mercy in him, but he was going home, now Pretoria was theirs and Oom Paul Kruger was fled. But if Kitchener took over, the K in his name did not stand for Knut, like the man in the music-hall song, the swell Gilbert the Filbert, the pride of Piccadilly and the Kernel of the Knuts. It stood for Killer, for that is what Kitchener was.

Hamilton had succeeded in getting the permission of the padre's wife to take her daughter Ellen-Maeve to a concert at the hospital. It might not have been quite the thing for a young lady, but there were more officers in Bloemfontein than there were in Aldershot, and if many of them were wounded, they would recover soon and be matchwood for marriage. And as for Naval Lieutenant Hamilton Sinclair, he was all in one piece, although inland. He had come to recuperate the naval guns, he said, although on the voyage over on the transport, the padre's wife had seen him often enough staring at Ellen-Maeve, too shy to speak – or so she had thought. But they must have spoken in secret, impossible as privacy was on a troopship. Or Ellen-Maeve would not have insisted with her quiet whim of steel in going to the concert with him. The padre's wife thought Ellen-Maeve could do better, but she also knew better than to try to change her daughter's mind when it was set. Ellen-Maeve might look like a buttercup with her forget-me-not eyes and body no bigger than a child's, but she was as stubborn as an Afrikander ox, and when she said pretty please, it was a royal command. And if she had Hamilton in her sights when he thought he had her in his, well, he would be holed below the waterline and sunk without trace before he could bring a gun to bear on this gillyflower.

The skits in the smoker were uproarious, if one judged by the uproar. But Hamilton never even smiled at *Punch* and his feeble and occasional laughs were followed by Ellen-Maeve, lifting her eyebrows and tut-tutting into her elbow-long gloves. She was, after all, a lady who visited the hospitals, and the humour was directed at her. And as for the fat old sergeant-major dressed up in a check table-cloth as a shirt and a frying-pan with paper roses as a hat, she did not think it was amusing that he sported a placard over his false bosom – OLD MAIDEN VISITOR – and spoke half in bass and half in falsetto, while a wounded Tommy with both legs in plaster reclined on an iron bed on stage.

OLD MAIDEN VISITOR: "Well, my dear man, and how are you today?"

WOUNDED TOMMY: "Me? I'm topping. How's yourself?"

OLD MAIDEN VISITOR: "Is there anything, but anything, I can do for you?"

WOUNDED TOMMY: (*Softly*) "Go away." (*Louder*) "No thanks, mum, I'll have a sleep."

OLD MAIDEN VISITOR: "Oh, very well, but are you sure I can't do anything for you?"

WOUNDED TOMMY: "Evaporate – I'll have a sleep."

OLD MAIDEN VISITOR: "But are you *sure* I can't do anything for you, my man. I can wash your face and hands. *Do* let me give you a nice little wash-up."

WOUNDED TOMMY: "All right, mum, take my bally hands and wash away. If it ain't the seventh bally time I've had my hands washed today."

OLD MAIDEN VISITOR: "Then I shall read you to sleep. *Little Women*. It is very suitable – Louisa May Alcott and *Little Women*."

WOUNDED TOMMY: "Perhaps you would read, mum, to my friend Mac in the next bed. He'd appreciate it."

OLD MAIDEN VISITOR: (*Offended*) "Then I will read to your friend Mac in the next bed. It is so nice to be appreciated." (*She turns her back and opens the book.*)

WOUNDED TOMMY: (*Settling down*) "Mac's been dead since morning."

As Hamilton took Ellen-Maeve away from the concert, he felt his cheeks burning at the mess that he had made of the entertainment. But she was all sweetness and light, hanging on his arm no heavier than a dandelion puff or thistledown. He had no idea of the mischief in her.

"I don't think soldiers are ever very funny," she said. "Plod, plod, plod – that is all they do. Boots, boots, boots, boots, marching up and down again – it does not sharpen the wits. But a sailor on the ocean wave – springing up and down, all that rum and hornpipes – it must be most stimulating."

"Routine, miss, routine." Hamilton racked his brains to think of one nautical joke, and could not come up with any. His brain was like a pea-soup fog on the Solent. "My brother-in-law Charles serves on the battleship *Terrible*. He's just had a good time, picking up some Germans sneaking in by Delagoa Bay to fight for Johnnie Boer. Dirty trick, that. And the Kaiser's our own Queen's grandson."

"Wagner," Ellen-Maeve said. "And Goethe. The Germans do have music. And a great deal of soul, especially soul."

"And big guns," Hamilton said. "And ships as good as ours. I wonder, in a scrap, if they'd fire Wagner at us? Pepper us with Mozart or sink us with Goethe?"

Ellen-Maeve laughed. Men liked to have their little jokes laughed at, and it was easy if one liked the man.

"I would rather be battered by Beethoven," she said. "And sunk by Nietzsche."

"Who?" Hamilton said.

"A philosopher," Ellen-Maeve said. "He believes in the Superman. And I must say, I think I see one around."

Now Hamilton's cheeks burned again. Never in his life had a young woman complimented him. He had long believed he was irredeemably ugly and born to be a bachelor. And now, this wisp of a thing, this sprite of mere ether, she was saying, Superman . . .

"Oh, I don't know – really . . ."

"Modesty," Ellen-Maeve said, "is not an attribute that Nietzsche gives to a Superman. But you must break the rule." She smiled and added, "And you must take me home now. Mother will be worried. And if we are late, Father will denounce you from the pulpit."

"Yes," Hamilton said in ecstasy. "But when . . . when will I see you again?"

"How long is your leave?" Ellen-Maeve said. "Or your mission."

"Nothing will take me away," Hamilton said, "if I have to spike the admiral."

"Then the day after tomorrow," Ellen-Maeve said, knowing that waiting always increased the mettle of a man. No young woman should ever be too available. "I will look forward to my Superman."

6

A MATTER OF
CONCENTRATION

Peg Sinclair was standing with the crowd on Trinity Pier at East
Cowes when Lord Roberts came home. The noise was deafening, all
the ships at anchor blowing their whistles as shrill as banshees, and
the horse artillery bombarding their ears with a nineteen-gun salute.
The little polished hero seemed too tiny for such a large welcome. But
off he went from the gangplank to Osborne to see the ailing Queen
Victoria, who had put the Victoria Cross on his tunic forty years
before and now made him an earl and a Knight of the Garter. The
honours were for giving Johnnie Boer a bloody nose, and they were
almost the last honours that the Queen and Empress would give.
For she herself would be needing the last rites in twenty days,
dying with Her grandson the Kaiser of Germany at attention at Her
left bedpost and Her eldest son, the new King Edward the Seventh,
at Her right bedpost. As the King had to leave for London to attend
the accession council, the Kaiser would make the arrangements for
the lying in state. He would order Union Jacks to be draped around
the walls of the room where his grandmother's coffin lay, covered
with flowered wreaths. He would even stay in England for Her
funeral and be made a British field marshal for his devotion,
although he was on the other side.

Peg's concern was not with this royal display of care. Her job was
with the wounded, who had come back with the new Earl Roberts on
the ship from South Africa. They were to be taken to St Thomas's
Hospital for further operations or to convalescent homes in Hastings
and Hove. She supervised their transfer from their sea-borne wards
to railway train seats, where the compartments had been converted to
ambulances for the journey. Of course, the new upholstery with its
bulging curves and scarlet and yellow dragon patterns was protected
from any contact with the bleeding by linen sheets. And the sharp
smell in the air was of varnish, not of ether or carbolic. But the soldiers
found their berths comfortable after the sea voyage, and the jolting at

49

the points on the tracks better than the pitching of the vessel in the Bay of Biscay. It was nice looking up at the nets of the luggage racks rather than at swaying hammocks. They were home on land where they had longed to be.

It was a heroes' homecoming, too. It was the last popular war. Peg met another trainload of disabled men, when Earl Roberts reached Paddington Station, and the new Prince and Princess of Wales were there to greet him – and a fine crowd, too, that nearly shattered the glass roof of the steam terminus with its hoorays and huzzas. While the earl and the countess – Bobs's wife had always wanted to be that – went off to Buckingham Palace with fifteen thousand troops lining the route, Peg again oversaw the shipping of the men from the train seats to the horse-drawn ambulances waiting outside the station. The stretcher-bearers were too rough with them. One trooper with an amputated leg was dropped on to the platform and swore like his rank. "Pig-dogs," was the best word he found for them. The rest was unprintable.

Yet Peg found that she could support these ceremonies at what was meant to be the end of the war more easily than she could deal with Marie's wedding in St Mary's Undercroft in the consecrated vaults below the House of Lords, with their painted arches and ceilings which showed saints and martyrs being boiled alive in scalding cauldrons. She had so looked forward to it. It would be the best occasion in her life – except for her own wedding. She had spent three months' pay on a pink silk dress, long and tight, but flowering at the bosom into the opulent petals of spring. Her white hat was wide and grew glass cherries; her white gloves made an eighth skin as far as her elbows and buttoned over her wrists with small pearls. But the condescension of the other guests killed her, the terrible talking down their noses and the cutting inflections of their voices that the English used to demean lesser breeds by the social death of a thousand slights. Her own family was the worst, her cousin May and the snobbish Charles Seymour-Scudabright with their mincing daughter Ruth; but she had to say that Murdo, allowed the day off from Harrow, was sweet to her, perhaps because his childhood in Peru had taught him that brown people could also be human.

The reception at the Café Royal after the marriage ceremony was in the wrong place and at the wrong time, but that was what Bill Dunesk and Marie wanted, and that was what they had. Peg thought that Marie's wedding-dress was miraculous and outrageous: ten thousand pearls stitched over a clinging sheath of a gown with a head-dress of osprey feathers that made her look like an Indian princess on the peace path. But her husband loved it, stammering in the receiving line to his astounded family and friends: "Meet my wife – all oyster seeds and wings; mermaid and bird – Marie." And her bronze beauty and quicksilver laughter won them all, whatever they were saying behind her back.

"I am so glad, darling," Peg said. "If you are half as glad as I am, you will be happy for ever."

At the reception, Peg backed herself into a corner. It was so much easier that way. To be ostracised was nothing. She was used to it. It was better than being patronised or having to explain why she was there or what sort of a cousin she was exactly to the bride. People would come to her, if that is what they wanted to do. But only one waiter did, to offer her a glass of champagne, which she did not drink. And Murdo came, all gangling and floppy-haired, and spoke to her about how topping it was to be a schoolboy at Harrow, all the fun and the games of it with a little work added. Latin was not for him, and Spanish, which he knew, was not on the curriculum. And then at last Marie reached her, ignoring the rest of the aristocratic guests as they had ignored her.

"Peg, my darling," she said. "Have I done the right thing?"

"You have done well for yourself," Peg said.

"That's just the sort of thing my mother Kate would say. I don't expect it, Peg, from you."

"His friends," Peg said. "You have to marry his friends and family too. And if these are they –" her right white glove swept in the stroke of a scythe to indicate the room – "then I don't know."

Marie laughed like a clash of cymbals.

"He won't have *them* long," she said. "If you think we will have the *same* kind of friends – but some of them I like. The poets and the painters and the architects and the designers."

"They're so decadent," Peg said. "And not very interested in women."

"I am."

"I know you are. The vote –"

"We'll get it now."

"*You* can do it?"

"I can do anything," Marie said. Then she laughed again, now in a descant of bells. "Didn't you know that?"

"But . . ." Peg was not quite convinced by her cousin's confidence. "Do you know you will be happy? With Bill? In *every* way?"

"What do you mean?"

"Oh . . ." Peg flushed. "I . . ." She looked for the right words. "You're so human – warm – strong. You are physical He is so withdrawn . . . inward. That male world. Clubs and other men. That is England."

"He can kiss," Marie said. "I know. And soon I'll know more, I guess."

Peg smiled and stroked the pearls on Marie's gown. Her nail caught a strand and snapped the stitches and white granules fell onto the carpet.

"Oh, Marie, look what I've done!"

As Peg bent to scramble for the pearls on the carpet, Marie straightened her.

"Don't," she said. "We'll find them later."

"People will step on them, crush them."

"So what? They're only pearls. Not people. Peg, I must go. But keep in touch. When you can manage after patching up our stupid men back from the war. I am honoured – truly honoured – you found the time to come here for this –" she found the right word for it – "extraordinary occasion."

Peg smiled and looked round the room, crowded with morning coats and cravats, diamond sprays and mellifluous voices, broken by cackles of malice.

"Yes," Peg said. "An extraordinary occasion. For an extraordinary woman, too. You, Marie."

At eighty, Mary Sinclair was another extraordinary woman. She had met a bustling, dumpy lady from England, Emily Hobhouse, who burrowed like a mole after the truth in the hole where it had hid itself. "The concentration camps," Emily told her. "We are killing Boer women and children there. You must come and see them with me, Miss Sinclair. They will believe your word in London – as they would believe the word of Miss Nightingale, God rest her soul. Even if they will not believe my word. For I am a liberal, you see. And a busybody. And a woman. And I do not think General Kitchener likes any of the three. He only listens to his moustache."

So it was that Emily Hobhouse and Mary Sinclair saw the conditions beside the railway sidings, after one of the great drives against the Boer commandos still on their flight over the veld. The bag of the game was women and children in open cattle trucks, sodden in the icy rain. And if they arrived alive after the rail journey, the camps were a shambles. Potchefstroom and Mafeking itself, these were a revenge. The Boer women thought it so. It was genocide, the killing of a nation. Because you could not catch their men on their horses, you killed their women and children by herding them into camps to die of disease and bad weather and poor feed. But people were not cattle. Even the Boers loved their oxen, their Afrikanders, better than the *rooineks* loved the *vrous* and *kinders* in their forced care. This was the matter of the concentration of them in the camps.

The thinking of it was army thinking in the divisions that set humans apart. There were the *hensoppers*, who put their hands up and got double rations, and the *bittereinders*, whose men were still fighting in the commandos and who did not fare half so well. Not that the rations were so good, anyway: a pound of meal and half a pound of meat a day, a scrape of sugar and coffee if you were lucky, and no fruit juice or vegetable or jam or milk, even for a baby. It made a *vrou* think. If they were killing her and her *kinders*, what was the poison? There were the blue things in the sugar, that were said to be making it whiter. There was ground glass in the meal and fish-hooks in the bully beef. Not that anyone had found them, but they must be there, because of all of the sickness that was going on. Certainly, the women and the children were dying in the camps in their hundreds and their thousands. And if it was meant to be typhoid and enteric from the bad water, and measles and dysentery, pneumonia and influenza and scarlet fever, malaria and bronchitis and diphtheria and whooping cough, why, these were just the names of the illnesses that the *rooineks* used to excuse the killing of the Boers. At Potchefstroom, there were no tents to put them in, only reed huts. Even the oxen were treated better in their *kraals*.

I call this camp system wholesale cruelty, Emily Hobhouse wrote to the Distress Committee of other ladies back at home. *It can never be wiped out from the memories of the people. It presses hardest on the children . . . Entire villages and districts rooted up and dumped in a bare strange place. To keep their camps going is murder for the children. Of course by judicious management they could be improved; but do what you will, you can't undo the thing itself.*

Sweat dropped from Emily's forehead and blotted the ink on her report. She put down her pen and wiped her brow and turned to Mary Sinclair, sitting like a still judge in a corner chair in their tent in the camp at Potchefstroom.

"Do you think they can be improved, Miss Sinclair?"

"Improvement?" Mary Sinclair sniffed. "Hell canna be improved. It willna stop the killing of the bairns. Thousands will die. Tens of thousands. I dinna ken how it was done, why it was done."

"Policy," Emily said. "It's the name men give for stupidity. Kitchener wants to win the war quickly. He does not mind how."

"Concentration camps," Mary said. "Now we have made them, they will be made again. It is a terrible invention. It will haunt us all our days, and the generations that will come."

"I cannot get Kitchener to close them."

"Then we must improve them, as you say." Mary tried to rise from her chair, but fell back. "Ach, my bones. They are set. Old bones set. Give me a hand, Miss Hobhouse." And Emily pulled Mary to her feet. "I am set in my ways like my bones are. But we must find new ways."

"In London, we have Miss Fawcett," Emily said. "Millicent Fawcett is *formidable*. She wants the vote for women. Then we shall change things."

"I dinna hold with that," Mary said. "It is not the time yet. But the women here – the Afrikaner women – I think they can change things. Women – all women – they can shame men into the changes. If there are children. Though they forget it, every man does – he was a child with a mother."

"The incorrigible women, the women who protest, they lock them in a barbed wire *laager*. They call it the Hog's Paradise."

"We will see about that," Mary said grimly and hobbled to the entrance of the tent. "And as for the sickness, I have sent for my nephew Seaforth to come here and help us to report. It is the more important to look for these prisoners than to care even for our soldiers. And Seaforth is the best doctor in all Africa, although he is my nephew."

Even the sentry could not refuse Mary Sinclair admission to the Hog's Paradise, although he had orders to do so. He quailed in front of the bent figure in black, whose power of command had more force than a brigadier's. Inside the *laager*, a dozen women lay in the dirt, wrapped in their single brown blankets. One of them stood up to shout at the two visitors, howling in an Afrikaans that Mary barely understood. "*Ons mans . . . kinders . . . broers . . . huis . . .*" She cut the edge of her hand across her throat as if slicing with a knife blade. "*Wat sal van ons word?*"

"She means" – Mary explained to Emily Hobhouse – "I think she means, what will be for us? What the now?"

"She will be out of here," Emily said. "And *now*." She started forward and caught the young Boer woman as she tottered on her broken boots and began to sag to the ground. "Look." A dark stain was spreading over the sand from under the woman's draggled skirt. "She's bleeding to death. Help me."

The old Mary and the dumpy Emily stood either side of the young prisoner – two living crutches to assist her out of the *laager* of her rebellion. The protest of the sentry died on his lips. In fact, he bowed a little as they passed and grounded his rifle. And so it was that Seaforth, arriving, met his aunt returning with a victim of the war, that was now a total war against family and house, the shape of the new war to come.

Seaforth could not do much for the woman, who had suffered a massive haemorrhage. There was no stopping the blood coming from her. And Mary and Emily, kneeling beside her in their tent, they could hardly understand her broken words in Afrikaans. But they did discover her name before she passed away in the evening. Annie Krug from near Ficksburg and Basutoland. Her husband was Piet Krug.

"That is a name I know," Mary said, as Emily helped her to her feet. "My nephew Hamish Charles, who is fighting here, he told me of a Piet Krug. He may not be the same. But if it is, he has lost a wife."

"It is shameful," Emily said. "Shocking." She began to cry silently, the tears rolling in glass beads down her cheeks. "I never saw a sister die like that before."

"Hundreds I have seen," Mary said. "Having a baby. Or not having a baby, like that poor Annie. A miscarriage."

"A miscarriage of justice, I think," Seaforth said. "I'll bring in the grave-diggers. Do they have one of those dark *predikants* round here? To bury her in her misguided faith."

"Aye," Mary said. "There is one. Find him, Miss Hobhouse." And as Emily left, Mary put her hand on Seaforth's. "You do not like their faith?"

"It does not like me," Seaforth said. "I am the son of Ham, the devil, really. Why, this woman would not have let my *coloured* hands touch her – and certainly not intimately – only she was too sick to stop me."

"They are women," Mary said. "They suffer. We all suffer the same."

"I know, Aunt Mary. I took an oath, the Hippocratic oath. To care for all equally. But as you know, all do not care for me equally. And these women, many are *trekboers* – they do not know hygiene, they have never seen a latrine. And their remedies! Their cures kill them. Fever – they put tar on their feet. They drink dogs' blood to feel better. Cow dung . . . horse dung . . . smeared on or boiled and eaten . . . that aids arthritis and enteric."

"I would it would aid my arthritis," Mary said, "if I could take the cure."

"A black chicken, cut open – its blood on the chest is the remedy for pneumonia. Shave a cat and its roasted fur will charm away bronchitis." Seaforth shook his head and smiled. "Witchcraft. And ignorance. Poor farm people still living in the Dark Ages."

"Poor people," Mary said, "who dinna deserve to be here."

"Right," Seaforth said. "Right as always. Indomitable and right."
He looked down at the dead young woman, whose cheeks were
bleached now in a sort of peace. "If I felt the pity I feel, I would not
do my job."

"I know, Seaforth. You are a good doctor, a good man."

"But this sight, Aunt Mary, how can you go on believing in the
Empire after this?"

Mary now looked down at the young woman, who had bled to
death. "Hold me," she said. And as Seaforth held her by the waist,
she managed to bend and close the eyelids of Annie Krug and cross
her hands, the one over the other. "There." Now she straightened
herself as best she could, and she answered Seaforth's question. "You
are right, Seaforth. I canna believe in the Empire. If it does this . . .
to the women and the children."

Seaforth did what he rarely did. He hugged his old aunt, who had
been as much of a mother as any he had had in his life.

"You were always the fair one," he said. "The only one who could
understand."

"Get away with you," Mary said, pushing at his chest. Then she
rapped his ribs with her bony knuckles, quite paining him. "Find the
facts. Write them for the report for the Distress Committee. We will
stop the dying. We must. It is a wrong, a great wrong, that canna be
forgot. But it will be a greater wrong if we dinna do something for
it."

There were a few commandos still loose on the borders of Basutoland,
but Hamish Charles knew that the war was over. He had already
applied to be released from his commission when he took leave and
rode from Ficksburg over the Karroo towards the blue mountains.
They were drawing him towards them. They were an answer to what
to do after the war. And he had to find Piet Krug. His Aunt Mary had
told him of the death of the wife of a Piet Krug in a concentration
camp, that shameful way of winning the war. Of course, Piet might
now be rotting in a prison camp himself in Ceylon, but Hamish
Charles had his doubts. Piet would have escaped again and be back
in his farm, if the British troops had not burned it when they took
his wife away.

The sandy road across the Karroo was caked and cracked, although
the hoofs of the horse kicked up pillars of powder. Here and there, a
dust devil danced with ragged veils among the milk-bushes that poked
out their dry leaves from the plain. Soon the coat of the horse and the
khaki uniform and pith helmet of the rider were matted with a clinging
reddish dust, while they plodded heavily towards the promise of the

far bergs. A song that the Boers were singing kept on haunting Hamish Charles, as he licked his lips that tasted like old ropes. It was written by a young woman when her sweetheart had been trapped and sent to prison camp after the surrender at Brandwater Basin. Hamish Charles only knew the first line in Afrikaans, the rest in English. He mouthed the words dumbly, unable to croak a sound:

> *Zeit gy Ginds de Blaawe Bergen*
> *Did you see those Blue mountains,*
> *Who will us betray?*
> *Taken prisoner by the foemen*
> *And sent so far away . . .*

That evening, he was singing the song loudly, after slaking his thirst from his water bottle, when a bullet flicked off his pith helmet and flung it against the charred wall of the abandoned farmhouse. As he swung round, his hand reaching for the butt of his service revolver, he heard a familiar voice say, "Drop it! *Soe*, it is you! You are a *schelm*. You have your domfool head shot off."

And there was Piet, lankier and hairier than ever, dropping the barrel of his Mauser, as he stood in the ruined doorway, fit to scare a buzzard in his patched dirty overcoat and clobbered slouch hat.

"You missed," Hamish Charles said. He bent and picked up his helmet and stuck his forefinger in the hole in the top of it. "You'll cost me a guinea to get a new one. I have two saddlebags of supplies, man. And a pannier of water. You must be starving."

"You come to look for me?"

"Yes. I did."

Hamish Charles saw the change in the troubled gaze of the Afrikaner. His eyes pierced with sudden certainty.

"She is dead. You come to say Annie is dead."

"After supper, Piet. I tell you then."

"Tell me now. She is dead."

"My Aunt Mary, she is a head nurse. She went to see one of those terrible camps, for the women . . ."

"They take her from my farm," Piet said. He shook his head slowly. "They burn it. They kill her. And you say, this is a war of gentlemen."

"It was fever," Hamish Charles said. "My aunt Mary is writing a report to the government. She says it is barbarous – immoral – the concentration camps. Making war on women and children. I think so. I am leaving the army. I will not fight like that."

"Your bloody generals," Piet said. "They lead you to our guns like waterbuck. Then with fire and barbed wire, they kill mother . . . *vrou* . . . *kinders*. Hyenas, *aasvogels*, *tijgers* –"

"I agree with you with all my heart," Hamish Charles said. "Kitchener is a butcher. The means don't worry him as long as he wins. But I came here, man, to find you and do you some good. There may be a way to build all this again – for you to start all over again." His hand swept quickly over the blackened bricks of the walls, then dropped to his side. "I love this country, I don't know why. I am damn sorry what we have done to it. And to you."

Piet looked keenly at Hamish Charles and believed him.

"You are here to say that," he said. "Eat. You are right. Eat. Then we talk."

They lit a campfire in the nearby *kopje*, where Piet was hiding until peace was officially declared. He had left the commandos, he said. Captured twice, he would not ride out again for a lost cause. He still had a limp from Paaderberg, he had no oxen or horses left, his home was in ruins. He lived on what he could kill with his rifle, but he was down to six rounds. The last two weeks he had lived on two ostriches and their nest of eggs – he had to kill both parent birds to be able to make his immense scramble of yellow yolks. "Man, they can take your belly out with one claw. And that old cock, why he sit on the eggs and hatch them like she sit. You can steal them not." He was even out of *biltong*, the salted and sun-dried antelope sticks of meat that kept the commandos going.

Hamish Charles's iron rations were a life-saver: biscuit and corn-beef and mealie meal and salt fish and dried apricots and coffee. He even had a hundred rounds for the Mauser, because he now carried one of the rifles himself. "Better than ours," he said, "German guns are."

Piet dribbled the brass cartridges through the long bones of his fingers, thick at the knuckles. A laugh like a death rattle made a hole in his beard, but the open mouth might have been a plea to put something in it. "God – it is not possible. A *rooinek* give me bullets. And we still fight."

"It's a stupid war," Hamish Charles said. "We don't need your land."

"The gold," Piet said. "The diamonds at Jo'burg. You want that. That Baas Rhodes of yours, he want everything. But the poor land . . . I think you leave it me."

"Actually," Hamish Charles said, "I thought – after the war is over – I might come and help you farm it. I mean, nobody wants it, do they?"

"The land here, take what you want. But there is grass not. For each ox, five acres to feed. If there is *vlei* not, wet land, then the ox die. But plenty *vleis*, plenty ox. You can make *trek*, pull a hundred waggon."

"Are there *vleis* round here?"

Piet's eyes were shrewd now, even if he looked direct at his friend and enemy.

"There are *vleis*," he said. "I had two hundred Afrikanders. I can show you *vleis*. Depend the land you want."

"And what I can do for you . . ." Hamish Charles poked at the charcoal under the cooking-pot hanging from a tripod of branches above the campfire. "I have a proposition, Piet Krug. When it is peacetime –"

"Peace? Time? Too long time for peace, I think."

"Four years? Too long, true. When it is peace, we buy – I buy with my back pay – two teams of oxen. You choose them, you know the beasts."

"My old ox," Piet said sadly, "they had names. Biffel, Bonteman, Witbles, Vaalpens . . . I know them. I say name, he do it. Not *sjambok*, whip not. He do it."

"We take the waggons to Delagoa Bay. We load up with supplies, what we need for building your farm again – and starting mine. Then we trek back here. And we pick up any surplus army stores on the way. When we win, you know, when we pull out of Africa, they'll sell all the army surplus stores for a song. War – it's a bloody wasteful business."

"That it is. Why you . . . you want to farm this dry country?"

"I don't know." Hamish Charles looked up at the black quilt of the night above, studded with Orion and Andromeda and the Plough and a myriad of stars, the Milky Way a bright scarf flung across the constellations. "It is so big, I suppose. And it's here, as they say."

"You are here," Piet said. "Let us eat."

Over their meal of stewed salt pork and beans, washed down with a pint of Cape brandy, Hamish Charles and Piet agreed their deal. When the war was over and the Seaforths had discharged Lieutenant Sinclair with his back pay, he and Piet would make the trek to Delagoa Bay and back again. Then they would set up on adjoining farms on the Karroo below the blue mountains of Basutoland. Then Piet learned that Hamish Charles had a cousin Robert from Canada who now wanted to join the Colonial Service and become an Assistant District Officer in Basutoland, for he also had fallen for the bergs and the *kopjes* and the riding wild. So Piet laughed and said, "Man, we have everything. Those Kaffirs over the border, they take ox, they no good. But if your cousin is the *baas*, the law, he hang them."

"I don't know, Piet," Hamish Charles said. "Robert never struck me as a hanging man. He's more of a cowboy, really. But he wants to be a Mountie now – in Africa. He was brought up on a prairie. Nothing as far as the eye can see. Worse than the karroo. But when he saw these mountains, he went ape. All Scotsmen love the mountains. It's in the blood."

"Your cousin in Kaffir country," Piet said. "I like it. But you ask everything, but not the one thing. Wife. You farm not if wife not."

"But I thought . . . your Annie . . . you have just lost her."

"Lost?" Piet's voice was bitter. "You found Annie here. You killed her. But did I say, my wife? I say, your wife. Not wife, not farm."

Hamish Charles felt his cheeks redden, but he put it down to the smouldering charcoal.

"I haven't had the opportunity lately . . ."

"Marry our girls – they lose their young men. In the war, in prison camp. I know sisters – van der Merwes – family with three sisters. If you like one, maybe I like other sister. Then we brothers, no?"

"If I like one . . ." Hamish Charles was hesitant.

"She know ox, cow, sheep, mealies, butter. How you run farm, my friend, my brother – and farm wife not?"

7

ALWAYS NOWHERES

Bain was the last of the three old Sinclair brothers. The other two, Iain and Angus, had always thought him the slowest and the least. But he did not care for their opinion. He alone had endured in Canada. He lived by the wind and the sky. The earth did not move for him. But the blades and heads of his wheat rippled and shook and shimmied to the gusts. The heavy and bowing winter grain stalks moved in eddies, while the spring wheat with its young seed-rows danced in the breeze. But the wind seemed to blow the horizon away even beyond the reach of human sight, which could only scan the edge of the world in the semi-circle of the watching eye-ball.

The pure light was scoured by the rush of the air, which blew everything clean and sharp except in the dry fallow falls, when the dust storms huffed and puffed grit into every crack and corner and room and mouth. Some folks would call the Canadian prairie before the Rockies a kind of desolation. But not Bain. By fence and post and seed and stock, he had made the land his own. Or he believed he had, unable to see his tiny irrelevance on the gigantic shield of the red grass plain, where the buffalo were reduced to a few bleached bones.

He worked the land with his son Gillon, who had stayed home while his brother Robert rode off to the war in Africa and now studied to become an assistant district officer in London. Gillon was no talker, but he was a worker, and he would stay from dawn to dusk behind the plough, turning up the furrows after the horse-teams. The work had built up his shoulders which topped his strong body like a cross-beam. But the work was killing Julia, Bain's wife. Although she was born stocky and powerful, there was always something out of sorts with her. Women – always complaining about their innards, and too delicate to say exactly what the matter was. And all the dosing and sulphur and molasses to thin the blood didn't seem to do a whit of good. She was not fading away, but she was swelling up, as if there was an ill water in her, as in the creek at the end of summer, near dry and poisonous until the snow melted and flushed it bright in the spring.

"We're nowheres, Pa," Gillon said around the kitchen table in the evening. "Ain't you never reckoned, this is no place, noville, nowheres, noworld, nix in the sticks."

"Where are we?" Bain said. "Right here. Right now. If you can't see it, you can't see it at all. Now your brother –"

"Pancakes," Julia said, bringing in three plates that looked like steaming dumplings. "And gravy." And that was a china sauceboat full of dark juice.

"What's in them?" Bain said.

"Don't you mind," Julia said. "Beef and stuff. I'm the cook."

"Sure are," Gillon said. He took his hot lump on his plate and cut into it with his knife. Vapours rose out, smelling of meat and herbs. He put a morsel on his fork, lifted it and breathed on it to cool it before he put it into his mouth. "Tasty," he said, not very well, for his mouth was full with the savouring.

"Very tasty," Bain said. Julia had to be praised for her cooking.

"That old stove," Julia said, "we need a new one."

"It's cast-iron," Bain said. "It lasts for ever."

"I don't," Julia said. "I'm not cast-iron. And I'll not be lasting without a new stove."

"All right," Bain said. "But the harvest this year – eighty cents a bushel, if we're lucky."

"Kill ourselves," Julia said, "working the land. What do we get for it?"

"Ma's got a point," Gillon said.

"It's my land," Bain said. "We was cleared from Scotland. Never had food. Now it's our land. Don't forget that. Our land. And we never had none."

"It's not the Highlands," Gillon said. "The mountains, I go for them. You remember that grizzly I shot, Pa?"

"Yeah," Bain said. "I remember the grizzly."

"On the mountains," Gillon said. "Not on the prairies. All you have here is coyotes and gophers. Not grizzlies and mountain lions."

"You got wheat," Bain said. "And stock."

"And nowheres," Julia said. "Gillon is right. Give me the dishes, I'll wash them."

"Good, Ma, good," Gillon said and handed back his plate, which he had cleaned out. "Kate, she's coming. We'll see her."

"Anyone –" Julia waddled to her feet. Her legs were so big now they almost stuck together – "any folks come here, it's a miracle."

"It's ours," Bain said. "What do you want? It's our land."

"I don't know." Julia stacked the plates and moved heavily towards the kitchen. "I want more folks. I don't want to live always nowheres."

When Kate did come along the dirt track from the faraway station where her husband Bob McDowell had dropped her off the Canadian Pacific Railway, she had not particularly wanted to come. Family – family – that was the word people in the family always talked about, because they were part of it. She felt she had to meet with the family in Canada from time to time; that proved there was a family there. But on the other hand, she knew she would only be walking into the censure of the family, because it had never approved of her marriage with a *métis* and half-breed, her daughter Marie being a quarter-Indian and a Crow. She was very defiant when she delivered the opening shot in the permanent family war.

"Now that Marie is the Countess of Dunesk –"

"The marriage," Bain said, knocking the bowl of his pipe on the table like drum taps. "The marriage – it is certain?"

"Like the railway timetable," Kate said. "You can catch a train to Scotland, and it will be there. Marie was married to the Earl of Dunesk. And a good Scots family it is, the Frasers."

Bain shook his head very deliberately. He was the master of his own land in Canada such as it was. Nobody could take away his soil and his creek. There was an absolute certainty in his manner, which weighed down the doubt in his mind. For all his air of conviction – and Kate knew that – Bain was a timid man. His caution and stability were actually a fear of moving and of risk.

"An actress," he said. "Your daughter."

"Sinful," Julia said. "Your daughter."

"And she married the Earl of Dunesk." Slowly Bain stuffed the head of his meerschaum pipe, stained brown with nicotine already, with a pinch of the stimulating brown weed. "That is why we left the old country. I reckon they are soft. They make the wrong choices."

"What?" Kate was indignant. "My Marie – she is not good enough for the Earl of Dunesk? She is better. She could be Queen. Mary, Queen of Scots, Marie, Queen of Scots. That's my Marie."

Bain stuffed his tobacco down into the bowl of his pipe as tight as an argument.

"She's part Indian," he said. "A Crow. I don't see a Crow sitting on the Stone of Scone."

"All I see," Kate said, "is a fool with a pipe sitting on dirt which blows away on the wind."

That started it. That is what family quarrels always are. Surely, there was a difference, but always about the same thing. One branch of the family disapproved of the other branch, not so much what they had done, but how it affected the family through the blood. Then it was nasty. But in the end, they had to make up. For they were family, were they not? Whatever they had done or had not done, blood would tell. They were related.

"Where's Gillon?" Kate finally had to talk about the son, who was missing that evening from the table. "Does he really not want to meet me?"

"He says he's sorry." Julia was adamant. "He cannot be here. He is . . . he is . . ."

"Courting," Bain said. "We do not approve."

"Good," Kate said. "I hope she's a Sioux or another Crow."

"Worse," Julia said. "A Russian. And still something too bad – a Christ-killer."

"A Jew?"

"A Jew."

Kate began laughing fit to burst. "I don't believe it," she said. "Gillon. The good boy who didn't run away like my Marie and your Robert. And now he's off with a Russian Jewess. You must be so proud – and pleased. What is her name?"

"Rachel." Julia's mouth closed in a tight ring. "Is that a name?"

"It's in the Bible," Kate said.

"What is the Bible?" Bain said, sucking on his pipe, which he had not yet lit. "The Scriptures, some of them are fitter than others. And their *names*! Nebuchadnezzar, Melchisedek, Zedekiah . . . you would not approve them all."

"There's nothing wrong with Rachel," Kate said.

"Nothing wrong." Bain tried to make his composure that of a Solomon at the judgement. "But all the same, Mary or Kathleen – and you are Kate – I think there are better names for the Sinclairs."

Kate rose to her feet. "I will not be resting here," she said. "I come in between trains, and it is a sore trial to reach you here on the carts before Bob and the CPR come back near here to collect me again. But I wish Gillon well with his Rachel. She will teach you a thing or two as my Marie has taught me. And I tell you, you can learn from a daughter – though never a mother can learn from her son." Now her glance was a dart in the heart of Julia. "Listen to your Gillon and your Robert. And listen to their women, wherever they may be. I have to go to Scotland the now, as you know. To the visit of my own daughter, the Indian – the Countess of Dunesk. And I will give her your love, Bain and Julia – what love I truly have of it, that is."

*

64

"What do you name a girl?" Marie looked accusingly at her husband. "I mean, boys are *easy*." And they were. He had dozens of names for boys: Andrew and Angus, Fergus and Malcolm, Stewart and Tralala, tralalee – but a *girl*. He had presumed it would be a he, it had to be a boy. Only it came out of her as the wrong gender. "So *what* shall we call her now?" Marie said. "In my language, I would call her Owl Feather."

"I do not think," Bill Dunesk said, "that we could have her baptised under that name." He hummed and hawed a little, as he did when he hardly knew what he was meaning to say. "There is a poem by Sir Walter Scott about a girl who lived down the glen."

"And what was she called?" Marie was holding her infant to her breast, as she sat by her four-poster bed in a lounge chair in their London house. The feel of the baby's lips sucking the milk out of her, the life out of her – that was the greatest giving, it was total love. "Is there a name for our child?"

"Rosabelle," her husband said. "Fair Rosabelle."

"Rosabelle," Marie repeated. The name had a lovely ring to it. She stroked the pink-brown crown of her baby's head, the hole in the top of the skull not closed yet, but breathing under the skin, the dark wisps of hair upon it. "Rosabelle – tell me."

"There was a dance at Rosslyn Castle down the glen," Bill Dunesk said. "And fair Rosabelle wanted to go there to meet her lover. Only a wind blew up across the Firth of Forth –"

"And Rosabelle?"

"She was drowned. She never reached her lover. But he was a Sinclair like you are."

Marie looked down at the baby feeding at her breast, hurting her, but making her feel a woman at last.

"She was to be a Sinclair," she said. "If she had not gone down. Well, Bill, I am now a Fraser. I have lost my name to you, with the marrying of you. But I am still a Sinclair from my mother and a Chatillon. And I like the name of Rosabelle, *la rose si belle* and beautiful. Tell me the poem, if you know it."

"I know some of it," her husband said and looked to the white ceiling of their chamber which had wreaths and posies plastered in to it. And he recited:

> Oh listen, listen, ladies gay!
> No haughty feat of arms I tell.
> Soft is the note, and sad the lay,
> That mourns the lovely Rosabelle.
>
> Moor, moor the barge, you gallant men!
> And gentle lady, deign to stay,

Rest thee in Castle Ravensheuch,
Nor tempt the stormy firth today.

Marie put her hand softly over her baby's head. "I don't like sailing," she said. "All that sea. I don't wonder Rosabelle was told not to go over the firth."

O'er Rosslyn all that dreary night

Bill Dunesk was in full flow now,

A wondrous blaze was seen to gleam.
'Twas broader than the watch-fire's light,
And redder than the bright moon-beam.

Blazed battlement and pinnet high,
Blazed every rose-carved buttress fair –
So still they blaze, when fate is nigh,
The lordly line of high Sinclair.

"Lordly, are we?" Marie laughed and took the baby from her breast. "You're a lucky one, Rosabelle," she said. "And you've had enough for now. Lordly on both sides, you are – or so we are hearing."

There are twenty of Rosslyn's barons bold

Bill Dunesk was intoning the poem like a psalm –

Lie buried within that proud chapelle.
Each one the holy vault doth hold,
But the sea holds lovely Rosabelle.

Marie rocked the baby in her arms. "Mummy holds the lovely Rosabelle. Are there truly twenty Sinclair knights buried in Rosslyn chapel?"

"In full armour," her husband said.

"Why? Were their women getting at them?"

"It was the custom then. The Sinclairs were always half-Vikings. Normans and Norsemen as well as Scots. Their being buried in full armour – and blazing when there was a death in the family – that's really a memory of Viking chiefs being buried with all their war booty when they died."

Then Bill Dunesk finished the poem.

And each Sinclair was buried there
With candle, with book and with knell.
But the sea-caves rung, and the wild winds sung,
The dirge of lovely Rosabelle.

Marie was rocking the child in her arms, crooning, "Rosabelle, Rosabelle, Rosabelle . . ." when her mother Kate came into the bedroom through the half-open door, saying, "I hope I'm not intruding," but Marie held up the baby towards her and said, "Meet Rosabelle, Mother. Isn't it a lovely name for her?"

"We never had one in the family," Kate said. "Not a Rosabelle." She moved to take the infant from her daughter and look at the clenched face of the baby, all tight in sleep.

"Well, you will have a Rosabelle now." Bill Dunesk stood up. "A Lady Rosabelle Fraser. It trips off the tongue. Dinner at seven. With those weird women you wanted to meet."

"Millicent Fawcett?"

"That's the one. She met your aunt with Emily Hobhouse over those concentration camps. I don't know if she's very amusing."

"The camps weren't."

"But at dinner?" Bill yawned. "I do like a bit of spice with my soup. Not stodge and seriousness. Anyway, enough of being domestic. It's not a role to which I am accustomed. But for love of you, my dear . . ."

"You will even put up with a baby girl," Marie said.

"Even that." Bill Dunesk smiled at Kate. "Marie must have been a baby girl once. Thank you for that. And seeing she grew."

"It was a pleasure," Kate said. "Having her, I mean. It still is."

"I have her," Bill said. "Or shall we say, she has me in thrall. Goodbye for now."

He left mother and daughter together to remind each other of what they had been before their long separation, and what the baby girl would be because of that past and that inheritance. "French, Indian and Scots," Kate said. "It's a lovely mixture. More than the *auld alliance*. It's the very old alliance. The civilised and the primitive and the savage – and the *Scots* are the savages."

Marie laughed.

"Rosabelle's father. He's Scots and very, very civilised. Too much so. And I bet she will be."

"Too much so? Your Earl? He's a perfect nobleman . . ."

"So perfect," Marie said, "he hardly dares lay a finger on me. For fear it will hurt me."

"You mean . . . ?"

"Not since she was born," Marie said. "It was like that with the Crows. A woman was unclean after giving birth. For months. I think for Bill I'll always be unclean now. Now I am a mother, a woman. No longer a beautiful pony-rider like a young man, except for having this –" she patted her breast, where a stain was spreading from her

67

milk on her muslin night-gown. "Maternity – it's not for our Bill. He liked me like Oscar Wilde liked Bosie . . ."

"Who?" Kate asked.

"Lord Alfred Douglas," Marie said. "He's still a friend in spite of the scandal. You'll meet him at dinner, though many people won't ask him any more. Oscar called him a slim gilt soul. And when I was a slim bronze soul – that's when Bill loved me. And now, a *mother* –"

"He'll love you the more," Kate said. "You see. I am your mother, and mothers are always right."

"I am Rosabelle's mother now," Marie said. "And I tell you, I'm right about Bill and me."

The dinner party that night was a fearful mixture of family and friends and foes. It was such a hotch-potch that it was bound to work or explode. Millicent Fawcett, the leader of the new women although she was getting on herself, was matched against the redoubtable Mrs Humphrey Ward, who believed that women were incapable of sound judgement, although her publishers did not think so when she screwed another extortionate advance out of them for her ornate prose. To partner this couple, it was Bill's idea of the incongruous to invite Lord Alfred Douglas, who admired formidable women, if he admired women at all. And then there was Kate, and her nephew Hamilton, the ship's engineer with his new buttercup of an Ellen-Maeve, looking for a job for him so that they could settle in England. And Marie, of course, her bare shoulders burnished above her low long gown of crimson crêpe that seemed to dress her softly for the warpath.

It was a curious dinner of pheasant that had been hung too long, with the women firing at each other across the plates of ripe birds and at the men, who were forced into silence or giggles.

"I met your Aunt Mary, Lady Dunesk," Millicent Fawcett said. "Splendid work she did for the Distress Committee –"

"You love Boers," Mrs Ward put in. "Personally, I can't abide them. Traitors."

"She helped us save thousands of the lives of those wretched women and children –"

"Those camps were perfectly adequate. Better diet there than they had at home on the veld. We *saved* them."

"Oh, do be sensible, Mrs Ward – if only for the novelty." So Millicent Fawcett silenced her opposition. "And can I count on you, Lady Dunesk, to help us gain the vote?"

"You surely can," Marie said.

"You already have mine," Bill said gallantly, seeing storm signals blow across the face of Mrs Ward.

"Why does treason – this support of the Boers and Home Rule for the Irish," Mrs Ward asked herself, "always go hand in hand with asking for the vote? If you *had* it, you *new women*, you would use it to betray our country. I'm afraid, our biological weakness does not lead to right conclusions."

"But you only speak for yourself," Marie said sweetly. "And if you are right, you can't be a woman."

"Mrs Ward's paradox is this," Bill said. "I am a woman. No woman is ever right. I am right to say this."

"Unless you are *not* a woman, Mrs Ward." Lord Alfred looked quizzically at the stern dowager beside him. "You could be in *disguise*."

"I believe I resemble my womanhood," Mrs Ward said. "While manhood is not a word to be confused with *you*, Lord Douglas."

Bill laughed and finished chewing a piece of pheasant. He picked some lead shot from his teeth and dropped it on his side-plate – *ping – ping – ping*.

"Careful, Bosie," he said. "She's holed you by the navel."

"Aeroplanes." Hamilton crashed in with another subject to save the day with magnificent irrelevance. "Aren't aeroplanes the most exciting things on earth?"

"I thought they *flew*," Lord Alfred said. "I mean, that is their point."

"They land again," Hamilton said. "They don't glide for long. It all depends on their getting engines. But if we can get an engine small enough – with enough thrust – we could fly over the Channel."

Everybody laughed. The idea was too absurd. Only Millicent Fawcett took him seriously, but then she took everything seriously.

"You're a ship's engineer," she said. "In the Royal Navy, aren't you? And you say it's feasible."

"It's feasible," Hamilton said. "I'm trying to arrange a transfer. A naval air arm. A fleet air arm."

"They'll land on water, will they?" Lord Alfred was amused. "Like ducks."

"Yes," Maeve-Ellen said, surprising herself. "Like ducks. And take off again. Like ducks."

"Sitting ducks," Lord Alfred said. "That's all they will be."

"That is the only sort you are able to shoot, I suppose," Mrs Ward said.

Bill Dunesk laughed at this.

"We will have to shoot your seaplanes, Hamilton," he said. "I can see it now. Flocks of seaplanes –"

"Squadrons. Like the cavalry."

"Bagging squadrons of seaplanes. An air machine shoot."

"They'll bag you," Hamilton said. "They'll drop bombs on you. They'll destroy whole cities."

"Don't be silly, Hamilton," Marie said. "All these scare stories. If we were made to fly, we'd have wings. But I do believe you. If we can't have wings, we'll put them on machines and fly in them." She put her foot on the bell on the floor to summon the servants for the next course. They had the new electricity in the house. Progress was not all bad.

"Exactly," Mrs Ward said. "We don't fly because we were born without wings. It is biologically impossible. Like women and the vote."

"Not technically impossible," Hamilton said. "That is the engine – the air engine – I mean to work on. And change the world."

"Nothing wrong in that," Lord Alfred said, "as long as you get it beautifully wrong."

"Like so many women do," Mrs Ward said. "They cannot think right."

"Except for you," Millicent Fawcett said. "You are the exception who proves the rule."

"Yes," Mrs Ward said. "Exactly that. I am."

He would never come. It was not that she really wanted him to come. And if he ever came, she would not imagine how he would look. Men were often disappointing, particularly when they were not very old; and when they were very old, they should be put out to grass, where nobody could see them. Virginia Callow had heard that the new Assistant District Officer was a horseman – you had to be in the job, there was so much country to cross, and young men usually cared more for their mounts than their wives. But he might not have a brain in his head or a mind bigger than a pimple. That was not necessary in the job, even if he had the power of life and death, or at least of flogging and taxing, over an area larger than Yorkshire.

As for his looks, Virginia told herself that she didn't care about that, although she did in those curious dreams of intruders which violated her sleep – a face as long and silver-white as the blade of a carving-knife approaching her. There were people in Vienna who said that dreams really mattered, but she had not read them yet. In case he did come, she put dabs of rouge on her pale cheeks, although it was a little fast, and it made her small school charges giggle and point and whisper, until she had to rap the desk with her ruler and say, "Children, the three times multiplication table. Three times one is three – and the three in one is God the Father, God the Son and God the Holy Ghost. And three times two is six – and you will get six of the best, Jonathan, if you don't stop that right now!"

When he did come to the Mission School at last, he was not what she expected. He was simply the only possible man around for fifty miles, she knew that. For she would not settle to be an old frump of a Boer farmer's wife, breaking mealies with a log and beating butter with a churn stick and grinding coffee between stones. She had a yellow Hottentot maid to do that at the school, but she could hardly pay for her servant. The wages were beggarly, twenty pounds a year, it did not buy her one decent dress. Sometimes she thought there was no sin in all the world save the sin of being poor, though there was the second sin which the Bible stressed – which was to be a woman like the original Eve and be cursed to labour for your bread if you were an orphan and there was nobody to look after you. But the man who would come to her would not care that she had nothing and was born nowhere. He was her only ticket out of oblivion, her passport back Home. In that way, he had to be a Galahad or a Young Lochinvar. And the man she saw entering her front room was not so wide of the mark. He was all wire and cord beneath his dusty riding-boots and jodhpurs and khaki jacket, while his face was as lean and sharp as in her dreams, but burnt to brick by the sun and the wind. His golden hair did not flow free, but was slicked to his skull so it looked like a shell for a field gun.

"Howdie, Miss Callow," he said, which was not much of a greeting, but had to do, she supposed.

"I am very pleased to meet you, Mr Sinclair," she said, then added, "at last," to blame him for his long delay in getting to her, as they had obviously already heard of each other at a distance.

Robert saw a tall thin woman with a pallid face under a cartwheel straw hat as big as a parasol to keep the glare from her milky cheeks, which blazed all the same with a red patch on either side. Her brown eyes were round and large and glistened as if they were washed, her thin lips were avid with desire and expression. There was certainly no woman like her for two days' ride anywhere, and if she was not the type of woman he had always admired, for these were of the soft and rounded sort, she was a lady and from England. And with that deference to the authority of a teacher or a mother, which had been drummed into him in the prairie, he said, "Duty kept me away, marm – duty." For he was the authority here even if he was only twenty-two.

"Well, I am very glad you came in the *end*," Virginia said. "And now you are here, pray do not *rush* away. Whatever your duty is, do let it wait."

"I don't know how it can," Robert said. "There's always a heap to do. It's crazy, but I am a sort of a father round here – a fixer for the Great White Mother."

"The Queen, you mean."

"The Indians called Her The Great White Mother where I hailed from, and I don't see as it may be different here. The tribes, they are all under Her blanket, aren't they? If there's room enough for them, which I reckon there is." Robert laughed at his own comment. "It sure is a big and beautiful country. These mountains, I could hug them."

"I consider it a bleak and barren land," Virginia said. "And it is a misfortune for those who have to live in it."

"But you came out –"

"No choice, Mr Sinclair. Needs must. Or should I call you District Officer?"

"Robert. Or Bob. We're not on parade. And you're Miss . . .?" His voice trailed away on the question.

"You are most informal," Virginia said coldly, but then relented. What was protocol in the wilderness? "Virginia is my name. But don't call me Ginny. Gin is a drink, I think."

"A pink drink. I never touch the rotgut. Scotch or beer."

"You do imbibe?"

"When I can track it down. I've a good nose for that spoor." Now he noticed two framed drawings on the wall, the rough outline in red and yellow crayon of a buck, but no buck looked like that, and some little black stick figures and a sort of serpent.

"Not bad, those paintings, for a Bushman."

"The Bushman is I," Virginia said and watched Robert scowl with shame. "Actually, I copied them off Bushmen drawings I was shown in a cave by one of my children – the children I teach, that is. I think there is something wonderful in primitive art, don't you? It is the first art. Primal – and so . . ." she reached for the right word to come up with, "simple."

They were just daubs to Robert, no better than kids' pictures, but he said valiantly, "I reckon they're great," and he hurried on to ask, "Now tell me, where can I bunk down? I guess I can stay over a couple of days. And I've got all my trek kit on my pony."

"There is the chapel," Virginia said, surprising herself by suggesting it. "It is all there is, except the huts, and they are occupied. You obviously cannot stay with me. But I am sure that God will not mind. You will probably be *good* company. And the chapel is really not much."

And it was not much – mud walls painted white with a zinc roof and twenty crude chairs and stools facing a table, on which stood a cross, delicately covered in black wood as a flower with four petals. That was the only sign of Our Lord. In front of it, Robert unpacked the kit he had bought at Walters & Co., the Recognised Overseas Outfitters – the Improved Compactum Folding Bed with its best rot-proof canvas and groundsheet and mosquito rods and net, his "X" Pattern Long Shape Folding Bath and Washstand and Tray and Latrine Seat and Collapsible Bucket with Rope Handle, items one of each, all contained in their special padlocked cover or Wolseley Valise in Waterproof Khaki Twill. It was all regulation gear, and now Robert Sinclair was living by the book, if not the Good Book. And he was looking for a regular woman, and there seemed to be one here. As he prepared to leave the chapel to send the Hottentot maid for some water for his ablutions, he saw the flowery black cross on the altar, and he fell on his knees. He should thank Somebody for striking it lucky, and that Somebody had to be God.

Virginia had done what she could over dinner for the two of them. The maid Tsutsie did not run to much more than corn mush and grilled deer, if you could call those tough antelopes and bush things anything to do with venison. But Virginia had hoarded a tin of Crosse & Blackwell vegetable soup, also of Christmas pudding, which she had not been able to face alone for the last festivity, a particularly hot and trying one. She concocted a hot white sauce out of the mealie flour and rather rancid butter, but as for the main course, she could only provide a roast salted leg of what looked like buffalo, so huge and dark it was, and an excuse of a Yorkshire pudding, which was the same as the white sauce with more flour and salt in it. It would have to do. Even if the way to a man's heart was through his stomach, she could only do her best with what she had. Mrs Beeton herself would have been in despair.

Yet Robert liked the meal and ate hugely. He even praised the faint taste of lime in the boiled water. He seemed to appreciate the trimmings, the embroidered napkins and damask tablecloth she had brought out with her – yellowing now from scrubbing with lye soap – and the candles which she had concocted from animal fat. The niceties were so important. If you let yourself go in the bush, you went native. Manners were really the rules you could not break. And though they hid a woman's true character, the needs and the wants that drove her, they were her weapons against any violation. So when Robert took out his pipe and pouch after dinner and began to stuff the bowl with coarse-cut tobacco, Virginia did rebuke him, although she did not mean to offend him, her only prospect of escape in any way.

"Would you mind if you *lit up* later? And perhaps outdoors. I really do find tobacco smoke a trial and not good for the disposition."

"Pardon," Robert said amicably and rolled up his pouch and put it in one of the side pockets of his drill khaki jacket and the filled pipe in the other pocket. "The bush does make you forget you're not alone. But that's what the ladies are for, I reckon. To tell you how to behave yourself in front of the ladies."

"There are more things than that in a relationship between the sexes." Again Virginia was surprised to find herself using so crude a term about human love. But she was hardly a sheltered woman. She was masquerading as a mission teacher. It was the only job she could find. And she had even read her Havelock Ellis. She knew what most women did not choose to admit yet – the desire of a woman for a man. "There is companionship and even a certain mystery." She rose from her chair and bent to fiddle with the brass knob, which adjusted the wick of the oil lamp. She knew its subtle light softened her face and suited her style. "I think when one meets somebody one *knows*. That is the loved one for life. It is immediate. It is there." She turned and fixed her huge and moist-bright eyes on Robert. "I have been waiting so long – and now . . ." She let her words hang in air as he might the smoke from his pipe.

Robert really did not know what to make of this. She seemed to have said a great deal, but nothing at all. She liked him, though. And she was a fine woman, no doubt of that.

"I'd have been here before," he said, "but I have all this work."

She sat near him and gazed into his eyes, until he had to look down. "Tell me about your work," she said. She knew that was the second way to a man's heart.

So he told her about how strange it was to be so young and yet have such power over people old enough to be his grandparents. Whatever the missions were doing, the witchdoctors were still in control. If there was a palaver you could not solve, they could, and what they knew about herbs and plants beat quinine and boracic into a back pocket, if you got fever or the runs. But all these cases and squabbles you heard, you weren't Solomon at the judgement, you really didn't know who was right and who was wrong, the natives were all such liars in court, if you could call his little meetings a court. So he would say almost at random, "Ten shillings fine," which was a hell of a lot for them, they might have to trek to the mines to earn it, or maybe a few lashes. But he did not like that, the *sjambok* hurt like the devil, it was only meant for oxen. But he had to do it. Black people did not feel as much as white people. Their skins were simply not so sensitive. He had met a doctor and a preacher in the army who had told him that.

"Tell me about London, your training there," Virginia said, beginning to dream of her escape as he was speaking. While he told her of classes and senior officers and learning the rulebook, she was seeing the spires of Whitehall and the red robes of the peers at the future coronation of the new King of England. Then she suddenly heard that very word in Robert's mouth, "Coronation – and my cousin's been asked." And at that moment, she knew that she might love him.

"Your cousin, who is she?"

"Marie? She's a countess now. Married somebody called Bill Dunesk, a nice enough fellow, but damp behind the ears. Still, she has to go to the coronation with him. All the peers are summoned by the earl marshal. Quite a shindig, I imagine."

Although she would like to have heard more, there was time enough for that. So Virginia asked, not quite at cross-purposes, "What do you intend to do with your first leave?"

"Well, this tour is two years, then I get six months. But my mother's real sick in Canada, and I reckon I just might go along there."

"But by London, through London –"

Robert laughed.

"The good old Union Castle Line, it does sail thataway."

"Oh, I should so like –" Virginia caught herself at being too forward. "I mean, don't you miss Home?"

"Home's a log house on the prairie for me."

"But Home – real Home – England. London. The real Home of all of us."

"It's a dirty great city," Robert said. "But it is fun. The Troc and the Long Bar at the Cri. But no ladies. I'm sorry."

"I just long for Home. I feel there, somehow complete. Whole. This life is a kind of exile, a trap." She gazed deeply at Robert until her eyes seemed to flood her face. "Anyone who would take me out of here, take me Home . . ."

"You needn't be looking far," Robert found himself saying. He certainly wouldn't round up anyone better here, and two years was a long time to wait for a woman. "A fine young lady like you, why, any man would be proud –"

"Any man will not do for me." Virginia snapped suddenly as if breaking the neck of her hope. "A particular man who will nurture . . . understand. I said there was a mystery in this." She rose to stand beside the oil lamp again, to adjust the flame, to look her best. The light flickered in little shades over her face. "I need a man who will engage all of me. And engage all of himself to me. For, you know, we women – if we are not held, captivated – we can be fickle. I promise you. I warn you. Fickle."

Now Robert was engaged by this threat of waywardness. His sense of possession was fired. He found himself on his feet and advancing on her at the lamp. His voice was thick. "I'd hold you," he said. "Tight rein. You'd never get away."

"Now, now," she said, eluding him and moving away. "Don't charge. You are not in the cavalry now." She walked to the door and opened it. "You cannot drop me with a shot between the eyes. We do not know each other, but there is time. I cannot run away, you know." And as Robert passed her to leave the room, she did not back off, but let him brush against her. A brief softness seemed to burn him.

"Tomorrow morning, will you breakfast with me? At seven. We start at sun-up."

"Seven, then. Good-night, Virginia."

"Good-night, Robert."

And he would have no good night of it. Robert knew that as he walked away. He ached for her, all because she was elusive. He had to possess her. Women were damnation that way, teasing a man. Like the Boer commandos, as you advance, they retreat. As you retreat, they advance. Female tactics. But just to make sure, Robert found himself kneeling by his folding bed again in front of the flowery black cross and saying his prayers, remembering Virginia Callow this time, just as his mother had taught him to do, if he loved somebody or they were family.

8

RAJ AND TREK

In the sprawling house above the valley at Annandale, Angus was enthusing to his older brother Iain about the railway that had just been opened up the mountains to Simla.

"When I built those mining railways in the Andes," he said, "I never thought I'd see my work done better. Certainly not here, in India. And not just to serve a hill station."

"Simla is the seat of government in the summer," Iain said. "The viceroy's here. And that American of his, Lady Curzon."

"But sixty miles of track – a continuous succession of reverse curves with a radius of one hundred and twenty feet – the steep gradients three in a hundred – rising to seven thousand feet. And a hundred and seven tunnels – in all five miles long – and fifty arched viaducts nearly two miles overall – and cuts and stone walls – all to spare the viceroy the eight hours on a tonga cart up the hill road. Though on that two-and-a-half foot narrow gauge, you sway so much you're sea-sick."

"You're still an engineer," Iain said. "You'll never retire."

"No more than you will."

"Planters never retire," Iain said. "You have to mow us down. Like hay."

"For eighty," Angus said, "you look hearty."

"I'm near the last one as fought in the Mutiny," Iain said. "No one remembers it at all. Not Lord Curzon. Nor that office-*wallah* Margaret's married to, Douglas Jardine. They're visiting soon, by the way. He's come up to Simla to report to Curzon. You will meet them the now."

"Good," Angus said. "I have come a long way to see the family. And this time, it may be the last time, brother."

"Aye," Iain said. "But it's been a wee while since we played bools at the dominie's in the glen."

Angus looked through the window down the wooded slope of the Himalayan mountain to the race-course in the valley below.

"You've made a glen better than Scotland here," he said. "Your Annandale."

"But it's no' the same," Iain said. "Ach, Anna."

A Gurkha servant wheeled Anna in her wickerwork chair into the living-room. She was handsome still, her face fine-drawn under the black lace cap that perched above the rest of her white hair.

"The world is coming to us," she said, "because I can not go to the world now. Peg also is coming – the doctor. She says your sister Mary wants her back in London. And she is your niece, Iain and Angus, in her way."

"But Seaforth," Angus said, "he will still be in South Africa?"

"Yes," Anna said. "It is best for him over there. It will be very embarrassing if Douglas and Margaret visit when Peg is here. In *his* position . . . mixing . . ."

"No," Iain said drily. "Peg is not a Maharanee. Douglas would mix with her, if she was. But she's better – a doctor."

"Caste and class," Angus said. "The British were made for the Indians, and the Indians for the British. A perfect understanding of what keeps us all apart."

But Peg was already at the house in Annandale when Douglas Jardine and Margaret and their daughter Ruby were carried by *jampanees* on their evening visit from Simla. Douglas Jardine had had a trying day, summoned by the viceroy to his camp. Lord Curzon could not abide the architecture of Simla, where all the public buildings were crosses between ironworks and chalets, and the viceregal lodge had been decorated from Maple's: lincrusta and pomegranate and pineapple patterns on the walls – fit for a Minneapolis millionaire in the opinion of Lady Curzon. So Curzon had fled to The Retreat at Mashabra and even further to a mountain camp on Naldera. There he penned his devastating and ceaseless minutes, while signallers informed him of the news of India by heliograph in the day and by flashing lamps at night. It was a devil of a journey there, Douglas thought, and just like a viceroy to put his staff to the greatest inconvenience. People did not come to Simla for the climbing, other than social climbing. Even if the Curzons found local society dull with the chief official sport 'hunt the slipper', not the tiger, it was filthy inconsiderate to drag a fellow over the Himalayas just to present a file no more important than a chit to the great panjandrum. But duty called, and Douglas always answered that call, however out of the way.

Yet duty had nothing to do with the sight of Peg at Annandale. Margaret's half-caste cousin was an official embarrassment to the Jardines. It was almost worse her being a woman doctor than being partially Indian. She even came under Douglas Jardine's department. He had to approve some of her requisitions at the hospital. Yet the only approval he had given willingly was her coming transfer to London to look after a ward of wounded soldiers for her Aunt Mary. At least she would be out of India. She was a relative, and in the Indian Civil Service one should never do a favour for a relation, and never accept a favour . . . Of course, it was different when the dollies came round at Christmas from grateful recipients of impartial imperial bounty. Then, if one found a hundred gold mohurs hidden in the bouquet, well, as long as the gift was anonymous, and one didn't exactly know who it was from . . .

"So glad you could come too, Miss Sinclair," Douglas said. "Margaret has not seen you for simply ages. And Ruby – our daughter – never."

Another galling fact was that Ruby and Peg were strikingly similar, with raven hair and long oval faces and large dark eyes. They even looked like relations. And Peg made this worse by saying, "I am glad to meet you at last, Ruby. Your mother and I were brought up here together as children."

"In a way," Anna said from her wheel-chair. "Peg's mother kindly helped us with our children. But Peg is a doctor. That is something I always wanted to be – but I was born too early for that to be possible. I met your grandfather, Ruby, when I was nursing at Nainital after the Mutiny."

"I can still feel the sword-cut in me," Iain said, "when it's cold."

"He gave me this emerald ring," Anna said. She moved to shift the brilliant blaze of green light round her finger so it shone from her palm. "I have been thinking about it. I mean to pass it on."

"Not the emerald." Margaret could not keep the quiver from her voice. "If you do think, Mother, it is time to pass it on –"

"I found it when we took the palace at Lucknow," Iain said. "Spoils of war."

"Then it is Indian," Peg said. She held out her hand to Anna, who had managed to pull the ring past the swollen joint of her finger. "Let me see." She took the jewel and rolled the ornamental gold hoop between forefinger and thumb, so that darts of emerald fire struck the eyes of the Jardines. "Are you giving it to this Indian?"

"Oh, Mother, you cannot –"

"Let me see it," Ruby said. She almost snatched it from Peg's hand. She examined the jewel closely.

"It's huge," she said. "But it's got a mark in it. A flaw."

"We all have a flaw in us," Iain said. "And yours is –" he held out a huge bent palm for the ring – "wanting something too much?"

Reluctantly, Ruby dropped the ring into her grandfather's hand. He closed his fist about it and did a slow uppercut in the air.

"I won it hard," he said. "I killed for that."

"Indians fighting for their freedom," Peg said.

"We were no' free neither," Iain said. "We were bound to the colours. Slaves to the regiment."

He opened his fist again to consider the ring, while Douglas Jardine said softly to Peg, "You're in favour of Indian independence, I believe. As is your brother, Dr Seaforth Sinclair."

"You know that?" Peg was not surprised. "In your official capacity?"

"We have our intelligence. Your brother is not thinking of returning to India . . ."

"Not immediately."

"We have heard of a lawyer called Gandhi organising something called passive resistance among Indian immigrants in the Transvaal, where we have rather decently allowed the Boers to have a say again. Now, we don't want him back here, trying to do the same thing. Agitators . . . they may seem to be harmless eccentrics – then, before you know it, suddenly they are national leaders."

"You know a great deal about us, Mr Jardine. In a country of more than a hundred million people, you know about the important few. Even when they are abroad. Will you know what I am doing when I go back to London?"

"You never know, do you?" Douglas knew he had revealed too much, which was unusual for him. "But then, it is better to know."

"Let us eat," Anna said.

"Tiffin time, Mother," Margaret said, but she could not resist adding, "but who *is* going to have the emerald?"

Iain lobbed the ring into the air and caught it falling and closed his fingers round it again.

"We'll keep it a wee while more," he said. "And then it shall go to our favourite child."

Anna smiled.

"And who would that be?"

"All of you." Iain opened his arms wide to include them all. "All of you who are good enough to come here and visit with us in our lonely life – while we are still alive, that is."

"Coming here is nothing," Douglas Jardine said. "You should have seen the miles I had to climb to visit the viceroy this morning. I know he likes to be inaccessible, but that was ridiculous."

"You should have marched across all India with the Highlanders," Iain said. "And then charged ten times over five miles a day in full kit at one hundred and ten degrees. That was moving. But who wants to hear the tales of an old soldier when life is so much *harder* on you young folk these days?"

Only Peg laughed, and then she put her hand on Iain's arm.

"You did put down the Mutiny," she said. "For the moment. You were brave to do that – so few against so many."

Iain opened his fist again and showed her the emerald ring, which now was dull green and shadowed.

"It was no' worth it," he said. "Or was it?"

Piet was a wonder with the oxen. When the tiny black *voorloper* drove them up to the waggon, they took up their places in double-span in front of the vehicle like two rough ranks on the parade ground before dressing to the right. Then Piet would limp up and down the team, calling each ox by his name: "Bakir, oy" – the wise front ox with horns as long as elephant's tusks – "Bantom . . . Rooiland . . ." and then his running joke on his new partner, "Hammie boy", and finally the big after-oxen which carried the pole or dissel boom, "Zole and Zwaartland." And each ox moved on command exactly into position beside the trek chain. And the *voorloper* and the big Zulus fastened the necks of the span to the yokes by straps of rawhide, which were then tied to the wooden slats of the *yukskeis*. Piet would now climb into the driver's seat and give a last call to any beast which had edged out of true, and it would sidle back.

Out of the blue, Piet would crack his long whip like a Mauser shot and yell like a trooper. The oxen would all strain to the yoke in one mighty heave, and the overloaded waggon would jolt into motion. Piet was so tender with all the beasts that he hardly ever scored their hides with his *sjambok*, though he could flick a fly off their rumps with the lash at twenty paces. He had bought good wheelers, and these were so trained that they swung out or turned in to correct the bumpy roads or bring back in line any unsalted ox in the double-span to their rear. But Piet was not so gentle to the strapping Zulu drivers he called "boys". He preferred most beasts to most men.

In the waggon behind Piet, Hamish Charles took weeks to get the hang of driving the oxen. Piet had bought him a good span, the front ox was old and wily on the track, but he could not work the long whip nor talk to the straining cattle as Piet could. He relied heavily on Din or Dingaan, a burly Zulu hired by Piet to teach Hamish Charles the way of the trek. But Din was savage with the *sjambok* and surly with his *baas*, flogging the beasts into their lurch forward and rolling on. And when one of them lay down in the middle of a path through a narrow kloof, blocking the progress of the whole convoy, Hamish

Charles had never seen crueller torments inflicted upon an unmovable object by Din and the furious Boer trekkers behind – giraffe-hide whips, blows from rocks on skull and spine, doubling the tail and biting it, stabbing the rump with clasp knives, even branding the beast again with hot irons. And then Piet woke up after a sleep on the forward waggon and asked the name of the brute and quietly went up to its dogged sprawl and spoke in its ear. And it rose at once, unsteadily as oxen do, then leant into the chain. Some swore that Piet bit its ear in the secret place no ox can withstand, but Hamish Charles knew he had only talked to it, man to almost a man.

The whipping of Buldoo showed the other side of Piet. The sound of the lashes broke the rest of Hamish Charles. He started up to hear the slow slap of rawhide thong against flesh and came forward to see a black shape tied against a waggon-wheel as he had seen Tommies tied when they had slept on sentry duty during the war. The flogging was banned in the British army now, but Hamish Charles had heard of men dying under a hundred strokes in the Indian Mutiny, when his uncle had been alive and fighting. But this was a cruel punishment, the *sjambok* cutting the back into red outlines of squares and diamonds as Piet inflicted a pattern of pain on his victim. Now the Zulu groaned and shuddered for the first time, and Hamish Charles caught Piet's wrist on the next back-stroke.

"Enough," he said.

Piet's look at his friend was bright with hate.

"Never," he said, "never come you between a *baas* and his boys. Or we will be dead all."

He shook his arm free and raised the *sjambok* again.

"I'll have him," Hamish Charles said. "He will work for me. He won't work for you after this. He's too proud."

"Have him." Piet lowered the whip. "You are hiring me also. You pay for us all. But he is useless, Buldoo. Always he ask for meat. Drunk on Kaffir beer. You have him."

"I will." Hamish Charles spoke to the watching Zulu drivers. "Set him free." He turned his back on Piet, who was rolling up the thong of his *sjambok*. "You do not whip him," he said. "When you use that lash, you whip yourself."

"You a *predikant*?" Piet sneered, but he mumbled in a sort of defence as he walked away. "You tell me, and you know nothing of the trek . . ."

Now Hamish Charles went over to the wheel and helped to catch Buldoo as he sagged back. "I have some boracic for those cuts," Hamish Charles said. "Bring him to my waggon. We'll wash those wounds."

Then Buldoo stood on his own feet. "*Inkos*," he said. "Chief. I work you. But this . . . nothing . . ."

Hamish Charles smiled. "All the same," he said, "you'll work better for me if we treat your back." And he did swab and dust with stinging powder the criss-cross of weals on Buldoo's back, in spite of the Zulu's protest that he did not need his back, for he would never lie down on his work.

And Buldoo never seemed to rest until the trek had reached the blue mountains. He was the same as Piet, patient with working beasts, hard on men, harder on men who were not Zulus, and hardest on himself. After Din had flayed Rooiland for a stumble from a broken *nekstrop* that jolted the span aside and the waggon off the track, Buldoo took the whip to Din and made the *nekstrop* good and talked the ox back into its plod and toil. He tormented the little *voorloper*, however, because he was a Hottentot and fit only to be a slave. "You stop the Zulus," he told Hamish Charles. "Or we kill these boys, we have all Africa." He had fought at Isandhlwana, when the Zulu *impis* had wiped out a British regiment and killed the cousin of Hamish Charles. He had been wounded at Ulundi, when the Maxim guns had cut down the Zulu kingdom. He was fierce in his loyalty, when it was given; he was terrible to his enemies; but he was firm and fair in his use of nature. From instinct, Hamish Charles had never thought to trust such an alien figure in the new landscape. But he found in Buldoo an education and gave him a grudging respect.

Perhaps the time of conversion came when Buldoo saved the pianoforte and the fowl coop, while they were trekking over the berg. Piet had laughed at Hamish Charles buying the musical upright which weighed half a ton and unbalanced the load on the waggon, perching on the top of the zinc sheets and coffee sacks by the squawking hens like a rock overhang. Buldoo was negotiating the double-span of thirty heaving oxen on the edge of a precipice round the stuck lead waggon, which had lost a wheel on the narrow cliff track. The hoofs of the offside steers tore loose stones from the rim of the gorge, which clattered down the berg in ricochets. The outer wheels stayed on the level only inches from the plunge down. And then the load began to sway behind Hamish Charles and Buldoo, who moved like a lion to the kill. He sprang up, threw the whip to Hamish Charles, swung round and pulled himself high on the sacks, then caught the weight of the piano, tugging against its ropes and threatening to tip the whole waggon sideways, over the drop. Man and object made a triangle of force against force on the top of the load with the fowls in their coop screeching at the struggle. The waggon lurched, the wheels crumbled the rimrock, the oxen swung in to safety past the stranded team, and

Buldoo wrested the piano back to straight. Hamish Charles could only swallow and clear his throat, useless in this time of danger.

Hamish Charles would see that Buldoo – with his craving for meat – was fed from the hunter's pot that the white trekkers kept for themselves. The iron cauldron on its tripod legs was a study in perpetual eating. It was always full like a horn of plenty. Something was put in as fast as it was taken out, anything killed that day which passed for meat – *dassie* or partridge, wild pig or *duiker*, ostrich or porcupine. The old bones were removed and given to the dogs, and new ones put into the stew. Any edible roots thickened the broth, but on the whole, it was flesh and blood and marrow, and the brew set in a cold brawn for a game pie breakfast without the crust at the start of the day. Hamish Charles took a double portion and left half of his plate for Buldoo, who could not abide the mealie porridge and mush for the rest of the drivers. Piet caught Hamish Charles at the feeding of Buldoo and warned him that he had no place in Africa if he spoilt his servants.

"Soft you are on man and beast," he said. "And you will end stropping them to death. And you were almost dead with that domfool piano. You do not play it even."

"No home is a home without a piano," Hamish Charles said stubbornly. "And you never know who will come to play it."

When Mary came to visit the farm of Hamish Charles by the blue mountains, he was almost ready to receive her. The zinc roof was raised on the joists above the stone walls, the pianoforte stood proudly in the middle of the drawing-room and its stool and two wooden lounging-chairs with green canvas cushions and flat arm-rests for perching drinks on. There was a working kitchen, too, with an iron oven and china willow-pattern plates and sacks of all the basic foods and a cold cupboard of stone slab and wire-mesh. There was a well in the yard for drawing up water, and barns and pens for the cattle, and *kraals* of piled boulders for the sheep. The chickens had the run of the house and they even laid eggs in one of the two beds from time to time. A dozen saplings of marula and mimosa were planted for a wind-break and for shade, when they were grown. Their bark was protected from the nibbling antelopes by wooden stakes, driven around their slim trunks and stems. Watering them every evening was the worst chore of all, but they would survive in no other way.

"You have done well," Mary said, settled too long on one of the arm-chairs, her joints set almost as hard as the wooden ones. She had the arthritis her mother had. "But I will see Piet Krug, for I must tell him of his wife. It will be hard. I have been telling of the dying of dear ones to the living for too long now."

"He comes this evening to see us," Hamish Charles said. He was uneasy about it. He had already been quarrelling with his Afrikaner friend about a *vlei*, where both of the herds went for water, and which both said were in their land, as if the open karroo could have any boundaries. "And there will be more people coming. I sent Buldoo over the border to fetch Robert. And he is bringing his new wife, Virginia. She taught at the mission school."

"A good woman," Mary said, and then added unexpectedly, "Good women are often the worst. They know they're good."

"That's very cynical of you, Aunt Mary. And I never thought you had any cynicism in you."

"Good works, that is all I have seen all my life. And I have worked too long with the women who say they do good works and don't at all. It is all in the saying and not in the doing."

A Hottentot boy came in with a teapot and two cups and saucers and a sugarbowl on a tray, which he set down on a low folding canvas table.

"Don't you move." Hamish Charles rose. "I will be mother." And he began pouring some green liquid into the cups. "I am afraid it's only bush tea. We've run out of Indian."

"First," Mary said, "I canna move. I am set. Second, if you are ever a mother, the Lord will have to change his creation. And as for bush tea, I drink everything that is hot, sweet and herbal."

Hamish Charles added two piled spoonfuls of sugar to the brew in the teacup, stirred it with a spoon and took it on its saucer to his aunt.

"I don't even know the bush it comes from. The locals pick and dry it for me. They know their plants."

"Now, is that Piet Krug coming over here before or after your cousin Robert and his bride? It is not a sociable thing to be telling him of the death of his wife in company."

"I hope so. But if not, I will take you aside, Aunt Mary. It is splendid to have you here."

And it was. Buldoo led Robert and Virginia on their ponies to the farm before evening. There was time for introductions and memories of the war against the Boers that was over now. The peace terms were generous enough. There were reparations, there was amnesty, as long as the Boers would give up their independence, which they could no longer defend. "There was conscience over those dreadful concentration camps even in the government," Mary said. "My report went to the War Office, very high they say. It would have gone to the old Queen, I dare say, but it was too late for that. Her son the King, I hear He does not muckle fancy the reading. But the thing is, when the

English are guilty, they can be generous. It is a generous peace. But some things can never be put right no more than broken china. I fear with Piet Krug –"

"He has forgiven us," Hamish Charles said. "He is a friend."

"I will see." Mary was not convinced.

Virginia's effect on the two Sinclairs at the farm was that of the opposite poles of a magnet. She attracted Hamish Charles immediately and repelled Mary less evidently. When Virginia laughed with joy to see the piano, and Hamish Charles led her over to it and she found it out of tune, yet still played Strauss and Chopin recognisably with the wrong notes, Hamish Charles thought a genius had ridden into the house. And watching her look up at her host with shy appraisal in her brimming eyes, Mary felt a stab of fear like a lancet to her heart. She called Robert over to her and spoke of Seaforth, now decorated for his medical services in the war and called to Johannesburg to help run a private hospital, endowed by the Apfelsteins with their vast mining interests in the Rand. "But he's coloured," Robert said and could have bitten off his tongue when Mary snapped back. "So are you. You just happen to be a different shade of bleach from most of the people in this country." And Robert remembered that Seaforth was the apple of his aged aunt's eye, who was blind to any blemish in him.

When Piet came unwilling into the room, passing the brim of his old slouch hat round and round in his long knobbled fingers, and darting suspicious glances at everybody in the room, Hamish Charles helped his aunt to her feet and waited by her until her bones unlocked enough for her to walk, then he said simply to Piet, "So good of you to come. Aunt Mary wants to talk to you about Annie. Perhaps you could take her out under the *stoep*." Piet took her by the elbow which felt as dry and bent as the crook of his walking-stick and supported her to the wooden seat outside and said, "Tell me of Annie. I must hear." And in her plain way Mary told him of the death of Annie and said that her last words were of her love of her husband, which was not true. But when Mary told a rare lie, it was always to the living about the dear dead, and she was always believed. And Piet wept silently, the drops and trickles from his eyes marking his beard as if with dew. Then he snorted and wiped his nose on the dusty sleeve of his jacket and said bitterly, "I hate all *Uitlanders*, then there is you. How hate you?" And Mary said, "You have good cause to hate us. But hate is useless. It destroys the hater. Thank you, Piet Krug, for loving. You have helped Hamish set up on his farm." Piet said, "Ach, that is nothing. He help me." And Mary said, "You must go on helping him. He needs a wife." Piet said, "And I need. We see sisters.

Bunjie and Lizzie van der Merwe." And Mary said, "That is good. I do not like the way he looks at his cousin's wife, when she plays the piano." Piet laughed and said, "Do not worry, Tant' Mary. Hamish is good, too good for a cousin's wife. Sometime I think – he is too good for this life, for this life here."

9

SOCIAL GAMES

At Lords, there were two games proceeding. On the cricket pitch in the middle, flannelled youths were playing the traditional game, with Eton in its second innings batting against the clock to make two hundred-odd runs to win, and Harrow bowling out the middle order like skittles, only the opener Plunkett-Drax looking like carrying his bat to defeat because nobody could stay in with him. Murdo Sinclair had taken three wickets for Harrow, but he was now fielding at long leg and keeping half an eye on the stands to see if he could find his father Angus and his sister Arabella, come over from Peru with his mother to meet the right sort of man, if she could.

For that was the second game being played in the stands and the promenade round the cricket ground back to the pavilion. Few of the thousands of strollers were watching the cricket. It was hardly the purpose of the attendance. Matches were being made, not played. Young women aimed the points of their parasols at their marks and hunted them down through the introductions of their parents. Two circles, an inner and an outer one, slowly perambulated in opposite directions round the green oval, where the thwack of willow bat and leather ball on bare hand sounded like an irregular flogging. Black top hats and straw boaters, morning coats with carnation buttonholes and grey check spongebag trousers, these were the male costumes, while the ladies had plundered pastel chalks and watercolour boxes for their soft colours, their tight linen or floating chiffon and lace. Now that the sun was shining, it was time to make hay and a bright future.

Angus had been to the crown colony of Hong Kong after his visit to India to discuss an engineering scheme for Kowloon, the leased lands across the bay. He had returned to Peru to retrieve his wife Isabella and daughter Arabella to sail with them to visit their son in England and see to his career, as he was leaving Harrow at the end of the term. Outside some business interests, Angus knew little of the London social scene, and he was hoping that Murdo would do something for the family when he finally left the cricket pitch. It would be better if Eton were bowled out soon, and Angus liked to hear the cheers as the wickets went on falling quickly, with only Plunkett-Drax soldiering on. There would be more time for the social game.

Brother Iain's daughter May was there with her husband, Charles Seymour-Scudabright, and their two sons, Gordon and Graham, although neither of the young men were good enough to play in the Eton team. The encounter between the cousins was almost like that of rival battle fleets, all evasion and suspicion under smoke screens of pleasure at the meeting.

"So good to see you *here*," Charles said, and then added, "and so unexpected."

"Our son is bowling you all out," Angus said. "Your sons don't represent their school."

"I am a wet bob," Gordon said.

"What is that?" Arabella asked. "You swim? You fell in?"

"I row."

"What is row?"

"A scull. With oars."

"A skull? You are a medical student?"

"Give it up," Angus said to his daughter, so like her mother when she was young that she seemed to her father an instant memory of a lasting love. "You will never understand public school games. At Eton, they even play a game with a wall."

"You cannot play with a wall," Arabella said. "It will hurt you."

"Beside a wall," Graham said. "But you get hurt all right. You can tread on the tugs, if you like, with your boots, as long as you don't kick them. And knuckle their faces. Like this." He switched the black top-hat he was holding from his right hand to his left, then made a fist and ground his knuckles against his brother's pink cheeks. "You knuckle them to force them away from the wall."

Gordon struck his brother's arm aside.

"You don't play the Wall Game at Lords," he said.

"I don't know if the battle of Waterloo was won in the playing-fields of Eton," Angus Sinclair said. "Perhaps it was lost there."

"What do you mean?" Charles Seymour-Scudabright was annoyed. "We have a tradition of service. Gordon will join the army, and Graham will follow me into the navy. Good God, there's Hamilton –"

And there was Hamilton, May's brother, joining in the skirmish of cousins with his tiny spouse Ellen-Maeve. He did not salute Charles, for all were off-duty from the navy in morning coats or black tails, the uniform of that day. But after the usual salvo of greetings, he did continue the provocation of the Seymour-Scudabrights.

"I am leaving the navy," he said. "Ships are finished."

"What?" Charles was outraged. "Britannia rules the waves. Where would we be without the Home Fleet?"

"Better off," Hamilton said. "The best thing to do is scuttle it."

"And you – a serving naval officer –"

"Not much longer," Hamilton said. "I am going to work on other kinds of engines."

"Hamilton believes that these gliding aeroplanes they have in America and France –" Ellen-Maeve said.

"Balloons, do you mean?" Gordon said. "Those spotter balloons our troops used in South Africa? Winston Churchill flew in one when we were marching to Pretoria."

"No, gliders," Hamilton said. "They will soon be powered with engines. Then they will be able to fly long distances."

"You can't intend to use steam engines." Angus was interested. "A steam engine would be far too heavy for an aeroplane to support."

"An oil engine," Hamilton said. "A petrol engine. As in those new cars we have. An automobile engine."

"Stuff and nonsense," Charles said. "A flying machine. It's about as real as Pegasus."

"What is Pegasus?" Arabella asked.

"A flying horse," Charles said. "He carried the Greek gods around. Only he did not. He never existed."

"They will exist," Hamilton said. "Flying machines. They will fly over your Home Fleet and drop explosives on them and all our ironclads will go straight to the bottom. If submarines under the water do not torpedo them and sink them first."

"Poppycock," Charles said. "Tommyrot and twaddle. You sound as if you had been reading that science peddler . . . what's his name? Wells."

"H. G. Wells," May said, always exact with other people's names.

"I have actually read Wells," Hamilton said. "You are right. He does believe in flying machines. So does Marie, or so she said."

"Is Marie coming here?" Isabella was now intrigued. "With the Earl of Dunesk?"

"We're meeting them by the pavilion," Hamilton said. "I don't think cricket is quite their game. But they wanted to meet all of you."

"We're not much of a family for reunions," Angus said. "But that would be splendid."

"You could hardly call this a reunion," Hamilton said, looking round the fluttering and floating assembly. "More like a dress parade."

"For those who went to School," Charles said, "it is a reunion."

"One big happy family, your old school?" Hamilton laughed and turned to Gordon. "Is that really how it is?"

"It's not so bad," Gordon said. "As long as you don't get a Pop tanning."

"What do you get that for?"

"I don't know. Smoking. Not training. Cheek."

"I'd rather even be a sailor," Hamilton said and gave Ellen-Maeve his arm again. "Shall we reunite ourselves with Marie?"

Arabella had always been proud of her own pallor and had fancied her chances of making a good marriage in England, but Marie was so bronze and bright and blazing in her clinging amber dress with her red hair piled beneath a golden hat like a sun, that Arabella could see why she had become a countess and the toast of London. In Peru, her family despised anyone with Indian blood; but in Marie's case, her ancestry had enhanced her beauty.

"I am so glad to meet you," Arabella said. "You are so beautiful."

"That from a young woman," Marie said, "and a cousin too . . . that really is a compliment. Uncle Angus has taken too long to bring you over from South America."

"It is a long way to travel," Angus said, "until we have one of Hamilton's flying machines."

"Oh, Hamilton –" Marie laughed. "Not more of your weird and wonderful inventions."

"There is an inn in Wiltshire called the Flying Monk," Bill Dunesk said. "A monk made a pair of wings, thought he was an angel, and threw himself into the air from the top of the local church tower. He only broke both his legs. Luckily, he landed on the town pig. Lucky for him, I mean – not the pig. It made nice bacon, though."

Gordon and Graham laughed, and Marie admired as usual her husband's gift of easing the uneasy by his drawling stories, rather off the point. It was the most pleasant thing about her new society, its understatement and its anecdotes. It was something which could not be taught. It had to be lived in until it fitted like an old ulster. She could see Arabella's fascination and envy at her husband's charm and languid distinction.

"Bill doesn't like these grand occasions very much," Marie said. "He would rather be with just a friend or two, discussing nothing very much, but very well."

"But you are going to the coronation." May and Charles had evidently discussed the unfairness of life that somebody as ill-born as Cousin Marie should go to the crowning of their new King.

"Without fail," Bill Dunesk said. "The King commands us to be there without fail. The trouble is, I failed pretty well everything at school, even when I was commanded by the beaks. Don't you, boys?"

Gordon nodded.

"Graham and I aren't swots," he said. "We don't have to be. We're going in the army and the navy."

"It's better to have nothing in your heads," Bill Dunesk said amiably, "if you're going to be cannon fodder. You make less of a target." He looked aside at the cricket ground, which all of them had quite forgotten, but now was echoing to ragged cheering. The batsmen and the fielders were walking back to the pavilion. The last wicket had fallen, Plunkett-Drax had carried his bat for seventy, but Harrow won by a hundred and two runs. "Another defeat for the old school," the Earl said to the young Etonians. "I hope it is not an augury for your military careers."

"We'll beat them next time," Charles said.

"That's what the British Army always says," the Earl said. "And rarely does."

Arabella found her cousins Gordon and Graham too young and shy. She felt almost old enough to be their mother, although she was their age. But when her brother Murdo appeared in his white flannels with another young man dressed in a pale blue blazer as soft as a spring sky, she did not find him too immature at eighteen. It was the celebrated Alexander Plunkett-Drax, who had stood at the crease like Horatius on the bridge, so that even the ranks of the enemy could scarce forbear to cheer. His lanky height made him stoop slightly to talk down to her, so that his compliments fell on her like guineas from heaven. He was certainly sure of his own attractions as well as hers.

"Where have you been hiding your beautiful cousin?" he accused Gordon and Graham. Then he turned to her. "In a dungeon, you're so pale. But now you've got out, we don't intend ever to let you out of our sight. Did you see me having my knock?"

"Knock?" Arabella said. "Don't you bat?" It was the only word of cricket that she knew except for one more, which she now used. "And ball?"

Plunkett-Drax began to laugh in a curious high-pitched way. Everybody laughed with him as the English always do at the unintended word of double meaning.

"Bowl," Bill Dunesk said. "You bowl a ball. Or if you are a beautiful young woman, you dance at it."

"I know no games," Arabella said. "I am hopeless at games."

"Then I shall teach you," said Plunkett-Drax. He turned to Arabella's mother. "Don't you play games in Peru? It must be very dull."

"Not young ladies," Isabella said. She did not know what more to say to the young man, but Bill Dunesk again came to the rescue.

"All young ladies play games, thank God," he said. He gave his hand to Marie. "Marie played with me and hooked me like a trout."

"I never fished you," Marie said, still getting the word for the sport as wrong as Arabella had. "But I rode you into the ground."

"Too true." Her husband opened his palms to include all her cousins and guests. "Shall we toddle off to tea? And celebrate such good company with strawberries and Veuve Clicquot?"

"Tea?" Arabella asked. "Veuve Clicquot is tea?"

Plunkett-Drax laughed again.

"You are as witty as you are fair."

"I am dark."

"There you go."

"Speaking the plain truth," Marie said, "is the funniest thing there is." She looked at the thousands of spectators who knew themselves to be the cream of the metropolis of the world. "Nobody here speaks the plain truth. That is why it is so funny." On impulse, she darted forward and kissed Arabella on the cheek.

"Come along," she said. "To tea with bubbles in it."

"Oh, Alexander," Bill Dunesk said to Plunkett-Drax. "Give my regards to your mother. I haven't seen Lily in an age."

"I never knew you knew each other," Murdo said.

"We're related," Plunkett-Drax said. "Vaguely."

"Everybody's related, aren't they?" Bill Dunesk shook his head at the little crowd around him walking towards their tea. "That's the trouble, isn't it? All these relations."

It had all started with the invitation, which was signed *Edward R.* in the top right-hand corner. Marie could hardly believe the language when Bill Dunesk gave it to her to read:

> *Right Trusty and Right Wellbeloved Cousin*
> *We greet you well*
>
> *Whereas the twenty-sixth day of June next is*
> *appointed for the Solemnity of Our Royal Coronation*
> *These are to Will and Command you and*
> *your consort to make your personal attendance on Us*
> *at the time above mentioned furnished and appointed*
> *as to your Rank and Quality apportioneth so*
> *to do and perform all such Services as shall be*
> *required and belong unto you.*
> *Whereof you are not to fail*
> *And so We bid you most heartily Farewell*

THE STRENGTH OF THE HILLS

*Given at Our Court at St James
the first day of December in
the first year of Our Reign
By His Majesty's Command*

"I am asked too?" Marie asked.

"Of course," her husband said.

"What do I wear?"

"You wear the same as the other peeresses."

"But I am not the same."

"I know, Marie, but . . . red velvet robes trimmed with miniver. And lots of chocolates in the linings because the Ceremony is five hours in Westminster Abbey, plus the wait before and after and the chore of getting there and away. Never go to a long occasion without chockies in your socks."

"And hats?"

"Tiaras. You have to wear a tiara."

"Do you have one?"

"In the vaults. Two or three."

"Will they fit me?"

"We'll find one which will."

"And if it doesn't?"

"My grandfather – Queen Victoria's coronation was so long ago – he told me the funniest moment was when She had the Crown put on. All the peers had to put their coronets on their heads. And sometimes their ancestors had bigger heads. I think heads shrink with too much inbred heredity. Anyway, when the peers put on their coronets, sometimes they slid down to the chin of the noble lords, wrapping his head up in the bag which is the velvet cap on top of the coronet. All those headless peers – it looked like the Wars of the Roses all over again."

Marie was worried.

"But if my tiara slips down when I put it on?"

"It won't. You have a beautiful big head and lots of lovely red hair."

"You could put a little coronet inside it. Then it couldn't slip down."

"We'll do that. Then a second Queen will be crowned. The Queen who reigns over me."

"You say the nicest things," Marie said.

"And I do not *do* them." Bill Dunesk bent forward and gave his wife a soft kiss on the forehead. "Well, I will this time. I swear you will be the prettiest peeress – the nonpareil – the goddess of the Abbey at this coronation."

*

94

It nearly never happened. The King was struck down with appendicitis. Sad crowds stood outside Buckingham Palace, waiting for the hourly bulletins about the royal recovery or decline. Sir Frederick Treves, back from the Boer War, was said to have been so overcome by his responsibility that his assistant had to complete the operation. But the news improved. The King mended. And a new date was set for August the ninth, with a shortened ceremony to spare the Royal health. "Fewer chockies," Bill Dunesk whispered. "We'll race through the show."

They did not. The crawl in the coach to the Abbey was slower than a slug's progress. But when the crowds lining the streets saw Marie through the glass windows, the cheering rose to a crescendo as well as the rhythmic chant,

> TAKE me,
> TAKE me,
> TAKE me, anee – WHERE!

"You are not forgotten," Bill Dunesk said to her. "Still the most famous woman in London."

"I don't want to be remembered," Marie said, "for that old number."

At the entrance to the Abbey, Marie saw the other guests ranged in tiers on either side of the long aisle. A page spread the velvet train of her robes, and she strode in with the lithe and bounding walk of her past, her back so straight and her head so high that it seemed to fly above her red robe. All looked at her in a sudden hush as she took her place in the transept among the massed scarlet and white fur and myriad diamonds of the peeresses. But they, too, looked only at her, whom they did not know, but now recognised as a rival, a solitary blaze among them.

Hours seemed to pass as Marie remained in her seat, rising only at the passage of minor dignitaries of the blood royal on their way to their due places. Then the comedy came, all the old lords arriving with their robes, tucking them under their arms or tripping over them, and holding their coronets in their hands like children with little hoops. Then the trumpets blew fanfares and the bells pealed and hundreds of choirboys sang hosannas and the organ intoned Parry's setting of,

> I was glad when they said unto me,
> We will go into the House of the Lord.

And the Westminster schoolboys in their surplices shouted hurrays for the King who was to be crowned, and the anthem rose in its praise of harmony.

Jerusalem is built as a city,
That is at unity in itself . . .
O pray for the peace of Jerusalem.
They shall prosper that love Thee.
Peace be within Thy walls,
And plenteousness within Thy palaces.

And all ended on the glorious high B-flat that only English choirboys and nightingales and thrushes can achieve.

Now the long procession was passing – the court officials with their white rods, the clergy with vestments of gold and green and blue, the bearers of the royal insignia, the crown on a red cushion held before, the tall cold Queen with Her train borne by eight ladies-in-waiting, then the rounded and bearded King, His pages holding His train. But as He passed the peeresses rising in their ranks of seats, He paused – perhaps He stumbled, although Kings cannot stumble even when They do. But He stood still for seconds and gazed at Marie, not at anyone else, directly at Marie, as though He had never seen such a woman before, as though she had an unspoken message for Him, as if there was already something between them. And all the other peeresses saw the new King looking at the new countess, and they began to whisper behind their hands. Then the King stepped forward again to the sound of the choirs. And Marie knew she had been chosen by Someone whom she did not wish to choose her.

When the Queen was finally anointed by the ancient Archbishop of Canterbury, Marie was standing near Her, helping to hold the canopy above Her. She saw the archbishop pour too much of the sacred oil from his spoon onto Her forehead so that a trickle ran down the Queen's nose in greasy tears. The Queen could do nothing but kneel and pray. She seemed to be weeping as a great cheering shook the Abbey roof when the crown was finally placed on the head of King Edward the Seventh. Marie wondered if the Queen were mourning the life of the sovereign that was to come. There would be no escape from it for Her. But as for Him . . .

Within a week of the ceremony, a note was conveyed through Alice, Mrs George Keppel, an intimate of the King, that the Earl and Countess of Dunesk would be welcome at a small function at Court, where Her Majesty the Queen would not be present. This invitation was hardly as formal as the invitation to the coronation had been, but it held the same implication – *Whereof you are not to fail.*

10

A LONG LABOUR

It was a long labour. A night and a day of it and now another night. Mary was too old for this, hobbling with her arthritis, always minding the birth of other women's babies, never her own, and in South Africa of all places. Of course, there was that story in the Bible of barren Sarah, ancient Abraham's wife, who brought forth well after her time of life because the Lord decreed it. But really, although the Good Book was always right because it was the Good Book, you could not believe everything you read in it. May God forgive me, Mary thought, for thinking so. Anyway, at eighty years old, she certainly couldn't hope for a blessed event, even if an angel had a hand in it. She could only hope to deliver Lizzie's third before the poor creature failed and her life ebbed away between the contractions she was almost too weak to have any more. The baby's head was too big for such a little woman, although she was broad enough at the hips, and Hamish Gordon and Martha had slipped out as easily and regularly as lambs in spring. "It'll have to be the forceps," Mary said to herself and looked in her black bag for them and found them, then turned to Virginia, who was useless at this sort of thing, having none of her own and not likely to have one by Robert, who was always away on trek and went on his leaves to see his sick mother in Canada. There was not enough pay to take his wife along.

"Get some more boiling water and towels, Virginia," Mary said. "I have to use the forceps. I hope I willna crush the wee babe's head." And as Virginia left the room, Mary went over to Lizzie, soaked in sweat and moaning with pain, and she said, "Have a last try, girl. And I'll pull his head out with the forceps." And Lizzie said, "Let me die, Tant' Mary. Not him. Do not hurt him. Cut me and take him out and save him. You call him Paul. Like Oom Paul. You call him Paul." And Mary said, "We dinna ken even if he is a wee lad. But with a big head like that . . . Now pull, girl, pull –" And she gave Lizzie the sheet twisted into a rope and knotted to the bedpost. "Pull. For the last time. Pull!"

Outside in the drawing-room, Hamish Charles stood. He caught Virginia's arm as she carried the kettle of boiling water and a towel back into the room, where Lizzie was now screaming. "I can't bear *you* suffering," Hamish Charles said, but Virginia shook her arm free, spilling some scalding water onto the man's boots. "What do you mean? She is suffering – your *wife* – you have all these children by her." And Hamish Charles looked down at his steaming boot caps. "Yes, she is suffering," he said. "But you are too. And I . . . can't you see I suffer? For *you*." Virginia kept her voice down, but there was anger in it. "How could you? At a time like this. But men are so selfish." And Hamish Charles found himself muttering, "But I care only for you – I live only for you . . ." And then there was the sound of a smack as sharp as a shot from a rifle, and the thin reedy wail of an infant, its first breath a small protest at all the trouble of being born.

"Thank God," Hamish Charles said. "Thank God." And he slumped down in the wooden arm-chair, his head buried in the palms of his hands as in a sort of praying.

When Virginia went back into the bedroom with her kettle and towel, she found Mary holding a squealing red small shape and cutting the cord and life-line to its mother and tying it and saying, "Have you ever seen such hair? That's what saved you, my lad, your hair. Though I pinched your ears a bit." And as Virginia poured the boiling water into the enamel basin and carried it over to the bed with the towel, she heard Lizzie say weakly, "Is it Paul?" And Mary answered, "Yes, it is Paul. And he has golden curls all over his head like a ram."

In the morning, Mary sat at the breakfast table with Hamish Charles and the two bairns, Hamish Gordon, aged two, and Martha, one year old, in her high chair. "You'll not be having any more," Mary said firmly. "It would kill your Lizzie. And these wee ones need their mother. You canna be so selfish."

"Indeed, there will be no more," Hamish Charles said. "I can promise you that."

"This one near killed her. The great big head on him, and born that way round. It is lucky for you I could be visiting. Oh, Hamish!" The man flinched as if the rebuke was for him, but it was for the tiny boy, who had tipped over his bowl of milk and porridge. "Will you no mind your food?" But his father was already mopping up the mess with a napkin, and saying, "He's too small to know how to eat." And Mary replied, "Nobody is ever too small to know how to eat, if there is precious little to eat. But it is worrit I am. That Virginia – she is asleep now – I think the birthing wore her out more than Lizzie. How long is she stopping here, Hamish? When will your cousin Robert be back to fetch her?"

"She is a great help to Lizzie round the house," Hamish Charles said defensively, wiping the face of his small son with the wet napkin. "She looks after the children . . ."

"She dinna ken a farthing about that."

"She taught a whole school of piccaninnies –"

"She has none of her own." Mary's judgement was final. "And in this house, with a fine man like you here –"

"She is my cousin's wife."

"I hope you mind it. And she does."

"Of course. You wouldn't suggest . . ." Hamish Charles looked out of the window as he went back to his seat. He had to hide his flushed cheeks. "Another scorcher," he said. "The drought will never end. The cattle will all be dead soon."

"So will I," Mary said. "And that is a matter that also makes me worrit. I am head of the family, if you can call our scatterings a family. And I must pass it on."

"There's still your younger brother Bain in Canada."

"He's failing. He will not live beyond Julia muckle long."

"Well, how about Hamilton –?"

"I like him well. But in fact, the best of all my nephews and nieces is Seaforth –"

"You *would* say that."

"He is doing very well at the hospital in Jo'burg. And he may . . . yes, Seaforth may be marrying. And to Miriam Apfelstein, too. What do you think of that?"

"She couldn't." And Hamish Charles couldn't believe his ears. "One of the richest families and Seaforth –"

"Coloured." Mary gave a short laugh. "Born on the wrong side of the blanket, too. Everything that can be wrong about him is wrong about him. And yet he is the best of you Sinclairs. She will be lucky to have him. Though she is not all I would want for him. Very radical. A socialist, she calls herself. And about the Empire, she is worse than I am. And you know what I feel since the war."

"You call it Your War," Hamish Charles said. "Not the Boer War. And they did start it."

"Did they now? Your War it was, Hamish, and you fought in it. So did that good neighbour of yours, Piet Krug –"

"He's not such a good neighbour now. Oh, Martha!" The baby had thrown her feeding bottle onto the floor, where it smashed into smithereens. Then she began to howl at the noise.

"Leave it," Mary said and turned to the little girl and fixed her with her eyes. "Hush," she said. "Little miss – you hush, do you hear?" As if mesmerised, the infant stopped howling with her mouth open, then put in her thumb and sucked it. "That is better," Mary said and turned back to Hamish Charles. "You will not be falling out with Piet Krug. He has married Lizzie's sister."

"His cattle still drink the last of my water."

"They are beasts. They go where water is. Who can stop them? Has he children?"

"Two now. Sannie and Pieter."

"You were married at the same time?"

"In front of a *predikant*." Hamish Charles smiled. "A funny old fellow in a black frock coat. He spoke in Afrikaans. I didn't understand a word of it, except where I had to put on the ring, and then Lizzie dug me in the ribs . . ."

"Your mother will not think you married at all," Mary said. "Roman Catholic that she is."

"It doesn't matter, Aunt Mary." Hamish Charles was embarrassed. "At Harrow, I didn't really say I was a Catholic. I was C. of E. like everybody else."

"The Church of England," Mary said severely, "is much more *soft* than the Church of Scotland. Or the Presbyterian. Or the Wee Frees. They will let in anybody. Including you."

"As long as you believe in God –" Hamish Charles said. "And I certainly do." He rose. "I must go and see how Lizzie is. And the baby. Thank you for all you have done, Aunt Mary. Really, we can't get by without you. I hope you'll stay with us as long as you can."

"Help me up," Mary said and Hamish Charles helped her to her feet and waited while her joints were loosening. "I must be going back to Jo'burg. You can spare Buldoo to drive me in the cart?"

"Yes. Of course. But you must stay –"

"As my father was saying, he would rather wear out than rust out. I ken I am past it, but Seaforth still asks my advice at his hospital. And there is the orphanage for the children of the war. We have to pay back, Hamish. We have to pay back."

Hamish Charles bent and kissed the thick white hair of the old woman.

"You have paid back what you have taken from us a thousand fold," he said. "If I was asked, what is a giving spirit – a good soul – I would say, Mary Sinclair."

Mary was secretly pleased at the compliment, but she was still anxious about leaving him in the house with Virginia, and his wife so sick in her bed. So she merely said, "You canna talk me round with that honey in your mouth. You watch what you do, Hamish. For if I canna keep my eye on you, God will – and not that soft English God you think is so easy on you."

The cave in the mountain had a fissure in the roof. A sun star sprayed light onto the sandy floor. "It must have been a natural altar," Virginia said to Buldoo. "A holy place for the Bushmen." But he stood contemptuous and silent as a boulder of granite, while she peered at the drawings on the walls and traced the outlines with her fingers. "Deer," she said. "Giraffe. A hippo. And, I wonder . . . It looks like a mammoth, but it is probably an elephant. Do elephants come this far south?"

Buldoo grunted. "Maybe sometime," he conceded. "Maybe old time. But why do you look for this Bushman trash?"

"It is not trash," Virginia said and began to take her crayons and her drawing-pad out of her satchel. "It is art. And I am going to set it down. I intend to become an expert, you see. Why don't you go and wait outside while I work?"

"The cattle, *baas* say I to take out ticks. And some they have *rinderpest*."

"*Baas* say," Virginia said, "you look after me, bring me home."

"You be long?" Buldoo growled.

"As long as it takes me, Buldoo."

So Virginia set to work to copy the Bushmen paintings, marvelling always at their exquisite simplicity, which seemed to catch the essence of a beast in a few strokes of red or brown pigment. In those early ages, the artist seemed to have lived in the animal, to be the antelope or the snake himself. It was not like that now. Even in her own body, there was a terrible distance between her nature and her spirit. Nothing was simple, all her desires were at odds. She had begun to hate her husband Robert – he abandoned her, he repelled her, he never took her to London, so far and so longed for. But she wanted the marriage to last, she could not bear scandal, she could not go off with his cousin, Hamish Charles, who wanted her and understood her as an artist and a free soul. But the dear fool had married a woman he did not love, just because he had to have a wife to run his farm, which he did not really want. He was no farmer, but something of a cavalier, that look of Quixote from his Peruvian mother – ascetic, melancholy, hollowed and chipped, with eyes that could both yearn for a quest and look as humble as a whipped puppy dog. A man would get himself into an inextricable mess, and then expect the woman he loved to get him out of it. But free in thought as she was for her time, she could not take a man away from his wife and three babies. She had no family to blame her, that was so. But that Mary Sinclair. She shuddered to remember how the old biddy had glared at her.

There was a shout from the outside, then another raised voice yelling back. Virginia packed up her work and ran through the star of sunlight falling from the crack in the roof of the cave into the yellow wall of the blinding daylight. There she saw Buldoo leaping down the slope of the berg towards a horseman, who was driving some oxen before him with his whip. He was shouting at Buldoo in Afrikaans, and Buldoo was bellowing back. And as Buldoo came at him, the rider struck with his long lash. But the rawhide thong caught round Buldoo's arm, and he held on to it, trying to drag the man out of the saddle. As Virginia ran down the hill, she could see the grotesque tug-o'-war played out between the Zulu and Piet Krug, whom she now recognised on his brindled pony. The contest ended with the thong of the whip slipping out of Buldoo's hands. He fell over backwards, while the Afrikaner raised the *sjambok* again. But Virginia ran under it to protect the sprawling Buldoo with her own body.

"Get out, *you!*" Piet shouted.

"I will not," Virginia said. "What are you doing on our land?"

"*Our* land? You have part, I suppose?" Piet's sneer gashed his beard below the shadow of his slouch hat. "My sister-in-law Lizzie, it is *her* land, maybe. And that fool Hamish. But now it is *your* land, *your* Hamish?"

"He take our cattle, miss." Buldoo now was standing behind her.

"They are my span. See the brand," Piet said. "They come over here. To the *vlei.*"

"Our *vlei,*" Virginia said.

"The water is for all to drink. It was a *vlei* for all. Until you come." Piet pointed his whip at Virginia, who did not flinch but stared proudly up at him on his saddle. "Now there is bad blood. Bunjie and Lizzie, sisters – now *you* . . . you take Lizzie's man."

"I am helping Lizzie with the children, as you know," Virginia said. "With the new baby, she cannot do much. They need me."

"They need you *here?*" Piet gave a laugh like a bark. "Drawing – it help Lizzie? You look for babies *here?* Go back to your home, woman. And your man. Or there will be blood here."

"Don't threaten me, Mr Krug. My husband is the law, over the border in Basutoland."

"Go, I tell you," Piet said. He cracked his whip towards his oxen. "Before there is blood, go!" He was denouncing her as if he were Ezekiel or some Old Testament prophet.

"Get thee gone too!" Virginia found herself shouting, as if she were casting out a devil. And as that was the last word and she had said it, she was quite proud at having stood up to the Boer so well.

*

Robert was due any day now to take her back to the quarters she would not call home over the border. Lizzie had not recovered from Paul's birth and still lay in the bed most of the day, leaving Virginia to supervise the Kaffir maids as they pounded the mealie grains with their wooden pestles and cracked and ground the coffee beans between two smooth stones. Virginia had bought Tsutsie with her, but the other African women would not listen to a Hottentot, so that Virginia had to give the orders herself. She was rarely alone with Hamish Charles. She took care not to be so, keeping the tiny Hamish Gordon and Martha near her skirts. But every evening when the children were put to bed, she would play the piano, which she had managed to tune herself. And her recitals of Liszt and Brahms and Chopin would plunge Hamish Charles into an ecstasy of gloom, sometimes filling his eyes with tears as he gazed at her. But this particular evening, when Lizzie and baby Paul were sound asleep and the door to the bedroom was closed, Virginia nodded towards Hamish Charles to come over to the piano while she played. As he approached, she said to him softly, "I know. We must talk. I know."

"I love you," Hamish Charles said. "I am desperate. What can we do?"

"Nothing, my dear. Your wife, your children, your farm. But if . . ." Her voice trailed away into the notes of the *étude*. "What would you propose?"

"I would leave all – risk all – for you." Hamish Charles's voice was broken. "I would take you away – start again – where nobody knows us."

"To London," Virginia heard herself saying. "Would you take me there?"

"Anywhere. If you would come away with me."

"You promise. To London."

"They would not know me there. You are right. I am not a farmer. My father Angus would help us. And you know, my mother does not even think I am married to Lizzie. It was not a Catholic wedding."

"But your children."

"Ah." Hamish Charles winced. "The children. Their mother would keep them."

"But you love them."

"I love you most. Wholly. Absolutely. If I must give up the children, I must."

Virginia's fingers ran up and down the keys. They were separate from her. She might have been playing in a dream. She was touching the ivories, the bones of dead things. She almost had forgotten why sweet sounds came from them.

"We met too late," she said. "Why didn't you wait for me?"

"You had already married Robert. You didn't wait for me."

"I hadn't met you. I had to get away. But you met me before Lizzie."

"Yes," Hamish Charles said. "I had to keep a wife to live here." Then he added bitterly, "Now I don't want to be here. I don't want to live."

"Don't say that." Virginia lifted her right hand and held it out to Hamish Charles. Her left hand still picked out Chopin's theme on the keys. Hamish Charles took her hand in both of his and chafed it between his palms.

"But could you – would you – leave Robert, if somehow . . . I was free?"

Virginia withdrew her hand and looked down as she finished the study in music. She spoke so softly that Hamish Charles could hardly hear her speak.

"I should not say this. But we are *modern* –"

"Yes. Tell me."

"Robert and I – there are no children – there is a reason. I can't say more."

"And with me? Do you *feel* –?"

"I feel . . ." Virginia watched her fingers moving to the end of the piece. "I feel – far too much. And far too late."

"It is never too late. Not while we have life. Virginia –"

Virginia finished the Chopin. In the silence, she looked up at Hamish Charles. Her large brown eyes spilled over. They seemed to flood her face.

"My dear," she whispered.

As Hamish Charles bent to kiss her, there was a burst of coughing from behind the bedroom door. The man drew back and listened. Then the summons came. "I need you. Paul is –" The words were lost in a thin wailing from the baby that cut through to the heart of Hamish Charles, and his face puckered in despair as if he was about to wail himself.

"There," he said. "You see. It is hopeless." And he moved towards the bedroom door.

Miriam Apfelstein came through Seaforth's bedroom door before their marriage. It was an act of defiance as much as love. She would show the world what she thought of convention. She would break the barriers between the castes and the classes. She was so open as she strode down the corridor into his quarters near the hospital that Seaforth thought she almost wanted the other doctors to see her going to bed with somebody they considered as Coloured – that was the official term for him. Neither black nor white, but ambiguous. Seaforth thought that Coloured rather suited him.

As he followed Miriam into his bedroom, Seaforth was glad she had not been seen, and also he was annoyed that she had not provoked a crisis with the law.

"You are too bold," he said, closing the door behind them, as she sat on his bed. "This may not be the right time to have us flung out of South Africa."

Miriam smiled at him, her lips spread and plum-red, her heavy eyelids masking the brilliance of her gaze.

"Don't you want me, Seaforth?"

Now Seaforth was kneeling in front of her, his head buried in her lap. His face was pressed against the warmth of her thighs, his hair against the small swell of her belly. He spoke thickly into the cloth of her skirt.

"You know I want you. My whole life – it is in you."

He felt her fingers combing the back of his head. Her voice sounded far away.

"Yes. My life too. In you."

He could feel the pulse of the beat of her blood against his cheeks, and after a silence, he laid his head sideways on the cushion of her seated body. His lips were muffled no more.

"I never thought," he said, "I could *feel* like this. Doctors, we are meant to be cold fish. No feeling. Or how could we operate and examine and cut people up?"

"You are warm, Seaforth."

"Even Aunt Mary . . . you know, she loves me, but she was always worried I could not love. But then, *you* come along. Aunt Mary always laughs about it. The Scots and the Jews, she says – they always got on well. Both are tribal – clannish. Loyal and suspicious. But I am an Indian, I say – and she just laughs and says, Seaforth Sinclair by name, Seaforth Sinclair by nature."

Now Miriam's hand was stroking the head of the man who would be her lover and her husband.

"I love you being an Indian too."

At this, Seaforth raised himself to look at this glorious woman, who would marry him.

"Not too much, I hope." The usual dryness returned to his voice. "I mean, I would rather you loved the man than the Indian in me."

"I do," Miriam said, "but –"

"I am not just forbidden meat, am I? Your proof that you want to end the class system? Your demonstration that you hate imperialism by going with an Indian?"

Now Miriam was stroking his cheeks with the palms of her hands. Then they caught his face and held it and made him look at the huge green stare of her eyes, glistening in her desire.

"You silly man. I want you. You, Seaforth. What you are. Yes, I hate the Empire, the class system, all this terrible exploitation –"

"As only the *rich* can ever hate it."

"Seaforth, shut up! I hate it. I can't help my family being rich off the gold-mines. They've given you your hospital –"

"I don't think they meant to give you to me too, Miriam."

"I do what I want. I'm a free woman. They brought me up to be."

Seaforth smiled his thin smile, although he dropped his eyes at the fierce blaze in hers.

"They wanted a good Bar Mitzvah boy for you."

"I am my own woman. I choose. I choose you."

"Yes," Seaforth said. He rose and stood over her, looking down at her. Her legs were spread open beneath her long skirt, her breasts were alive beneath the little embroidered waistcoat she was wearing. He ached with the want of her.

"You," he mumbled. "You. I want you. And you –"

"Yes," she said and fell back as he sank upon her.

II

A MINE

Marie never thought she would ever go down a mine, but Keir McBride had insisted on it. Her husband was away more and more in London with his amusing friends such as Lord Alfred Douglas. And she had to flee the capital after the King had pressed his attentions on her at the private dinner arranged by Alice Keppel. So she was left in charge at Dunesk with her Rosabelle, who was now four years old and would not be detached from her mother's left ankle. Marie loved her daughter's dependence on her, and through that absolute love, she worried over the future that her daughter would inherit. There were the coal mines between Dunesk and Rosslyn as well as the paper mills. And when there was trouble at the pits, and Keir McBride came to the castle to tell her husband of it, Marie took it upon herself to solve it. And as she could not decide without seeing for herself – for what was the use of a man's word unsupported? – she said she would go down a pit.

"Women," Keir McBride said, "they nae go down. Never."

"I will go down," Marie said. "You will take me."

"Aye, the countess, down pit." McBride set his hawk's face into a hard mask of denial. "You will nae go down." He twisted his black cap in his hands as if he were strangling her in the cloth.

"I will," Marie said. And she did. There was no man who would dare to stop her. That Scots toast, "Here's to us, who's like us? Damn few and they're all dead." She drank to that, even though she was a woman.

She wore her Indian buckskin leggings again, trousers like a man, also a flat Roundhead helmet, which Cromwell's troopers had left behind when they had stormed the castle after the Battle of Dunbar. The pit-cage was a slow descent to hell, while the grim galleries that spoked out to the coal-faces from the shaft were so low and dark in the patches of light from the oil-lamps that she had to stoop and stumble over the rails for the coal-tubs, which the pit-ponies were dragging between their limbers. Ahead, the flickers from the lamps of the miners hacking at the face. Behind, a pitch darkness and a burial in the deep earth. Then they went through a door worked by a trapper-boy no more than fourteen years old, his job the opening and closing the barrier for the putters with their ponies and coal-tubs. And one time of danger, with Keir McBride's arm crashing her against the side of the gallery as a set of sixty empty-coal tubs came hurtling back down the slope to be filled again. And the shouting of the over-men to keep the miners working, the echoes of their screams to hurry the lumps of the black diamonds to the surface. And the water dripping from the cracking shives of stone on the roof down the props, the threat that Keir McBride had brought her see, a catastrophe waiting to happen.

"When it breaks," he said, "there will be the flood. And we will all drown."

"So what is to do?" she said.

"Close the gallery. With explosive."

"Close the whole mine. It would be safer."

"And your husband's fees? His royalties? He willnae." McBride's twist of a smile gashed his sooted face.

"The earl," Marie said, and was surprised to hear herself use his title, "the earl cares for human lives more than profits."

"Nae earl dinnae."

"I will ask him. And answer for him."

"But the wages," McBride said. "The families will starve wi'out the wages."

"So you don't want the mines closed?"

"A piece of them. This wet piece." McBride put his dark hand on a soaking side-prop, a trunk of oak. "You could be in a wee boat. 'Half o'er, half o'er to Aberdour is fifty fathom deep/There lies the guid Earl and Countess wi' the Scots lairds at their feet.'"

Marie laughed.

"I've heard that poem from my husband," she said. "It should be Sir Patrick Spens, not he and I. But you're right. We are under water. And he'll never come down to see it."

"And you . . . never you should."

"I am here." Marie smiled and put her hand lightly on McBride's sopping shirt. "And I am safe with you. And we will have this piece closed, I swear it."

And she did persuade her husband to close it, although he had one of his rare fits of anger when he heard that she had been down one of his coal mines. "It's that pernicious McBride," he said. "He says he is *organising*, as if he could organise a game of marbles. He talks of a union, when the only time a group of Scotsmen comes together ends in stabbing and bloody noses. Does he say he is a socialist?"

"You do," Marie said sweetly. "Like your old friend Oscar Wilde did."

"Oscar's socialism was purely aesthetic," Bill Dunesk said. "And he was right. Men should not be slaves to their work. Machines must do that work. And the machines should be the new slaves. Unfortunately, civilisation needs slaves so that artists can be artists."

"You can be an artist now," Marie said. "Only because your miners are slaves."

"Yes," the earl said. "I cannot change the system. But I do try to understand it."

"But the point is to change it."

"What?" For once, Bill Dunesk was sneering. "You come from nowhere – you are now a countess – and you want a change of the system? Or perhaps you would like to be Cinderella in reverse. Back to the bare-back riding and the Music Hall, which you have so successfully risen above."

"Bill," Marie now rose above her husband as he sprawled back on the Empire sofa in the drawing-room of the castle, "you know I am not ungrateful."

"Two negatives do not make a positive, Marie. Simply, you are not grateful. Gratitude is not part of your wild nature."

"I married you . . . part of it . . ." Marie tried to pick her words carefully. Anything she said would be wrong. "I thought, if I was your wife, we could change things. We could have the power –"

"Ah, yes – being a countess, you would have the power –"

Marie went off at a tangent, seeing herself in a trap.

"Rosabelle is there. Don't you think . . . isn't that the best thing about our marriage – Rosabelle?"

"She is not a boy – an heir."

"In Scotland, women can be heirs. Mary, Queen of Scots –"

"We could still have a boy."

"If you were more *interested*."

"Or if you appreciated me more. My particular ways." Bill Dunesk stretched up his arms from the sofa towards the hovering Marie. "Descend on me, Marie, from heaven like a shower of gold. For that is what you are."

"That was Jupiter. A male god, descending on a girl."

"Well, let us reverse roles," he said. "If you will not be Cinderella backwards, then let me be your Minnehaha, and you be my Hiawatha, my Indian brave."

Marie stooped and kissed her husband, then broke free from his arms and walked away to look out of the keep window, down to the glen with the brown Esk river curling below.

"*We* could change so many things," she said. "And make a better world for Rosabelle."

Bill Dunesk sat up on the sofa to consider his wife by the window.

"You really are quite an *upsetter*."

"And you're a spectator, like your friend Oscar Wilde. You do know what to do, but you won't do it. It would upset you if you did. You merely want to be free to pursue your art . . . and your fellow artists. But you're not a socialist. You just say you are. You're selfish."

"Aren't we all?" Bill yawned. "Of course, we're all sorry for the poor and needy. But it's *word*-deep. We say it to soothe ourselves."

"Then *don't!*" Marie swung round on her husband. "It's wrong. Don't *say* you're with your miners. You can't be, you're the earl. That's what Keir McBride says."

"I do not need to take my words from him. But I am closing the wet part of the pit."

"Yes. To stop a tragedy."

"To save lives."

"Yes, but, oh, Bill, can't you see?" She ran towards him as he rose to hold her. "Don't just stand back. Don't make your little jokes. Engage. You must commit."

Gently, the earl put her away from him and gently he shook his head.

"Perish the thought," he said. "Always retire and stand back. Always have a little joke. One only *engages* servants. One *commits* perjury – or commits people to prison. Engage – commit – you really don't know what they mean, dear – and they are not words for people like us."

"Really, to have to be selected," Charles Seymour-Scudabright said. "It is lucky for them that I choose to represent them." The former naval captain from H M S *Terrible* spoke as if he were issuing a command, not having an opinion.

"I agree," May said. "But it should not be too embarrassing."

"To question me about my private affairs? And my beliefs, which are between me and my God? It is degrading – blasphemous, you might say."

"It is only a selection committee for a seat you will certainly get. It is a formality."

"Then they need not go through the process. They could merely select me as their next member of parliament."

"They are often *nice* people," May said. "Very *nice*."

"That is their trouble," her husband said. "Nice people are often very nasty. I cannot abide nice people."

"I am sure there will be no impertinent questions," May said to soothe him. "They will be too scared of you to ask about any horrors."

"There are no horrors in my career. As someone who was a captain in the Home Fleet – a defender of the realm – as well as having a family connection with North Mimsbury for generations, I would have thought that examining me before selecting me –"

"Charles, you will toddle it."

"May, to tell you the truth, I don't approve of all those Reform Bills. My great-grandfather served North Mimsbury for decades when it was a rotten borough. And he served it well, as I will. But none of this fuss about *selection*."

"I wouldn't say that to the committee," May said. "Not if I were you. You know what a collection of nonentities it is – they think they really do matter."

"Then I will not speak more than I must. I will say nothing very much – but very well."

"You usually do," May said.

Charles Seymour-Scudabright gave his wife a sharp look. Sometimes he suspected her tongue was a little on the tart side, but she smiled sweeter than a syllabub, so he always forgave her.

"I will follow your advice, my dear," he consented graciously. "My service in the Royal Navy, my wife an angel, a son at Cambridge before he joins the army, another at Dartmouth Naval College, what could be better for a country constituency?"

"Ruth," May said. "Our daughter is your problem."

"But she has not caused any trouble yet."

"She will. Her ideas –" May threw up her hands and said no more, as if Ruth's thoughts were too shocking to express.

"We can pack her off," Charles said. "She can visit relations. Or we can marry her off. That will shut her up. Marriage always does."

"No suitable man is presently on tap," May said. "But she has had an invitation to Ireland. To stay with my cousin Arabella, who married that Alex Plunkett-Drax."

"He's a bit of a devil, isn't he? Didn't he marry her for her money?"

"Yes. Uncle Angus married rich himself. A Peruvian nob's only daughter. So Arabella went with a dowry – too, too Spanish South American, but that's how they are out there."

"What do you think? Shall we pack Ruth off there to hunt and fish a bit?"

"Do her the world of good, don't you think?"

"And no bloody books. That's one good thing about the Irish, brains isn't their line."

"No – they have bogs there, not libraries." May contemplated the florid bluff face of her husband that had once seemed so masterful, and now appeared overdone. "Brains isn't a line that ever does a man any good. Or a single girl."

The selection committee was, indeed, a walk-over. All the Tories were male solicitors and tradesmen with two brace of squires and landowners. Presenting himself as a hero of the Boer War – the naval guns at Spion Kop – as a commander of battleships and an opponent of votes for women and any radical change, Charles Seymour-Scudabright seemed to have inherited the seat for which he was being chosen. When he added that he believed in protection for English corn and English beef against cheap imports and free trade, he turned a certainty into a sanctuary. He was the right man in the right place at the right time doing the right thing. He had always known he was. It was only that, when he had been asked to take early retirement from the Royal Navy because of his inability to concentrate or navigate, other people had not appreciated his true qualities. But he knew what a good man he was. And the electors would certainly know. After all, it was a seat which had always sent a Tory to parliament, and always would. Particularly if he was top-notch, as Charles indubitably felt he was.

At first, Ruth thought that Normanton was worse than the Slough of Despond, where the poor Pilgrim fell in and stopped his Progress. The grey stones, the draughts as keen as slivers of ice, the wet grass sopping through her boots, it was a cold store for human beings. And isolated in glowing patches amid the general darkness, a few peat fires and one of wood in the hall, as lonely as light-buoys in a sea channel in a storm. It was not a question of living in an Irish winter, it was a matter of surviving. And Ruth did not see how she could keep on until spring, when her exile would be over and her father elected.

There was another bright spot, to be sure. And that was Alexander Plunkett-Drax himself.

"I am rather beyond the Pale," he used to repeat to her, in his favourite joke and explanation. "But we live inside it. The Pale, of course, explains the name of this friendly mausoleum. Normanton. The family estate, God help us. I wish Father had lived a little longer, he might have spared me this at least, until I was too gaga to mind about it. Normanton. The Normans took this part of Ireland and put a pale – a fence – around it to keep out the savage Irish. But personally,

I wish we had let them in. Then we wouldn't have to live here. Like them, we too would be beyond the Pale."

For all his pretences, Alexander seemed to love his land. His complaints were really an appreciation of his possessions. For fear of seeming to value his inheritance too much, he ran it down in the way that the English often do. They mock what they hold most dear. There was no other reason, Ruth thought, for him to have married her cousin Arabella, except for having her money to pay for all the repairs to the house and for the draining of the fields. Arabella really was sinking fast, both personally and literally. The juices were running from her into the ground. But it was easier to drown than walk in County Kildare. The big house itself might disappear like the House of Usher into the dark tarn, swallowed up by the swamp of the land.

Arabella had retired upstairs with one of her *migraines*, the smart French word that had taken over from the vapours or fits of melancholy. Now her husband went beyond the pale. He pounced on Ruth, who had long expected it, as had all the servants and Arabella. He did it under cover of helping Ruth, as he did everything. It was never his intent, she must be positively begging for it. Ruth was sure that the embroidered low stool which she stumbled over had been laid in her way as a trap by Alexander, so that he could catch her as she fell into his waiting arms, and not onto the carpet. Before she could resist, his grip of concern had changed to the claws of desire, one hard arm locking her against him, his other hand pulling her head back by the hair so that he could bite her neck and ears with hurting kisses.

She could hardly breathe, she could not say no, her protest was smothered by his mouth, which clamped on her lips as in the jaws of a vice. When he freed her to crush her face against his throat so that she could still not speak, matting her hair with the pressing of his mouth, she had to twist her head to the side to utter a word.

"No – Arabella –"

"Don't speak," she heard. "It spoils everything. Bloody words."

She was forced back against the sofa, her dress ripped and hoisted high, a thrust into her was a fierce pain. She did not scream, her throat was locked.

"Virgins," she heard. "Always such a mess, virgins." Then he did not speak, but lunged and panted, then shook and trembled, then lay heavy on her for a moment, then sprang back from her, recoiling. She closed her eyes, lying spent on the sofa, waiting for him to say one word of want or of love. But all she heard was, "It's awful first time. Much nicer next time." Then a caress of her cheek as if it were the light flick of a whip. "You'd better do something about that blood. It'll stain the sofa. Before the servants come in."

He presumed correctly. She should have told Arabella, and she said nothing, for shame and fear of scandal. She should have left Normanton that night, but she had nowhere to go, her father was in the middle of his election campaign and she had no money. She should have resisted his next attack on her two nights later, when his wife was sedated with opium, but his assault was too sudden, and she would not shout in case the butler heard. And this time, she did feel a certain response to his driving need. Something in her answered to his cruelty and his anger at his desire for her. She almost revelled in the knowledge he would reject her. It was not that she wanted to be a martyr, but she did want to be a rebel. And this rape of her, it severed her scruples at cutting off from her family and its pompous decency.

"I can't stay now," she said to Alexander Plunkett-Drax, as he lay against her side, still tensed in an arched bow of lean flesh.

"You've nowhere to go."

"Marie Dunesk, she'll take me in. She's wild too."

"A savage. An Indian. Very alluring."

"She'll take me in. I want to be free."

"With *your* father and mother?" Alexander laughed in his shrill way. "They are *so* conventional. And they get a wild one. You never can tell what sort of a brat you will get." He paused in order to make everything worse. "I didn't tell you. Why Arabella is so under the weather. She's expecting something – he, she or it."

"And you –"

"Exactly. She won't be in service for quite a while."

"You're a pig, Alexander."

"That's what you like." Alexander rolled himself onto one elbow to look down at her in the moonlight that shone through her bedroom window past the open shutters. "I knew it when I first saw you. Like a good filly, you like to be broken. A touch of the spur and the quirt."

"I do not." Ruth beat against his bare chest with her right fist, until he caught her wrist, nearly crushing her thin bones. "Women aren't horses," she sobbed.

"No," Alexander said, releasing her. "A better ride." He lay back beside her, and then did the unspeakable, making it her fault. "I knew what you wanted. I gave it to you. If you think I *enjoy* being a bit of a bastard, I don't. I'd much rather play Sir Galahad or Young Lochinvar. But you wanted a pirate lover. So I had to oblige."

"I'm to blame?" Ruth could not believe her ears. "You can't think –"

"It's the truth," Alexander yawned, then sat up in her bed, rising as a pale spear from the shadow of the canopy over the four-poster.

"I must get back to Arabella. She may wake from her druggy dreams and *want* me. Oh God," he drawled, "the wants of women. How can we ever satisfy them?"

12

TO SHOOT A DUCK

The news of the death of his mother Julia had recalled Robert back to Canada. Again there was not enough pay to take Virginia with him; the Colonial Office was mean with the servants of the Empire. So Virginia was once more staying with Hamish Charles to help with the three children. Lizzie did not want her there, but Hamish Charles had insisted in the name of charity and mercy and the fine words used by men to get their own way. Only the little ones, now two, three and four years old, kept the brew from boiling over. Looking after their love absorbed most of the emotions of those who were now grown, but unable to cope with their hearts.

It had to begin one day. The star cave with the Bushmen paintings in the foothills had become Virginia's refuge. In the recesses and cracks branching from the entrance cavern, she found with her oil-lamp amazing drawings, which suggested a primitive religion. There was a complicated pattern of geometry something like a maze. Out of its wavy lines stuck the heads of bucks and giraffes. The pattern even ended inside the neck of an ostrich. The wandering paths were a labyrinth that led her to the inwardness of living things – long ways winding within to the animal in her.

Buldoo no longer guarded her at her paintings, but he told Hamish Charles where to find the star cave. And when a shadow fell across her closed eyelids as she lay back in the blaze of light falling from the hole in the roof, Virginia knew who had come to see her. She only blinked to check the outline of the dark head above set against the glare, then she closed her vision again. She did not speak or recognise that he was there. She knew what he would do, if there was enough of a man in him. Any word from her would foil his will. And he was so hesitant, so controlled, so *good* – she could not stand it.

She felt his weight on her, his dry lips fierce on her cheek, her eyes, her mouth. She heard him mumbling and rasping sounds that might have been his desire or her name. She felt his hands tearing at her skirt, lifting it. She knew a dry piercing of her that became a soft entrapment. Then she heard his cry and howl, and she found herself crying out as well in answer or from her own need. She could hardly hold him to her within her arms, he trembled so violently in a spasm of shivering. Then the burden of him pressed her down into the sand until she was the earth itself. And then he spoke at last, his lips against her ear.

"I am sorry, Virginia."

"Don't be."

"I did not mean –"

"I hope you did."

She was laughing now. The silly man with all his apologies. She would have to make him bolder than that if he was going to do what he said he would do for her.

"Move over," she said. "You're crushing me."

"I'm sorry," he said again, rolling across her to lie at her side.

"No, *don't* say that. I might *like* being crushed."

"I never thought of that. Virginia . . ." He sounded almost frightened. "You didn't mind that I . . .?" His voice trailed away.

Virginia was laughing again. She sat up and smoothed her skirt down on her bare legs.

"Hamish, you know what I minded about – why did you take so long to come and find me?"

Now he began to laugh, almost uncontrollably. Their mirth reverberated within the rock. There was a sudden clatter, a ricochet of wings, a squeaking and a screeching. Thick bullets whirled through the air. Virginia flung her head onto the man's chest and hugged him.

"Bats," he said. "Only bats."

"I hate bats."

"I won't let them get in your hair." He kissed the long black waves that hid her head. "They eat insects. Bats are good for us."

"That doesn't stop me hating them."

The clatter in the air had died away. The sun in its falling had foregone the hole. It was growing dim inside the cave.

"I'll take you home," he said. "How did the painting go today?"

"I must show you something," she said. She sat up and found her oil-lamp, its flame still guttering.

"Here, on the wall. Look." Two long flat shapes seemed to crawl towards each other on splayed legs. "The Bushmen drew these lovers like two lizards. Just like us. How long we took to approach each other . . ."

"I do see," Hamish Charles said. "You're quite right. These primitive things – they can be relevant, I suppose."

"Better than that," Virginia said. "Stimulating. Look at this one I drew. It's in a crevice a long way in." She pulled her sketch-pad out of her satchel and opened it and held the picture out for the man to see. The mixed bag of crocodiles and wild dogs and zebras and wilde-beeste and hunters and snakes and scorpions was clear in its meaning to her. But Hamish Charles did not seem to understand, but shook his head, puzzling.

"Don't you see?" she said, almost exasperated. "It's all one for them. Creation. They're part of all of it. That's what's wrong with us. We divide things. This good, that bad. This spirit, that flesh. This do, that don't. We don't need this and that. We should just say, I want. And I do it."

Hamish Charles smiled and put his arms round her waist and grabbed her so tight that she thought a rib or her spine might crack.

"I wanted – and I did," he said. Then he let her go.

She breathed in deeply and breathed out again with a sigh.

"So I noticed," she said drily, and then she said, "darling," for the first time to him.

The cattle lay dead or dying about the *vlei*. It was not the drought, for there was still water in the muddy dip. Piet Krug scooped up some of the brown liquid in the hollow of his hand and put his tongue in it. Then he spat out, his face contorting. As he looked up past the lying beasts, their horns sunk into the land, he thought he saw a movement among the stones of the nearby *kopje*. One figure – two? Or was it the heat-haze making a couple of rock points dance? He would have known in the Boer War. He would have picked them off both with his Mauser. Two single shots and both of them dead.

"Keep down," Hamish Charles was saying to Virginia. They had dismounted behind a boulder, and the man was peering round the obstacle down towards the plain. "I think it's Piet Krug. I don't know whether he's seen us. Most likely he has. He's got eyes like a hawk."

"What if he has?" Virginia said. "We were out on an innocent ride."

"It won't work. I'll ride down, brazen it out. I'll say I'm alone. Give me five minutes. Then you ride back and round to the farm. Then nobody will know for certain."

Virginia stroked the hanging head of her pony. "Lizzie already knows for certain."

"I haven't told her. I've always denied it."

"She knows." Virginia knew the wife knew. "Women always know."

It was not the time to argue. So Hamish Charles said, "I am going down." And he led his horse round the boulder and mounted it and rode towards the *vlei*.

Piet Krug took his rifle from its sling by the saddle of his horse. He was shaking too much to control his hands, but he willed himself to be still as his brother-in-law rode towards him. Hamish Charles was not carrying a weapon. He had not ridden to the star cave to shoot, but to make love. He dismounted near his Boer neighbour and walked towards him, ignoring the rifle in the hands of the other man.

"Where is *she*?" Piet asked.

"She? I don't know who you mean." Hamish Charles tried to sound puzzled, but his worry made his voice quaver. "I have been riding alone."

"*She* was riding. You were riding her."

"Piet!" Hamish Charles was shocked. "Don't be so crude."

"I see two people on the *kopje*. You and she."

"I am alone. I swear it."

Piet moved the barrel of his rifle forward. He tapped the end of the muzzle on his brother-in-law's knee.

"Now you are alone. And you lie. Bunjie say, you sleep with her. Lizzie say, you sleep with her. In there." Piet now jerked the gun-barrel towards the mountains. "Where the whore, she paints."

"She is not a whore." Hamish Charles rocked on his feet, waiting to strike at Piet, but fearful of the rifle. "Never say that. She is the governess of my children. My cousin's wife."

"That? It stop *you*?" Piet gave a dry, short laugh. "You poison Lizzie, your *vrou*. She is sick. She die slow with your bad heart. Now you poison the ox. My ox. I taste the *vlei* with my tongue. Arsenic. Are you crazy, Sinclair? You want for we all are dead?"

"Arsenic?" Hamish Charles was shocked. "I saw the cattle. I thought they were resting."

"Dead. Dying."

"Arsenic. I can't believe it. I couldn't do it. Some of the cattle are mine. Why should I poison my own stock? This is my water."

"Your water. My water. If it is not you –" Now Piet was raising the muzzle of his Mauser to aim casually at the other man's chest. "Then it is your *dom* miners. You let them on your land."

"I cannot stop them. They come anyway. You can't keep off a wildcat prospector."

"Chase them. I do. Chase them like we chase you in the war."

"They're looking for gold. If they strike it rich, so do we. Mineral rights – ever heard of them?"

"They start the *dom* war. Gold on the Rand. And now, they put poison in the *vlei*. To wash the ore down. For shiny metal, they kill

– they kill." Now Piet was tapping at the chest of his brother-in-law with the gun barrel. The blows were as quick and hard as the beak of a pecking vulture. "I kill you not, Hamish, in the war. In my sights, you were. I kill not. Now you are in my sights. And I kill, I think."

"I have no gun," Hamish Charles said. "You can't shoot me. I can't defend myself."

"Get on your horse," Piet said. "Go home. Send the whore away. I give you one week. If the whore is there, I kill you."

"She is not a whore. She is innocent."

"She is arsenic in the *vlei*. She kill us. Now get on your horse." Suddenly Piet hit Hamish Charles on the chest with the metal barrel, bruising his ribcage and knocking him two paces back. "One week, man. Or I hunt you. I kill you like a buck."

Hamish Charles walked back to his horse. With one foot in the stirrup, he turned towards Piet, who was still aiming the Mauser at him.

"You'll never get a Dutchman to recognise the truth."

"Lie," Piet said. "But true – you kill Annie, my first *vrou*. Now you kill Lizzie, the sister of my second *vrou*. I do not think. I think you die first."

In face of such unreason, this lack of thought and logic, Hamish Charles had to ride silent away. The trouble was, the Dutchman was right about the main points. There was poison in the home and out here in the open.

On the fatal day, Hamish Charles never knew, or believed that he never knew, what made him pick up the wrong gun. Or if he had picked up the right gun, he never knew why he said he was shooting the wrong thing. That was the case against him. Why did he say he was going to shoot duck with a rifle? Unless it was a sitting duck, as his wife was. He should have taken a shotgun or said that he was hunting buck, not duck. But then Lizzie would not have gone with him. She would not let Virginia go, she was too jealous. Their guest and governess had to remain behind with the three small children. And Buldoo could not leave the poisoned cattle, which had survived the dose of arsenic in their dip. So Lizzie went out with Hamish Charles, to shoot duck with a rifle.

They had driven out to the marshland in the light cart, pulled by a single pony. Lizzie seemed almost happy, her broad face breaking into smiles or appeals for sympathy, her yellow curls almost golden in the setting sun. "We will have roast duck," she said. "Then soup from the bones. Then a brawn and a paste. There is four thing to do with duck. I know them. You are lucky, Hamish, you marry a wife know how to do."

Yes, Hamish Charles thought, he had married a wife who knew how to do. And she knew how to do when they came to shoot the duck on the marshland just over the border. Piet had made and given him the two decoys, when matters had been better between them. He set the wooden and painted toy ducks in the marsh and sent Lizzie a little way off to hide in the reeds. She had an unexpected gift, which she used to amuse the infants. She could reproduce bird-calls – the screech of the black stork or *groot-swart sprinkanvoël*, the hoot of the spotted eagle-owl she called *steen-uil*, the croak of the pied crow, the *bont-kraai*. The quacks of the ducks were child's play to her. So she sent up her coarse siren calls to the skies in the evenings, when the birds were settling down.

Later, Hamish Charles was to point out one factor in his favour. If it were he who was intended to be the victim of the bullet, it would have been the mistake of a marksman – a Piet Krug or a Robert Sinclair, for the border had been crossed into the district of his authority. A straight line could be drawn from the peak of the rise behind the marshland through the back of Hamish Charles, where he was standing to shoot, and on to the place where Lizzie was squatting in the reeds, calling down the ducks. A bullet aimed from the high ground at his head could have missed him and hit Lizzie instead. It was an explanation. Only there was nothing to prove it. And nothing to show why he had taken his Mauser to hunt fowl. He would have needed birdshot for that feathered prey.

As it was, when the teal and the pochard and the dwarf geese, the *rooibek-eendjies* and the *bruin-eends* and the *dwerg-ganses*, came skidding down the twilight, Hamish Charles discovered what a fool he was to bring the wrong gun. His mind must have been elsewhere. It had obviously been on Virginia and the impossible situation at home. Still, he thought he would risk a shot with the rifle, and he fired once at a fluttering shape descending down the air. The shot seemed to echo in his ears, as if he had shot twice, a left and a right. Then there was a cry, a human cry. Then silence. Even the wings of the birds ceased their beating. And the false calls of Lizzie in the reeds were hushed. She would never call again. A bullet had hit her head.

"Lizzie," Hamish Charles shouted. "Lizzie!" Then he began to blunder across the wet ground towards the reeds. He could only hear the squelching of his boots in the muddy soil. "Lizzie!" His fear grew with her silence. "Lizzie!" Parting the reeds with his hands, he looked down. His wife lay on her back as if she were asleep. A small red spot, no bigger than a wedding ring, was in the centre of her forehead. But the moss behind her was a red cushion to the scarlet curls on the back of her head.

Hamish Charles did not remember what then he had done. Virginia was his witness. An hour after he had driven from the farm with Lizzie, she had discovered that he had left his shotgun and taken his rifle to shoot duck. Some premonition, or perhaps a touch of guilt, had made her turn over the care of the children to her maid Tsutsie and ride on her pony towards the marsh in Basutoland, where her husband Robert was already overdue on his return from his leave. The darkening sky had made her ride full of terrors. Her pony had stumbled on an ant-heap and she thought it had broken its leg. But no, it was slightly lamed, and she could go slowly on. As she reached the rise before the wetland, she heard two shots. She was adamant about that. The second sound was not an echo. There were two shots, fired close together. She rode round the rise to the marsh and she heard Hamish Charles's voice, as he was calling out, "Lizzie!" When she reached the reeds on her pony in the gathering dark, she could just see the shape of the man standing by the body of his wife. He was putting the barrel of his rifle in his mouth. "No!" she shouted and fell off her pony and picked herself up from the mud and ran towards him, screaming, "No, no, no!" And he did not pull the trigger before she came to him and took the rifle in her hands and led him away behind her.

Virginia kept him from killing himself. She told Buldoo to remove all the guns from the house and hide them. She concealed the sharp knives and even the hanging ropes. He was inconsolable and guilty. He said he hadn't done it in one breath. Then in the next breath, he said he had and he could not forgive himself. He had to die, too. The infants asking where Mama was sent him into tears and despair. And this was the witness, and perhaps this was the murderer, whom Robert found when he arrived at the farm early in the morning after the shooting to collect Virginia. She thought that his arrival was so timely he might have known of the killing. He might also have followed them home from the marsh.

"Robert," she said. "Thank God you've come. I'll take you to the body. It's just over the border, in your territory. It's your case."

So she rode with her husband to the marsh in the morning. They had so much to say to each other, to confess to each other. But there was nothing to say but the unsaid and the understood. The silence between them was fused with meaning. And in the end, Virginia said, "Whatever I've done, Robert, don't let him suffer. It was an accident. You judge. You try it. It's in your jurisdiction. Don't let the Boers judge it. They'll hang him. It'll be the Boer War all over again."

"Why do they hate him?"

"Because of me," Virginia said flatly. "They think he and I . . ."

"Is it true?"

"It's a lie." Virginia had to save her lover. "I swear it's a lie. We like each other –"

"Natural, I reckon. We are kin." Robert's voice was dry with disbelief. "But it's bad, real bad, he's a Sinclair, she was an Afrikaner, you're an Englander. And her sister married to Piet Krug. I can see Black Week all over again."

"You'll save him?"

"I'll do my duty," Robert said, and he thought he would try to do it, whatever he felt.

Robert spent a while examining the body, which was still lying undisturbed in the reeds. He heard Virginia's story of the two shots. "But you say Hamish only fired one – we can check that." He made Virginia sketch the body, its position in the reeds, relative to the geography of the place. She shuddered as she drew, the lines of the pencil wavering on the paper. Then he picked up the dead woman, putting her over his shoulder. And he walked heavily back to the position of the hide, where the huntsman had concealed himself. He laid down the body and searched the wet ground. After a time, he found one cartridge ejected from a Mauser rifle. He did not find another.

"Two shots, you reckon?" he asked his wife. And when she nodded, he looked at the line between the rise and the hide and the place of Lizzie's death. "So he could have shot at the duck," he said, "and somebody shot at him. Only they missed and shot her." Virginia nodded again. "If there were two shots," he said, "it doesn't say who the second gun was. Though there were folks with a reason to hate him. Piet Krug, you say. A threat to kill him, if he didn't throw you out. It's possible." But then Robert paused and shook his head. "But one thing I don't get. A man, he won't take a rifle to hunt duck. It's not natural. However much he had on his mind."

They brought Lizzie's body back slung over the saddle of Robert's horse, her bloodied yellow curls trailing down. She would have to be buried on the farm. Already the news had reached the neighbours, and Buldoo came in to say that twenty Boer farmers were riding in with their rifles, for they did not trust the justice of the *rooineks*. So Robert gave Buldoo the concealed shotgun and put him in the barn in front of the porch and told him to fire to wound, not to kill, if he lifted his hand. And he told the rest of the farmhands and the maids and Virginia and Hamish Charles and the children to stay inside out

123

of harm's way. He would deal with it. So he waited on the wooden bench of the *stoep* with his American carbine and the Mauser of Hamish Charles and the cartridge belt. He had checked the magazine. It was true, only one shot had been fired. Unless Hamish Charles had fired twice and reloaded with one cartridge. But that was unlikely. Even so, Robert reckoned he might need some evidence, if only to save his wife and his cousin from the vengeance of the Afrikaners. So he fired the Mauser once in the air and put the spent case in his pocket with the first case he had found in the hide. And he reloaded the rifle with a single cartridge, so that he could say it had only been fired once.

An hour later, Piet Krug and twenty Boer farmers came riding in with their rifles. Only Krug dismounted and limped towards Robert, sitting on the porch.

"Don't get in the way, *rooinek*," Piet said. "This war you lose."

"There will be a trial," Robert said. "The tragedy took place in my district. I will try it. I swear I will."

"*You* try him? A cousin?" Piet's savage smile gashed his beard. "That is justice?"

"It will be a fair trial. And Piet Krug, you will come to it."

"I will?"

"You may be tried, too. For your mistake."

"What? *Rooinek*, you want I should kill you –?"

"Here." Robert took a risk and tossed the Mauser of Hamish Charles over to Piet, who caught it in surprise. All the time Robert kept his carbine trained loosely on the Afrikaner. "Check it. One shot fired."

Piet broke open the magazine and checked that one cartridge was missing, spilling the others on the ground.

"So? One shot, that kill Lizzie."

"There were two shots, Krug. My wife heard them. So did Hamish Sinclair."

"They lie."

"They do?" Robert fished in his pocket and brought out the two cartridge cases, rolling them together in his fingers. "I found one of them in the hide – Hamish was there. The other one – on the rise behind Hamish. Squashed grass, too. Somebody was there. You, Krug? You fired at Hamish. You missed. You killed your sister-in-law instead of him."

"You lie. Three times you lie." Piet's face was blotched tan and scarlet above his beard. "Your cousin kill Lizzie. Your wife lie. You lie. And maybe – it is *you*, not me. You jealous of your wife. And that devil. So you shoot him. And you miss. And you kill Lizzie. So?"

"I go for your evidence," Robert said. "It will sound great in court. But there is a hitch –" Again he rolled the brass cases against each other. "These are both Mauser cartridge cases. I use a carbine. Made in the US of A."

"Then you make the two cases. You lie. You *Uitlanders*, you always lie."

Piet raised the barrel of his rifle, but Robert was too quick for him. He flicked up his carbine, shooting from his chair as if from the saddle. The bullet struck Piet's Mauser and sent the gun spinning away and left Piet crying out and wringing his bruised fingers. And as the outriders – the new Boer commando – as they raised their weapons on their horses, the blast of Buldoo's buckshot behind them sent their guns falling back on their saddles or to the ground.

"You're surrounded!" Robert shouted. "I'm not crazy!"

He could see Buldoo, grinning from his revenge on the Boers as he emerged from the barn with his smoking shotgun, which he reloaded. But the Boers did not know if Robert had twenty Zulus waiting in the barns with rifles trained on them. He had the advantage, so he shouted, "Go home! We bury her here tomorrow! I swear! And there will be justice, I swear. No more blood now! No more blood!"

Piet turned back towards the outriders. He had clenched his hands and now he raised them into the air in a great fist.

"We will go," he commanded in Afrikaans. "We will come back. We will bury Lizzie. We kill him and her. This is our land." And all the outriders answered him, "This is our land." And then they rode away.

Virginia was proud of Robert for what he had done, and her guilt pricked her heart at what she had done to him. Hamish Charles could only mumble his thanks in an incoherence that made him sound drunk. Nobody could resist Robert's suggestions, which were really orders.

"Pack all you can," he said. "They will be back in the morning to kill you. We take the children and Tsutsie and Buldoo with us over the border into my territory. They will not follow there."

"But what about burying *her*?" Virginia asked.

"They will do that," Robert said. "With a *predikant* – their faith. If you stayed for the funeral, they would lynch you. We go tonight. Tomorrow – it's too late."

At last, Hamish Charles managed to speak, for all the shame and guilt clogging his tongue.

"Why, Robert . . . why are you . . . why . . . all this for *me* . . . and Virginia?"

"She is my wife."

"Yes, but –"

"You *are* my cousin? I think you are."

"Yes."

"Well, then." Robert patted Hamish Charles on the shoulder. He was clamping his feelings, keeping his anger to himself. "Blood is thicker than water. Bain always said that. Fathers are always right." He paused. He could see that his cousin and his wife could not judge his mood or his intent. "Now there's blood in this," he said, "we have to be thick. Thick as thieves. Thicker than water, I think."

So that night, there was a trek over the border to British colonial law in Basutoland, as administered by its district officer, Robert Sinclair. And Lizzie's body was left washed and groomed lying on her bed in her best nightgown, her hands folded together in silent prayer, but the dark ring of death still on her forehead.

13

NOT PROVEN

Not proven is a Scots verdict, and it has no value in English law. But Robert Sinclair was a Scotsman before he was a Canadian, although he now served the British Empire and carried its passport. He knew of the old country's judgement. Not proven in a murder trial did not mean the accused was not guilty. It meant that his guilt was not proven, so that he might stand trial again, if there were new evidence or if he admitted the offence. In a way, not proven was the worst of sentences. It was truly life-long. The noose was always hanging over the head of the one who was charged with the crime. If he were guilty, daily he feared discovery by conscience pressing him to confess. And even if he were innocent, the world might get to know that his innocence was not proven, just as his guilt was not. It was a permanent torment that only ended in death, natural or legal.

At the inquest, however, Robert could not give that verdict. It was the great fortune of Hamish Charles that the killing of Lizzie had taken place over the border in Robert's district, and that he had fled with Virginia and the children to stay with his cousin, who was also his coroner and his judge, before the court met and the trial took place. It was also his great misfortune. For Robert knew that his wife loved Hamish Charles, and that his cousin loved her to the point of folly, and perhaps murder. But of course, that was not proven.

And there was the outcry from over the border, and the press. The Boers wanted blood for blood. They were furious that the accident of a frontier had placed the inquest and trial in Basutoland. The neighbours had ridden back the next day to find the farm deserted except for the hands they called Kaffirs – and the dead body of Lizzie, lying decently in her marriage bed. They had called in the *predikant* and buried her in their Old Testament way, refusing to say, "Vengeance is Mine, saith the Lord." They wanted the vengeance to be theirs. They threatened raids over the border to kidnap their quarry and execute him. And they could easily have done it – they were trained commandos, after all. And the newspapers in Ficksburg, their reports of the case reached Cape Town. And when they reached Cape Town, they reached the Colonial Office in London. And it was a scandal. And scandal was the one thing which the Colonial Office abhorred, particularly if it had to do with a District Officer in a sensitive colony. And that District Officer was Robert Sinclair.

"You're riding me into the ground," Robert said to Hamish Charles on the night before the inquest. "Yeah, a life's gone, and maybe you had something you done with it. But now it's my life."

"I'm sorry." Hamish Charles was stooped in front of his cousin. "I didn't mean to . . ." His shoulders slumped even more.

"Never say that," Virginia snapped at him. "Never *say* that. You did nothing."

"Sure," Robert said. "He did nothing. But I still need to know a thing or two before the inquest tomorrow. That is, if the brothers don't ride over the hills and make a Magersfontein out of us again."

"Oh, yes," Hamish Charles said bitterly, "your cowboys weren't there. That's why we lost. That's why our uncle was killed."

"Right," Robert said. "Right for once, Hamish. But the cowboy's here now and he wants to know a thing or two. Tell me – come on – the truth. Did you shoot Lizzie? Did you?"

Hamish Charles looked at the straw mat on the floor. Then he looked up. "I don't know," he said. "Truly, I don't. But I swear I shot at a duck. Not at her."

"With a rifle?"

"With a rifle."

"And the second shot?"

"I heard it."

"And I heard it." Virginia spoke a sort of hatred. "I told you. Don't you believe your *wife*?"

"Yes – on this," Robert said. "But not, I reckon, when her feelings are in question." He swung back on the accused. "So there was no intent? It was an accident?" Then he said, as if almost to convince himself, "It had to be."

"It was an accident," Virginia said.

"Let him say," Robert said.

Hamish Charles tried to remember what had been said, then groped for the right phrase.

"It had to be," he repeated. Then he paused in the silence, and he added, "An accident. That's all it was."

"That won't get you off," Robert said.

Virginia could not stand her husband being an inquisitor over them. She had too much guilt to hide.

"You *dare* question him? He's innocent."

"I am trying to teach him the questions he will be asked," Robert said.

"By you?"

"By me."

"Why?"

"Because I am the law. If I don't ask them, they will kill him – the Boers. And they will fire me – the Colonial Office."

"Ah." Virginia was silent. She never knew Robert could be so discriminating. "So how do you, as you say, get him off?"

"I go for your evidence," Robert said. "I say there were two shots. I say I found two cartridge cases – both of them from a Mauser. I produce those cases. Just as I did to Piet Krug on the porch in the farm, when you were hiding inside. Two shots – only one from you, Hamish. Another killer – aiming at you, hitting Lizzie. You get off. Accidental death. Or death by persons unknown."

"Christ," Hamish Charles said. "I should thank you. Why are you doing it for me?"

"I don't know," Robert said. He searched in the pocket of his khaki jacket and took out the two brass cartridge cases.

"The trouble is, it's wrong. It's phoney-baloney. I shot off your rifle on the porch. I made the second cartridge case. As you fellows say, I manufactured the evidence."

There was a silence longer than a memorial service.

"So we're at your mercy," Virginia said. "And you are giving it to us. Why?"

Robert rose from his low canvas chair with the flat wooden arms, where the servants set the sundowners. He walked over to the thin mesh that covered the window from the mosquitoes. He looked out into nothing.

"I hate you, Virginia," he said in a small voice. "And you, Hamish. You were made for each other. You met in hell. But you were always there. You are damned for each other. And it's nothing to do with me. I was in the way." He kept his back turned on the shocked faces behind him. Then he said, "So you met. So she died, the woman in your way. So she had to die. It doesn't mean *you* killed her, Hamish. You didn't mean to kill her. And if it wasn't you, somebody else killed her. Somebody did. From that rise behind the marsh. Shooting at you and hitting Lizzie, because she was in line behind you. I reckon somebody did that."

There was a hush that extended time. Then Virginia with that quickness of hers seized upon the implication.

"It was *you*, Robert. You shot at Hamish. You hit Lizzie. That's why – why you give us *your* mercy."

Robert turned back from the wire mesh of the window. He was smiling, almost debonair. Lightness played on his face, almost a joy at being found out.

"You're crazy, Virginia," he said. "But if I let you go – not proven, I mean – you'll never forget it, will you? You'll never forget me – how I let you go. For all you did to me – you bastards – *I* let you go."

Then Virginia learned, and later she was to know for certain, that the Sinclairs might seem to forget, but they never did forgive. A mercy from them was a sentence for life. No one could ever repay.

Mary knew that it was the last visit of her life. She could not endure the chaise as it jolted and bounced over the karroo towards Basutoland. Each shake stabbed at her locked muscles and bones. It had been the same for her mother. Arthritis had crippled her at the end. Mary had even had to retire from her consultancy at the Apfelstein Hospital in Johannesburg and live with Seaforth and his new wife Miriam. Most of that family had hated the marriage, but Seaforth was working at the hospital which they had endowed, and nobody could deny his brilliance. Too many people owed their lives to him to talk against him. Poor Seaforth, Mary thought, always bitter just because of his colour, yet with the best hands on a surgeon she had ever seen. But Miriam loved him, even if she saw him through pink spectacles, a victim of discrimination, an exploited colonial, a slave of the Empire. She would grow out of it. Or so Mary hoped. Most people did.

But the killing of Lizzie. Mary knew Hamish Charles, or she thought she did. Even if he were head over heels in love with that foxy Virginia, he would never murder his wife. It had to be an accident. But Robert, the wronged husband, being the judge and the jury. It was a wicked thing. And then there was the farm. What would happen to that? And the children? It was a mess as well as a tragedy. But Mary had spent her long life cleaning up messes. She was the effective head of the family, and this was the last, the very last thing she could do.

She was too late for the inquest when she reached the District Officer's bungalow, the verdict had already been given. Accidental death. Two people shooting at the marsh, one of them unknown. Hamish Charles given the benefit of the doubt. No evidence of his relationship with Virginia or of his falling out with his wife was submitted to the coroner or allowed to be heard. As the chief witness, Virginia was cool and composed, even distant from Hamish Charles. She was merely a governess on the farm, helping out the family while her husband was away on leave. There was no need to refer the case to trial, whatever the scandal might be. Accidental death. That was Robert's verdict.

Helping the bent old lady in dusty black from the chaise, Hamish Charles trembled. If there ever was a true judge, it was his Aunt Mary. Her verdict was inescapable. But she kissed him, as he stooped down to her, and said, "Dinna worry, Hamish. It is the future the now for you. What will be." And she leaned on his arm as he took her into the bungalow, where she took up her position on the only wooden chair as if on a throne or a chief's stool. "I want to talk to you one by one," she said. "Or we will never get anywhere at all."

Virginia was most frightened of Mary's judgement. She knew the old woman disliked her. She had meant to be scornful, refusing to admit Mary's right to make a second trial of the accident or of her love for Hamish Charles. But the blue stare of Mary's eyes from her lined face, as crushed as a crumpled towel, broke Virginia's resolve, and she found herself weeping and kneeling, her face buried in Mary's lap, and saying between sobs, "We never – I did not mean – I don't want to hurt Robert – we met too late – it was an accident, too. But love – it's so strong –"

"Sit up, girl," Mary said. "You may not think it, an old one like me, but I ken love. I ken what love is."

"You do?" And Virginia straightened herself and looked at Mary, but stayed kneeling beside the ancient woman on her chair.

"Ach, yes. Robert tells me he will let you go. It is over. Hamish tells me he loves you. He will never leave you. But that is a terrible thing. Divorce. It is a terrible thing."

"Yes," Virginia said. "But I will stand it, if I must."

"Not here," Mary said. "Where will you go?"

"London," Virginia said. "Hamish says London. And I want –"

"Ach, I see." Mary shook her head. "Why every fool girl in the bush wants to go to London is a mystification to me. But there you are. And what will you live on? Hamish only has the farm. And who will sell it?"

"I don't know," Virginia said. "The Boers will kill us if we go back. That Piet Krug, he's married to Lizzie's sister –"

"I will do it," Mary said. "I know Piet Krug. He will not kill an old woman. I had to tell him how his first wife Annie died. In our camp. Now I will tell him – his sister-in-law – an accident."

"He hated Hamish Charles. There was a quarrel. Arsenic in the water. Miners."

"I will give Piet Krug what he wants. Water, land, whatever. A reparation, if you can ever repair a death. The rest, I will sell and send you the money. But, Virginia, tell me true – one thing – you will care for the wee ones."

"I will. I swear I will."

"As if they were your own folk?"

"I swear."

"And if you and Hamish Charles, you have a bairn? It is a terrible thing to be a step-mother. To try and not love your own more. And not to see the other mother in the step-family."

"They are Hamish Charles's children. I will love them, because I love him."

"You will try, I think." Mary put her hand on the shoulder of the kneeling young woman. "I wish you luck. Hamish will have written to his father Angus in Peru about this and about you. His mother's folk are a wealthy family. They will help. And he has a brother Murdo in London, he has kin there. And there is the house in Vancouver in Canada, which Angus bought for my old mother and father. They are buried there, and Kate is still there. You will have help, if you truly love Hamish and the three wee ones."

"Thank you, Aunt Mary," Virginia said. She rose to her feet and looked down at the shrunken figure in black that had been sitting over her. "Then – I have your blessing."

"For what it's worth," Mary said in her dry way. "And for what you are worth."

When she reached the farm, Mary had expected it to be burned. But it was not. So she sent for Piet Krug, and he was not long in coming to her. In fact, he came to see her so quickly that she hardly remembered that she had sent the message. But when he entered, gangling and lanky, the long beard and sprouting whiskers covering the face under the shadow of the slouch hat, Mary felt a pity for him that almost obscured what she had to say.

"Nice," she said. "Very nice. You come to see me, Piet Krug. And you did not burn the farm."

"It is also Lizzie's farm," Piet said. He stood in front of the seated Mary. Now he took his hat off and rolled it between his hands. "They come not." His voice was as bitter as an aloe. "They send you."

"You would kill them." Mary smiled up at the scarecrow with the beard. "But you canna kill me. I know you, Piet Krug."

"And I know you." Piet bit his lip. "The dirty tricks, the *Uitlanders*. They know us. They send in old ladies."

"You send in commandos," Mary said. "Dirty tricks, you Boers, you did them all. But then, the English they did dirty tricks to my folk, the Scots. So we ken you – and we ken the English."

Piet laughed. "You are worse than the *predikants*. You tell me. The *Uitlanders* are so clever. Their soldiers, they hate the *Uitlanders*. But they fight for the *Uitlanders*. Then they come to us, they say. We hate the *Uitlanders*, too." Piet laughed again. "Now, Mary Sinclair –"

"It is true," she said. "Yes, it *is* true. Now, Piet Krug, I will say what we must do."

"I listen," he said. "But only to you."

"I have to sell this farm," Mary said. "The folks here, they canna come back again." And Piet nodded, wagging his head. "I have said, they will all go away. Robert, he is to be transferred to West Africa, because of all the talk and the feeling. He willna rule your border no more." And Piet nodded again in satisfaction. "My nephew Hamish Charles – and *that* Virginia –" Piet smiled at the emphasis Mary put on the woman – "they are going to London. But with the children, I am afraid."

"I want the children here."

"I know," Mary said. "But as Lizzie is dead, they must stay with their father. Now, Piet, if you are right, and you may be –"

"I am."

"They will come back to you. Believe me, Piet. The bairns are *your* bairns too. I am still a Scotswoman, against the English. They will come back to you, if you are right. But now, the law is they stay with their father. Lizzie is dead."

"They will come to me," Piet said. "They are Afrikaners. They must be here."

"No," Mary said. "I bring you peace. Hear me."

"I hear." But Piet was moving his teeth against each other, splitting them.

"You have the *vlei*, the water. You have the land you want. It *is* your land, as you say. You give some to me to sell, as the law says. You get rid of the prospectors – the miners. You are right. They are greed. They kill us – they kill all of us. For metal."

Piet laughed at the old woman.

"You are the enemy. You are the friend. You come to confuse."

"No," Mary said. "I will be dead, Piet, before you see me again."

Piet laughed once more.

"You never die. You live for ever. You bury us all."

"I am dying," Mary said. "And I am like the people you call Kaffirs. You are wrong. I know the day I die. They know. They could teach you."

"A Kaffir teach me?" Piet laughed for the last time. "Tell me, Mary Sinclair, why? I take all the farm."

"Tell me, Piet, will you break the law? I know this is *your* land. But not all of it. Some must go to the bairns. The rest I give to you."

"You cannot give for a death."

"I agree," Mary said. "You canna give for a death. But this is no blood money, Piet. This is an answer. This is an end. This is peace. This is your land. This I give to you." Piet shook his head, swaying from side to side. He said nothing, so Mary went on, "Ach, dinna you ken. You win a war, you lose a war. But you lose a war, you win a peace. You have won, Piet Krug. And you have lost. And we are winning, too, the Scots, who lost to England. We are winning the peace."

"Wicked," Piet said. "Wicked, it is you."

"The war is over," Mary said. "It is peace the now. I am dying. An I am dead, it will be peace. I saw your Annie die. I will give you peace, Piet Krug. And you will have it. You are so proud – as terrible – as all the Sinclairs are. You will have peace from me, Piet Krug."

At this command from the little woman in black, Piet shook his head, but smiled and asked himself, "Who shall say no to you, Mary Sinclair?"

"No' very many," Mary said. "But I want your peace with me, Piet Krug."

"Two killings I have," he said. "Annie and Lizzie."

"Then it is two pardons you have to give," Mary said. "Annie and Lizzie. But now you have the land you want and the water, *your* land."

"Devil," Piet said and walked away and returned. "No," he said. "Devil you are."

"Now then," Mary said, "my lad – I need an end of it. I am to die. I will live to sign the damned lawyers' paper – to give you the land, to sell the rest of the land. Then I die. I know. I am a Scots Kaffir, a Scots Indian. I know when I die. That is why, Piet Krug, you will believe me. You will end the war."

"*Soe*, you," Piet said. He walked to the old woman and bent and kissed her hand. He had never done this in his life. Then he said, "You."

"When you are near dead," Mary said, "it dinna matter. All you wish for, it is, all is in order. You canna meet your Maker . . . he willna let you in through the Pearly Gates . . . if you canna say, The Ledger, it is in order. I did what I could. It is in order. There is no sin, you see – and I was told all is sin. You live in sin for ever. But there is no sin. I have lived so long – too long – and I ken, Piet, I ken – there is no sin. There is only peace to be found. We must forgive, even if we canna. There are no judges. Listen, Piet. In your thinking, God knows. He says – forgive. I am an old woman. I know folks. Let them be. And wait for Heaven, till God is your judge, your only judge."

"Oh, Mary." Piet said her first name at last. "Mary – it is the name of the Mother of Christ."

"And of the Magdalene," Mary said. "The sinner."

"Mary," Piet said, "I wish for vengeance."

"Too late," Mary said. "Peace the now."

"But we will have our land."

"Yes. The peace is good to you."

"And if we have children –"

"If –"

"It will be our land. We will be the most in it."

"There might be the blacks," Mary said. "Your Kaffirs, you know."

"This is our land," Piet said. "And you will give it back to us."

"Aye," Mary said. "But not I. If you have a majority –"

"We will have many children – *kinders*."

"Then the land is yours. Or the Kaffirs'."

"Our land." Piet smiled at Mary Sinclair. "I will stop the commando. We will not go over the border. Your Robert, your Hamish, they will be gone?"

"Yes," Mary said. "They will go."

"I show you something?"

Piet took out of the pocket of his jacket a brass cartridge case. He put it in Mary's hand. And he said, "I find this yesterday only. On the *kopje* down where Lizzie is killed. And the inquest say, somebody aim at Hamish and kill Lizzie. Two shots. Look, Mary – American cartridge. Remington cartridge. I know. The bullet is Robert Sinclair. That is why he let Hamish go. He kill Lizzie. A mistake. He mean to kill Hamish. For his wife."

Mary rolled the cartridge in her old fingers, which would hardly close, the arthritis had clamped her bones. Then she took this brass bit and tucked it down the black bosom of her dress.

"Piet," she said, "it is too late. You were my enemy. You are my friend. You have the land. And as for *this* –" patting her bosom – "it is over. We have peace." Then she sighed and said, "There is no truth in the peace. But we must have it."

She was set solid. She could not move. She knew it would happen. The stiffening of the bones, an absolute paralysis. But it did not reach her mind. Her thoughts were flowing free. Ach, just in time. The signing of the papers done. The sale of the rest of the farm done. And her lying in the old iron bed, where dead Lizzie had lain with Hamish Charles, now in London with his Virginia. All tidy now, that was the way to go. All in order, the last things done for the living, who must go on. Poor wee ones, what a world for them.

God had now locked her in the cage of her joints and her bones.

She would never shift for herself again. But she was alone. She would die alone. That was good. She was never the one to look for others to look for her. She had always looked for others, never for herself. And surely, never for her old bones. She had had her time. It had come to an end. And she had done well, or well enough. When she passed those Pearly Gates – and pearl they were not, old oak at the best of it – and she came to the final Accountant, sitting by his Book of Lives, and he would say, "Mary, you didna do this, you didna do that," why, she would draw herself up on her bones and say, "Wee angel, but I did this, I did that, I did, I did, I did so. And muckle more." And so she had done. It was more the doing of it than the not doing of it. That was what the Sinclairs were about, at the end of it all. The doing of it. And so some of the clan might slip into Heaven . . .

14

TEA, GRIT AND CARBOLIC

The meal was highly coloured and they ate their way through the rainbow with their fingers. Saffron rice, red peppers, brown curry, green chutney, and even fine silver paper over the top of the sweet rice pudding, which gave it a bitter aftertaste. Rather like the Empire, Seaforth thought – then he caught himself thinking that sour thought and smiled at himself. Marriage must be softening him. And he looked at his wife Miriam, who was still embarrassed at eating with her hands, and he said, "Darling, use a piece of the *chapatti* like a shovel, and scoop the food in. It's like digging a ditch."

"Thank you," his sister Peg said. "My cooking – like a ditch?"

Seaforth laughed, and Miriam said, "If all ditches were like this food we'd have them instead of restaurants. This is *grande cuisine*."

"I don't think so," Peg said. "A humble Indian meal. Would you like some Bombay duck?"

"Please." Then Miriam looked at the proffered blackish hard slices of dried fish, and she said, "Duck, this?"

"Fish. They salt it and squash it and dry it on the pavements."

"No, thank you. Not the sort of process of curing food I care for."

"You prefer tins."

"Well, they're cleaner."

"Natural foods," Peg said. "That's what I always recommend." She ate her last piece of filled *chapatti* and licked her fingers as delicately as a cat licks her paws. "Anyway, if you do get to like India –"

"I do already."

"Then you will find us very natural. Almost too near to nature."

"Not in our religion," Seaforth said. "I have warned Miriam – sacred cows, corpses in the Ganges, even *suttee*, the burning of widows, although it is forbidden by the British. And *caste* – how I hate caste."

"Only because we are outcasts," Peg said. "Literally, born out of caste. Eurasians. Neither one thing nor the other. We are worse, really, than the untouchables."

"Touching Seaforth," Miriam said, "is quite a pleasure."

Seaforth laughed and stroked the back of his wife's hand.

"Miriam likes men who are tall, dark and brilliant."

"You, of course."

"Of course." Now Seaforth was suddenly melancholy. "I have to tell you, Peg, now we're home in India at last –"

"I know," Peg said. "We can't put it off. I must know."

"She died peacefully – and alone. That neighbour of hers, Pie Krug, he found Aunt Mary. He was fond of her, though he is a bastard of a Boer. He hated us coming to the funeral. And as for me being married to Miriam – why, he treated me as if I was contagious, while Miriam was a walking mortal sin. I tell you, I would rather be out of caste here than a Coloured over there. Anyway, Robert came over the border, and we buried Aunt Mary in a cave in the mountain – in a place where the sun shines on the grass every afternoon. There was bad blood between Krug and Robert – it was over the shooting of Hamish Charles's wife. But they didn't have a fight – they were burying Mary. We all disliked each other, but . . . I can't explain but you know how Aunt Mary always was with us. She always made the family get on with each other and get on with the job, even if we refused to do it. She may have been dead, but her spirit – I don't believe in spirits, so let us say, her memory – her memory kept us all at our prayers, those of us who had prayers to say – and being civil to each other. Peace – that was her message from below the ground."

"Yes," Miriam said, "that funeral out in the veld, it was so tense and strained, just the four of us and a Zulu Buldoo as a grave-digger – yet there was a strange calm in the air, a truce in nature."

"I loved Mary," Peg said. "She was the only one of the Sinclairs who ever did a thing for my brother and me."

"It wasn't what she did," Seaforth said, "it was what she was. And I never thought I'd say that old chestnut about anyone, particularly not a member of our Scots family. But Mary – there's not a truce in nature now, Miriam. There's a gap in nature. You know, Peg, I can't believe she's gone. It's like an amputation. I feel I've lost a leg."

"Her work at the hospital in Jo'burg was miraculous," Miriam said. "At her age, too. I once asked her, 'What keeps you going, Aunt Mary?' And she said, 'Tea, grit and carbolic.'"

Seaforth laughed and shook his head.

"One of a kind, Mary was. You couldn't help but like her. Even that damn race-hater Krug did. And Cousin Robert, colonial copper Robert, he was sentimental about his old aunt. He read a poem over her grave, which was the worst thing ever written, but somehow it seemed right at the time. Absolute tosh, but it expressed all the loving

that the Roberts of the world feel about running the Empire. And
Mary, in her way, would have felt the same too. It was written by a
Scotsman called Murray – Robert met him in the Boer War. He
pressed a copy of the dreadful verses on me when we left Mary's
grave, and here they are –" Seaforth handed over a folded paper to
his sister. "*Scotland our Mither* – it's the only memorial service you
will ever receive for our dear Aunt Mary."

Reading the verses, Peg did not know whether to laugh or cry, but
the last line blurred with her tears for her dead beloved aunt. Her lips
moved as she read silently:

Scotland our Mither – this from your sons abroad,
Leavin' tracks on virgin veld that never kent a road.
Trekkin' on wi' weary feet, an' faces turned fae hame,
But lovin' aye the auld wife across the seas the same.

Scotland our Mither – we've bairns you've never seen –
Wee things that turn them northwards when they kneel down at e'en;
They plead in childish whispers the Lord on high will be
A comfort to the auld wife – their granny o'er the sea.

Scotland our Mither – since first we left your side,
From Quilimane to Cape Town we've wandered far an' wide;
Yet aye from mining camp an' town, from koppie an' karroo,
Your sons right kindly, auld wife, send hame their love to you.

Peg wiped her eyes.

"It's impossible," she said. "Even the messages on Christmas cards
make me cry. And Scotland is not even our mother. India is."

"And Scotland," Miriam said. "Your father's home."

"Not really. He was always fighting for England here and all over
the Empire. If we have a Scots home, it's at Simla in the Himalayas.
It is even called Annandale. Uncle Iain's house."

"A sort of baronial bungalow," Seaforth said, "where our uncle
lives in some state with his wife, entertaining the viceroy in summer.
He's come a long way since he was a Highlander in the Mutiny."

"Will we go there?" Miriam said.

"In time. There's no hurry. I must take up my job first. At Lahore."

"A military hospital?" Peg said. "That's unlike you."

"Oh, some soldiers are humans," her brother said. "In fact they
are all humans and only too human. I found that out in the Boer War.
Unfortunately, it was the best post I could get, once Miriam and
I decided to come back to India. I have these wonderful military

recommendations from the King's Surgeon himself, old Treves. Even the man who married our cousin Margaret, Douglas Jardine, couldn't block my appointment."

"I wrote to you in South Africa, didn't I?" Peg said. "About how suspicious he was of you and your politics. He hates the idea of independence."

"You wrote to me. But, as I said, he couldn't stop me getting the post at Lahore."

"Perhaps he wants you under his eye. To see that you don't get into mischief."

"I think I can outwit Douglas Jardine."

"He's in Intelligence, more than the Civil Service – "

"The Great Game? Really?" Seaforth explained to Miriam. "We call Intelligence here the Great Game, because that is what our imperial bard Kipling called it. And it is so British to call Intelligence a game. That is because they think independence is play – child's play for silly little Indian boys like me."

"People in Intelligence," Miriam said, "are rarely intelligent. They use the name to disguise their mental deficiency."

"Douglas Jardine is brighter than he seems," Peg said. "Never underestimate him."

"I have no need to," Seaforth said. "Because he is bound to under-estimate me. A *shi-shi*, that's what they call the half-and-halfs."

"*Chi-chi?*" Miriam smiled. "That means very smart in France."

"Miriam," Peg said, "you must get Seaforth to take you to Annan-dale soon. Anna's on her last legs – I didn't mean to say that. She *is* in a wheel-chair, but she's dying. It's cancer, like our mother."

"Something in common at last." Seaforth could have bitten off his tongue at his tart comment when he saw the look of shock on his wife's face. "I mean, the same sad disease. How long will Anna last?"

"A week – a month – you should go. I don't think Uncle Iain will survive without her, any more than Grandfather did our granny's death in Canada."

Miriam put out her hands to cradle Seaforth's left hand in her palms.

"I made Seaforth promise that we would die together. Not just leave one of us behind. Isn't that silly? It will have to be on the barricades."

"No," Peg said. "It's right to try and die together, even if it does not always work that way. You know, Seaforth, if Iain goes, that's the end of a generation in India. The men who won the Mutiny. It might be the time for a change, a great change."

"It is." Seaforth stood. "Thank you, Peg. Miriam and I must go. To make that great change in India."

"That soon?" Peg laughed. "Only you, brother dear, would be confident of throwing out the Raj by tomorrow breakfast."

"I only give them till midnight," Seaforth said.

"You're always asleep at midnight," Miriam said. "That's no way to run a revolution."

"No man can change the world," Peg said, "without his beauty sleep. That's what Mary would have said."

"And carbolic," Seaforth said. "No revolution without carbolic."

Douglas Jardine found that being in Intelligence made him more of an office-*wallah* than ever. It was not a Kim's game, the fairy-tale that Kipling had recently published, all disguises and boyish ambles along the Great Trunk Road. It was permanent sentry-duty against going to sleep. Goodness, it was so soporific in the hot season, the creak or crackle or chortle of the revolving *punkah*, the rustle and flutter of flimsies under the paperweights, the pens of the *babus* scratching as though they were irritated by an incurable itch, and the padding of the bare feet of the *chaprassis* as soft as floor-rags as they moved files from one desk to another or brought another cup of sweet and milky tea. The temptation was to do nothing except what Lord Curzon had done, to write a minute answering another minute and to file it away to be unread until the hereafter. If there was work to be done, the clerks or the subordinates would always do it for one, and if they did it wrong, one could disclaim them. A velvet tongue and a sharp ear were the only qualifications necessary for keeping the position. Intelligence was a desk-bound affair.

So it was with anticipation rather than disdain that Douglas Jardine waited for Seaforth to come and see him. It was bold enough. The Eurasian doctor wanted to survey his surveyor. It was the case of the goat hunting the tiger. But arrogance was written all over the file which was already being kept on Seaforth. And the file was not wrong. The bounce in Seaforth's walk into the Intelligence officer's room was almost impertinent. But courtesy was always the best concealment. Douglas Jardine rose from his office chair to greet his wife's cousin.

"Dr Sinclair," he said. "It is good of you to want to come and see me. Do be seated."

"Thank you." Seaforth sat. His skin had been burned dark in the sun, which framed the intensity of his eyes as sparks glow in anthracite. "Better come and see you, Mr Jardine, than wait for you to come and see me."

"How is the hospital at Lahore? It is near one of our largest cantonments. Do military manoeuvres really interest you?"

"Oh, I am not a spy." Seaforth smiled. "I leave that to British Intelligence, whoever they may be." So Seaforth showed his knowledge to Jardine, who knew that the doctor knew he was not just in the Indian Civil Service. "I cure the sick. I am not interested in boots, boots, boots, boots, marching up and down again. Or where they are marching."

"Knowing you were coming, Dr Sinclair, I hoped you might return with me to see the family. My wife Margaret and daughter are with me, although my son Wallace has left us to go to Cambridge – much brighter than his father, I can tell you." Jardine gave a self-deprecating smile of total pride. "You did come back to India to see the family again, did you not?"

"It was one of my intentions. I will bring my wife, if I may?"

"The famous Miriam Apfelstein. What do they call her? The Red Rand Robin."

"No, no." Seaforth smiled again. "The Boer Bolshevik. Only my wife's family, as you know, is Jewish."

"They would hardly approve of your marriage . . ." Jardine's words were both a statement and a question, for this was a meeting and not an interrogation. "But you might have *converted* . . ."

Again Seaforth smiled.

"Convert from what? I am not a good Hindu. And I would be a worse Jew. We are both, you may say, free-thinkers."

"Socialists and anarchists and free-thinkers . . ."

"To be short – yes, no, yes. There's not a law against it."

"No, not if you are not against the law."

"Your law?"

"Our law."

"Shall we say," Seaforth said, "how highly I regard your code of medical practice?"

"And our law?"

"Your law for the rich? Or your law for the poor?"

"There is only one law."

"Two," Seaforth said. "Ask the rich, ask the poor. You will have different answers."

"Don't you think, Dr Sinclair, that doctors are best as doctors. Your *medical* opinion I would value . . ."

"And I your intelligence?" Seaforth shook his head, then stared at Jardine. "Let's get down to it. You don't want me back in India. I may be a trouble-maker. What are you going to do about it? If you try to intern my wife or me – like those vile concentration camps I saw in South Africa –"

"Why should we? For what cause?" Jardine was almost honeyed in his tone. The doctor seemed frightened. He might break easily. "We do not intern people here. Unless they threaten the state."

"You know – we make no secret of it – we hate imperialism. We want Home Rule for India, like you are giving the poor Irish at last."

"Freedom of speech –" Jardine swung his swivel chair to one side and slowly crossed his legs, fastidiously pulling the crease of his trousers to one side. "It is a principle of the law here. You may say what you wish and you may think what you like. But do not say it so as to cause a disturbance."

"Or incite a Mutiny."

"No, not another Mutiny." Jardine gave his broad fatherly smile to Seaforth. "You know the law. You are intelligent – and *almost* one of the family. You are a cousin of my wife. I do not have to tell you. You *know* – and I am sure that your wife knows – even with her rich and radical connections –"

"Don't spy on us," Seaforth said. "Don't bother us. I am telling you. My wife does have rich and radical connections."

"Oh, yes, the Jews – they *are* meant to run the world." Jardine yawned and hardly bothered to hide his pretence of boredom with his hand. "But I simply don't believe it. The Jews are really quite an insignificant and dispersed people with only a minor talent for making money."

"Christ was hardly a financier."

"Not that, *please*. How odd of God to choose the Jews. And odder far that Christians choose a Jewish God and abuse the Jews. One has heard that before."

"You have heard it all before." Seaforth rose from his chair. "We will not come and meet your family just yet. We must get on with our work."

"I *am* sorry." Jardine also rose. "Margaret will be *desolated* not to see you. She longs to meet Mrs Sinclair. But what work is it exactly that you must get on with?"

"The hospital. Medical work."

"And your wife?"

"As you say, her politics are her own affair. Unless you interfere with her."

"As a gentleman, could I?" Jardine walked round the desk to usher Seaforth out. The *punkah* now swished as regularly as the strokes of a cane on flesh. "It was good of you to bother to come and see me. We shall meet again . . ."

"In different circumstances," Seaforth said.

"I have no doubt."

The way the Great Game ended was hardly great and not a game. Fearing that the Russians were taking over Tibet and threatening India across the Himalayas – if trying to traverse those celestial mountains could be called a threat rather than a folly on ice – Colonel Francis Younghusband led a thousand Gurkhas and Sikhs, four thousand yaks, seven thousand mules and ten thousand porters into the snows of the uplands. The Dalai Lama decided to resist. From Lhasa he sent a band of warrior monks in orange robes and fifteen hundred troops with matchlock guns and sacred charms, each one sealed by His Holiness Himself to make the wearers bullet-proof. Quite kindly the brigadier in command of the Indian Forces, James Macdonald surrounded the Tibetans with his men. And shortly, the only person who spoke their language, Captain O'Connor, told the monks and the local warriors to lay down their museum pieces. But the head monk had a revolver, which he drew from his robes and used to shoot off the jaw of a Sikh. Four minutes later, seven hundred Tibetans were dead or dying.

"A terrible and ghastly business," Younghusband told Iain Sinclair on his way home through Simla. "We shot down monks with machine-guns as they were *walking* away. And there was a Tibetan who lost both legs and laughed with our doctors and said, 'Next time I will have to be a hero, because I can no longer run away.'"

"And did you find the Russians in Lhasa?" Iain asked. Then he had to catch his breath before he could continue. He was very short of wind now. "Were they there?"

"No," Younghusband said. "They are all being killed by the Japs in Manchuria. Who would have thought it? Europeans being beaten by yellow-bellies."

"The Ivans are bonny fighters," Iain said. "Dinna I know it? That Crimea – they gave us a hard time of it."

"I had forgotten, Mr Sinclair – you were there."

"I am that old," Iain said and laughed. "But the Ivans, they had the worst generals in all the world. Did I not hear their navy shelled our fishing boats in the English Channel, thinking it was the Japs come all the way from Japan with their torpedo boats?"

"I have heard that," Younghusband said. "But as you know, I have been away from home over the Himalayas. I was sorry to hear about Anna."

"We must all come to an end," Iain said. "Hers was merciful. But I canna do without her." He felt tears prickle at the corners of his eyes and blinked furiously. No self-pity now. "I willna be aye here myself at Annandale."

"You must," Younghusband said. "You and your Gurkhas, you have been our eyes and ears for forty years and more on what is happening over the Himalayas."

"Old soldiers never die, they say," Iain said. "But they do, and they do not fade away." He wheezed and had to suck air into his lungs in order to continue. "They run out of steam."

"You're not an old engine –"

"I am. I need coal to stoke me up."

"As coal goes," Younghusband said, contemplating the brown spirit that trapped the candle-flames like yellow lilies in his clear glass, "it's good stuff. How do you get good malt here?"

"Whisky travels." Iain drained his own glass. "Whisky and Scotsmen, they travel well."

"And age well. But there are very few of you left in your own country. Thank you, I'll help myself. And you." Younghusband leaned forward and found the decanter and filled both of their glasses again. "Here's to you and Scotland and all you've done for us."

Iain did not drink again. Something was worrying him.

"You said it was a Macdonald, the one that had those poor Tibetan folk killit. You canna trust a Macdonald."

"Now the clans are talking. If you had ever got together against the English – instead of killing each other – you would have beaten us instead of fighting yourselves and then having to fight for us."

"Aye, that's a fact." Iain did drink to that, and then he said, "Younghusband, will there be no more fighting here? Will we be having peace with the Ivans?"

"Yes," Younghusband said. "The Japs will beat them, and then they will make peace with us. In Persia, in the Himalayas, in China. In the end, you know, it will be Europe – the white races – fighting Asia, the Yellow Peril. And there are many more of them – India and China, hundreds of millions of them – they can swamp us. Now the Japs have won and proved they can beat us."

"We shall lose this? Annandale?" Again Iain paused to breathe, as rackety as a cog-wheel missing some teeth. "Aye, the Indians shall have it back one day. My niece Peg, she said that. So she shall have the emerald. As a pledge."

"What emerald?"

"Anna's. I had it at the siege of Lucknow. When we buried her –" Now Iain was fighting for breath, for his throat was thick with feeling. "Only my daughter Margaret came. And her daughter Ruby. The others were *occupied*. They askit me, Iain, the emerald ring, can we have it the now? And I said –" Iain coughed and coughed into his hand. The spasm seemed to ease his lungs. "Not yet, I said. Not till I am gone."

"You will be with us," Younghusband said, "always. India needs you."

"Ach, get away with you." Iain laughed. "India dinna need us. Those mountains –" He nodded at the window panes. Beyond them the crags of the white and indigo Himalayas were piebald in the night. "They were there for aye. They will be there for aye. When we are come and when we are gone." He breathed in, the slow pistons of his lungs still just in trim. "This talk – this Home Rule – this independence for India –" Again the slow chug of his search for breath. "My brother's boy and girl – wrong side of the blanket – their country, they will have it of us –" A gasp and a sigh and a slow filling with air. "But they . . . they are no more than we were –" A long pause, a silence. Then Iain said in a loud voice, "Stronger than us – and them – the strength of the hills."

Younghusband put down his glass and rose and went over to the window to look out into the night and the striped slopes of snow crevasse and pitchblende rock.

"I do not know how we passed those mountains in winter, Sinclair. We killed poor people, we reached Lhasa, we found little, we achieved nothing, we returned. And Tibet is independent again under the Dalai Lama. And he will persist, for there is always another Dalai Lama. Almost as eternal as the Himalayas."

"We do nothing," the old man's voice said behind Younghusband. "And we are right proud of what we do."

Younghusband turned his back on the ambiguous barrier to the north, where nothing was ever done by man.

"We do what we can do," he said. "And we are not the judge of what we did. Another . . ."

His voice trailed away into the deeps of the night.

15

A VOICE WITHIN

Bain found himself talking to Julia's grave. There was never an answer, but he talked to comfort himself. "Three years of the drought," he said to the tombstone. "Like the plagues of Egypt. But it canna be a judgement. Look, there's no flowers to your grave – and it is the first time I have put no flowers to your grave. But there is not a one here the now, they are withered with the grass. You ken, Julia, the bones – they are showing through the dust before it blows away. The bones of all the buffaloes we killed when we first come here. A prairie of bones all the way to the mountains, and the dust blowing through the wire . . ."

So Bain would talk to himself, squatting by the headstone to his wife. He told her of Robert, so far away in Africa and transferring to the Gold Coast and the jungles, he would not like it there, the malaria and the blackwater fever would have him. And his wife running off with Hamish Charles, who might have murdered his own wife. Blood was blood and kin was kin, but if his brother Angus had to marry a woman from Peru, he could not count on all his bairns being right, they would have the Spanish and perhaps the Indian in them, which Hamish Charles did, and that was why he was what he was. And as for their son Gillon, well, he had stayed on the farm, but there was no living on the dry land any more. Gillon got three bairns quick from his wife Rachel. She had the hips for it, but there again, perhaps not the blood for it, her family coming from Russia, Jewish peasants driven out by a *pogrom*, the Cossacks beating them with whips and firing their houses. But Leah and Fiona and Colin, they were fine wee ones, and the family would go on. That was surely the point of it. But they could not all go on here. The land would not stand it.

Bain never thought that Julia would answer him. And when he heard her voice, he knew it was inside his own head. But the voice was so real, it was herself speaking. He was not speaking to himself, it was the wife he had lost who was talking to him and saying, "Bear up, Bain. The drought will end. The rain will come, because the Lord

God will not forget you. Only bear up. It is your land and the only land that will ever be your land. Do you not run away over the Rocky Mountains."

Hearing her with his eyes closed and her repeating to him so close and clearly, Bain almost expected to see her dear self when he opened his lids, but all he saw was the tomb with her name, JULIA SINCLAIR – BELOVED – REST IN PEACE. Even then, at her dying, the farm could not pay good dollars for more letters from the mason to be writ on her stone.

"Gillon himself says we canna bide here. The land will not feed us. The mortgage for the machines and the wire is not paid. The bank will foreclose. He says we must away over that McDowell's Canadian Pacific Railway to the house in Vancouver, where Kate is, and where we have room. And we must sell the land and start again. But I canna start again. It is the end for me, Julia. With Iain gone the now in India, I am near the last of my brothers and sisters – the last of them, but for Angus and Kate. And the last of our land, it will be going with the last of me."

A wind blew up over the dry plain and dust beat at the stubble on Bain's face, peppering his unshaven cheeks with the buckshot of the dirt. And he could no longer hear his wife's voice inside his head for all the noise of the powdered earth blowing into his face. So he cupped his palms over his nose and waited to hear Julia speak her final words to him. For he had to know what she must do.

"Go, if you must," she said within his mind. "Go, but do not sell all of the land. Our son will come back, or our son's son. For God will provide – if not for us, then He will provide for them. And they will return. Our land, Bain, my beloved. Our land."

The wind had been banging at the shutters on the farmhouse, crick – crack – crash, and Rachel was looking from the door to see that her father-in-law was coming home from his wife's grave before the hot blast that would surely follow that day. And she saw him bent against the force of the air, but smiling as he walked towards her. And he said, to her surprise and her relief, as he passed her to join the children in the farmhouse, "We will be going to Vancouver, Rachel. But Julia says, we will keep the land." And Rachel knew that his old wife was long dead, but if she still gave such good advice from beyond the grave, long let her live in him.

They had hardly been in London. Virginia could not believe it. She had spent most of her life and her feelings on getting back to the artists in Piccadilly and Chelsea, and she had no sooner arrived back in England, when they were shipped off again to Vancouver. They had no money, that was the secret of existence. If you had no money, you had to do what your paymaster said. And her rich father-in-law Angus had insisted that they go to the family home in Vancouver to wait, until a post was arranged for Hamish Charles in the Far East. Angus now had his connections there. Yet however grand the connections of Angus were, they always seemed to be in the most godforsaken places. If Angus was your bankroll, you were rolled out of the way, as far as he could send you.

"There's nothing wrong with Vancouver," Virginia told Kate. "But you have lived so long here, only you know what is right."

Kate laughed and said, "Even if mother and father died here, it is not our house. As far as I reckon it, it's a stopover between Bob's trains."

And Bob McDowell did come and go according to the timetables on the Canadian Pacific Railway. So assiduous was he in his duties, he might almost have had a timepiece ticking in his head. But he was approaching retirement. And there was no way that he would give the Company any excuse to lay him off before his pension. He did more than live from the rule book, he breathed it, he ate and drank it, and he would only quit on the due observance of it.

"We are putting you out," Virginia said. "We must be most unwelcome guests. All *five* of us – and . . ." She looked down with horror at the swelling beneath her own loose blouse. "Another one on the way." That had been the consequence of her marriage to Hamish Charles in London, after her divorce. She would never admit it was the cause. "I am sure it will be a girl and if she is – as she will be – I shall call her Clio. After the Muse."

"That's not a Sinclair name," Kate said. "Italian, is it?"

"Ancient Greek. Classical."

"It is not right for a girl," Kate said. "But if you and Hamish wish it –"

"I do. So he does."

"You rule the roost."

"No," Virginia said. "I do *not*. Do you think I would choose to *roost* here?"

"You're very welcome," Kate said. "It's good to have children round the house."

"Step-children."

"Children, for all that. They are good little ones. But how will you manage them, now you will have one of your own?"

"Not very well," Virginia said. "To tell you the truth, I am not *domestic*. Primitive – I favour the primitive. More Lapsang Suchong, if you please." She held out her porcelain teacup with the blue dragons

149

on it towards Kate. "You are so kind to get me China tea. It must be difficult . . ."

Kate filled the cup.

"Not at all. We face the Orient. Two lumps?" At Virginia's nod, she dropped the sugar cubes with silver tongs. "And will you really be going to that plantation in the cannibal islands? My nephew knows nothing about it. Growing copra – it sounds like a snake-farm."

"Cobra, you mean," Virginia said. "And needs must. For it is Angus who insists. He says there is no other job available for his son. Well, Hamish did not know how to farm in Africa. So it will be no handicap that he does not know how to farm in the Pacific."

"Some say it is paradise in the South Seas. Do you read our Scotsman – Robert Louis Stevenson?"

"Paradise for me," Virginia said, "is not a coconut palm on a deserted beach. It is a street lamp in Regent's Street. I look for London, and I am in exile."

"You will find work to do there," Kate said, "helping your man."

Virginia stirred her cup of tea, dissolving the last residues of the sugar-lumps with her silver spoon.

"Men help themselves," she said. "Very rarely do they help women."

"You sound like my daughter Marie," Kate said. "She is quite for the women now. Votes – and she will not let the men stop her."

"I did not meet her in the brief time I was allowed in London. I regretted it. But when my penance in paradise is over . . ."

"Ach, stay here," Kate said. "And I will show you Vancouver is a finer city than your old London. That is in the future, that is."

And Kate might have showed Virginia just that, only she did not have the chance. For her brother Bain arrived, and Gillon and Rachel and three more little children, so that the old house was bursting at the seams, and the sound of half-a-dozen tots squealing and squalling together fair drove everybody to distraction. Kate loved it. An old woman now, and suddenly to be mother to these six wee things, thinking she was the be-all and end-all of everything, because their mother and their stepmother could not really cope – that was a satisfaction, and Kate had waited long for the moment, while pretending it was too much for her, too. And, of course, it was also the future of the family.

The men in their usual silly way thought that they were providing for the future of the family. As if their talk raised a single child or solved a single problem. But Gillon was set on never going back to the plough and the bad soil, while Bain his father was too sick and ailing to leave his room and answer back. So there was only her

husband Bob to speak for the railways, when the timetables let him
rest – and handsome Hamish Charles, who knew a very great deal
about everything and nothing worth saying about anything at all. The
three of them had retired to the parlour with a bottle of malt whisky,
which men said was a medicine as well as a stimulant, and women
knew to be a blaze of foolishness as well as a black tongue.

"You do reckon, Mr McDowell," Gillon said, for Bob was a stickler
for the right title, "your trains wouldn't run on time bar the Morse
Code. It runs a sight faster than your locomotives and waggons."

"There is a use in it," Bob said, playing with the chain on his
hunter that spread over his dark waistcoat like the Milky Way over
the bulge of the night sky. "But it is for buying tickets, meeting
goods. The trains ran before the Morse Code, and they will run after
it."

"But I saw a cinematograph –" Hamish Charles said.

Bob McDowell glared at him.

"You do not attend those *arcades* – those penny arcades –?"

"It is a wonderful invention, the cinematograph –"

"Dumb illusions. What is the film of a train running into a station
compared with a train running into a station? The first – trumpery.
The second – majesty."

"The film was called *The Great Train Robbery*. And the Morse Code
. . . the operator at the station, he gave away the robbers. They were
caught because of him."

"So, your cinematograph, it is the tinkle of a warning bell. A police-
man's whistle. Child's play – and I would not bother to see it."

"Maybe," Gillon said. "But I guess there's a future in it. That
wireless. What do you think, Hamish? You were in London. What
do they say over there?"

"There's a Mr Marconi –"

"Sells spaghetti, does he?" Bob McDowell laughed. "Pasta
vendor."

"Radio waves, that's what he calls them. He has them on the ships.
They may talk to the shores from the seas. Now they want the radio
waves all over the British Empire. It's one of the biggest things in
London. Cousin Hamilton, he's in it."

"He's in the navy," Gillon said.

"He has left it," Hamish Charles said. "He is not interested in
ship's engines. He talks of air engines. And wireless. He has met
two brothers called Short. There is something – seaplanes for the
navy. Seaplanes that will fly the Channel. There is a Frenchie called
Blériot. He says he will *sail* across on his wood struts and canvas
wings."

Bob McDowell could not contain his laughter. His breaths made the top of his malt whisky seethe and bubble.

"They'll run like trains, will they?" he said. "In air? Seaplanes. Only a bloody gull can do that."

"I believe you, thousands wouldn't," Gillon said. "Do you have Hamilton's address?"

"Of course. I'll find it."

"Will he help? A cousin? A Canadian cousin?"

"Yes, I'll see he does." Hamish Charles was embarrassed. "After you have been so decent – I mean about me and your brother's wife . . . I mean, you could have taken his side –"

"I don't reckon I know what happened. That's between you and Robert. And Virginia. Well, lucky for some . . ."

"What do you mean?"

"Lucky for you," Gillon said, smiling. "You're some man."

And Hamish Charles did not quite know how to take the remark, but he had never understood the local idiom. And it was as well that they were going off to Polynesia soon, where this damned plantation might be. For Virginia was getting sick and tetchy with her baby on the way, and he could not stand the racket of all the toddlers in the old house, his own three and Cousin Gillon's brood. It was touch and go, really, whether Virginia gave birth or Uncle Bain expired or he himself went mad from the stupidity of trying to be a family man, which he was not cut out to be – or the clipper came in on time. Fortunately it did, and it carried him away with his second wife and four children including an infant called Clio, while he left an uncle breathing his very last behind on the Canadian shore, never to be seen again.

If there was a civilising mission to clean up the world, copra was certainly a means to do it. Sending the coolies or the blackbirds up the thin trunks of the palm-trees like monkeys on sticks, dodging the fall of the clumps of coconuts crashing down in green cannonballs after their hacking on high, cutting them open to extract the kernel, drying it in the sun, then grinding out the oil to use in soap for million on million of pale skins. Whale blubber and animal fat had been used, but vegetable oil was better to soften and make supple the fairest of the fair. Naturally, working conditions were hard, and Hamish Charles could never have exploited his imported Indian and Chinese and his kidnapped Solomon Islanders as Bulberry did, a sweating hulk of an overseer, who drove on the work gangs in between hangovers and bouts of fever. When he heard the screams of the workers after Bulberry's assaults with truncheon and cat-o'-nine-tails made from strips of sting-ray skin, Hamish Charles always walked the other way, preferring to ignore what he could not stomach. He knew there was no other way to treat the labourers and get the work done. But it was not a way he chose to see.

Virginia kept to the house by the sea, except for long expeditions into the interior, when Hamish Charles sent four armed house-boys with her. She was making a collection of devil-masks and totems and carved sacred paddles and prows. To her husband, it was all primitive junk, but it was art to her. And one evening she returned with carved and painted doorposts, rather like the gargoyles on medieval cathedrals. Indeed, they were made by a European, she said, who called himself an artist, and who had gone native. Gauguin was the name. But his woodwork and daubing seemed to Hamish Charles even inferior to the products of the pagan natives. Art was the opposite of the savage and the wild. If it was not, there was no point in being in this hell of a paradise. All the soap from all the copra in the world would not scrub out one more cruelty of the white race to lesser breeds.

Virginia was on another collecting expedition when Chung killed Bulberry. Hamish Charles had not noticed the Chinaman among the others. Not that all yellow faces were the same to him, but he flinched from their looks at him, their passive resentment and loathing. So he had not noticed Chung's long and hangdog look or his stooped height. But when the guards brought the man to the big house, his body red with his victim's blood, also flayed and bruised by terrible beatings, and his hands bound behind his back, Hamish Charles saw a fierce and haughty culprit, who stared at him in judgement and contempt.

"He killed Bulberry?" Hamish Charles asked. "How?"

"Boss Bulberry beat him many time," the head guard said. "Look. No skin Chung. Then Chung catch whip. He kick Boss here." The guard kicked up one leg high and tapped a weal on the side of Chung's neck. "Bone break. Boss fall. He dead. Chung here."

"Did you do it, Chung?" Hamish Charles could hardly bear to look at the prisoner, who was staring so intensely at him. "Translate. Ask him if he confesses he killed Bulberry."

The head guard spoke in Chinese to Chung, who nodded. Then he answered rapidly, darting sidelong glances at Hamish Charles, as if he were referring to his master. The head guard shook his head, refusing to translate what he had heard. But Chung's voice became angry. He pointed at Hamish Charles, accusing him and forcing him to insist to the guard, "Tell me what Chung is saying. Tell me. Translate."

The head guard hung his head.

"Is no good. He say name Chung Sin Chu. He say same name you. He say Sin Chu him *maman* Peking by and by. No good."

Hamish Charles looked at the long face of the Chinaman, pale with loss of blood and fear. Yes, it was possible. Certainly, he had the large nose and frame, the drawn features of the Sinclairs, but with narrow Chinese eyes. And Uncle Hamish Jamie had been at the sack of Peking. And he had had two children by an Indian woman. Why not by a Chinese woman, too? But it was impossible, because it was intolerable. To admit to a relationship with a coolie, who had just killed the overseer, merely on a delusion that a name was somewhat the same. As if he had not had enough scandal with his marriage to Virginia. He could not condemn her and the four children to more shame on a claim on the family guilt.

"No good," Hamish Charles said to the head guard. "He lies. He lies to get off. Take him to prison. Tell him if he repeats his lie or his false name, Sin Chu, to the judge, he will certainly be executed. Tell him, he lies. I know he lies."

When Chung heard what Hamish Charles had said, he crouched as if to spring, but was caught by his bleeding arms by the guards and dragged away. The last that Hamish Charles saw of him was a grimace of such bitterness and despair that it wrenched his master's conscience. Hamish Charles wanted to absolve himself and tell Virginia, but he did not. He could not confess to her another cause for dirt to be flung at them. They had hidden the news of the killing of Lizzie and the divorce of Robert from the other Europeans on the island; but they lived in daily worry of being identified by some sea captain, sailing round from South Africa and knowing their story.

"Truth will out." Hamish Charles had learned the phrase from his Aunt Mary before she had died. He had denied it, but he believed it secretly. Everything was always known in the end. But for the moment, to admit to a false kinship with the Chinese murderer of a white man . . . They would have to flee again. No island would be remote enough to take them in.

So all that he said to Virginia on her return was, "A terrible thing. Bulberry was killed by a coolie. He is mad. Raving. He does not know what he is saying."

"Anyway, you wouldn't understand it," Virginia said. "You do not speak Chinese."

"I do not understand him," her husband said, "killing Bulberry."

"I would kill him. If he beat me like he does them. But look –" She unrolled a canvas and held up the picture for Hamish Charles to see. Two yellow women in red and purple skirts lay in front of green mangoes and yellow gourds. "Another Gauguin. A painting this time. Do you like it?"

"It's ghastly," her husband said. "How can he paint such subjects . . . so sloppily?"

"I'll keep it," Virginia said. "You see, it will make us rich."

"That's rich." Hamish Charles laughed at the absurdity. "Only copra will. And that is a rotten way to make money."

16

WITH WINGS

"We are Official Aeronautic Engineers to the Royal Aero Club," Oswald Short said in 1913 to Hamilton, "but we started in balloons. We used to supply them to the Balloon Company of the Royal Engineers for observation work. But then with the Green engine and the Sunbeam and the Rolls – all those automobile engines – why, air *ships* did not seem the big thing, but aeroplanes."

"And seaplanes," Hamilton said. "I am sure you will go to that."

"Yes, yes." The stocky businessman smiled at his new recruit. "I see you are still a naval engineer at heart. You want flying *boats*. But the fact is, the navy is far more interested in our aeroplanes than the army is. Ever since we won that *Daily Mail* prize for an all-British flying machine that could cover a closed circuit."

"That is what brought me to you," Hamilton said. "I am sure the future of the navy lies in the air."

The aircraft manufacturer laughed.

"That's a contradiction in terms," he said. "Navies are for seas. But you are right – the seaplane will be their salvation. Spotting enemy fleets –"

"Bombing," Hamilton said. "And why not aerial torpedoes?"

"Steady on. We don't even have seaplanes yet."

But Hamilton was soon set to work on the design of them. They were based on the Short biplane with a Gnome engine, basically a training machine with tandem seats, the pilot in front. Hamilton put two long pontoons into water-tight compartments under the wings with subsidiary floats at the tips, and he added a small float on the tail with a rudder to steer by while taking off from water. At first, there was not enough power to lift off the seaplane, so a twelve-cylinder 275 hp Sunbeam-Coatalen "Maori" engine had to be installed. But if there was a swell running, let alone a choppy sea or small waves, the seaplane would tip up before taking off. A dead calm was necessary for success, and that was rare enough at Calshot on the Solent, where

Hamilton supervised the trials for the first pilots of the Naval Wing of the Royal Flying Corps.

It was there that Hamilton had the first of his two revolutionary ideas. And they were so simple. "Wheels and floats," he told Oswald Short. "Then it can fly off a ship and land in the sea."

"Fly off a ship?" Short was amused. "What do you think the navy's coming to? A sort of aircraft carrier?"

"Exactly," Hamilton said. "That's the right word. An aircraft carrier. They have your old balloons on board some ships already – blimps for spotting. Why not seaplanes or flying-boats? If you had a ship with a flat top – the funnels projecting out of the side or an elevated top deck – then your aeroplane with wheels and floats could take off the deck and land in the sea."

"Can you really see the admiralty slicing the superstructure off a battleship and making it into an iron airstrip?"

"Seaplanes could even land on deck, if there was a net to catch them in."

"Steady on, Hamilton. That's going too far. First, think how long your aircraft carrier would have to be to allow for a take-off –"

"Catapult them, if necessary. Or steam into the wind."

Oswald Short laughed again.

"Now, really. So you shoot the aircraft off and catch them in a net to get them back. Why the floats?"

"Because you could use a crane to lower them into the sea and retrieve them after they landed in the sea."

"Wings. What are you going to do about the wings? They are far too long for lowering and storage."

And here Hamilton had his second inspiration, which came to him out of the blue.

"Fold them," he said. "Like a bird or a butterfly. Fold the wings."

"I don't believe it. Wings on hinges? They have to be fixed. You can't have folding wings and a stable aeroplane."

"Let me try," Hamilton said. "And then there will really be a Royal Naval Flying Corps."

He was living with Ellen-Maeve and their two children, Hamish Henry and Titania, in a curious edifice known as Luttrell's Tower, only a mile away from the base at Calshot, where hangars in dazzle camouflage now surrounded the castle, built by King Henry the Eighth as a defence against the French. The tower was six storeys high and had smugglers' caves beneath for the storage of illicit brandy and silks tax-free from over the Channel. It was a children's paradise, a pebble beach beneath the sea-gate, and gardens leading to the big house inland. It was also nearly grand enough for Ellen-Maeve, whose social aspirations were as lofty as the folly she lived in. When Hamilton joked that he was in the right profession now, his seaplanes would take them higher and higher, his wife failed to see the point.

"On your pay," she said, "we will always remain at the bottom of the heap. And this place, those winding stone stairs – it is not even a country house, and certainly not a stately home."

"But think of the man who had it before us." Hamilton looked out of the window of the high octagonal drawing-room across the dark Solent towards the lamp-lights of Ryde on the Isle of Wight. "Marconi himself. He did his wireless experiments from here, flying his wires from kites."

"Marconi? Isn't there some big government contract with his company? Are they not going to base telegraph stations all across the Empire?"

Hamilton had to admit Ellen-Maeve was always very well informed, although he never knew where she got the information, as she was at home most of the time with the children. But he said, "Yes, you are right, naval communications will be very important. But do you know, Ellen-Maeve, Marconi could communicate with old Queen Victoria Herself at Osborne in the Isle of Wight from this tower? And his family saw from this window the *Titanic* sail out. Look – " And, indeed, through the window he could see the lighted floating palace of another transatlantic liner – "And when the *Titanic* hit the iceberg, it was his wireless on board tapping SOS which saved some of the passengers. He would have been on the *Titanic*, but he decided to leave by an earlier ship so that he could greet the *Titanic* on her arrival in New York. Only, she didn't sail in. She sank. You know, stewards on liners, they always give the toast, 'Bottoms up,' every time a ship passes over where the *Titanic* went down last year."

"Don't be morbid," Ellen-Maeve said. "And don't say *Titanic* so often. It's unlucky. It's so like the name of our darling little Titania. And I don't want her to go down with anything else."

Both of the children had chicken-pox. And that was after mumps and measles and whooping-cough with scarlet fever still to come.

"Childhood," Hamilton said to his wife, "does seem to be one disease after another."

"They have to have them," Ellen-Maeve said. "It makes them immune later. Anyway, nanny's had them all, and you have, and I have. So we won't get it. But their being sick is sickening! We never go to London, even when Marie asks us."

"I thought she was in Scotland. Did she not have to avoid the previous King's attentions? But he's dead and gone now, I agree."

"Oh, that's all over." Ellen-Maeve came to stand beside her husband, her yellow curls no higher than his shoulder. "She is very active now. Votes for women. And socialism, I hear. And the new labour unions. I do not think that is very feminine."

"But you are." Hamilton put his hand on top of his wife's head. He gently felt her hair with his fingers, and she did not protest. "Some of the family are coming down here. Murdo, Uncle Angus's boy – the one we met at Lords, playing cricket. He wants to be a pilot. And so I've pulled a few strings with Murray Sueter, the airship man at the admiralty. Murdo will be one of the first air seamen."

"He was a nice boy," Ellen-Maeve said. "But please stop messing my hair." She put her hand up to take away her husband's hand from her curls. The lights of the liner were distant now on the dark channel. "He introduced us to Alex Plunkett-Drax. Who is being beastly to Murdo's sister. And didn't Ruth Seymour-Scudabright have to come back very *suddenly* from staying with them in Ireland? There was *talk* –"

"There is always talk," Hamilton said, "when two women get together. And more talk, if the subject is another young woman."

"You used to like to talk to *me*. Now all I hear about is your beastly engines and flaps and floats."

"I will take you up in a seaplane one fine day, Ellen-Maeve. And then you will see that it is all worth it."

"You will never do that. I will never fly."

"You will." Hamilton put his arm round his wife's shoulder as she was too tiny for him to encircle her waist. "Flying – it will soon be as natural as breathing. Mark my words."

"Gamma minus. Bottom of the class."

"Flying. We will all have wings."

The extremes of the different lives which she lived in London stretched Marie to the brink of breakdown. Other women seemed to cope with the abyss between what they said and how well they lived. Perhaps society was immutable and could not be avoided. So it was better to accept and not resist, to live in luxury and think like a seamstress in a sweatshop. As a girl, Marie had been poor. As an actress, she had worked hard. Even now, she paced her appetite and kept her body lean. But there were other actresses among the aristocrats – and other North Americans. The waspish and chinless pecking parrot, Maud Cunard, the willowy and witty Consuelo Marlborough, the devastating Nancy Astor. But with their socialist friends like George Bernard Shaw or the leaders of the rising Labour Party, Keir Hardie and Ramsay MacDonald, they would praise Marx and pass round the port. Their lip service to the poor did not affect the banquets made by their servants. They digested more treats than social change.

Yet Marie did agree to go with her husband to the most terrifying dinner party of her life. They were estranged now, almost separated. She went her way and had her flings with the vital people she knew like Keir McBride, the miners' leader at Dunesk. And her husband Bill certainly went his own way with his male friends, who claimed to be making a new world by reviving the gothic and the flamboyant, a sort of pretty gloss on the slums and the black truth of the time. Where Marie saw squalor and degradation, Bill saw a beautiful veil drawn over the harsh facts. They stayed together, opposed in mind, divorced in body, for the sake of Rosabelle and what was called society.

Yet they had come together for a dinner. "It is better than with the Asquiths in Downing Street," Marie's husband had quietly informed her. "There you have nothing but the Souls – and their repartee is greater than their aesthetic gifts. And you may walk through a green baize door directly into the Chancellor of the Exchequer in the next house, who is more rewarding, but less witty. So let us toddle along to Consuelo's in Belgravia. She was a supporter of your sainted Aunt Mary, you know, in the Boer War. She does good – and what is worse, she loves your votes for women."

It was an intimate dinner party, which seemed to Marie a show trial. Round the long table with oval ends, twelve people were ranged on their isolated hard chairs like witnesses in the box. Their role was to testify to their reputations and their intentions. The great hostesses were there and the *literati*, Shaw and Barrie, who alone looked wistful, as if Peter Pan had just flown out of the room. The butler moved round between the conversations, which died like shot birds between the serving of the seven courses and the four wines.

"Those who can, do," Shaw said, "and those who can't, eat." His red beard wagged as he masticated another forkful of game brawn.

"I thought you only ate greens," Maud Cunard said. "Peck, peck, peck, like an Irish hen."

"I eat what is put in front of me," Shaw said. "It is called hospitality. The Irish are good at it. The English often fail."

"Please don't think you are being force-fed," Consuelo Marlborough said. "Like our poor Emmeline in that dreadful gaol."

That started the real discussion, the feeding by force of the imprisoned suffragettes on hunger strike led by Mrs Pankhurst. "It was a dreadful business, the forcing of the rubber tube down the throat, the pouring of the gruel down the aperture, the saving of life by violence. Must anyone be made to stay alive, must women be denied their power to protest?"

"You can go too far." With horror Marie heard her husband's provocative drawl at the end of the table. "That deluded girl, who threw herself in front of the King's horse at the Derby – he might have won the race."

"She died, damn it," Nancy Astor said.

"He lost, bless her," Bill Dunesk said and smiled. "Only the bookies were happy. And as for chaining oneself to iron railings to make a protest to parliament, I don't think the fair sex has been worse off since that lady who was rescued by St George from the dragon was chained to the rock."

"And what do you reckon you mean by that?"

"Only that we men will give you dear ladies the vote, which you richly deserve, as long as you don't bully us into it. My dear Marie, for instance, has never picked up a tomahawk –" and seeing Marie's look of fury, her husband changed his words – "I mean, picked up an axe to defend her rights. She has them, anyway. She is free of me."

"She does not want her rights from you," Shaw said. "She wants them as her rights. For herself."

"Right." Bill Dunesk smiled to himself, appreciating his point. "Precisely right. But we do live in odd times, don't you think? Right's not quite the word for what's happening now. Your lady friend, Dr Stopes, and all this *contraception* –"

"Personally," Marie intervened, looking hard at her husband, "I believe nature should take its course. Or not – if not."

The others laughed. Her estrangement from her husband, his style of life with his male friends, these were known in the small circle of metropolitan society, so small it often seemed like a hangman's noose.

"Nature," Barrie said softly, "is something we are given to rise above. If anyone says nature, I run out and mow the lawn."

"Darling Peter Pan," Bill Dunesk said. "And you never grew up, either."

"Who wants to?"

"Nobody."

The two men looked at each other in silent agreement.

"Women are rather more practical," Consuelo Marlborough said. "We do want our male babies to grow up. They become men, and they sometimes listen to their mothers – even Winston. And they may listen enough to give us the vote." She rang the bells. "We are eating duck and truffles, if you can stand it. English truffles. Somebody has trained a pig in the New Forest to find truffles, and these are they. Wonderful noses, pigs have. They're more use than just pork."

Over the main course, the conversation turned to falling standards. It was something which Marie had always noted. Things were always worse than they had been before. The older the guests and the speakers were, the better it had been in years gone by. Now the worry was not Russia, but the rise of Germany. The new King George the Fifth was a sailor and almost as stupid as the Danish Queen Mother, who still concentrated on keeping one of the smallest waists in London. Yet the fact of a blockhead on the throne need not be a disaster, if the Liberal government under Asquith could put through old age pensions and Irish Home Rule and income tax, some of the things that might drag Britain into the twentieth century.

"We want the future," Marie said. "But you all look at the past and regret it. Why, why, why?"

"Because we were born into it," her husband said. "Or some of us were. We did not just *arrive*."

There was a silence after his remark. Few men cut down their wives in public, and Dunesk was usually known for his subtle tongue. But Marie was writhing. She would have no more of it. She would not.

"When I arrived here," Nancy Astor said "– and I'm sure it goes for you, Consuelo – we didn't feel we were joining the old . . . other than our spouses, I mean." The women at the table smiled, the men looked down. "We were bringing in the new. Only it's taking a hell of a long time to arrive."

"We will retire," Consuelo Marlborough said. "And leave the gentlemen. As my husband is never here himself – he rarely arrives except to depart to his club, we are rather separate now – will you, Mr Barrie, preside and ask the other gentlemen to join the ladies in due course – if that is what they want to do?"

With the other women in the old bedrooms and bathrooms of the Belgravia mansion, Marie found another scene, a new world that was overcoming her life. She loved men, she was rejected by her husband, she even had the occasional dangerous moment with her miner in Lothian. But women were her friends. They would change society. Only they had the power to do it.

"I thought I was free," she told Consuelo Marlborough, "when I was a girl, riding an Indian pony on the prairie. And when I was an actress, I was free. But . . . I guess I didn't know. No woman was free. She had nothing for herself. But I didn't know. And now I do."

"Sweated women, Marie. Will you join me in that? Women working for nothing in factories. Prostituted labour. You will join me to end that?" The intensity of the duchess's face, her belief in her cause, almost made Marie feel that the other woman was a Keir Hardie, a social evangelist for her truth. But she was as much the wife of the man whom she had married as Marie was – the peeress in a silk gown, cosseted by servants. "You will help me?"

"But we live like this," Marie said. Her hands spread and drooped. "We are . . ."

"Hypocrites? I don't think so. If I was a Poor Clare, I could do little. Feed a few miserable people and pray for them. But we have the power to change the lives of millions of women –"

"That's why I married Bill Dunesk," Marie said. "I thought . . . with the power to change . . ."

"And what went wrong?"

"Living like we do – that changed me while I wanted to change things for others."

"Look, my dear." Consuelo Marlborough put her hand under Marie's chin, tilting her face into her blinding gaze. "You said, you did not know you were unfree. Your marriage, your life with us, it has educated you. Without riches, we do not have the time to learn. Without power, we can do nothing. Having this position, I mean to do rather well." She smiled and released Marie's cheeks from between her hands. "Privilege – it's only an opportunity to do better for other people."

"If I didn't feel so guilty about it," Marie said.

"Don't. Guilty is a word people use to do nothing, because they can excuse themselves." The duchess rose from where she was sitting on her great quilt of silk roses with the question, "Shall we join the gentlemen? They need us to tell them what to do."

"I am leaving Bill," Marie said abruptly. "I can't stand it. Even at dinner, he says things about me . . ."

"Stick it," the duchess said. "Like I do with my intolerable man. So we keep a bit of power to do what we want."

Marie Dunesk joined the Duchess of Marlborough's campaign for sweated women in the East End garment factories. She also went to Calshot to fly with her cousins Murdo and Hamilton in one of the new Short seaplanes.

"You are the first human duck which ever took off the waters," Hamilton told her. "Nobody will ever shoot *you* down. You have wings."

"Maybe," Marie said. "But there's a man who still reckons I am tied down."

"You?" Hamilton laughed. "You're a bird. You have always been free."

17

SWEATED WOMEN

She believed in it, but it had hardly ever happened to her. When Ruth intruded on her life, Marie had expected to be distant to her little cousin. But there was an immediate recognition between them. The girl was both defenceless and reckless, shy and fierce, stammering and pouring out her heart. She told Marie about her time with Alex Plunkett-Drax, her shame at his rape of her and also of his repulsive attraction. She had to leave Ireland and return to her home, but some gossip had reached her father, the member of parliament, Charles Seymour-Scudabright, or it had got to Alex's wife, her cousin Arabella, who had hinted at something in a letter. Anyway, the affair was now a common suspicion, if not knowledge. She had to run away. Could Marie house her and find her something to do?

Marie could and would, feeling in Ruth's need that she had found a sister soul in the crusade for exploited women. She had become fiercer in the struggle, raising money for the militants, visiting those who were put in gaol for disturbances of the peace. Yet she did not wish to compromise her husband. She was now separated from him, as Consuelo Marlborough was from her husband, the duke. But the parting of the ways and Bill Dunesk's coldness towards his wife had fuelled her fight for women. She was also involved, through the pits in Lothian, with the cause of the miners, who were striking at long last for higher pay and better conditions. There again, it was a personal involvement, this time with a man, the union leader Keir McBride. Their closeness in Scotland had turned her own daughter of thirteen, Rosabelle, back towards her father, especially as the child now looked like a pre-Raphaelite dream, her long red hair curling down to her waist from a pale oval face with heavy lids that drooped over green jade eyes. This fey beauty was the toast of her father and his friends, enthralled by the swirling designs from France and a new style. Rosabelle was also no sexual threat, as she was on the far verge of childhood and wanting never to grow up.

Ruth became a secretary to Consuelo Marlborough, who was organising a conference on sweated women, working seventy-hour weeks
to earn a few shillings. If she could set a social trap, the Liberal
government might do something about it. Lloyd George had forced
through a National Insurance Act, and the Conservative House of
Lords, fearful of the creation of hundreds of new peers, had not
thrown it out. But the anger on the Tory side ran high, and in no one
higher than in Charles Seymour-Scudabright, who stormed in one day
to her office in Sunderland House, where the conference was to be
held.

"You will come with me at once," he said. He was more corpulent
now and seemed to carry a cushion under his waistband, while his
cheeks were two red balloons, waiting to burst.

Ruth remained sitting. Her heart trembled, but her voice was firm.

"I shall stay here, Father, where I am."

"You are a disgrace to the family."

"Not to all of it."

"The Dunesks, if you mean them. They're in trouble."

"If you mean Marie – women's suffrage, sweated labour – the disgrace is that you do nothing about it."

"We are for England," her father said. "Its proper values. None of
these seedy share dealings, the corruption of the nation."

"Oh, the Marconi business. That is mere slander."

"The attorney-general – the postmaster-general – buying shares in
a company which is awarded a government contract. It's disgraceful.
And the head of the company is an Isaacs too, the attorney-general's
brother."

"Just because they are Jews, Father, you suspect foul play for
money. Like Mr Belloc. If they were good Catholics or Protestants –"

"They are degrading the ethics of the nation –"

"Which God sent the Conservatives to protect."

"You will wash your mouth out with mustard, young woman."

"I am too old for that. Calm down, Father. Anyway, what has it to
do with Marie?"

"Her husband, Dunesk, has been involved in the Marconi share
dealings. Through another of your disreputable cousins, Wallace –
Margaret's child from India – the one who left Cambridge to go into
the City. University, it never does anyone any good."

"Oh, brother Gordon survived it before the Grenadiers got him.
And brother Graham didn't need it before he started messing about
in boats."

"Hold your tongue, young lady. Both of your brothers are serving
their country. And the way the Kaiser is behaving, they may be most

necessary sooner than we think. But I don't know if we are worth saving. With a corrupt government . . ."

"It is not corrupt. Just because it cares for the poor and working people –"

"Its ministers buy shares in firms which profit from government contracts."

"But we need those wireless stations, don't we? For your blessed navy. In Egypt, East and South Africa, India and Singapore. Graham will be able to sail anywhere, and you will always know exactly where he is sinking."

"This is the last time I shall warn you, Ruth, to show some respect. I shall cut your allowance –"

"You haven't paid it in months."

"You may expect to inherit nothing."

"Good. If I inherited your politics –"

"You will give up working here immediately. I have just found you a job in a law firm."

"Do you think working for the Duchess of Marlborough is not respectable?"

"Her views are insupportable."

"But her character?"

"If a woman has wrong thoughts, her character is affected."

"But you will come to our grand occasion, Father. Look." Ruth added her father's name to the list on her desk. "I have put your name down with only the most distinguished people – bishops and law lords, half the peerage and *you*, the most influential of all the members of parliament. You are to come to Sunderland House –"

Her father paused. He was never one to refuse a glittering social occasion, which might advance him.

"For your sake, I may not say no. But what is it for?"

"Sweated women."

"Then I will not come. People who work for low wages choose to do so. It is what the market will bear." Her father smiled sourly down at his daughter. "And what does the duchess pay you? Enough for stockings?"

"A living wage," Ruth said. "So I don't have to depend on a man."

"You call your father a man?"

"No," Ruth said. "If he is not man enough to help sweated women."

Her father did not come to the conference, although most of the high and mighty did, believing it to be yet another charity event with strawberries and champagne at the fag-end of the Season. Instead, Consuelo Marlborough and Marie Dunesk produced twelve old women on a platform. Each told of decades of working for nothing, not the song of a shirt, but its requiem mass. One of them did unfold a real shirt she had made as if it were a white flag.

"A dozen of them, and I get ninepence. Last week me and my old man, we sat from five thirty in the morning till eleven at night – fourteen dozen shirts. And we got ten shillings less ten pence for cotton. A penny, that's the price of our dinner. Never more than a penny for twenty years."

There would be a trade board on the matter, a minister promised Consuelo, but Marie did not believe anything would happen because of that. "Sweated women," she said. "That's all we ever are, unless we marry out of it."

On the top of the stone tower that stood as a marker in the paddy-field, a brother and a sister were looking across the green rice-blades towards the blue ridges of the Himalayas. Seaforth had taken Peg out to the country to show her what he called the only triumph of the Raj, the great survey of India by Captain Everest.

"Triangles," he said. "He mapped our continent out in huge triangles. He started down at the tip in Cape Comorin, and then in base lines of seven-and-a-half miles, he plotted this continent all the way up to the north. And when the distance was too great to calculate on the ground, he built these stone towers we are sitting on. Just to get the measurements right to one inch in a mile. The thing is, Peg, what was he doing? Was it worth it?"

"*You* think so."

"I do. I don't know why. It is not there to see, but it is enduring."

"These stone towers are. We sit on them."

"Yes," Seaforth sighed. He stretched out an arm towards the mountains. "A grand illusion – like the British in India – which is ours and always will be. But it is a fiction like Mr Rudyard Kipling writes, even if these are monuments. Most of them will become target practice in time. But this one – absolutely useless – a tower in a paddy-field, it marks something marvellous. A madman with his instruments who correctly plotted the true length and breadth of India in giant triangles all the way to the Himalayas. You know, Peg, when he was paralysed by malaria, Everest had himself hoisted to the top of these towers, just to be sure his measurements were right. He was a fanatic for the numbers and the rules. That is why the British will lose India to us. It is not the way of this country."

"But you admire it. Their method."

"I do. Old Uncle Angus did it, you know, when he was a young man. He surveyed what he called the Medicine Line, the frontier between Canada and the United States of America. It was an artificial line, but it mattered. Canada is still there and fairly independent. It took him years. Surveys are a kind of truth, Peg. You cannot see them, even if you sit on their towers. But they define your land for ever, even if it does not belong to you." Then he added, "Yet."

"Angus is dying. I heard that from Cousin Margaret, over at Annandale. She has it now."

"They all have to go. Like our father in that silly Boer War. And Iain's gone and dear Mary. Angus now and Kate soon enough. A generation passes, and they leave us. The future." Seaforth showed his thin and bitter grin to his sister. "Do you feel like the future, Peg?"

"Not much," she said. "But I will survive it. As long as they need doctors."

"And pay you." Seaforth smiled again. "They will need doctors and pay you. They have wars to come. Imperial wars."

"You are a doctor, too, Seaforth. You treat anyone. Soldiers. Anyone."

"Yes, I do. Peg, there will be a great war, a world war. I know it. And when it comes, we will serve again, as we did in the Boer War. But this time, we will ask our price. We serve you, you give us our freedom. What do you think?"

"They will say yes. Then they will not do it."

"They might. If we send for Mr Gandhi."

"Your Mr Gandhi. You think he walks on water."

"No. He sits down and does nothing. So he moves mountains. Talking of that, you see *that* mountain." It was such a clear day that the eye seemed to travel through infinity. At that range, one peak looked as another, even to the discerning eye. "There is Everest."

"How do you know?"

"Because I do. The great surveyor died before he finished the survey. So the team went on, and when they first came to the Himalayas, they used his methods, theodolites and triangles, and they worked out the height of the peaks from the plain. And when they came to Peak Fifteen, a young surveyor did his sums and said, 'It's the highest mountain in the world. It is twenty-nine thousand and two feet precisely.' And perhaps it is and perhaps it is not, but it is the highest mountain in the world. And it was called Everest."

"Is that a good story or a bad story?" Peg looked away from her brother towards the blue ruffle towards the horizon.

"Both good and bad. The great surveyor Everest, who had never seen it, had the highest mountain called after him. But nobody would have known it was the highest mountain without the great surveyor."

Peg smiled now. She liked her brother best when he was ambiguous, and not too fanatical.

"I think you admire them, really," she said, "for doing and building what we could not do." Then she was malicious. "At least, the *Sinclair* in you does."

She touched a nerve. He was still too raw at his age to take gentle teasing. Even Miriam had not taught him to laugh at himself.

"Don't say that," he said. "You heard of that case in Polynesia. That Chinaman convicted of murder on Hamish Charles's copra plantation. He was a Sinclair, he said. Our half-brother. When our father was in Peking."

"You don't believe it."

"I don't know. I can't prove it." Seaforth began to bite his thumbnail, a bad habit of his middle age. "What if he is?"

"They did not hang him?"

"No. a life sentence. Extenuating circumstances, they said." Seaforth gave a short laugh. "As if life is not a sentence, anyway. With no extenuating circumstances."

"If you could hear yourself talk, Seaforth, *you* would not believe what you say."

"That is what sisters are for – to tell their brothers what bloody fools they are."

Seaforth hugged Peg, drawing her into his arms.

"Look," he said, "you should get married, I recommend it."

"Some have asked me," Peg said. "But I take after Aunt Mary. There's a while yet. And Seaforth, I would lose my independence."

"Independence?" Seaforth smiled. "We have not got it for a whole country. Why should *you* worry? One Indian woman."

"I'd rather be a free spinster," Peg said. "And walk my road to the river. And as for you, brother, you should not be with your old sister up here. You should have brought your wife."

"Miriam has to look after the children. She's not English. She won't leave Shankar and Solomon alone with the *ayah*."

"Our mother did."

"She was the *ayah* to our cousins at Annandale. But you, Peg – if a man is lucky enough . . ."

"I take after Aunt Mary, I told you so. A doctor has to remain alone."

"Mary did marry, in the end."

"It isn't the end. Thank you for bringing me up here, brother."
Again the sweep of the eye seemed to comprehend all India, green and growing by the Ganges, the garden of the world in the right

season. "We have time to talk and think. There's nothing of that down there."

"Serving the Raj," Seaforth said. "They don't give you time to talk and think. It's part of their policy. Oh, can you come to Bombay some time?"

"Why?"

"Communications. They're setting up a Marconi station there. We will be able to talk to South Africa directly – and Gandhi."

"And our family."

"One of them is coming. I heard it from Margaret. Gillon, a cousin from Canada. He is mad about the wireless. The farm there is a desert. Like this, before they put in the irrigation."

They looked down over the green paddy-fields. It was hard to credit. Such fertility, it must have been there always.

"The British put in the irrigation," Peg said. "I remember, Uncle Iain worked on it."

"More mouths to feed," Seaforth said. "More colonial mouths till we have independence."

"More rebels." Peg smiled at her brother. She knew how to switch his words. "More supporters for you. More people to throw bombs at the viceroy."

"The bomb missed," Seaforth said. "It only blew up the viceroy's howdah and hurt his elephant. But it made the Durbar in Delhi go with a bang." Peg smiled. "But, you see, the power of the new communications. All the world heard immediately of the bomb under the seat of the Raj."

"And saw it. The cinema."

"I have seen that. In Bombay." Seaforth looked down across the pattern of the paddy-fields, which was not a survey but the skein of irrigation canals which made rice grow on the earth. "In Bombay, too, there is the P & O coming in. Hamish Charles cabled Margaret that his wife was on it. That Virginia, the one he killed his first wife for."

"Aunt Mary said, no, he did not."

"Aunt Mary was wrong. I think she is leaving him. Like she left Cousin Robert. A fickle Virginia. She is on the way back to what they call home."

"Home." Peg looked over the verdant quilt below. "They use that word too much. Home is here." She thought that now. She had not thought that before.

"The only way I excuse our father – and our cousins that call our India a kind of home." Seaforth's left leg seemed to have gone out of control. It was tip-tapping the stone. He had to hold his calf with his hands to stop it. "They were forced to wander. They were driven like cattle from their lands. Their own Scotland."

"They can go home now."

"Cousin Margaret is going. She may be on the boat with her darling daughter Ruby. But she will return to Annandale. She loves Annandale. She waited long enough to get her hands on it."

"It would never have come to us. It was Uncle Iain's."

"He gave you the ring."

Peg twisted the emerald on its gold band till its green stone caught the light and blazed round the flaw in it. It filled her sight.

"Yes, he did. Conscience – they do have conscience. Something makes them give it back, the Scots, give back what they took. In the end."

"In the end? We may not be here to see the end."

"We will be," Peg said. She rose on the top of the tower like the statue of a dark victory. "You have just shown me all India, brother. In the end, it must be our land."

18

FIGUREHEADS

However much she might dislike Virginia, Margaret had to admit a certain splendour in her pose against the rails in the bows of the P & O liner, the *Viceroy of India*. The hard, rakish lines of her face made her seem a fierce figurehead. Both of the Sinclair wives were travelling POSH, of course, on the starboard side of the ship to avoid the worst of the sun. The women passengers outnumbered the men. There was a giggle of Returned Empties, those young hopefuls who had come out in the autumn under the name of the Fishing Fleet and were being shipped back in the spring without a catch in the Indian Civil Service to a spinster future in Dear Old Blighty. Margaret was bringing her daughter Ruby in the opposite direction, looking for a match in England. And Virginia, although evidently running away from her husband Hamish Charles and her step-children on their copra plantation, was taking her child Clio, even if she was only seven and rather a distant prospect in the marriage stakes. But calculation, Margaret knew, was something that Virginia was never without.

"My dear Virginia," she said, "who would have ever thought we would be on the same boat?"

"We aren't," Virginia said. "You export India with you. And your little castes and classes. Here sit the Civil Servants –"

"The heaven-born."

Virginia smiled at Margaret, sensing a sister in malice. "The heaven-born. And there are the military, all *pukka sahib*. And they don't speak to the planters or to each other. And then there are the rich unmarried girls going home, and the poor governesses, equally segregated. Then the real pariahs like me, who come from somewhere far too far east. So we don't count at all."

"You do pretty well, Virginia – not being counted, I mean. You always stand out in a crowd."

"But do I add up? That's what I ask myself. And the answer is nought. I add up to nought. A mother with a seven-year-old. Hardly a desirable proposition. And I don't even know how to dress for dinner. There's the Punjab Club wearing white jackets and black trousers, and the Calcutta Club wearing black jackets and white trousers, and the Lahore Club wearing blue shortie jackets and pink trousers – "

"Bumfreezers and cherrypickers," Margaret said.

"My God," Virginia said. "I didn't know you *could* speak like that."

"Oh, you can't avoid the army in India. You have to listen to troop talk till the bitter end."

"So what is a woman to wear? I feel I should come on in a chess-board back and front with a geranium hat."

"You do all right," Margaret said.

And Virginia did look good, the wind blowing her long white dress flat against her leanness, showing the small curves of her body.

"In fact," Margaret added, "you do better than all right."

"Your Ruby is simply beautiful," Virginia said, lying through her teeth about the young miss with her sausage curls and milksop face with huge eyes bright as new pennies.

"And so is Clio," Margaret said, talking of the little monster, who tore around always in a temper and had even bitten the purser in the leg. The way to ingratiate oneself with another mother was by praise of her child. Both Virginia and Margaret knew that, and they also knew that the other knew it and discounted the compliments.

"I'm glad to be taking Clio home," Virginia said. "She has never seen it. Never seen home."

"Ruby has. And to tell you the truth, if we can find the right situation, she may even remain there. Her brother Wallace is doing so well in the City . . ."

"Really?"

"He is a financier, interested in scientific advance. Wireless telegraphy. Curiously, not a British invention. An Italian called Mr Marconi, I believe, did it first."

"Oh, they've had a few bright ones outside the ice cream parlour," Virginia said. "Leonardo da Vinci and the rest. But that was a time ago. But tell me, do you think there's anyone really interesting on board? I mean, who will pass the time of day until the gully-gully men come on ship at Suez and find chickens in your bosoms?"

Margaret smiled. "If there was someone special, you would have seen him."

Virginia smiled back.

"No, you would have seen him. For Ruby."

Both women then smiled at each other and left the deck. For both had seen the most intriguing, and perhaps eligible, man of them all. Always dressed in a spotless white suit – he must have worn three a day in the heat – Maurice Walter exuded the quiet arrogance of wealth and the secret knowledge of power. His manners impeccable, his behaviour imperturbable, his only faults the chain-smoking of thin black cheroots and the using of violet *cachous* to scent his breath, Walter gave no hint of his trade or his reason to travel back from the East on the *Viceroy of India*. Before she engineered her introduction, Virginia noticed one of the cavalry captains, the beanpole Alistair Abercrombie, keeping watch on Walter in a nonchalant way. There was something mysterious about the man, and she would find out. And she would use none of the usual methods which Margaret might use, dropping a glove or pretending to stumble near him. He was too sophisticated for such an approach. She would brazen her way to him.

She walked straight up to Walter as he lay in his steamer chair, smoke trailing from his cheroot in a miniature parody of the liner's funnel.

"You look the only sort of man on board who would know what I am talking about," she said, leaning down to look at him directly under the brim of his white panama hat with its scarlet-and-black band. "What do you think the value of primitive Polynesian art will be? And a painter called Gauguin?"

Walter climbed slowly to his feet and took off his hat.

"May I have the pleasure of knowing who – ?"

"Virginia Sinclair. You are Maurice Walter."

"You can read the ship's list. And perhaps there are some aboard who know me."

"I feel you know about the primitive."

"Dear *madame*, a little. My interest is, indeed, the import and export of things from the Far East. *Les choses qui puissent frotter l'avenir* – shake the future."

"That's very well put, *Monsieur* Walter."

"If I may see your primitive works, *madame*, I should be honoured. But, in general, you are correct, if you wish to enter that trade. There is already an appreciation of the violent and the primitive in Europe – *l'homme sauvage* is the new man in Paris and Milan. Ferocity is quite in fashion. And as for Paul Gauguin, if you have any of his works and hold onto them for a while, you will have your fortune."

Walter appreciated the ceremonial masks and carved clubs and paddles which Virginia was bringing from Polynesia. He was ecstatic over the Gauguin paintings, though reserved over that artist's carvings. "The brush," he said, "is mightier than the chisel." He even showed an interest in Clio, who was fascinated by his elegance and his cheroots and displayed a tendency to flirt, which almost made her mother jealous, though her daughter was only seven. When she apologised for Clio's innocent forwardness, Walter merely smiled and said, "Girls mature early in the tropics. And if she matures into half the woman her mother is . . ." His compliment trailed away into a silent suggestion of some complicity between them. And that night, they danced together to the ship's orchestra, twined so tightly together that they seemed like a single reed swaying. They were the scandal of the ship, and Margaret told Virginia so in the morning.

"You were being simply shocking."

"I hope so," Virginia said.

"Everybody knows you're married."

"So to say, and you say it."

"Well, you are married to my cousin – or *cousins* – and your name is Sinclair. I can hardly avoid informing –"

"On me. You wanted him for Ruby."

"I did not. But to see you making such a spectacle of yourself. As if you had not already had enough scandal in your life. That dreadful murder of Hamish Charles's first wife . . ."

"It was an accident." Virginia pricked Margaret with a look like a hatpin. "If you say murder to anyone, it is slander. The verdict was an accident."

"Robert's verdict. Your *husband*."

"Then. Not now. And didn't he have every reason to call it a murder, if it really was? But he told the truth. An unhappy accident. And if you tell a lie on this ship, I shall know. And Margaret, if you do, I shall sue you. Or scratch your eyes out, whichever you prefer."

Margaret quailed before Virginia's fierceness. Of course, she had already spoken about the murder, for that is what it surely had been, to Alistair Abercrombie, when she had been to him to find out all about Maurice Walter. Anyone would have. Why should she lie to hide the shameless Virginia's past? But she did lie now, to save herself from Virginia's menaces.

"Of course, I haven't said a thing. You know I wouldn't. One always stands by one's relations. But it is very difficult, with you stuck to that man in front of everybody. Alistair Abercrombie said you might have been *glued – welded* like the ship is."

"Why don't you weld Alistair Abercrombie to Ruby? Then he would stop spying on us."

"If you think I have my eye on Abercrombie –"

"Ruby has. She shone her eyes on him like a lighthouse."

"You are merely trying to change the subject. To accuse Ruby of the designs you have on Maurice Walter."

Virginia laughed and said, "Well, I am a designer, but I assure you,

Maurice Walter may have his own plans, and perhaps I may not fit in with them."

"You *fitted in* very well last night on the floor."

"Dancing together does not mean sleeping together," Virginia said coolly, watching the shock freeze Margaret's face. "It only implies it. And frankly, one's chances on a ship as crowded as this beggar probability."

"You are shameless," Margaret said.

"Because I say what you think?"

"All the same, I must warn you. Abercrombie says he's dangerous. He's under surveillance." Margaret's voice dropped to a whisper as though somebody was listening, hidden in a lifeboat on the empty deck. "He may be a foreign agent."

"I do hope so," Virginia said. "Anyway, we have a lot of time to find out about one another, Maurice and I – and simply nowhere else to go, unless we jump overboard in a lovers' leap. Actually, I think the sharks' jaws would be kinder than the local comments."

So Virginia continued to flaunt her relationship with Maurice Walter, which always stopped just short of going with him to his luxurious cabin in the First Class (she was travelling Second with Clio sleeping in the bunk below her). But as they approached the Red Sea and the Suez Canal, the weather became so sultry that Maurice must have been changing his white suits six times a day to look so serene and uncreased, while the *dhobi-wallah* on board was on permanent duty, washing and ironing and starching in his hell-hole of an oven below decks. The *Viceroy of India* had not yet been equipped with the new electric fans in the cabins, so the passengers began to sleep on deck, which was sweltering enough.

The sexes were segregated, but Maurice Walter bribed a steward to erect for him almost a caliph's tent on the foredeck. And there he seduced Virginia, his lovemaking so sensitive and assured that she was confounded and destroyed, clinging to him and bursting into tears and sobbing, "Never, never . . . how can you? I never knew . . ." And he soothed her and stroked her into silence, then gently made love to her again until her pleasure became intolerable, and he had to hold his hand over her mouth to stop her cries waking the other passengers. She bit into the side of his hand like a panther.

Now she was even more a pariah than she had ever been, shunned by the servants of the Raj returning from India and the English women who had not found a husband out there. Her affair with Walter made her an outcast worse than a murderer, for she was sinning almost in public, and she had her small daughter with her. She was an affront to every standard of morality. But Walter himself became more amused and immobile, saying to her, "When everybody disapproves of you, you know you are right."

"I am right," Virginia said. "For the first time, I follow my heart. And I do not care."

"You are reckless," Walter said. "And that is what I love in you – besides your obvious charms. And now, because your dear Wilde said, nothing is more repulsive than the British in their occasional fits of morality, I shall give you this, to wave in their faces and shock them more."

And so he gave his first of many gifts to Virginia, a pearl-handled small revolver, inlaid with gold. "It was for a maharanee," he said, "but I kept it. The deal with her husband – *kaput*."

Virginia looked at the revolver, which fitted as snugly in her hand as a toy.

"Thank you," she said. "Curiously, I have always wanted one. You deal – in arms?"

"Didn't you know?"

"No. I had not suspected."

"How else can one become rich? Or be so suspicious?" Walter drew on his black cheroot until the tip blazed like a gun muzzle. "Weapons are the one thing everybody always wants. I supply them. A commodity like any other. And these days there are more and more buyers, especially in the East."

"They may be used against us –"

"Us?" Walter shrugged. "Who is Us? You and I? The people in this boat? A so-called nation? The human race? All of these are Us. And we all want weapons to defend ourselves against Us."

Virginia shook her head and smiled.

"You are very convincing, Maurice, and corrupting."

"Inspiring, Virginia. I inspire you to know the woman you really are."

"The woman who loves you."

"Yes. She."

For Robert, arriving on the Elder-Dempster or the Union Castle steamers to Nigeria was rather like trying out the attractions of a fairground. The heavy seas made him find his way down to the surf-boats in a mammy-chair, a wooden box hanging on a chain from the ship's derrick, which also lowered all his bags and baggage. The surf-boats took him to a tender, which dumped him and his possessions on the Customs wharf. And even though he was a district officer, he was searched as if he were a smuggler instead of an importer of regulation kit and chop boxes. His food for his eighteen-month tour of duty had all been packed by the Army and Navy Stores for getting by in the bush. His pride and joy was his Lord's lamp, which indeed appeared to be a gift from the Almighty. Its kerosene flame on its four legs scared off everything from crocodiles to mosquitoes like God hurling fire against Sodom and Gomorrah. And the sternwheeler up the Niger to his district was a journey through humid swamp and mangrove to a protracted hell. In a box slightly bigger than the mammy's chair, he sweated on the top deck, while an African village spread itself over the lower deck with chickens and goats and mounds of yams, floating to nowhere very much.

Life on his station in the three larger boxes of his bungalow was ruled by quinine and calling-cards. When his boy brought in his pink gin on a tray, a bottle of quinine stood by the glass. Not taking five grains a day was held to be a sort of suicide and worthy of a reprimand. Not sleeping under the drooping aisle of his mosquito net was self-mutilation. If malaria did not strike, blackwater fever would. The only thing that kept a man from falling victim to alcohol or infectious bites was the strict observance of convention. At every new station, Robert had to leave cards, even before he unpacked. No matter that the extent of his calls was a dozen bungalows much the same as his own and a ramshackle club, where one was likely to be knocked senseless after an hour at the bar, but protocol demanded the dropping off of tiny pasteboards with one's name at every door where a European might be malingering. Two cards were the rule, if somebody had a wife, but wives were a rare commodity and severely discouraged. Few of the few wives survived more than a tour or two.

Patience Silvers was the special case, the matron in charge of the infirmary which bore the good name of the Lugard Hospital, the only one for a thousand miles around. She had survived seven tours and was reckoned to be a walking pharmacy. Scratch her skin, the story went, and anti-fever bark would come off. Her pale-blue eyes were yellowed with medicines, her body thickened by endurance. Yet she was a handsome woman, and even if she was formidable, she could mock herself and drink among the men at the club as if she were one of them. Their forgetting of her sex was a compliment in her eyes.

Only Robert saw her differently. It began with her getting rid of the worms which afflicted all the men. The usual way of getting rid of the jiggers that came from flies was to wait until their tunnelling under the skin reached a hole and then to wind the tail of the parasite round a straw and slowly draw it out over the succeeding days. When Robert had an attack of sudden blindness in one eye, he went to Patience Silvers and told her. And she said, "That's the *filaria* fly and you're very lucky, we can get rid of it." And she took out a needle, as if truly to blind him, but instead she took away with the point the tiny thing working its way across his eyeball. Her delicacy was extraordinary, her touch exquisite. Robert felt nothing but relief. And as he blinked and wept involuntarily, she said kindly, "You're not crying for the jigger, I hope."

"No," Robert said. "And thank you, Miss Silvers. I sure am happy you took him off."

They became friends at the club, and the other members noticed with disbelief a little lipstick on Patience when she knew she would meet him, even a hint of scent. But Robert was, as they were, a confirmed bachelor during his job in the White Man's Grave, and hoping to survive enough tours to earn his pension. Both because he trusted the matron and wished to discourage her, he told her the story of his divorce.

"It isn't that I hate Virginia," he said. "I just don't trust women. Not you, of course," he added. "But it was the accident, the shooting of my cousin's wife."

"You gave the verdict," Patience said. "An accident."

"Yes. I think it was."

"Weren't you being . . . merciful?"

"Right, I guess." And here Robert made an admission that surprised even himself. "I had a carbine up above the *vlei* myself. I guess I must have thought . . . an accident . . . it might have been me."

"But it wasn't?"

"No. No for sure."

"Then you are a good man. And you do not want to admit it." Patience looked severely at Robert, as though to blame him for that quality. Then she suddenly broke into one of her rare smiles that illuminated her set face. "I like that you are better than you want to seem."

"Worse," Robert said. "You don't know me."

It was the nightmare he could never escape in his sleep. He would wake under his mosquito net in a pool of sweat, shuddering and shouting incoherently, knowing that he had done a crime, knowing that he would be judged for it, hanged for it. The nightmare was the truth, the waking was the dream. Everybody on the station knew the verdict. Living through each day was waiting for the just sentence to be carried out. He had fired at Hamish Charles, intending to kill him. His bullet had hit the Boer wife in the reeds by mistake. He was guilty of murder, and yet he was set in Nigeria to administer the law. The killer was the saviour, the condemned was the magistrate.

Only Patience knew – without knowing the cause – that Robert had lost the will to live and dragged through his days. It was an explanation of his recklessness in the riot. He wanted to go down for ever. When he heard that his fellow officer Sanderson was surrounded by the mob and was being beaten to death, he did not wait for his Ibo policemen, but ran to the compound without his pith helmet or his boots. He was carrying only his special hand-made truncheon in his hand, black leather hiding the lead weight at the end of the rattan cane with its wrist thong. Reports said that he beat the backs of the crowd, shouting, "Get out! Sinclair! It's Sinclair!" And the howling rioters parted for him. He charged through and found men beating Sanderson's head with stones. The brains of the man were spilling out of his smashed skull. Robert pointed his truncheon at a random five of the screaming attackers in their white robes. "You – you – you – you – you! You hang if this man dies!"

There was a sudden silence in the front of the crowd. At the back, the yells became muttering. The five men who had been singled out began to edge away, but the press behind them was too great for them to escape. They watched Robert kneel and rip off the shirt from his back. Then he rolled up the cotton into a rough bandage and wound it round Sanderson's head below the jaw and tied it in a tight knot. This held the brains in place and stopped Sanderson from moaning.

"Now – you five – lift him up! Just his body, I'll hold his head. And if you drop him, by God –" forgetting he had left his revolver behind – "I'll shoot you!"

And so the five chosen men picked up Sanderson's body between them and staggered through the crowd, carrying it, with Robert holding the victim's head up in its bloody bandage. And nobody lifted a hand against the district officer. Later, Robert never knew why. Was it fear of retribution? The myth of the invincible white man? A belief that he had some secret power that made him do such a foolhardy thing? He had never thought about it. He had done it. But Patience Silvers knew that he had done it because he did not care enough for his life not to risk that.

Incredibly, Sanderson lived. He broke every medical rule and survived. The five men did not hang, but were sent to labour gangs to build roads for twenty years. Patience would find a shape standing at the end of Sanderson's bed every midnight for two hours, keeping a silent vigil when the rest of the bungalow boys, as she called them, were drinking at the club.

"There's no need to do that, Robert," she said. "He can't talk, you know. We have to feed him through a straw. There may be damage to the brain. We don't know."

"If he sees me, he'll know I'm there. When he needs me."

"You were there when he needed you."

"He didn't know that. He was unconscious."

"And you, my dear, will be unconscious if you don't get some sleep. Don't you trust me to look after him?"

"I do trust you."

"Then go home. I'll call you when he needs you."

"What in hell is the point of going home? You've seen it. Nothing there but my camp kit. And bottles of gin."

"You need somebody to look after you, too."

"No takers."

"You might find a wild card."

"You play poker, Patience?"

"I do. And I play hard. Haven't the bungalow boys told you?"

"They don't know a darn thing about you."

"And you do? I order you, Robert – go to bed. Doctor's orders."

"I don't like sleeping. I get . . . bad dreams."

"Take this." She put a bottle of dark brown fluid in his hand. "If this doesn't knock you out, Jack Johnson wouldn't."

"You know about boxing too. The first black heavyweight champion."

"It won't be the last. But it will be the last of you, my lad, if you don't go home and knock yourself out."

The brown drug was an uppercut, as Patience had promised, and Robert had his first straight and guiltless sleep in months. And as his head began to mend, so did Sanderson's. And three months later, Robert found himself giving a dinner party for three in his bungalow with a borrowed canteen of cutlery and the club's cook, who knew how to add game and tasteless river fish to the tins of bully beef and peas from home. For the patient's sake, drink was banned. It might go to his head.

"You can't be here," Patience said, raising her glass of lime juice. "But here's to you being here when you're an impossibility."

Sanderson raised his glass. His wounds still showed in black ridges through his cropped hair. He spoke slowly, but he made sense.

"Here's to . . . being here . . ."

"Hear, hear." Robert smiled. "Though being here isn't plumb the here where I'd go for being in."

"And thank you . . . for –" Sanderson winced at some sudden pain – "saving . . . my life . . ."

"I didn't," Robert said. "She did."

"He did," Patience said. "He wrapped his shirt round your brains and held them in. You're still all there."

"Here." Sanderson smiled. "Anyway – thanks."

"I thank you," Robert said. "You did something for us." He smiled at Patience, and Sanderson noticed she was wearing a red ring, a ruby or a garnet. She had never worn one before. "I guess you brought us together."

"You knew . . . Patience . . . before."

"In a way."

"Not at all," Patience said. "I didn't know him. Now, he's quite a hero, you know."

"I am not," Robert said. "A damn fool."

"That, too."

"You're not," Robert said. "There's nobody like you in the whole world. Except my Aunt Mary –"

"Your old Aunt Mary, the one who died?" As Patience spoke almost dourly, Robert could see his error. She was older than him, it did not matter to him. But the comparison had made her think it did. "She was a matron, too."

Patience gave Robert a quick, thin smile. "Perhaps you love only people who can be an *aunt* to you?"

"No. You know that."

"Who can look after you."

Sanderson intervened.

"We all . . . want . . . to be looked after." He was pleased to manage four words in a row. "And by you – that is best."

Now Patience shocked them. It was the last thing the men expected her to say.

"Can you conceive," she said, "that I might want to be looked after? All this time caring for others – and who cares for me?"

"I do," Robert said.

"How much?"

"Enough to marry you." Robert looked at Sanderson. "I want you to be the witness. Patience and I, we will marry."

"Congratu –" Sanderson had to draw breath. "Congratulations."

"They are premature," Patience said, "like a baby can be. We are not married yet."

"But we *will*," Robert said.

"Not here," Patience said. "Perhaps on our next leave. It is true, you do need looking after." She turned towards Sanderson and showed him her red ring. "Ruby for the heart, ruby for remembrance. Robert got it off a Syrian trader. Probably illegal, but – he took a risk. He likes taking risks."

"No longer," Robert said. "Unless you want me to –"

"I don't," Patience said. "I want you here with me."

"I am . . . his last risk," Sanderson said.

"We'll drink to that," Robert said. "In lime juice with a dash of bitters."

So they drank to that, and Patience thought how vulnerable Robert was despite his hard good looks. She would have to run him to the top, for he would never make anything of himself. She was tired of running a bush hospital now, she was weary to death, all the sap dried out of her. But running a man in his career, catering for his comfort and her own, that would be a challenge. She doubted if they would have children, she had only a couple of years when that might be possible. But he would be her child, and he would think himself the man about the house, as men always did, when the woman arranged it.

Peg also thought of marrying. But it was a general thing, no particular man to marry. She wanted to have a child. Her blood stirred her, her womb gripped her. In the nights, a fist clenched inside her that doubled her up and demanded a baby to be born to her. But all the suitors seemed impossible, mostly other doctors and an occasional civil servant, men withered with duty or plump with self-satisfaction. But there was Shilendra Menon, who had distinction and had even studied at Cambridge University. He was too small and too plausible, but he was gentle and persistent. And there was a glance and a gleam in his eyes that made his courtship appear more as a need than an arrangement.

"Peg, you must give up," he was saying to her. "You hold out longer than the Statue of Liberty. You have not seen that. I have, I tell you. And her torch – it only has the electric light in. You, you need flesh and blood in you."

Peg considered the smiling, little man in his white suit, so immaculate that he could have been at a first communion, which she had once seen in England.

"Shilendra, I would accept you – but you are too good to be true. You have a good family, you have money. You are in the government of our India. You are a Brahmin – even your caste is right. How can I refuse you?"

"Indeed."

Shilendra's eyes glittered at the prospect of this improbable denial.

"But that is why I do refuse you." Now Peg laughed at him. "Can't you understand? I am a doctor. I deal with bodies breaking down. Nobody is perfect. You come to me, perfect Shilendra. All I know is the imperfect. Human people, full of flaws. So how can I refuse you, Shilendra? I hate the perfect. I want life – raw and beastly. Like that Darwin says, nature red in tooth and claw."

"A tiger hunt," Shilendra said. "Perhaps that is more your style."

"Oh, come on, Shilendra – I am not being totally serious!"

Shilendra laughed now, but he was watching her too closely, almost cruelly.

"You like to tease. You learn that in England. When I was there, the ladies did tease me. I learned to call it amusing – fun – but –" Shilendra paused and looked for his words. "Pride, it hurt me. There can be insult to a man, you know."

"You would not want me to think you perfect?" Now Peg was smiling at Shilendra. "The perfect husband. What every Indian male person wants his wife to believe that he is. You know, drink my bathwater when I am away."

Shilendra shook his head. His mouth was a purse drawn tight.

"No," he lied. "Not that."

"You want it."

Shilendra broke out of his embarrassment. His smile would have won over the world, but perhaps not Peg.

"That is why I come to you. A woman, educated in England. A woman who knows who she is. A woman who is a doctor. A woman to share my life."

"You don't mean it."

"I do."

"You do not. Even my brother Seaforth –"

"Ah, the famous doctor. The radical. The man who wants our independence now –"

"My brother Seaforth is married to a white woman from South Africa. She is very independent – more of a radical than he is. Yet, he thinks she should stay at home with the children. But then, even my darling brother is an Indian man."

"*Achta*," Shilendra said. "You do not make it easy for a man who loves you."

Peg fixed him with the intense search of her eyes.

"Would you let me go on being a doctor? Swear it."

Shilendra looked directly back at her with his arrogance and his need to believe what he was saying.

"I swear it."

"And a child. I want a child. Or it may be too late."

"A son. I want a son."

"A daughter. A child."

"Yes. A child."

"And you will *always* stay. *Always* stay with that child?"

"Yes."

"Swear it?"

"I swear it."

The stares at each other had never wavered. Now both looked down at their own ground at the same time. Finally Shilendra looked up.

"So you say yes, Peg."

Now Peg looked past him, almost shyly.

"I did not say that."

"But I may hope."

"Next Wednesday," Peg said. "You visit at the same time next Wednesday." And she took his arm and almost pushed him out of the door. But as he left, she brushed her hand against his cheek. And then she was ashamed of herself. He might think she was encouraging him.

19

MEAT CLEAVER

Perhaps because she was the daughter of a member of parliament Ruth Seymour-Scudabright was not the hatchet woman. Yet she took the meat cleaver into the National Gallery in a carpet-bag. Something about her look of innocence stopped the guards from searching her. They did investigate the handbag of the real avenger, who was to take the axe to male lust and the degradation of women. But they found nothing – no orders from the militant suffragettes, no Pankhurst proclamation to destroy the art treasures of the nation. So Mary Richardson passed through to her rendezvous under the *Madonna of the Rocks* so remote from the concerns of modern women. There Marie was waiting with Ruth and the weapon, rolled up like Cleopatra in its rug covering, to be revealed for a different effect.

"Ruth and I will be at either end of the gallery," she said softly. "We will give you the go-ahead. Then you are on your own."

"Yes," Mary said. She took the carpet-bag. "They are now destroying the most beautiful woman in history in gaol. The Cat-and-Mouse Act of that horrible man Asquith. Bringing Sylvia Pankhurst in and out of Holloway Gaol at the government's beck and call, just because of a false bomb charge."

"Well," Ruth said, "we did blow up Lloyd George's villa. It quite spoilt his golf. And there was that arson at Kew, which did not help the gardens."

"There is something else I can spoil," Mary Richardson said.

Watching from the door of the gallery where the Rokeby Venus was hanging, Marie felt a vicious excitement. Perhaps it was the Crow Indian blood in her, the thrill of anticipation before the charge. But there the picture was, the naked woman admiring herself in a mirror the inverted vanity of her sex that allowed the domination of men. And the painter was a man, a genius they said, but still a man, who lingered over female flesh like a voluptuary, enjoying the self satisfaction of a beauty in her own form. Now it would be violated chopped open. And not violated by a man, but a woman with a cleaver fighting for the rights of women with a butcher's blade. Even the languid Asquith would take note of that. But Marie had to take note of where the guards were as well as the spectators. She looked to the next gallery. Only two dawdlers were nodding over a masterpiece.

She flicked her hand towards Ruth at the far entrance. Ruth flicked her hand back. "Now!" Marie called. Standing in front of the naked lying Venus, Mary Richardson put a hand into her carpet-bag and pulled out the meat cleaver. She dropped the bag and set about the canvas, stroke after stroke. Cut breast, cut waist, cut thigh, cut and cut and cut again at slavery and lechery, hack at the male use of female self-abuse. See, the canvas curls back like skin from open wounds. Venus is dead.

The noise of the blows of the chopper hitting the gallery wall alerted the guards. Men in blue uniforms ran past Marie and Ruth at the entrances and rushed towards the suffragette with the axe. Mary Richardson had only time for one more blow at the revealing mirror on the painting before she was dragged down to the ground by three men. Marie's blood boiled to help her sister in distress, but she had her orders. She and Ruth must get away to report the reasons for the attack. It would be called an outrage when it was a legitimate protest. The truth must out.

"Don't you think you were going a mite too far," Bill Dunesk said to his wife. "It is a dreadful picture, all that expanse of too, too solid flesh. But to take a chopper to Venus. Couldn't you have used a cut-throat razor?"

"It wouldn't make the same point," Marie said.

"It rather reminded me of that surgical husband of your favourite Aunt Mary, Harry Lamb, who was meant to be Jack the Ripper. Only it was a woman doing the disembowelling this time. And it might have been you."

"It was not me," Marie said. "Anyway, how do you know it had anything to do with me?"

"It always does, Marie, these days. But thank you for keeping my name out of it. It would not have done."

"I was the cover," Marie said. "I managed to get Ruth away with me. Who would believe the Countess of Dunesk had anything to do with a lunatic lady with a meat cleaver?"

"Respectability is the best disguise," Bill Dunesk smiled. "I always use it myself."

"Oh yes," Marie said. "Congratulations. You and the government over the Marconi share scandal. Cleared at the libel trial. Not a stain on your character."

"But a few thousand pounds more in our pockets. Money, my dear, is such a messy business. I wish I had more of it so I could ignore it."

"I wish you would spend it on your miners and your pits. They're still a disgrace."

"The disgrace is what you do with them. And him, their leader, Keir McBride. I do know, my dear. I do keep my ear to the ground."

"You should keep it down the mine."

"*Touché*. But I would point out that all your radical activities are financed by my money – immoral earnings though they may be."

Marie could not answer that. It was too hurting and too true. She must counter-attack.

"But I turn a blind eye on your *artistic* activities. With Douglas and your *friends*."

Her husband shook his head slowly and smiled again, looking down.

"Blackmail," he said. "I never thought you would stoop to that."

"I would never betray you. You know that."

"Yes, I do. But reminding me – pointing out the truth – that is a personal betrayal."

"You point that out to me."

"True. But that is why we will not divorce. My finance for your discretion."

"And for the sake of Rosabelle."

"Her, too. She is simply the most divinely beautiful creature in London." Bill Dunesk rose from this rare visit to his wife, and, as usual, his gallantry got the better of him. He bent and kissed Marie's head. "Except for her mother, of course, who is even more divinely beautiful."

"If I could believe a word you said –"

"The trouble is," Bill Dunesk spoke as he left the door, "that you always do."

Discretion did not stop Marie's activities for her cause. Soon she found herself advancing on Downing Street with unlikely allies from her own family. For reasons of boredom and snobbery, since so many duchesses and countesses had now joined the suffragettes, including Marie, Ellen-Maeve had thrown her caution aside to aid her social progress in London. And Virginia, newly arrived from Polynesia to set up her art business, had also swelled the ranks of the marching women, although she was rather more credible in her beliefs. Marie took to her cool ambivalence, while Ruth was bowled over by her flaunted independence. So the four Sinclair women marched on the home of the prime minister, escorting the released Sylvia Pankhurst as an honour guard. She was frail and emaciated after her forced feeding. She had to be released or she would have starved to death. For Asquith and the opponents of votes for women could not stand another martyr after the sacrifice of the suffragette who had died under the hoofs of the new King's horse on Derby Day. Better an on-and-off imprisonment of the militant leaders than a dead heroine to inspire more rebels against the rule of men.

The police were waiting for them, blocking off the cul-de-sac into the hidden corridors of power. Their charge into the double line of bluebottles was a foredoomed affair. Hack and kick and scratch as they could, knock off a helmet and pull a copper's hair, the women were hustled off to the police-waggons or were routed down the Mall. Ruth broke through and reached the black iron railings. There she handcuffed herself to the metal uprights before the police could handcuff her. They broke her poster – DON'T FEED SYLVIA – GELD THE LIBERAL CAT – but it took three hours and two blacksmiths to cut her loose and take her to gaol, where Sylvia Pankhurst had also been returned for breaking the conditions of her brief parole.

The worst of the ordeal for Ruth was a visit she could not avoid from her outraged father – the furious Tory Member of Parliament had had his name dragged through the mud and Fleet Street. Any more jokes in the Members' Tea Room of the Commons – "I say, I say, I say, who's got a daughter behind bars today?" – and he would have apoplexy as well as having to forgo preferment. He raged at Ruth across the table in the visiting room at Holloway, the wardress behind her scarcely able to contain her sniggering.

"You damned peahen!" Charles Seymour-Scudabright shouted. "How dare you?"

Ruth had meant to reply, "Very easily," but she found herself hanging her head and saying meekly, "I really am sorry." It was exactly what she had not meant to say. But that is what a father's anger did.

"You have ruined my career. I shall lose my seat. What will I say to the Association in my constituency? Did you think of that?"

"No."

"Of course you didn't. You don't think of me. Only of yourself. I suppose you are under an evil influence. That is the only possible explanation. If you would say so to the authorities – how Marie Dunesk or Sylvia Pankhurst have misled you. If you would testify – "

So that was it. The law of betrayal. Sneak and escape scot-free. It had been the same at school, but then her father had never grown up from his old school disloyalties. Ruth found her nerve again.

"What I do is entirely my own fault," she said. "You have always told me to be responsible."

"Not when you are led astray."

"I believe in what I do."

"Handcuffing yourself to the railings in front of Ten Downing Street –"

"It showed how I felt."

"Do you realise, Ruth, you are a traitor to your country?"

"I am trying to save it."

"Don't you answer back, my girl. We are going to be at war with the Kaiser soon. All that fleet he is building, as though the seas weren't ours as they always have been. We have had to bring back the Home Fleet from the Mediterranean. And even I had to cross the House to vote for that pipsqueak Winston Churchill's navy budget – forty-five million pounds for four more dreadnoughts, eight cruisers, twenty destroyers and some of those new-fangled submarines I don't hold with. Though I must say, the Prince of Wales went on one and it didn't sink Him. But you are sinking us, you and your bloody women friends. You are trying to sink the whole country. Thank God you are not representative of your sex. Your mother says she will have nothing to do with you –"

"Send her my love," Ruth said sweetly.

"She doesn't want it. And she told me, on no account to appeal on your behalf, to engage my lawyers –"

"You are too mean for that. And merciless."

"What!" Still more blood pumped into Seymour-Scudabright's purple face. "I who have reared you, paid for you, I who have forgiven you outrage after outrage –"

"I would not be grateful to any man now," Ruth said. "Even to you, Father."

"Well, I do not mean to do anything for you anyway."

"Then you will not."

"You will serve your full sentence, as you deserve."

"Oh, I shall go on hunger strike. Then they will force-feed me and Sylvia again and let us out under the Cat-and-Mouse Act on our good behaviour. And then we won't behave. And then we will be here again."

"You revel in your infamy! And you bear my name!"

"I did not choose to." Ruth smiled at her choleric father, who did seem on the point of breaking a brace of blood-vessels. "You gave me my name."

"I wish I had not. You are not my daughter!"

"But I am. You told me so. If I am not –"

"You are not."

"Why did you sign my birth certificate if my mother is a whore?"

It was the first time Ruth had succeeded in rendering her father speechless. He rose on the other side of the table and raised a fist to strike her. Then he gasped and straightened up, breathing heavily. Then he glared at her and walked out of the visiting room, never looking back.

Ruth also rose and slouched back towards her cell and managed a smile at the wardress and the words, "Happy families."

Above them at Brooklands, the Blériot monoplane was doing the impossible. The Sinclair cousins had talked to the French pilot before, and he swore that he would loop the loop, a somersault in air. He had boasted that flying upside down was as easy as sitting at home in an armchair. There was no rush of blood to the head, merely *élan* and *esprit*, those wonderful words the French used to excuse their daring. And he rolled his aeroplane over in a circle as easily as a child spins a hoop.

"That's something," Murdo said to Hamilton. "We can't do it in your Short Folderwing."

"Ah, but you can fly from ships, Murdo. And that fancy Blériot with all its tricks, it can only go one way. Even if it takes off on a platform slung between the big guns of a battleship, it will have to ditch in the sea at the end of its mission. I'd rather get back than do cartwheels in space."

As they started to leave the air display and return to the Short works at Rochester, a gentleman in a white suit was waiting to meet them. He introduced himself to them as if he had known them all their lives.

"You must be Hamilton Sinclair," he said. "And you Murdo Sinclair, the test pilot. Your relation Virginia, she described you to me so accurately that I felt I was meeting old acquaintances who should never be forgot, as your 'Auld Lang Syne' says. Maurice Walter, at your service."

"You know Virginia?" Hamilton said.

"I had the fortune to be on a ship with her from India. She told me so many interesting things, particularly about your seaplane with the folding wings. A stroke of genius, and –" he smiled at Hamilton – "your genius, I believe."

"I did have the idea," Hamilton said. "You say you are at our service. But what service may we do for you?"

"No," Walter said. "I insist I am at your service. I believe that your company is a commercial enterprise."

"It is, indeed. Although the navy is buying some of our seaplanes."

"Then I shall be your second navy. I wish to buy some of your seaplanes."

"That's good," Murdo said. "Good for business."

"And good for who?" Hamilton asked. "Who would they go to?"

"Those who wanted them. Please – " Walter extended a flat platinum case towards the two Sinclairs. It snapped open to reveal slim black cheroots packed as tidily as bullets in a magazine. "Would you join me in a smoke? No?" He took out a cheroot himself and lit it from a Lucifer match. "You will excuse me. It is my only vice." He drew on his smoke. "I should say, my only obvious vice."

"You deal in armaments?" Hamilton said.

"Exactly."

"It must be profitable. All the great powers arming for the war to come."

"And the little powers. The thing about the arms race is everybody has to catch up."

"Ireland," Murdo said, thinking of a letter he had just had from his sister Arabella, married to the Irish estate of Alex Plunkett-Drax. "You don't dabble in Ireland?"

"I do, naturally. An admirable situation." Walter blew a white puff that hung briefly in the air. "Ulster needs rifles and machine-guns for its volunteers. They will not tolerate Home Rule from Dublin. And the Irish also court independence for their island, they also want rifles and machine-guns. There is prospect of civil war – and most uncivil it will be. But for me, it is an opportunity. And most civil the Irish are, north and south, to give the opportunity to me."

"You don't *care* where you sell?" Murdo was shocked. "What if our own weapons are used against us?"

"I am a businessman," Walter said. "I am not a moralist. I leave that to your bishops who will say it is a just war, when you go to war against Germany, as you soon will. But then, the German bishops, they will say exactly the same. Do two just wars make one just peace?"

"We may go to war." Hamilton considered Walter. "You know, Jerry has Zeppelins. We are afraid they may bomb London and our fleet."

"I would supply you with the plans for the Zeppelin," Walter said, "if you would sell me six of your seaplanes with the folding wings. I hear one of the models can even carry a torpedo."

"We hope for that. But tell me, Mr Walter, would you sell our seaplanes to the Germans?"

"The highest bidder is always my best client. And – " Walter smiled at his own statement – "I always pay the highest price for the best."

"I am not sure that the Short brothers would accept your offer. If we did not know where the seaplanes are going."

"Money talks, as you say. And its message is this. If I buy your seaplane, you will have more money to develop the next model. The aeroplane which carries the torpedo. Money talks, don't you think?"

"You are very persuasive," Hamilton said. "But I am not sure if I like –"

"I did not ask you to like," Walter said. "I ask you to accept a large sum of money. Of course there will be a commission for you two gentlemen in it. Shall we say, five per cent?"

"We do not do business that way here," Hamilton said rather stiffly.

"Pity. It makes things so much easier. Wheels are made to be greased. I hope your other cousin, what is his name? A Canadian, I think Gillon. I hope he will be more amenable."

"He's working on the new Marconi telegraph system. Across the Empire. You're not seeing him too?"

"Virginia has been most lavish with her introductions. Would you say, Mr Sinclair, that communications – in the air and in the air waves – will win the next war and the wars to come?"

"Yes," Hamilton said. "The next war and the wars to come."

"It will take millions of troops on the ground," Murdo said. "These are early days."

"But the early bird, as you say," Walter said, "does he not catch the worm? You are not at war, Mr Sinclair. You are a commercial company. You are obliged to sell your early products to a fair bidder, who is not at war with your country. If I wish for your seaplanes or for your telegraph systems – and Marconi is so commercial a company that it can buy and sell governments, including your own, apparently – you will sell them to me. And I will resell them where they are most prized."

"In Ireland, I suppose," Murdo said. "I have just heard from my sister. You are right. There will be a civil war there. And you may be arming both sides. And you don't care."

"I care like God for each single sparrow," Walter said. "Each human life is as precious to me as a diamond ring is to a *fiancée*. I only supply the weapons. And some men are stupid enough to use them. That is not my affair. For I do not pull the trigger. I do not drop the bomb."

Then Hamilton remembered that he had heard of Maurice Walter before. Cousin Margaret had told him of the arms dealer's affair with Virginia on the liner from India and what Intelligence knew on him.

"We may be commercial, Mr Walter," he said, "but we do draw the line. And that line is between you and the Shorts. The seaplanes are not for sale."

"Have you told that to your chairman? And to your shareholders?"

"They will follow my recommendation."

"Pity." Walter dropped the stub of his cheroot onto the tarmac at

Brooklands and ground out the spark with the sole of his black patent leather boot. "I will have your seaplanes, Mr Sinclair. But by other means."

They were only wearing cloth shooting caps and jerseys and riding britches and boots, but they were an army, no doubt of it. And they were a hundred thousand men, all against Home Rule and dedicated to keeping northern Ireland free for Protestants to rule, as God had decreed since the Battle of the Boyne. As an ex-officer, Alexander Plunkett-Drax was high in the chain of command under Sir George Richardson in the Ulster Volunteer Force. It was he who had brought in the smuggled shipment of five thousand .303 Mark 3 Lee-Enfield rifles with a million smokeless cordite cartridges and six Vickers machine-guns. With this firepower, they could put paid to any Catholic plot to make the Pope reign in Belfast, where Old Red Socks would certainly be murdered if he tried to say a Mass.

He had also been the bagman who had carried two hundred thousand pounds in used Bank of England notes to the depository in advance. It was curious that an obscure cousin of his wife Arabella had been an intermediary. He had never had anything from Arabella's family, which seemed to dislike him. The women were radical, the men so stiff they might have been wearing corsets. But Gillon, fresh arrived from Canada on his Marconi training course, was desperate for money to buy a house for his wife and three children, Leah and Fiona and Colin. The mysterious Maurice Walter had found an ally in him and a go-between. So Alexander went to London with the price for the weapons plus another thousand pounds for Gillon himself.

"I am a good Protestant, I guess," Gillon said as he counted the white five-pound notes which Alexander gave to him. "Otherwise, I couldn't take the cash. I'm for your cause all the way."

"When money and morals mix," Alexander said, "it is very convenient. Where is Mr Walter?"

"In the next room, buddy."

And so Mr Walter was, waiting for his price. He did not even count the notes in the two suitcases. "If they are short," he said, "you will have short guns."

"How do we know we can trust you?" Alexander asked.

"You must. Necessity means belief."

"You have a bad reputation."

"Except in delivering the goods I am paid for."

"You do that." Alexander looked at the arms dealer, so imperturbable in his white suit, even with a fortune in his grip. "Tell me, how do you get modern British Army supplies?"

"A trade secret."

"I suppose British civil servants in the War Ministry are underpaid."

"That helps."

"You have thought you will be depriving our army of these weapons, if they are suddenly called upon to fight?"

"More will be manufactured. It is good for trade."

"If you do not deliver," Alexander said in a flat voice, "we will kill you, you know."

"That is normally said, Captain Plunkett-Drax. But it is unnecessary. I always deliver. I value my life."

"But not the lives of those killed by your guns."

"Naturally not. My own life is the one I care about. Other lives are the concern of others, who value their own."

"How did you get to my wife's cousin? The Marconi man."

"We are expected," Walter said, "by a beautiful lady, who is also related to you. Virginia Sinclair, who has married two of your wife's cousins – although not at the same time."

At Virginia's house, Alexander Plunkett-Drax was astounded at the decorations. He had never seen the like – weird coloured squares and oblongs called Cubism from Paris, devil-masks and tribal gods from the South Seas and Africa, crude oil paintings of native women or peasant life or French landscapes. He bridled his scorn, knowing that it might appear to be ignorance. For he found Virginia fascinating, and the way she looked at him with frank appraisal was a signal of a future meeting of bodies, if not minds. She was older than him, but she had the lean grace of a whippet. Only Maurice Walter seemed to dislike the mutual attraction between the two of them. Was it possible that the serene and assured merchant of weapons could be jealous? Well, if that was the case, Alexander Plunkett-Drax would give him cause. Only he would have to be careful, for once in his life. He had threatened to have Walter killed if he did not deliver the weapons to Ulster. But Walter was equally capable of having him killed. He was sure of it.

"I hope you will both remain very happy." Alexander Plunkett-Drax raised his glass of pink champagne in a toast to Virginia and her lover. "I am sure you will. Unless there *is* a great war. But that will only mean more business for you, Mr Walter. And, I should think, your absence from London."

The skies over the Summer Isles spoke of conflict. They were a madness of changing light. No day was ever the same for an hour, no pattern in the sky or on the water. They had a fitful beauty in glower or in shine. In her retirement from Canada, Kate McDowell could not count on them, wayward and dangerous as they were. The clouds might graze like sheep in a blue heaven, then a high wind would shear their rumps and the bright fields above would grow dark. Then the falling of the day would put armoured scales on the sky and sea, leaving the isles as black dreadnoughts, striped in camouflage by the broken and bright ribs of their superstructures. And when the sun slouched in its long setting below the horizon, red and orange flakes spilled onto the water from the bleeding of the last light. Night killed the day so slowly that it made the evening retreat insidiously, not with the sudden ambush of the tropics. Even then, the spume of the waves made bright wounds on the stricken Atlantic loch. With the bad news from Europe in her ears, Kate saw a battlefield where there had been a peace on earth.

"Ach, the war will not come," she told her husband Bob, slumped and heavy in his armchair before the peat fire that smouldered daily in the hearth, for he always felt the chill in every season now. "It will not come," she insisted, trying to convince herself against her fears. "Folks canna be so daft."

"Because you say so?" Bob was rarely ironical. "People are crazy. Now that they have killed that prince in Sarajevo."

"What's that to do with us?"

"Nothing. But people fight for nothing. It is the armaments. Men never pile up weapons unless to use them."

She and her husband were sitting in their decline in their converted crofts at Achiltibuie opposite the Western Isles. Kate had wanted to return to her Scots homeland from Vancouver for her dying, and there was Fraser land near where she remembered her melancholy leaving for Canada as a child on the ship that foundered. Two adjoining crofts had been converted into one cottage home for them, but all around stood the ruins of other abandoned cottages like Pictish barrow graves, the wrecked stones of a lost race. And their invaders and destroyers, the Cheviot sheep, cropped the land barren up to their walls. Bleat – bleat – bleat, like the hiccups of a slow-firing gun, this was their requiem to the folk who had gone before.

"Now Angus is gone," Kate said, "I am the last, you know, of the sons and daughters of Hamish and Hannah Sinclair, that left this land so near to here."

"Enough children," Bob McDowell said, "there are enough children from all your dead brothers and sisters to people this Scotland all over again. Breed like rabbits, you do."

"I only have Marie, and she Rosabelle. I wish she would spend more time with her girl, instead of leaving her to her father. But she will have her votes for women."

"I am grateful to the father," Bob said. "For he gave us this house."

"He could well afford it." Kate rose stiffly from her chair. Her old bones ached. "I will prepare the pheasant, for it is the first that I have ever eaten. When I was a bairn, we couldna eat a pheasant. It was the laird's. You were hangit for the taking of it, or sent to Australia."

"There's laws to save the crofters now."

"Ach, too late for us."

Kate hobbled into the kitchen. She had plucked the bird that morning. She picked up a sharp knife with its bone handle in her right hand and held the claws of the bird in her left. She would do as she was told. A pheasant was no chicken. She must take out the crop, or it would poison her. She slit the cold puckered skin of the bird below the neck and put down the knife and scooped out a small pale dumpling with her fingers. Now the innards, that was the next thing to do. And she plunged her hand into the stomach of the pheasant, feeling for the heart and the lights to pull out. And on the sudden, she thought of the chill of death on her father's cheek, when she had kissed it at his laying-out before his burial. And she thought of the drawing down of her days and those of her husband, that they might not last until the coming of the great war, which would as surely come as the conflict of the sea and sky each night over the Summer Isles.

20

WAR AND CHRISTMAS

It was cold. There was no protection from the whiplash of the high air. Tears formed under the goggles, making a mist on the glass. Murdo Sinclair, on the run in to the Zeppelin sheds at Düsseldorf, felt like an icicle in pursuit of the improbable. Guns were firing at him, useless stuff whizzing past, random bullets in space. Attack from the air was a new tactic, and there was no answer to it yet. But a stray piece of lead could put an end to the whole enterprise, so Murdo jinked the wings of his Short seaplane and stayed on target. Then he came in slowly over the sheds where the Zeppelins were hidden like queen ants hatching within the hive of London's future destruction.

Behind him, his observer and bomber sat. It was so elementary. He released the bombs like a hen laying eggs. And down they went onto the sheds, all three of them. One hit, one missed, and one failed to explode. But the huge detonations and the twin puffs of black smoke, that was success. One Zeppelin perhaps was destroyed in its hangar, so Murdo banked and turned. He could land in the sea off the Heligoland Bight, and then he would be winched onto the Dreadnought. Then he would fold his wings, as a bat did after its hunt at night. And he would report to his cousin Hamilton that the sea battle had taken to the air, the era of the battleship was numbered.

On the Marconi telegraph, another cousin, Gillon, reported the success of the mission to Hamilton before Murdo had returned with the Home Fleet. "A-one OK," he said. "Mission accomplished. Out." And Hamilton, sitting on the threshold of a new age of war, did not know what to believe. They had accomplished so little. One Zeppelin was destroyed, when millions of men were massing on the western and eastern fronts in Germany. This prelude might be an overture to what was to come, but how long, Oh Lord, how long before the curtain went up?

Fighting at Mons was a pleasant shock. Captain Gordon Seymour-Scudabright with his battalion of Grenadier Guards watched the execution of the hordes of Huns on the barbed wire. His trained riflemen fired their Lee-Enfields with their rugged oiled bolts until the barrels grew red-hot and the linseed oil boiled from the wooden stocks and burned their palms. The worst marksman could not miss, there was hardly need to aim. He only had to fire into the grey of the evening, charging in mass into the concentrated fire of trained guns. So great was the point-blank murder that the Germans thought that they were being mowed down by the Vickers machine-guns, when there were only two of these issued to a regiment. But the steady stutter of the Lee-Enfields at their rapid fire was a fusillade without mercy or end. Thousands fell and screamed and writhed as the German advance came in. It sickened Gordon and exhilarated him. Slaughter was just so, and a joy.

The British Expeditionary Force was broken by the Boche artillery. At first it had been a game, the salvoes passing overhead and crashing in the rear like cymbals at a pantomime. Gordon's Guardsmen had poked their heads over the shallow pits, which they had dug with their entrenching tools. "Look," they had shouted, "a black bastard – four whities – a washout – another miss – lower your sights, blind-eyes!" Then the enemy gunners had adjusted their range, and the lyddite and the shrapnel began maiming and carving open their ranks. And when the order for the retreat came, they were glad to fall back. Of course, the Brigade of Guards never retreated, everybody knew that. They were merely taking up new positions. But this time, they were regrouping rather near Paris and not on the Belgian border, where the Germans had sliced through.

Day after night, and night after day, they slogged back along the dusty roads under the plane trees. Lurching about himself with fatigue, Gordon had to wave his revolver and curse his men awake at dawn. "Damn you, I'll shoot you if you don't get up! What do you want? Spend the war in a Boche concentration camp?" So he swore and threatened, and all his Guardsmen fell in and slouched on towards the Marne and the Aisne, sleep-walking in a nightmare of retreat. And their sergeants made them polish the toe-caps of their boots every night, even when the soles had worn away and they were walking on bare feet. And on their flanks, the cavalry hovered as angels of death.

One evening, Gordon saw someone he knew, Alexander Plunkett-Drax, as he dismounted to report. He was attached to the Fourth Dragoon Guards, which were screening them from the German First Army. It was ridiculous that these mounted troopers could actually deter the shot and shell of the concentrated firepower of the Huns. It must be the last grand illusion. Some folk memory of Mongol hordes on horseback or Crusading knights stopped the German corps from annihilating the routed British forces. Or perhaps the Boches were as tired as they were. They had advanced too far and too fast. They had run out of steam.

"Alex," Gordon said, "what the hell are you doing here?"

"Not running away like you."

"They'll shoot your nags to smithereens."

"They'll put you in the bag."

"What you need is armoured cars. The Belgians had some. Better than a bloody horse."

"Says you. I can ride off, while you plod on."

And so Alexander Plunkett-Drax did, when he had delivered his message to regimental HQ. But the retreat became harder, because the soldiers became mixed up with the refugees. On farm carts and on hand carts, on prams and wheelbarrows, the French of the northern villages were taking to the road. The Guardsmen broke ranks to help out the old men and women pushing their grandchildren and few goods towards Paris. The British Expeditionary Force became a fleeing rabble, khaki tunic and blue blouse mixed in a straggle of disorder. Sleeplessness led to a form of mass insanity. After ten days and nights of stumbling along, the soldiers began to dream as they walked, to talk nonsense or to their distant mothers and wives over the Channel. A fearful babble filled the dusty air with jabberings, while foot dragged after foot to the safety of the south.

Somewhere near the Seine, they could eat and sleep. There were stocks piled there and bedding. After twelve hours of unconsciousness, an Orderly Room was held, and some sort of discipline was remembered and enforced. "You're a bloody lot of cripples," the sergeant-major shouted. "A disgrace to the British Army." But reinforcements arrived, all plump and clean and tidy from Blighty, and raring to have a go at the enemy. They had good boots, while the mob in retreat had rags wrapped round their toes. And the order came to regroup and counter-attack as far as the River Marne and over it. Paris was saved, and the war ground to a halt in the trenches and below the earth along the banks of the Aisne.

It was the day they brought the aeroplane down that also brought the Guardsmen back together again. Yesterday and the day before, the maniac Hun in his Spad Albatross came screaming along the lines of troops, firing a scatter of bullets and sprinkling a bomb or two, which exploded nowhere in a puff of dust. The third day, every man had fifteen rounds ready and the belts were on the Vickers and the Lewis guns. As the shrieking machine came down, the machine-guns and the rifles poured their iron tracery into the sky. The din was terrific. A ragged wall of steel and lead darts stood up before the flying engine. It could not pass, although its charge on high carried it past its holocaust, trailing black smoke to its crash two miles away. The cheer that split the sky was the noise that Gordon had been waiting to hear. His men had recovered – in the bond of the death of their lone foe.

"Aeroplanes," he told his sergeant. "They will never win this war."

Although Marie wanted her all the time for the hospital work that now engrossed nearly all the suffragettes, Ruth found Virginia's modern art gallery more exciting. She had collected the work of the Futurists, our allies from Italy, who exalted speed and machines, violent action, and even war. "Burn the museums!" they cried in their riots. "Drain the canals of Venice! Kill the moonlight!" The aeroplane and the racing car were their Madonna and Angel Gabriel. The swirling motion and raw colours of cyclists by Boccioni, the expansion of lights by Severini, and the flight of swifts by Balla, these hung with the Gauguin primitives of the savage state on Virginia's walls. Maurice Walter had brought them over from Milan on the eve of war, before his disappearance. "It is good for trade," he said, "that Futurist leader Marinetti. When he said war was the only true hygiene of the world, business went up two hundred per centum."

Yet Ruth did not expect the violence in her own feelings on the evening she let herself into the Bloomsbury gallery and went up the stairs to the maisonette above. There was nobody in the living-room, decorated with the brown blocks of Cubist paintings from Paris, by artists with names like Picasso, that were unknown and would always be. There was a noise from behind the closed door of the bedroom, and soon Virginia came down the treads, her hair a black tangle, but her flowing wrap of spring flowers painted on chiffon making her float above the steps in a picture of fresh innocence.

"Oh you, Ruth, I wasn't expecting you."

"I hope I am not inconvenient."

"Oh, you could never be. You are always welcome here." She enfolded Ruth in her arms, crushing her face against her breasts, so that Ruth could sense the scent of sex on her. "You might as well know."

The man who followed Virginia, buckling the copper mirror of his Sam Browne belt, was the man Ruth loathed. How could Virginia have fallen to Alexander Plunkett-Drax? She swung round on her friend, who was saying, "I believe you know each other –", with an accusation, "I told you about him! What an utter swine he was!" And all she heard was him mocking her through his nose. "I told you, Ruth, some girls love swine. They make us what we are."

Ruth found herself blocking Alexander with her body from the approaching Virginia.

"You are a swine because you always were. What are you doing here? You should be getting killed in France."

"Leave, and I earned it. And some tommyrot. They want us to move from horses into tin toys and I have to check out some contraption with tracks and armour on."

Virginia now held Ruth round the waist from the back, stopping her from attacking her tormentor. She answered for both of them.

"I heard about these armoured things from Cousin Wallace. He's joined the Yeomanry. And you know how interested he is in backing new inventions."

"If Maurice finds you here," Ruth said, "he'll kill you."

"Oh, Maurice Walter won't get back here." Alexander Plunkett-Drax walked over to a decanter shaped like a shell-case and poured himself a brandy. "He's had to hotfoot it to points east. British Intelligence got onto him. Gun-running to Ireland."

"To you, I bet."

"Those were the old days. Ulster, who cares? The Paddies have joined us in fighting the Huns. So have the Springboks, our old Boer friends. All those things are post-war problems now. When we've won."

Virginia released Ruth, who was shivering from a turmoil of loathing. Now the girl would not attack her past lover.

"War is a great solution," Virginia said. "All our troubles – strikes, votes for women, Ireland – all postponed till the next truce. Perhaps our dear Marinetti is quite right. War may not be hygiene, but it bandages our old wounds. And we can't take off the plaster till the peace."

"It's disgusting to hear you talk like that," Ruth said. "I always thought, Virginia, you're so sensitive – your fine feelings –"

"She likes the real thing," Alexander said complacently. "A real man. Like you do too, Ruth. Don't tell me there's not a streak of violence in you. And you want it satisfied. You know the only thing better than having a woman?" The two women looked at him, knowing and fearing what he would say. "Killing a Hun. Sticking him with a lance. I got an uhlan right between the shoulder-blades as he was getting away. Going in . . . ah –"

Whether the story was true or not, Alexander smiled at the shock of it on his audience. Virginia spoke first.

"You like killing?"

"Who doesn't?"

"I hate it," Ruth said.

"You don't admit you like it."

"We spend much of our time at hospitals, trying to patch men up. What they have done to each other."

"Don't you want to kill them, really?"

"If it was you," Ruth said, "I would."

"There you are. Women are so perverse. They always want to kill the men they want."

Virginia laughed.

"Don't think we only want you, Alex, because you are so intolerable. Even you can go too far."

"I doubt it." He finished his brandy. "I must amble off and win the war. Till next leave, Virginia."

"*Au revoir*," Virginia said. "Or rather, *adieu*."

"Break your neck," Ruth said.

When the impossible man was gone, Ruth fell into a storm of accusation of her friend, which ended in a fit of weeping and consolation with camomile tea. Virginia did say she was sorry, but what could she do? Maurice Walter had vanished for ever, Alexander wanted her, the average life of an officer in France was now six weeks only, how could she deny his need? "For me," Ruth cried, "for my sake!" But even she knew that however strong the bonds were between women, when they wanted the same man, they slipped the knot. In fact, the more she confessed how terrible Alexander was and had been, the more attractive he became. He traded on that, the conspiracy among women which made him the demon lover. He was not as great as all that in bed, but his reputation made him so.

"I do love you, Ruth," Virginia said, "and we won't let that Casanova *manqué* come between us. With any luck, he'll stop a bullet before he bothers us again."

As she said it, Virginia knew that both of them did not really want that. They still wanted him.

Another war was being fought in India, but only a family row. Peg was dandling her baby in her arms – another Shilendra, the father had insisted on that – when Seaforth and Miriam had burst in upon her. Seaforth was quivering with rage. He shook as an arrow fixed into a tree, trembling with the impact.

"I can't bear it," he said. "Orders from England. Back there to patch up the victims of another of their bloody wars. And you, Peg – you with your baby."

Peg put her baby down on the divan behind her, holding the back of his head as if it were an eggshell.

"I don't mind," she said. "But Shilendra's not coming with me.

His father's got a wet nurse who is a cousin. Anyway, I cannot risk him." She smiled at Miriam, who smiled back at her. "I don't mean to shock you, brother, I will miss Shilendra awfully, but . . . to be a doctor again, in England again, I will feel I am doing what I was meant to do."

Seaforth stood still, as if she had struck him in the face. He was shocked into silence. Miriam spoke for him.

"But working for British soldiers," she said. "In an imperialist war. German Empire against British Empire."

"Oh, just men," Peg said. "They do expect us to look after them when they are dying for their eternal stupidity."

Now Shilendra came into their drawing-room, hung with Moghul rugs and bright with brass jars and hanging lights. He shrugged and spread his hands.

"She's your sister, Seaforth. I am only her husband. What can I do with her."

"Tell her to be a mother!"

"I do tell her. And she tells me, when she married me, I said she could be a doctor. Always. I said it – and now she tells me."

Seaforth walked across to his sister. His eyes were hot embers.

"Stay with your son. Don't go!"

She taunted him back.

"*You* are going, aren't you? They ordered you to go back. They ordered me. And you, Miriam –" Now she swung on her sister-in-law. "You have agreed, haven't you? You will stay with the children in India. You will see the work through here. While Seaforth is away – patching up the agents of British imperialism because he has to, he's a doctor – *you* will keep the cells going here, the flames burning for a free India – that free India we all want."

Seaforth was silent, and Miriam too. They had no answer to what Peg had said. But Miriam had to say, "I will be going with Seaforth. I will have to leave the children here, Shankar and Solomon. But we have excellent *ayahs* –"

Peg's look at her was as a steel blade. Now the baby on the divan began to wail in a voice as thin as one note on a reed pipe. His mother picked up the infant and challenged her husband.

"Do you think I don't love him? I gave him your name, Shilendra."

Shilendra could not look at her. He dropped his eyes and said softly, "If you did love him and me, you would stay here in India. It is not for you, my dear Peg, it is not for you to bandage our oppressors. Your brother is right. This is not your war. It is, in fact, our opportunity."

Seaforth smiled at Shilendra. They did not like each other, but in families, even opponents might say the right thing.

"Peg, darling," he said, "your husband is correct. It is not your war. It is our opportunity to make India free."

Ah, the hypocrisy of men! Peg could not stand it, even with her baby in her arms.

"You are going, Seaforth. Why not me?"

"I have to. I have orders."

"So have I."

"But as a mother with a baby. You know the British. On compassionate grounds, you can get away with murder – "

"Or birth, apparently."

Again there was a silence. Even Seaforth did not know his sister could be so formidable. So he said weakly, "You do not have to go."

"And if I feel I should. It is my job. Even if I must leave the child I love."

Miriam was torn. She had to love the woman in Peg, who had to do what she must do. She hated the war for the Empires, which she hated more than all the past. But she was leaving her children in India to go with her husband. So she said, "Peg, do what you have to do. But this is murder – exploitation – shame. Do not go to help these murderers."

"Ah," Peg said. She put her baby in her husband's arms, and he received the child gently, loving him. Then she walked over to Miriam. "My dear," she said, "you and I know, we must do what we have to do. And perhaps be mothers after."

Miriam hung her head and mumbled, "Perhaps . . . what you have to do . . . it's all wrong." But she knew in her heart that Peg was right.

"God knows," Peg said and challenged her brother Seaforth with her stare. "Doctors have only one thing to do. They save lives. There's nothing else. They cannot choose. That is it. What, Seaforth?"

And Seaforth looked gloomily at the tile floor.

"Women," he said. "Sisters. What else do we have?"

Marie's war efforts were directed at the Women's Emergency Corps and the Wandsworth General Hospital. When Virginia and Ruth were not involved with their art dealing, they were starched into service, as was Ellen-Maeve, up from the country at last, and Ruby, dead set on picking up an officer too wounded to run away from her. Her grandfather Iain, after all, had picked up his wife that way in a Himalayan hospital after the Indian Mutiny, when he had been hamstrung and fancy-free. For the wounded, wards were another way of meeting women. Many a match was the result of an accident in the field.

Most importantly, Marie had her friend Peg recalled by the War

Office from India for service at home, and with her came her brother Seaforth and his wife Miriam. Again, there was an understanding of women, rather to the exclusion of men. Miriam had already become a firm supporter of Peg in India in her battles for higher appropriations for her hospital. She found in Marie another fighter for her favourite causes, although Marie's wealth and title stuck in her craw, and the Countess of Dunesk had to disarm her suspicions.

"You're quite right," she said. "I am a filthy capitalist and class enemy. But you come from very wealthy parents, Miriam."

"They don't help me any more," Miriam said. "They know I want to destroy them and their mines in Jo'burg."

"But you still love them, in their way, which you cannot alter."

Miriam was silent and scowled.

"Yes," she said.

"Well, I was born poor – and the American Indian in me hated the British aristocrats. And now I am married to one – in a kind of a way – I love what I have the power to do. Surely, the thing is to *change* things –"

"That's what Marx said."

"And you cannot *change* things without the power to change them."

"We should not use your sort of power. Workers' power."

"Not with our sort of workers," Marie said. "Not yet. You don't know them. They have no idea of their own power."

Seaforth reorganised the Wandsworth General Hospital. He insisted that soldiers only understood rules. The problem was that army rules were not the same as hospital rules, although there were coincidences. So he drew up a wounded warrior's guide and order book, which ran:

- NEVER DESERT YOUR BED WITHOUT PERMISSION

- STOP TALKING WHEN SISTER SAYS SO

- NO DODGING OF TAKING MEDICINE

- IF YOUR TEMPERATURE CHANGES, SAY SO

- SISTER IS ALWAYS RIGHT AND DOCTORS ARE RIGHTER

- DON'T DISCUSS YOUR CASE – ACCEPT IT

- DON'T FLIRT WITH THE NURSE. YOU ARE HER PROBLEM, NOT HER OBJECT

Come home to catch her officer, Ruby Jardine from India was one of the volunteer nurses who disobeyed the last rule. She was very popular in the Senior Ranks ward. They always asked for Ruby to bathe them. At first, she had been delicate about too much contact with male anatomy. But she warmed to the work and caused considerable jealousy when she seemed to prefer treating a stricken lieutenant rather than a maimed major.

"Seniority," the older officers would say. "That's what the army's all about."

"Hospitals aren't," Ruby would reply demurely. "I'll get round to you when my rota says I do."

But Ruby's rota was a moveable feast. And when Alisdair Ogilvie was brought in with his shattered leg and shrapnel in his left cheek, Ruby tended to him as if he were a relative. Certainly, his right profile made him appear the best-looking man in Britain, and once the bandage was removed from his wounds, his whole aspect would prove it. And as for his character, Ruby loved the mordant streak in him that made her laugh, although he always implored her not to be amused in case he followed suit.

"You know, Miss Jardine," he would say, "it hurts me to laugh, but it does tell me I still have a face."

Alisdair had no hope of leaving his bed before he was engaged to Ruby. She then allowed him to limp with her round the garden. And before he was returned to the front, they were married in the absence of her parents, who were in India, but her brother Wallace came to the short ceremony, dressed in his new Yeomanry uniform. He was being kept back in Britain to attend trials of a new armoured fighting weapon.

"It won't be in good enough time to save me," Alisdair Ogilvie said. "I'd love some steel plate between me and the Hun machine-guns."

The honeymoon was only for forty-eight hours. Exhausted and wounded herself in body and soul, Ruby could not see her husband for the storm of her tears at Victoria Station, where she had to suffer his leaving for France.

"No, no, no," she was shouting. "Don't go!"

She provoked shock on the faces of the other deserted women. "They must go," an old dowager said to her severely. "You must let them go to fight, and not make such a fuss about it."

But Ruby could not stop crying out, "He won't come back. I know it!"

And she was right. On Christmas Eve, 1914, Alisdair Ogilvie was killed in action on the Western Front.

On Christmas Day, Gordon Seymour-Scudabright heard the Germans singing from their trenches. He knew the tune, "*Stille Nacht, heilige Nacht*". And then a lone violin sent out its sad sweet notes – Handel's *Largo*. By God, who would believe it? It was better than the explosions of the *Minenwerfer*, the Minnies. And then his own Guardsmen gave three cheers and began to sing, "Home, Sweet Home". As if this were home, this foul morass of muddy shell-holes and tangles of wire. And the firing stopped. No sniper bullet flew. He could hear a blackbird sing, too.

Yet he could not stop his men dropping their rifles, leaving their trenches, and wandering into No Man's Land. The Germans brought over wine and *schnapps*, the English took bully beef and Christmas cake. Hoarfrost glittered on the soggy ground, a million million brilliants of light as if the Milky Way had fallen down to carpet the bog of death. And there was a football game of sorts, if you could call kicking an old German bucket helmet through a pair of splintered stakes football. Down where the Gordons were, the ball was a hare, and the beast jinked and swerved between the two roaring teams of captors, until a German bagged it from the kilted Scots for the stewpot that night.

Alexander Plunkett-Drax was savage about the voluntary truce of Christmas. He threatened to shoot any of his dragoons who went out to make a private peace. "They're bloody Huns," he shouted. "Baby-killers! They spit children on bayonets. They burn cathedrals. Look at Arras!" And his rage was only exceeded by that of Charles Seymour-Scudabright doing his war duty from the Ministry of Information at home, keeping up the morale, which the troops were letting down so badly at the front.

No newspaper was allowed to carry the story of the Christmas peace in northern France. The Hun had to be labelled as he truly was, a butcher and a rapist and a fire-lighter. Even apostate daughters like Ruth had to be told to toe the line. Being a radical might mean being a traitor to one's country. So her father studied the proof of the poster in front of him:

TO THE
YOUNG WOMEN
OF LONDON

Is your "Best Boy" wearing
Khaki? If not don't YOU THINK he should be?

If he does not think that you
and your country are worth
fighting for – do you think he
is WORTHY of you?

WAR AND CHRISTMAS

Don't pity the girl who is
alone – her young man is
probably a soldier, fighting
for her and her country –
and for YOU.

If your young man neglects his duty to his
King and Country, the time may come when
he will NEGLECT YOU.
Think it over – then ask him to

JOIN THE ARMY – TODAY

"Myrtle," Charles shouted. "Myrtle!"

He approved of secretaries with the names of trees or flowers. A Violet or a Lily, an Iris or a Petunia, these names reassured. They reminded him of the English Roses which the Tommies out there were defending, and who would wait by their window boxes until the men came home.

When Myrtle entered, she was enthusiastic over the poster, her smile opening in petals to a patriotic glow.

"Oh, yes," she said, "we should all be worthy of the sacrifice. And then they will not neglect us."

Charles Seymour-Scudabright gave her the address of a certain gallery in Bloomsbury, where his daughter Ruth was said to be living with a cousin's wife, Virginia Sinclair. His strict instructions were to plaster the neighbourhood with this particular poster, to recall the women to their senses and their duty. He did not know that it would remind both of them of Alexander Plunkett-Drax, who was not worthy of either of them and neglected them both. But he did loathe the brief Christmas peace of the Great War as much as Charles did. And in their hatred of the enemy, both men were able to come to terms with their own selves.

21

MY ENEMY, MY FRIEND

Below the Short seaplane, the mangrove swamp spread out its claws
and crooked legs like ten thousand thousand crabs scuttling towards
the grey Pacific Ocean. At the controls, Murdo Sinclair peered down
as best he could through his steaming goggles. His observer and wireless operator, Boggis, was also on the look-out when he was not tinker-
ing with his set. And there, suddenly, in a channel of the Rufiji River,
were two different sorts of trees, straight with crosses upon their
trunks, the masts of the missing German cruiser *Königsberg*. Murdo
put the seaplane into a dive, then levelled out to follow the twists and
turns of the tributary to where the warship was lying, concealed off
the swampy river. The sound of a machine-gun firing from the
cruiser's deck putt-putted in his ears, and the crackle of rifle shots.
Holes were punched in the fuselage and the upper wing as they flew
past the grey side of the warship, its 4.1-inch gun pointing uselessly
at the empty sky. Then Murdo banked and nosed, turning in a lazy
half-circle to report.

"We're like a ruddy sieve," Boggis shouted to him.

"Good for lettuce," Murdo shouted back.

"Where are we?"

"Down the drain. Camera ready!"

He brought the seaplane down over the superstructure of the
Königsberg, ignoring the bullets whizzing as useless as hornets past
the floats of the biplane. Boggis was hanging over the edge of the
cockpit with his rosewood camera. "Got her!" he shouted. "Head for
home!" And Murdo did just that, clearing the mangrove trees and
flying over the forest to the sea creek, where the monitor *Mersey* was
lying, its one vast Howitzer pointing up from its iron platform. He
put his aircraft down bumpily on the muddy waters and waited for a
cutter to take him and his observer aboard.

Hamilton Sinclair was quite impressed by the quality of the aerial
photograph, while the captain of the *Mersey* thought it near to magic.
"It's clear enough," he said. "We'll fire over the trees. She's a sitting

duck." Then he turned to Hamilton. "Your seaplane, it can observe and report. Where our shells land."

"Of course," Hamilton said, then verified with his cousin. "That will not be a problem?"

"A tea party," Murdo said. "As long as the wireless works. And the wings don't fold up on us."

Hamilton laughed. It had been a long voyage round the Cape for the seaplane to East Africa, where Von Lettow and his black *askaris* were leading the British armies a dance through the bush in Tanganyika, and the German fleet still had a major warship on hand to sink the troop convoys from India. The Royal Naval Air Service was slowly proving that flying was an answer to the big guns of the battleships, even if Nelson was turning in his grave.

"We can have them now," Hamilton said. "After we have refuelled."

As he took off, Murdo could see the vast antique cannon on the monitor elevating to lob its shells one by one in an arc onto its target. It would be curious if a haphazard coincidence put a steel projectile from his own side through his wings. But there was a lot of room in space. And the Short seaplane had not reached the moorings of the *Königsberg* again before the British bombardment was detonating mangrove trees in flying umbrellas beyond the enemy cruiser.

"Four hundred yards long!" Boggis was shouting into the wireless. "Two hundred right. Over. Roger. Out."

Now the *Königsberg*'s cannon were replying to the heavens, hurling their reply over the swamp at their hidden enemy. But the explosives were closer now, fountains and plumes of river water spraying the hostile deck. And then, a direct hit, the funnel of the German cruiser cartwheeling in flocks of metal birds from the force of the black strike. And as he saw, Murdo was struck himself. A fragment hit him in the shoulder. And looking behind, he glanced at Boggis sprawling forward, his flying scarf crimson from his blood. The joystick would not pull back. He could not gain height. He dropped to fifty feet above the brown channel and headed for the sea, following the sinuous course of the Rufiji.

Cousin Robert Sinclair was also aboard on the *Mersey* to watch Murdo bring down his crippled aircraft by the ironclad monitor. It stalled on landing, tipped forward and began to list, half of one of its wing-floats shot away. But it could be salvaged. It had other missions to do.

"You have destroyed the *Königsberg*?" Robert asked.

"We have crippled her. She will not sail again."

"But her guns, her naval guns?"

"They'll rust with her hulk."

"Von Lettow will have them off her. They're better than anything we have."

"That's your problem," Hamilton said. "You're on the ground with your West African Rifles. You stop Von Lettow. We have, from sea and air."

"It's so bloody frustrating," Robert said. "It's our stupid generals. There's only one good officer, a bullyboy called Meinertzhagen. The rest are so dumb they wouldn't qualify as animals. And Von Lettow's real smart. He's like the Scarlet Pimpernel, I guess. We seek him here, we seek him there – and he's always got a march on us. We've transferred troops from all over the Empire – India, West Africa, South –"

"How's the wife? Patience?"

"Had to leave her behind."

"She's older than you, isn't she? A matron?"

"You shouldn't ask that. Yes, she is. It doesn't matter. I'm happy now." Robert looked at his cousin. "And Virginia – do you ever see her in London?"

"She's doing all right," Hamilton said, not knowing what to say exactly to his cousin. "But Hamish Charles isn't happy, and nor are his children. They're all dumped at boarding schools. She's pretty well left them. I suppose that might give you some satisfaction."

"It doesn't." Robert looked over the sails of the *Mersey* to the cutter heading for the stricken seaplane. "I haven't got anything against Hamish Charles."

"But he did kill his first wife. And ran off with yours."

"Did he now?" Robert turned on his cousin, his face both set and desperate. "How do *you* know?"

"I don't, I just heard –"

"Don't hear. *Know.*"

"You said, it was an accident. We – the family – we've always thought how good you were . . . how generous."

Out by the sinking sea-plane, sailors were lifting free the body of Boggis, crimson with blood even at that distance.

"Don't be too sure." Robert's voice was bitter. "I don't know why I gave that verdict. I would say who killed her was a matter of doubt."

Over the water, the sailors dropped the corpse. It fell into the creek. There was a thrash of water. The sailors beat at some creature with their oars. The body was dragged away. A sailor in the bow of the cutter picked up a rifle and began to fire aimlessly at a crocodile heading towards Africa.

"We are killing so many now," Robert said. "And it doesn't matter who kills who any more. Why should one little death matter? So long ago? Why one?" He looked towards Hamilton for an answer, but Hamilton could give him none. So he had to add, "But it does matter. To me."

As the gas casualties came into the station, Hamish Charles was also thinking about the death of his first wife. He remembered her blonde hair red with blood as she sprawled in the reeds by the *vlei*. The soldiers on the cattle-trucks were dead or dying too. No one was breathing. Those who were living were coughing and retching. Thick green and yellow phlegm came out of their mouths. They twisted and arched from some internal agony. They cursed and groaned, their blankets drenched in their sweat. They were on the racks of hell. No inferno could be worse.

Hamish Charles, the transport officer at Rheims, moved away the men in torment. He directed the stretcher bearers to some, the grave-diggers to others. They had been conveyed back day after night, and night after day. Hamish Charles had lost count. Another stupid push over the top into the machine-guns. But this time, the breeze had been blowing in their faces, and the Germans had added mustard and chlorine gas to the wind. Chemical warfare, it was worse than poisoning the wells with arsenic to kill the African cattle. These men were slaughtered like vermin and worse than vermin. No rat should die so.

Hamish Charles dreaded to find a face he knew among the myriad of the wounded. But on the third sleepless night in the railway sidings, drinking cognac openly from the silver hip-flask covered with crocodile skin which he always carried and used too much, he came across the aged death-mask of a young man he had met recently and long ago. The Grenadier uniform was streaked with sulphurous stains, the worn young-old face was stubbled and grey with dying. The voice gagged at the sight of Hamish Charles.

"I'm Gordon," the soldier croaked. "Save me."

Hamish Charles knelt by his cousin and opened his hip-flask. Drop by drop, he tilted the brandy into the open mouth of the Grenadier. Gordon Seymour-Scudabright coughed, but mercifully held down the poison in his lungs.

"Save me."

"I will try, Gordon."

There must have been some reassurance in his voice, for Gordon closed his eyes. Then a spasm shook him, a fit of twisting and screaming that added to the cacophony of pain in the carriage. And when he arched up, he choked and fell back. And he did not breathe again.

Hamish Charles closed the lids of the dead man's eyes with his forefinger. He tried to cross his cousin's hands in a prayer for such a release, but a sort of stiffness had already set in. He looked in Gordon's breast pocket and found a wallet and some creased letters from England. He would send them home.

He rose to his feet. The stretcher-bearers were hovering.

"Take him to the hospital."

"But he is dead, sir."

"To the hospital. Tell Dr Seaforth Sinclair it is his cousin Gordon. I want the body shipped home with the wounded. He'll be buried in England. Understand?"

"Yes, sir."

Hamish Charles jumped from the charnel-house of the railway waggon onto the gravel by the tracks. He took a pull from his flask again. He had worn the scaly skin of the river beast chestnut and smooth with the palm of his hands. Again he took a swig of brandy. It did not help much. The pleasant haze in his head had become a lump of lead. Why had they not killed him too? Why make him a Charon, a ferryman of the dead? He was the one who should have died. He had killed a woman once, an accident, but he wanted her to die. And the woman he had married, Virginia, she was a tart by all accounts, whoring with a French arms dealer, and too damned clever for him. He did have four children, Hamish Gordon and Martha and little Paul – and one by the tart, sweet Clio – but boarding schools had engulfed them, as they swallowed up all colonial children in their harsh regime so like the British Army.

There was money enough to pay for that, since his father Angus had died. There was no need ever to return to the slavery to copra in the South Seas. But why survive? Who needed him, a failure all his born days? Perhaps the children did. But it was a wise child who knew his own father, and a bad father he had been. He still loved little Clio, but Virginia would not let him see her, even on his leaves, which never seemed to come. Altogether, for everyone's sake, he was better off dead. But he was living, and the moans and the screams of the dying were all about him. Even in war, being killed was so bloody random.

He finished the brandy in his flask and staggered towards the bar in the station to fill it. As he lurched along, he felt in his pocket for his talisman. Under a light on the platform, he studied it – a white fleur-de-lys set in red glass surrounded by a lead border – a fragment of the stained glass windows of the torched cathedral. The three petals on their stem were a flowering cross.

"Thank You for Your mercy," Hamish Charles mumbled to God. "I don't deserve it."

*

The *Ben My Chree* had been a passenger ferry between Liverpool and the Isle of Man. It had been refitted for the seaplanes with a hangar on the upper deck and a testing and repair workshop. It had reached the Dardanelles to reinforce the *Ark Royal*, which could only winch up its ten aircraft on steam-driven hoists from their hangar in the hold. Transferred from East Africa because of their expertise, Murdo and Hamilton Sinclair had sailed through the Suez Canal up to the Aegean Sea. For Lawrence of Arabia was already beginning to assault the Turks in the southern deserts, and soon there would be a fresh crusade to recapture Jerusalem.

"I don't know," Murdo said. "Do you think it will work?"

He was looking down from the deck of the aircraft carrier to the Short "Shirl" seaplane bobbing at the side. It was heavy in the water. For an eighteen-inch torpedo was slung beneath it.

"You know the specifications," Hamilton said. "Rolls Eagle 8 engine, 400 horse-power. That's enough thrust to get your tub airborne. And you've got six and a half hours' flying time at a top speed of a hundred miles an hour. Think where we were only five years ago. We got a prize at Shorts for flying round one closed circuit on an airfield!"

"If I didn't trust the engineers," Murdo said, "I'd never bloody fly."

"And I'd never send you up, Murdo, if I didn't know you would stay up till you came down."

So Murdo set off in his single-seater biplane on his epic journey towards his Troy across the Dardanelles. The entrance to the straits was heavy with the hulls of British and French battleships, their names a register of an ancestry which Homer might have written himself – the *Majestic* and the *Agamemnon*, the *Vengeance* and the *Albion*, the *Triumph* and the *Indefatigable*, the *Charlemagne* and the *Queen Elizabeth*, with the *Lord Nelson* and the *Swiftsure* and the *Prince of Wales* in reserve. With their lineage and nobility, how could the Allies lose?

Heartened by the evidence of the grey invaders beneath, Murdo found his target in a harbour on the near side of Asia. The old Turkish transport was low on the waterline, almost beached. It was a straight run into the ship, as direct as a cavalry charge. He dropped to fifteen feet above the swell and released his explosive cargo. The mechanism worked. He jumped another twenty feet in the air from the loss of weight. The aircraft skipped with joy. The propeller still whirred round and about in a blue blur. He rose and banked and swerved and looked back and underneath. An explosion rent the ship, a tiara of smoke blazoned the horizon. Smack dab in the middle, the torpedo had gone home – and that is where Murdo went.

"It is history, naval history," Hamilton told him that night in the mess of the *Ben My Chree*. "The first ship torpedoed by an aeroplane."

"I've hit a submarine, I think," Murdo said. "In the North Sea. With a hand-bomb."

"But if that U-boat had been under the sea – its proper habitat – instead of recharging its batteries . . ." Hamilton was smiling. "You could never have hit it. While a ship, its place is top of the water. Not under it, until you send it there."

"True. So?"

"The war is ours. In the future, all will be air wars. Including the sea."

Certainly, Hamilton proved right in the evacuation of Gallipoli. All the heroics, all the courage, all the sudden deaths to gain inches of beaches, these were as useless as the ten years the Greek Allies had spent assaulting the walls of Troy, before they took it with their feigned retreat and the deceit of the Trojan Horse. But this Allied withdrawal was for real. And it was by sea. It was no good the great poet on a brief visit writing about the beauty of the slaughter of the troops from the far dominions. *With all the fury and the crying of the shells, and the shouts and cries and cursing on the beach, the rattle of the small arms and the cheers and defiance up the hill, and the roar of the great guns far away, at sea, or in the olive-groves, the night seemed in travail of a new age. All the blackness was shot with little spurts of fire, and streaks of fire, and malignant bursts of fire, and arcs and glows and crawling snakes of fire, and the moon rose, and looked down upon it all. In the fiercer hours of that night shells fell in that contested mile of ground and on the beach beyond it at the rate of one a second, and the air whimpered with passing bullets, or fluttered with the rush of the big shells, or struck the head of the passer like a moving wall with the shock of explosion. All through the night the Turks attacked, and in the early hours their fire of shrapnel became so hellish that the Australians soon had not men enough left to hold the line.*

So all departed by sea, with the great poet well in the lead. But it was not the great departure that it might have been. For the British Army – except from Afghanistan – had almost always been perfect in its retreats, which were never admitted, rather than in its advances, which rarely succeeded. It was the fleet that had to take them off in old steamers brought over from the English Channel, the peacetime notices in French and English still painted on the gangways: PRENEZ GARDE – MIND THE STAIRS.

As the last of the soldiers strolled softly from Suvla and Anzac at night over the hulk of the *River Clyde*, beached as a jetty, they found that the rearguard had to wait for the final lighter to safety and the battleship *Prince George*. The problem was that General Maude had lost his valise. And only as dawn was breaking did he find his missing bag. He just made it to the ultimate barge from Gallipoli rather as King Arthur did on his terminal voyage to Avalon, before the first of the ammunition dumps were blown up, the signal to the sleeping Turks that this was another failed crusade.

Like Ichabod, the glory of the Allies had departed. But one of them, Naval Lieutenant Graham Seymour-Scudabright, had not. In charge of the Marines who were igniting the abandoned heaps of explosives and stores, he had stood for a moment between the rising light and the phosphoro waters of the Aegean, used by the ancient Greeks to sail across to Troy. A Turkish sniper had a clean shot. And Gordon's brother died on land as he had done, but with a pain so quick that it was gone as it was felt, in a classical land that bred the myth of heroes. Only he would rather have been alive, as all heroes would.

May Seymour-Scudabright had never seen her husband Charles cry. But now he wept for hours on end. He would not come to terms with his grief. To lose one son and then both sons, he who had done all that was right in this world. There was no justice in it.

"Gordon and Graham," he blubbed to her like the schoolboy he was under all his bluster. "Taking them. They could have left me one." He did not think of her. She was only their mother. "One boy to go on with my life. Just one boy. It would be enough."

"You are always saying," May said, dry-eyed because she only wept in the silence of her bedroom, "what a just war it is."

"It may be a just war. It is. But it doesn't mean they should take both my boys."

"They. Who are they?"

"I don't know. The people who killed them."

"Gas. A sniper. Just another target."

"Gordon. And Graham."

"I know. Our boys."

They fell into silence, and May looked across at the man she had thought she had loved once for more than his wealth and air of command. Now he was a sad fat man nobody could love. Except her. For he was now at his depths. And there was the past between them, two boys were dead. She rose and walked over to him sitting in his plaid chair and took his head out of his hands and pressed his face into her soft middle through the cloth of her dressing-gown.

"There," she said. "There. I'm here. And we do have Ruth."

Muffled the voice she heard below her.

"Don't talk of her."

"I must. She is the last one left to us. And just because she is rebelling now – that modern art with that awful Virginia – it doesn't mean that one day . . ." May had to be positive. "She is nursing. She is out of gaol. No more of those dreadful votes for women. No more Cat-and-Mouse Act. She is helping to heal our soldiers. She may *meet* somebody. You never know."

Charles Seymour-Scudabright brought up his tear-streaked face from the security of his wife's dragon silk material.

"I know about Ruth. She will never – "

"Never say never, as they say, if you are a parent."

"She will never love us. Or respect us."

"Those are very different words. Charles . . ." May looked down on her obese, slouched, dependent husband with some affection. "She still loves us. We are her mother and father. But *respect* us? That is too much to ask in wartime."

"But here I am, running the war with my *propaganda* – that's the new word for it." Charles was almost pleading for reassurance. "I mean, morale is very high, is it not?"

"When the Zeppelins don't bomb us. Or the Gothas."

"Very high on the whole. And something to do with me."

"Very much to do with you, Charles. We simply don't know what to think until we read your posters. Britain's New Million Army – Complete the Second Million – Men wishing to join – Fall in and follow the band. Come and help us – For Honour and Freedom." May paused for effect. "If I was a man, I'd join up at once. As I am a woman . . ." She paused again. "I vote for you to keep us enlisting."

"Oh May, what would I do without you?"

It was the first time Charles had expressed any need of her since the war had begun. It was hard that it took the death of two sons to make him admit the truth. Then May repressed the thought. It was too cheap. She had not had the time to mourn herself, to lament the void of this double loss of the flesh which had been born of her. But she had to console him first, her biggest baby as he had always been.

"I am here," she said. "I always will be. England has to do without our sons. But she does not yet have to do without you."

And in his look of surprise and gratitude and sudden hope, she had her sort of reward. She had helped the man who lived.

22

THE LIONS COME HOME

The tank was a ship, really. Wallace Jardine knew where it had come from. It was born out of the Admiralty Landships Committee. Clambering inside one was like entering the gun turret of a battlecruiser or the steel lozenge of a submarine. But this was the flat ground before Cambrai, not the North Sea off Jutland. It took four men to steer the Mark IV tracked monster with its Daimler six-cylinder engine working a worm differential and the pressed steel plate revolving tracks, which only lasted twenty miles at the full speed of four miles an hour. Inside the groaning and clanking tin of claustrophobia was worse than being processed into bully beef. But three hundred of them did break through the first time they were used properly. They cleared the German machine-gun nests with their Lewis guns and 57mm cannon. They bridged the trenches with fascines of stakes and brushwood dropped off their turrets, and they cleared the barbed wire for the following infantry with grapnels and pulling power. They changed the face of future war as much as the armoured knight had in the time of the Crusades.

Watching the assault with his dragoons, Alexander Plunkett-Drax had to admire the ingenuity of these rolling iron dragons. They were camouflaged like chameleons and lurched from side to side, but never turned over. They would plunge down a shell-crater and come up from drowning on the far side. They belched out petrol fumes that he could smell a mile away. This black smoke was their own screen against the enemy. Their caterpillar wheels crunched barbed wire as if it were spaghetti. And the sound of bullets ricocheting off their scaly sides was as ineffective as the buzz of a distant swarm of bees. They would cut a swathe in the Hindenburg Line for the cavalry to charge through and roll back the Huns to Berlin and beyond.

As the horsemen moved forward behind the foot soldiers, who were consolidating the ground overrun by the tanks, Alexander saw the first disaster. A tank was lying on its side, its wheels still revolving, its tracks askew. It looked like a gigantic beetle on its back, flailing at nothing. The rent in its blackened flank showed where the German shell had punctured it and incinerated the humans in its metal belly. Another armoured insect straddled a stream, bogged down in mud, showing only its top gun-turret like a crocodile would poke out its snout in a swamp. And then a third tank waited, immobile, a wireless aerial betraying it as one of the new command centres of modern war, relaying signals back to headquarters, which would not know how to respond, or if they could, how to respond in time.

The dragoons never had their charge. The forty thousand cavalrymen behind the armoured attack were stopped by a few German gunners in a village on the flank that the tanks had forgotten to take. In Flesquières, an anti-aircraft 77mm gun manned by Unter-Offizer Krüger knocked out seven tanks before he was killed beside his artillery piece. The Highland Division never stormed its way into the strong point. All the kilted Jocks did was get into a muddle with the mounted men. Ahead was a canal, and nobody had a pontoon bridge to cross it. Yes, horses could swim, but who was going to start a water charge of the Light Brigade into Hun machine-guns? That sort of glory and folly had gone out with the Crimea.

Then the tanks came waddling home. They had run out of steam and spare tracks. And Alexander Plunkett-Drax and his forty thousand horsemen who had ridden through and beyond the Hindenburg Line, now rode back again. Over their heads flew the Sopwith Camels, which had cleared the air of enemy spotter planes and enabled the attack to be a surprise. There was some talk of them fighting duels in the air, of jousts and tournaments as if they were knights on wings. Even the Baron von Richthofen had left the saddle for the cockpit, and his unseating in his red triplane was held to be an encounter of chivalry in space. The Lewis gun was the lance now, the propeller was the hoofs of the charger. Alexander Plunkett-Drax felt demeaned by the machine.

A later meeting with a wireless operator at headquarters did not improve the mood of the dragoon officer. The man, who had the rank of captain, bore the name of Gillon Sinclair and turned out to be a Canadian cousin of his wife Arabella, whose relations were legion and usually unspeakable. Gillon enthused to Alexander about wireless and war. The messages received back from the spotter planes and balloons and tanks and infantry wireless sets with their long cables rolled back behind the advance had altered the planning of battles. Instant information was the secret of success. The enemy would be beaten in the air waves, not in the trenches.

"Tommyrot," Alexander said. "In the end, there's only the bayonet and the lance, the bullet and cold steel."

"I reckon not," Gillon said. "The right info and you won't know what hit you. You won't even see it. Bombs and gas from the air, mines and long-range guns, tanks and submarines – they'll win wars in secret."

"Men win wars. Weapons don't." Suddenly Alexander remembered something his mistress Virginia had told him about this Canadian cousin. "Didn't you deal with Maurice Walter? Sell him some of our secret weapons?"

Gillon flushed. He had almost forgotten that early episode, when he had come to England to work for Marconi. But how could this cavalry captain know anything about it?

"You know Walter?"

"Yes. I dealt with him. Over Ulster. We bought rifles, machine-guns. But I never *supplied* him. Like you did."

"I did not." The lie direct came easily to Gillon. "Your info is plumb wrong."

"It's right. It's the best. You always get the truth between the sheets."

"Someone I know?"

"She knows you. What happened to Walter? I would like to know. You with all your information."

"I last heard of him in the Balkans. Supplying the Turks. He wasn't very popular here, when the war broke out."

"I'll say." Alexander Plunkett-Drax smiled at Gillon and stared him down. "Mum's the word over Walter. I bet you'd like him dead."

"Yeah. I guess I would."

"Snap. So would I. For reasons of my own."

Maurice Walter was facing a firing-squad. On the Salonika front, he had been captured in the advance on Bulgaria. He had stood out in his white suit in this dirty war, the only immaculate being on the whole front line, even though he was found hiding in the wine-cellar of an old taverna. "I am merely a trader in curios," he had told his captors, who had then told him that he was a merchant of death, the fashionable phrase those days for the international arms dealers like Nobel in Sweden, who were supplying every side in the Great World War and would institute peace prizes when the conflict was over for the cripples who survived. What Walter did not know was that on the Salonika front was a man who might wish him dead, the husband of his London mistress.

Hamish Charles had another problem on his mind. As a transport officer seconded to Greece, he had to deal with mules and donkeys as well as the rare railway train, and now an aeroplane had landed on a strip which had been cleared in the mountains, and the local peasants were frightened. They had never seen a flying machine before. Greek they might be, but Ancient Greek they were not. They were hardly soothed by folk memories of Pegasus, the airborne horse of the Gods, or Icarus, who had flown too near the sun on his feathery wings until the wax had melted and he had crashed to his death in the sea. They took the bomber from the sky as a visitation like the plague, and only Hamish Charles having his photograph taken with the village chief beside the Handley Page with its hundred-foot double wingspan persuaded the locals that this omen might be a blessing from Heaven, and not a curse.

The photograph was to be his memento of the war, and he would send it home to show that he also was helping to win the struggle and not only drinking himself to death on *ouzo* now, a local liquorice drink that looked like milk and burnt like blazes. He got on well with the bomber pilot, who had trained with Murdo in the fledgling Royal Naval Air Service before the start of the fighting.

"If you had told me," the pilot said, "that five years on I'd be flying a bloody big boat to bomb Constantinople, I'd have said you were barmy."

"Constantinople?" Hamish Charles was impressed. "We lost at the Dardanelles, but we can bomb Constantinople?"

"Yes. Like another Crusade, isn't it?"

"Like another Crusade."

And it was now. The Christian armies and navies and airforces were defeating the Turks. Hamish Charles had heard from his Cousin Robert, his enemy and his friend, that he had been transferred with a man called Meinertzhagen from East Africa to Allenby's army, advancing upon Jerusalem. Again, Crusaders would take the Holy City. Onward, Christian soldiers, marching as to war . . .

"I don't know," Hamish Charles said, passing his flask of *ouzo* to the pilot. "I suppose this war, when we win it, will be good for us."

"Thanks," the pilot said and took a swig from the flask. "Cor, bloody awful! Is this the local petrol? We'll lose the peace, I bet. Even if we win the war."

"Right," Hamish Charles said.

And right he was, Hamish Charles thought, watching the Handley Page fly off after its refit. Against the savage mountain range, its size diminished to a speck, its engine roar to a drone and silence. Its passing was evanescent against the northern peaks, which still blocked the British advance. Nothing that was hurled against them, aeroplanes and armoured cars and artillery, made the least difference to that barrier of stone and gorge and ravine. "You shall not pass," was the unspoken message of the crags, and they did not pass. That was the strength of the hills, that was the irrelevance of all this military effort, of human existence.

Hamish Charles kept his thoughts to himself. He knew that he might be projecting the failure of his own life onto the failure of all lives and all endeavours. He had killed his first wife, or he believed he had. He had lost his second wife. He had abandoned his children, for the war had taken him away from them. There was nothing left for him to do. Except that evening, when he returned to brigade headquarters, he was told of the capture of Maurice Walter, the merchant of death, condemned to be executed in the morning as a spy and a traitor, whatever the legal niceties might be.

"I know the man," Hamish Charles told his brigadier. "I mean, I know of the man. He kn-kn-knows my wife." He betrayed what this Biblical knowledge was by a slight stammer, which he corrected. "Knew her before the war."

"You think you could get some intelligence out of him before he gets the chop?"

"I'll try."

Walking into the cell and seeing Walter for the first time, Hamish Charles felt the satisfaction of revenge. He was not jealous. How could he be of this haggard figure, his face blotched with bruises and stubble, his white suit fitting no better than a canvas sack?

"Maurice Walter," he said. "You don't know me. I know you. I am Hamish Sinclair, the husband of Virginia."

To his credit, Walter drew himself upright and even essayed a little irony.

"Destiny, to think it could be so shabby," he said. "What a fate to meet *you* here? I am hardly at my best, you are my executioner."

"Not exactly. The firing squad will be twelve men. I shall ask, however, to be the officer in command."

"And if they miss –"

"They will not."

"You will finally execute me. With your revolver."

"Did you supply it?"

"In the back of the head. Will you do me a favour?"

"Why should I?"

"To prove your generosity to your enemy. That will make you feel better about yourself. Virginia told me –"

"Do I want to listen?"

"You do. All men like hearing about themselves. Virginia told me that you are uneasy with yourself. You cannot forgive yourself. You killed your first wife, took Virginia from your cousin. You suffer from that idiocy called guilt. *Ce n'est pas la logique*. But what Anglo-Saxon was ever rational?"

As he talked, Walter seemed to recover his confidence and his dignity. He might have been judging Hamish Charles, who was his judge.

"You feel no guilt for all the killing from the weapons you were selling?"

"One death. That is all that matters to you. One particular death rather than the ten million who will die in this war. The wife you killed, Sinclair. Your wife. And now you will kill me. For no crime –"

"For killing thousands of our men."

"I do not kill. You do. You use my weapons. But . . . the favour I ask –"

"What is it?"

"If you will not let me escape –"

"Don't be absurd."

"No, you are too limited – too military – for mere magnanimity. Then kill me yourself. Cleanly, quickly, and now! One bullet to the back of my head. With your service revolver. So I do not have another night of anticipation before my execution."

"It would be against regulations."

"I attacked you. You were defending yourself."

"A bullet in the back of the head? It would not look like a defence."

"Think of the satisfaction. True revenge –"

"You will die, anyway."

"Not by your hand. And it will not be murder. As killing your first wife was."

"It was an accident, Walter –" Hamish Charles heard his voice rising at the taunt. He must control himself. "An accident."

"Not as I heard it. It was a *crime passionelle*. You wanted Virginia. And now the killing of me, because you are jealous of me and Virginia, that will also be a *crime passionelle*, but a *legal* one. It will lay the first illegal act to rest. Kill me with the blessing of your military law. And you will satisfy your honour – and save the name of your wife."

The mockery in Walter's voice influenced Hamish Charles. His hand dropped to his holster. He undid the flap and drew out his weapon and thumbed loose the safety catch. There seemed to be an obstruction in his throat. He spoke thickly.

"Have you thought you may get what you want?"

"I hope so."

"Well you won't. I wouldn't give *you* the satisfaction."

Walter shook his head as if in regret for what he was forced to say. "Virginia, she is a courtesan. Of all the *poules de luxe* I have ever had, she excels in the arts of love. Breasts like a nymph, thighs like a leopard –" The barrel of Hamish Charles's revolver hit Walter across the mouth, splitting his lips on his provocation. "Ach." He fell to the floor.

"You will be executed in the morning," Hamish Charles said.

Walter looked up at him, wiping at his lips, which were streaming red.

"You fool. You will never live her murder down. Or mine. You will never live us down."

The new searchlights stitched the night sky over London with their seams of light. They criss-crossed in moving patterns, searching for the pale coughdrops of the Zeppelins and the vultures of the Gotha bombers, coming to void their high venom on the city. The anti-aircraft guns hiccuped at the armada above, sailing the dark sky, suddenly trapped as targets in the shifting beams of brightness. This was no night for a reunion, and yet it was. For it was to celebrate a death that was the herald to a new generation. Kate was dead in the third year of the Great War, nine months after her husband Bob the Railwayman had passed away. And her daughter Marie had called the clan together in memory of their forebears, who had begat them. If there was a war in the heavens, it would not stop their memorial feast. It was apt, in a way. The death of Kate was marked by fireworks over their gathering.

The arrival that morning of the postcard from Hamish Charles in Greece had also suited that night. He must have bought it after it had been imported to the canteen there. It showed young lions walking towards an old lion, lying on his stone hill and tagged ENGLAND. The other lions were tagged by the names of the dominions: CANADA, AUSTRALIA, SOUTH AFRICA, NEW ZEALAND and a distant yellow cat called INDIA. This was the true gathering of the Empire in the defence of the mother lair. A pride of lions walking across a dry plain under a sun that flew the Union Jack above its rays. The caption of the whole postcard – THE LIONS COME HOME.

The message on the back was curt, but it confirmed that Hamish Charles was still alive. Addressed to the Countess of Dunesk, it read:

Dear Marie,

I am in the pink. Here's hoping you all are. Murdo is fine and flying high, and Robert too. Tell Virginia a fellow called Walter met a sticky end. And a good show too.

Best
Hamish

It was all a game to the men, Marie thought. Death and retribution, envy and emotion, the men played it as a game. Play on, and play the game. She could not tell how Virginia would react to the news of the death of her lover and financier, but probably not too badly. After all, she had the ghastly Alex Plunkett-Drax in her life, and Walter's end would solve a problem for her. She was lucky or unlucky with Alex, because he was never exposed to any danger in France. The cavalry were kept firmly far behind the lines. Civilians were more likely to catch a bomb unloaded on their bonnets from a Zeppelin than the fancy horsemen were to see action over the Channel.

They could have been sitting in the basement of Sunderland House, which Consuelo Marlborough had kindly opened as a shelter for the duration of the air raids. But this was not the night to duck for cover. They were meeting in the Pall Mall, which was naturally not there, but in the Haymarket. If places had been where they were named to be, German spies or bombs might have dropped in there. The old biddies were presiding over the theatre bar as they always did, Bunnie and Mac – Helen Macdonald, the *doyenne* of the trade. And there talking to her sat a little man in a khaki tunic with a vast sunflower stuck between his brass buttons. "Roses and chocolate creams," he was saying, "nectar and ambrosia. The world has no greater pleasures." Except for his uniform, Marie thought, nobody would ever know there was a war on.

Her daughter Rosabelle was there, tall and angular with her wild red hair long enough to sit upon; and Ellen-Maeve, more like a daisy than ever with her yellow head and white flounces, along with her husband Hamilton, home from Africa at last for more research on his blessed seaplanes; and the young widow Ruby in black with black ribbons in her ringlets, and her hard mother Margaret from India, where husband Douglas still connived with the Civil Service to keep the Raj in order; and Ruth and Virginia, still bosom friends in spite of their shared lover; and her own friend Peg from India, hating where the war brought her and what it made her do. But Arabella would not come over from Ireland with her son Peregrine, what with all the troubles there after the Easter Rebellion: somebody had to guard the house while Alex Plunkett-Drax defended the whole British Isles from his stables near Rouen. Nor had her husband come, Bill Dunesk. Their estrangement was total. He seemed to shrink from touching his wife as though she were infectious, so he stayed apart to hide his aversion.

Marie called the table to order. She was used to public speaking now.

"We are met to remember my mother Kate," she said. "She is

226

buried now in the Scotland she left and always loved. She has come at last to her home. I know you could not be there. The war calls us all to serve. But she lies at rest, where she would be, looking over the sea to the Western Isles. Do not cry for her. She had a full life. And she lived her span and is done. For never any rest she had in all her long life. She is at peace now – and we are not. To my mother Kate."

Here Marie picked up her glass of pink champagne and made the others drink with her, shocked as some were at this kind of a memorial service in the Pall Mall theatre bar.

"She asked me to give this tribute to her going. She never stood on ceremony. She was proud of me, of what I have become. But she never understood what I was doing – working for women and for miners, for the rights we shall have when the war is over. She was the old school. We are the new. When I remember, how I came to London – a music-hall turn on my pony – that's why they know me here at the old Pall Mall."

"Take me, take me . . ." Virginia said. "Even I have heard of *that* number of yours."

"And now – a war to win – a peace after which women will be free – and poverty over with fair wages for all. India and Ireland given Home Rule . . ."

"Steady on," Margaret Jardine said. "You sound just like Seaforth."

"My brother," Peg Menon said. "Saving your boys."

"And all that tosh you talk about independence. Douglas says you are positively *dangerous*. As bad as those Irish rebels."

"At the moment," Peg said, "we *Indians* are mainly in France, saving you on the Western Front."

"Darling Marie," Hamilton said, "more about your mother, less about saving the world. No politics in the mess, you know our golden rule. Nor in the Pall Mall." He rose for another toast.

"The Sinclairs, God bless them, may they always meet again wherever they may roam."

"The Sinclairs."

The clinking of the glasses in tiny chimes made Ruby begin to cry for her brief lost husband. Already a baby kicked in her belly, and there was no father for it. Her mother Margaret put an arm round her daughter. "Hush, it'll be all right. We can cope back in India. We'll go back to Annandale." And Ruth thought of the dead, not of her Aunt Kate, but of her two brothers killed within the week, and now of her coming together with her mother and even her father Charles again, vain and censorious though he was and always would be.

"Isn't it a terrible thing," she said to Virginia, "that dying brings us together, and living never does?"

Virginia had already heard of the sticky end of Maurice Walter, and that her husband Hamish might have had a hand in it. But she did regret her loss. She had, indeed, met Alex Plunkett-Drax through Walter and his arms dealing.

"People introduce you before they die," she said. "What do they say? You pass away. But before you pass away, you pass on – you pass on your friends, your lovers, to people who are still living."

She now rose to her feet, her glass held high.

"To Kate," she said, "and to the others who serve or have gone in this war –" to Ruby – "to your Alisdair –" to Ruth – "to your Gordon and Graham –" to Peg – "to your Seaforth and Miriam –" to herself – "to a friend and helper of mine –" and raising her glass – "to all those who have passed us on so that we may know each other better and be together now."

All drank to that. Outside, a siren wailed over the night streets. Marie put her arms round the thin shoulders of Rosabelle. "Come on out," she said. "You'll be able to say, I was in the Pall Mall the night they bombed London."

"And out of it," Rosabelle said. "If I go out with you."

Mother and daughter went out into the Haymarket, where no hay was sold now, for the horse-buses had given way to petrol buses and electric trains on rails above and underground. And in the darkness, a ragged comet was falling, a sign of the beginning and the end. An English fighter-plane had soared above a Zeppelin and had dropped on it bombs and flechettes sharper than the arrows of Eros's bow in Piccadilly. The great gas bag had burst into flames and was descending slowly on the great city, trailing rags of fire in a burning trail. Around it the searchlights crossed their beams, drawing a blaze of peaks and crags, making outlines of ranges and hills against the dark nothing of the night, sending up bright pillars to hold up the heavens from London. And Rosabelle spoke softly to her mother the opening lines of her favourite poem from William Blake:

> The fields from Islington to Marybone,
> To Primrose Hill and St John's Wood,
> Were builded over with pillars of gold;
> And there Jerusalem's pillars stood.

Marie watched the dancing buttresses of light as the fiery debris of the airship floated down the dark.

"Robert's in the real Jerusalem," she said "He wrote back that we have just taken it. It is ours."

"It always was," Rosabelle said. "It is here. Can't you see?"

"I can see."

The burning tapestry against the night sky sketched towers and walls, summits and spires. And Marie stroked the red fall of her daughter's hair that streamed down while the last embers of the Zeppelin were buried in the far roofs of London.

"I can see," Marie said, "why we pass on."

ANDREW SINCLAIR

THE FAR CORNERS OF THE EARTH

When the glen is cleared, the Sinclairs are scattered.

With the rest of their clan and neighbours, Hamish and Hannah Sinclair, together with their seven children, are driven from their home as the Highland landowners replace people with sheep and deer.

Desperate and hungry, the family is split up, the parents and five children setting out for the New World aboard an overcrowded, fever-ridden emigrant ship while two sons enlist in the army.

From Canada and India, the Crimea and Africa, farming, fighting, nursing, constructing railways, always struggling for survival and security, *The Far Corners of the Earth* begins the epic story of a family spread across the world, building, whether they willed it or no, an empire for Britain and her Queen.

HODDER AND STOUGHTON PAPERBACKS